W9-CPK-341

FICTION

MESSENGERS

By

David L. Arnett

MESSENGERS

By

David L. Arnett

Books

Unity Village, MO 64065-0001

MESSENGERS
First Edition 2011

Unity Books titles are available at special discounts for bulk purchases for study groups, book clubs, sales promotions, book signings or fundraising. To place an order, call the Unity Customer Care Department at 1-866-236-3571 or email *wholesaleaccts@unityonline.org*.

Messengers was originally published by In His Steps Publishing under the title *Swing High, Sweet Chariot: The Gospel of Jake Daniels*.

Cover and Dust Jacket Design: Jenny Hahn
Interior Design: The Covington Group, Kansas City, Missouri

Library of Congress Control Number: 2011921045

ISBN: 978-0-87159-355-9

Canada BN 13252 0933 RT

SWING HIGH, SWEET CHARIOT

(Variation on a popular Negro spiritual)

Swing high, sweet chariot,
Coming for to carry me home.
Swing high, sweet chariot,
Coming for to carry me home.

I looked over Jordan and what did I see,
Coming for to carry me home?
A band of angels coming after me,
Coming for to carry me home.

Swing high, sweet chariot,
Coming for to carry me home.
Swing high, sweet chariot,
Coming for to carry me home.

Sometimes I'm up, and sometimes I'm down,
Coming for to carry me home,
But still my soul feels heavenly bound,
Coming for to carry me home.

Swing high, sweet chariot,
Coming for to carry me home.
Swing high, sweet chariot,
Coming for to carry me home.

If you get there before I do,
Coming for to carry me home,
Tell all my friends I'm coming too,
Coming for to carry me home.

Swing high, sweet chariot,
Coming for to carry me home.
Swing high, sweet chariot,
'Cause I ain't ready to go.

FOREWORD

The words in the following text belong to Jake Daniels alone, although I have divided the text into chapters to promote ease of reading and provide a clearer sense of time and context. I have written the epilogue myself, as I believe most objective readers will be seeking further validation of the events described in Jake's text. I have also collated and arranged the various supporting documents, including Appendix A, "Psychiatric Evaluation and Incident Report," and Appendix B, "Letter From Dr. Tomas." It is my hope that the short afterword following the appendices will remove any lingering questions in the minds of some readers.

CHAPTER I

IN THE BEGINNING

Maybe I was not out of my body long enough. I did not pass through a dark tunnel and reach the light, where the whole of my life and its effect on other people were revealed to me. No, it just didn't happen that way. I was hovering over my body just long enough to see that it was a bloody mess stretched out on the ground next to my crumpled, smoldering SUV—and to see the mysterious woman again who had signaled to me just before the truck crossed the center line and plowed into my car. I didn't wonder how it was that she could stare into my disembodied eyes floating several feet above my body or what she was doing at the side of the road in the first place or how she had reached me so quickly. I didn't wonder about any of that then. All of that came later—after the blackness struck and my ordeal began.

There were no dreams, no voices, no lights, not even pain in the beginning. Consciousness returned slowly in short, bleary intervals. Shadowy figures lifted my eyelids, as if searching for a tiny spark in the depths that might just be kindled into something resembling a human being one day. Mostly, there was … nothing. Does that surprise you, or frighten you perhaps? I had always imagined the nothingness of Zen, for example, as containing awareness, with the burgeoning potential, almost the promise of nothing ready to explode into something.

And maybe that is what happened after all, without the explosion and without the brooding awareness of a spirit rushing over the dark waters, as I slowly rose from complete oblivion into dim consciousness—and excruciating pain—after three weeks in coma.

You need to know that I am a painter with a particular talent for sketching. That is important. Otherwise, my search would have ended only in the same vague awareness of the transcendental that probably arises in you when you are alone and trying to remember that one small thing that will unlock the whole mystery for you at last. I am also a vegetarian.

You need not know the extent of the pain from the broken bones and the ripped tissues and the surgeries. In fact, you cannot know it unless you have experienced it yourself, and even then you cannot really remember the pain itself. All you can truly remember is the anguish—for that rests in the mind and not in the body—of not being able to bear any more and yet being forced to do exactly that.

As the pain eventually receded, and the drugs for the pain were slowly withdrawn, I began to remember the accident, slowly at first, very slowly, as fragments of images began to assemble themselves into something coherent that almost resembled actual scenes just before the collision.

The doctors said that I might never remember anything concrete about the collision, that this is common in vehicle accidents because there is not time enough for the sensory input to be imprinted in long-term memory. In my case, moreover, the skull fracture, severe concussion, and "insult" to the brain, as one doctor put it, should have wiped the slate clean, not just memory of the accident. In fact, let's be honest, I shouldn't be writing this. I should be dead.

Add to that the broken hip, arm, and collarbone, along with the internal injuries and the fact that I no longer have a spleen, and you will imagine that I am a lucky man, right? After all, I am here, writing, still among the living, uncrippled, and barely scarred, physically. Tell the truth, though: Would you wish to experience such luck?

So yes, the memories began to return as fragments, and they probably would never have progressed beyond that point, except for that one instant as she looked me dead in the eye when the eyes of the bloody and unconscious heap below me were swollen shut.

Let me try to explain that—as well as I can, anyway. I was released from the hospital almost four months after the accident. My fiancée Allison had been incredible from the moment she got the call. My parents told me afterward that she had come every afternoon during the week after school and had spent most of every weekend as well in my hospital room. She wept as the first signs of consciousness appeared. She talked to me constantly, and at times I think I can remember some of it, but that is probably not true. She talked to me about our wedding plans and the power of love to overcome all obstacles. She talked to me about the first-graders and our own children to come. She talked to me about miracles. And then I awoke, not all at once, of course, but gradually, and I suffered, and she soothed me as best she could, and the miracle actually began to occur, as even I became aware through the pain that I was healing. And then one day, the doctors congratulated me on my extraordinary recovery, a pretty young nurse pushed me out to the curb in a wheelchair, and Allison drove me home and cared for me there.

One month later, with the doctors' permission and the promise of a generous settlement from the nationally prominent moving company that owned the truck that had smashed into me, we flew to Bermuda from Indianapolis for the sun, sand, and sea air, but mostly for the crystal clear water itself. We both love skin diving, and Allison is a true mermaid, both as swimmer and long-haired beauty. She dove beneath me at one point to look more closely at a triton shell as we drifted along one of the more magnificent reefs. Floating above her, admiring the long legs and utter grace of the woman who was soon to be my wife, the memory struck me *hard*, so hard that I raised my head from the water and ripped the snorkel tube from my mouth in my panicked need for deep breathing.

You know how it is with only a few dreams in your lifetime, when everything is in brilliant color, and when you wake abruptly and can remember every detail? This was more, much more than that. I'm a painter, remember, figurative not abstract, and I try so hard to capture a single instant on the canvas in a way that at least suggests what came before and what may come afterward. But nothing I have ever done comes remotely close to the timelessness of that moment, as if infinity had been contained in that instant and nothing else is necessary or even thinkable. There I was again, floating over my twisted and bloodied body and suddenly becoming aware of the need to turn my disembodied head toward the side of the road, and there she was, standing there just a few feet away, alabaster skin without a line in her face, and then her eyes fastened on mine, and the flash in my mind's camera flared, and the image was somehow etched in the finest detail in my mind or something that served as my mind in a state beyond my experience and even my belief.

And the earlier circumstances came flooding back as well. I was in the Forester again, returning from the central police station to my home by the lake, driving smoothly on the two-lane blacktop, easing into the self-hypnosis where your reactions are automatic and the body drives the car rather than the mind. It was dusk, drizzly, the sky was gray, the wind was blowing, and I had just hit the base of the steep but short hill that signaled the five-minute mark before I would turn off toward the lake.

4

And there she was with her feet actually on the pavement and her right arm extended fully with her index finger pointing to my left. If I had swerved immediately, just at that instant, the truck might have missed me altogether, which was probably the way it was supposed to be, but I used that instant unwisely to look at her and wonder what she was doing. When I looked up, I saw that the truck barreling down from the top of the hill had crossed the center line and was eating up my lane. I jerked the wheel hard to the left automatically to avoid the head-on strike, not caring in that instant what might be waiting for me in the ditch on the other side of the road or the trees beyond it. Time slowed. I saw the truck driver's face. The car skidded. The truck plowed into the right rear. The car flipped and rolled … and I was floating above my bloody body and I felt the compulsion to look to the side of the road and our eyes met and the camera flashed … and I was swimming in the blue waters of Bermuda with my memories intact but my mind in shreds as my real body, or at least the one I was used to, floated above Allison.

As soon as she surfaced and lifted her mask on to her forehead, Allison knew there was a problem. "You're terribly white, honey. What's wrong?"

"Help me to shore," I said. "Please."

I don't really remember reaching our room, but I know that I was shivering badly and I asked Allison to turn off the air-conditioning. She climbed into the bed with me and held me close after the resort's doctor had left. "Too much sun probably," he had said. "Keep drinking the water and stay inside the rest of the day. I'll check with you tomorrow."

That night, I told Allison about the accident, the out-of-body experience, and the woman who could see me. She asked the right questions, and she gave me the right support. Nevertheless, I don't think she believed me. Not then.

I called my neurologist in Indianapolis the next day, and he actually returned the call no more than an hour later. I told him that my memory of the accident had returned but with a twist that was troubling me.

"I would like to see you next week," he said, after I gave him some of the details. "You may experience odd mental effects for years, including false memories that you would absolutely swear were true. Come in Wednesday afternoon if you can."

We cut the trip short a few days. Allison was wonderful about it. The tests were good, and the doctor assured me that I was doing exceptionally well and that I shouldn't worry about strange memories that might appear periodically. Worry was not the right word—*obsess* captured my mood much more closely.

What is important for you to understand is that the single instant of eye contact was burned into my consciousness in a way that I cannot compare to anything else. The brightness and clarity of the image was not only unlike any other dream but also unlike any moment of my waking life. And how—if I really was in a dis-embodied, "astral" state—could the woman lock on to my invisible eyes in my invisible body floating several feet above my pathetic visible body?

I think she made a mistake, you see. She should not have made eye contact with me, because the shock of contact with the transcendental imprinted itself into my soul, if that is what we are really getting at here. And, even then, my bodily consciousness would have forgotten it if I had not been floating above Allison in the crystal blue waters off Bermuda and the similar sensation of looking down on a body had not triggered the memory of the out-of-body experience.

And there is more. I am an artist. Do they really not know these things? I am not only an artist, but a sketch artist who worked part-time for the Indianapolis Police Department. Oh, I had other ambitions, of course, like everyone else with a flair for drawing. I did formal portraits, oil on canvas, for increasingly attractive sums of money. Allison was impressed. But the police work was steady, and I had a knack for it. There is a subtle psychic element that separates those who can extract just the right contours and shadings from the information provided by the victims and those who do the journeyman work that usually fails to produce an image that leads to an arrest. I was also unusually good with names and always had been. My mother said that I would point at objects as a very young boy and call out their names, particularly animals, which always fascinated me. The ability to remember names also helped on occasion with perpetrator identifications, as the face on an emerging sketch could trigger the name of a suspect in a mug shot that I had seen months before. I was in demand—and apparently far more than I had realized.

I went directly home from the neurologist's office to my studio at the lake and produced the first pen-and-ink sketch of her. The eyes were the hardest, but I got them too on the second try. I had never had a subject like her, you see. The image was so intense in my mind that I could see her staring at me from the paper the entire time I was working on her. It was more like tracing than sketching. I had the ideal subject for my portrait—a woman who never moved, who gazed at me from within my own psyche. I kept staring at the second sketch. Staring. And then I called Allison and told her that I would need two days of intense work alone in order to finish a portrait. I told her that I loved her, and it was true. She was understanding, as always.

I did not understand, however. I only knew that I had to do a color portrait. The only way to soften the burning image from my mind—soften, because I knew that I could not remove it—was to transfer some of its fire and sharp-edged clarity to the canvas. I unplugged the phones. And I began.

I didn't eat for two days. I barely slept. I drank only water. Alcohol would have sickened me. When the colors were not right, I paced. I would lie down for a minute or two and then return to the 30x40 canvas, and then repeat the process, and the image began to grow in size and power. I wanted crisp detail, almost but not quite photo realism. I had to have the emanation, the crackle of raw power contained and softened within a woman's body. I had to compress that and focus it in her eyes. And yet the task was easy, because I felt the very force that I was trying to capture flowing into my hands and into the portrait.

When the creative energy is flowing, you can reach a point of inexhaustion, a point at which strength builds on strength, when the body seizes full control of the metabolic processes and frees the mind and the spirit to soar. And then, if you are blessed at least once in your lifetime, the mind itself breaks away like a spent container for the vehicle that is lifting you into space, and you penetrate at last into the silence of the living void, where invisible energy shoots through you and from you, and the work that is produced does not really belong to you at all but to the source of inexhaustible power. "Weave a circle round him thrice, for he hath drunk the milk of paradise."

When I awoke on the couch late on the third morning, I knew that the painting was finished, and I knew that it was good, but I truly could not remember exactly what it looked like. I put on the coffee in the small kitchen adjoining the heavy-beamed great room, showered and shaved, and then returned in a towel to pour the coffee into my favorite mug. I drank it slowly and looked out across the lake. The autumn sun was shining brightly through the glass of the sliding doors that led to the terrace. Still I delayed. I threw on a flannel shirt and chinos and stepped into my old fleece-lined slippers. I plugged in the phones and left a message for Allison at school to ask her if she could come by for dinner. Then I called my father, Hank Daniels, who lived in Chicago with Mom and still handled a few law cases, one of them being mine. I left a message on his machine.

Finally, with nothing else to serve as a decent excuse, I entered the studio on the other side of the great room and approached the easel. It's funny about the word "breathtaking," because that's not the way it is. You suck in your breath quickly when something stuns you. It's breath-giving, as if you need the extra oxygen to deal with the event. And there it was, the image I had been carrying in my brain and beyond since the breakthrough in Bermuda. It's funny, too, because I hadn't realized she was beautiful until then. I had been so jolted by the electricity in her eyes that I had not been able consciously to encompass the whole woman calmly and clearly. Yet something in me had been able to do so. The hypnotic, almost seething blue eyes drew me deeply into the canvas.

I blinked and purposely refocused my vision around the eyes instead and gradually expanded my view to take in her head, shoulders, and hair—her hair, blond, long, and full, yet wispy the farther it fell from her face, as if pushed outward by the electricity in the eyes. She had a small, straight nose, full lips, no lipstick. Her smooth, flawless skin glowed with health. Her face was so lovely and her eyes so powerful that I did not even notice the light green raincoat at first, but, yes, that was what she wore, and somehow that unflattering garment only added to her beauty. The painting stopped at her chest. It was as if I had zoomed in on the image in my mind and taken a head-and-shoulders snapshot of her. The background was dim—dark blue sky and a few trees fading into the gloaming. A subtle aura of light surrounded her, perhaps the rays of the sinking sun. I couldn't take my eyes off her. I had to take my eyes off her. I draped a cloth over the painting and returned to the great room and the kitchen to pour another cup of coffee.

By the time Allison arrived, I had cleaned up the studio and the rest of the cabin, marinated the steaks and prepared the vegetables for the grill, uncorked the cabernet sauvignon, changed into a sport coat and sweater outfit more appropriate for dinner with my fiancée, and lighted the wood fire in the great room. The scene was set, and the male lead was in place, but I wasn't at all certain that I knew my lines. Is there any way at all to describe an obsession without seeming to be obsessed and very likely as mad as a hatter? Allison, I would like you to meet a beautiful mystery woman who is more important to me right now than you are. I know you'll understand. No, somehow I imagined she would not understand.

But I had not calculated on the power of the painting. I had not been at all sure that others would feel the same power emanating from it. As we drank our wine, I invited her into the studio to see the work that had kept me from her. I lifted the cloth … and she simply stared without saying a word for at least a full minute. She slowly set down the glass of wine on a side table without taking her eyes from the painting.

"I can't look away from her eyes," she said, pronouncing each word slowly and distinctly. "I'm stunned. This is the most spectacular thing you have ever done, Jake. I don't know what to say. Is she the one from the accident?"

"Yes," I said. "She is the one who tried to warn me, the one who stood next to me afterward, and the one who could see my spirit floating above my body. I know it all sounds crazy, my love, but every word is true. You need to trust me on this one, not the doctor."

"I love you, Jake," she said tenderly. "I almost lost you. I will love this woman too, if she is the one who somehow prevented your death." Tears started to flow down both cheeks. "But can anyone like the person in that painting really exist?"

The phone rang as I started to say that the painting itself could not capture the full aura of power streaming from the image in my mind. It was my father calling from Chicago.

"Congratulations, son!" he said exuberantly. "You can now care for me in my old age!"

"What do you mean, Dad?"

"I mean that I had them over a barrel. The evidence is all there—the driver behind you, the skid marks, even the statement that the truck driver gave to the police before the corporate attorneys stepped in. They will continue to pay all medical expenses

10

as necessary—and they have agreed to damages of ten million dollars if we drop all other claims and help them a bit with the media. What do you say?"

It was my turn to be stunned. Dad had handled the negotiations with the moving company pretty much on his own. They had been good from the beginning about the medical bills. But ten million dollars?

"I say you're a genius, Dad, and I will gladly help them in any way in return. Thank you."

"Genius does appreciate recognition. On the other hand, you should be dead, you know. Instead, you're about to marry an incredible young woman, and now you're rich to boot. I would say you should thank your guardian angel, son!"

CHAPTER II

ARIEL

*W*hat I couldn't understand, you see, was what was so special about me, thirty-year-old Jake Daniels, sketch artist and aspiring painter. I had always loved the forest and animals. I have to smile to admit it, but I actually had been an Eagle Scout, until I went to the University of Indiana in Bloomington and learned that the young women who interested me there had not been Girl Scouts. I was tall for my age in school, and I played some basketball, like every other boy in Indiana. My main talent, though, was always drawing, going well back into grade school, and I had a particular talent for sketching wildlife in biology classes. My lawyer father was never overly pleased with that, but he didn't let it show much, and he actually supported my ambition to be a professional artist when a few of my projects began to win awards.

I was certainly no criminal—I had one speeding ticket on my record. I did genuinely try not to hurt other people. And Allison liked the fact that animals, kids, and older people all seemed to take to me. Nevertheless, the only person who might ever have nominated me for sainthood was my mother, who was, shall we say, constitutionally unable to look at her son with a critical eye. The same was certainly not true of a number of women in my life who were no longer in my life, largely because of each other. So a saint I was not. Why me?

I needed to know why an intervention had occurred that defied the normal laws of existence in order to save my life, for that is what I firmly believed had happened. I needed to know if there were others like me. And I needed to know more, much more about angels. If they existed, there would have to be records of their contacts with humans—many in the Bible, of course, but many more, I suspected, in other texts and contexts.

I began the search on both the mental and physical levels, in academic research and old-fashioned police work. Money was no longer an obstacle to anything. I paid for the right to conduct research at Butler University, complete with a study carrel of my own at the library and access to the Internet. Then I set out to find the truck driver, whose shocked face was also firmly set in my memory. More to the point, the record of the accident was firmly set in both the police files and the legal documents in my father's office. The driver's name was Jimmy Harrison, and he lived outside the city in Carmel.

My first response was pity when he opened the door to his run-down rambler. He was forty years old, out-of-shape, and bleary-eyed. I also knew that he was unemployed.

"Who are you?" he asked gruffly.

"I'm the man you crushed with your truck," I said. "But I'm here to give you some money in exchange for some information," I added quickly as he was about to shut the door.

"I'll tell you anything you want. I don't owe those bastards *nuthin*!"

The truth is he wasn't such a bad guy. He had been cited by the police for failure to control his vehicle, and the company had fired him within a week of the accident, in part because he had given honest answers to the police before calling his company. Unless he hired himself, his days as a truck driver were over.

"It was all so fast," he said while sitting across from me. "The blinding light, that damned wind, the skid, your car, me fighting to keep the damned truck on the road. As soon as I got it stopped, I came running over to you and what was left of your car."

"You said 'blinding light.' What blinding light?" I asked.

"I dunno. You must've switched to brights. But it seemed like it came from the side a little. I dunno. I just know I was blinded and then the truck was moving over the line with the wind howling, and I couldn't fight it back in time and then you swerved in front of me. And, damn, it all happened so fast!"

"Did you see a woman standing next to my body?"

"That wasn't a woman, buddy. That was the guy driving the car behind you. He had stopped and pulled his car across the road to head off traffic. He was standing over you when I got there. 'He's dead,' he said to me. 'I'll call the cops. You call an ambulance.' We both had cells, and we both called 911. I don't know why. But as I'm talking to the operator and giving her the message, I hear the sirens and I look up and there's the ambulance and a police car both. It all happened so *fast*, you know. It don't make sense really. Maybe I was in shock too. The other guy starts running back to his car and waving the ambulance in, and I turn to look at you. And it was so beautiful, man. The light from the sun, I guess, bouncing off the clouds. I dunno. But it was like you were glowing. And I'm thinking maybe the guy's not dead after all. Please, God, don't let him be dead, I said. I'm glad you made it, buddy."

"I know that you did what you could," I said. "But, look, there was a woman on my side of the road who tried to warn me that your truck was crossing the line, and then I saw her again standing next to me when I was stretched out on the road." I opened my briefcase and showed him the sketch. "This is what she looks like."

"Wow!" he said. "That is one lady I would never forget. But I didn't see any lady that night, either before or after the accident.

And you gotta believe me when I tell you: You didn't either. You were as close to dead as it's possible to get—and I've seen some bad smash-ups on the road. I thought you *were* dead, and so did the other guy. I guess the emergency guys getting there so fast saved your life." He stopped for a second and stared out the window. "You know, I still don't know how they got there that fast. It don't make sense to me."

I put the sketch back in the briefcase and closed it. "Thank you for your time," I said. "And thank you again for doing what you could." I handed him the check for ten thousand dollars. "I hope this helps a little. I've seen the report. You weren't drinking. You cooperated fully with the police. Visibility was poor and the road was slick. I don't know about the light, but I think maybe you got a raw deal. Get it back together, brother. We only have one life, you know."

We shook hands. He thanked me and returned the grip hard, looking me square in the eye. I liked him. As I walked back to the car, though, I thought that maybe I had lied to him. The line was automatic, something I had said a few times before, but I have never used the "one life" thing again.

* * *

If you are the way I was then, you probably do not know much about angels. Oh, you will remember that the angel appeared to Mary and told her that she would be bearing God's child. If you are a devout Christian, you will know the entire story of the Annunciation. You will also think about the angels on high announcing the birth of Christ in Bethlehem. You may think about the angel that rolled back the stone on the first Easter, and then you may recall some of the florid text in Revelation that you didn't understand as a child and that nobody truly understands as an adult. You will probably have to stretch to get beyond that, although some of the references in the Old Testament are interesting, and I will get to that later.

If you are a Mormon, things cut closer to home, since you believe that the angel Moroni appeared to Joseph Smith in the United States in the nineteenth century and delivered the golden tablets to him that constitute the Book of Mormon.

If you are a Muslim, you may also be more comfortable with the idea of angels than I was back then. The Prophet refers to them frequently, and the Quran was revealed to him by the angel Gabriel.

In fact, almost all religions bear witness to angels or at least to supernatural beings that serve the Almighty both in heaven and on earth—and to demons, unfortunately, including Christianity.

And, of course, you will joke about guardian angels after a near escape, although something in you will hope that they are real.

There is a fraternity of people, though, who go way beyond these things. If you are among them, I can only apologize for the simplicity of my understanding then. I knew nothing at that time about those who devote their lives to the study of angels. Some of them, to put it gently, are a card or two short of a full deck. Others are frauds. Some are merely gullible. Some are all of these. And then there are those who study seriously and sincerely, who compile the stories, and who try to subject the data to some structured and rational analysis.

I began to read at the university.

Did you know, for example, that the various orders of angels have descended to us from the obscure sixth-century pseudo-Dionysius or Dionysius the Areopagite? Neither did I. Nor is it particularly important, as it seems clear that he misread one of the letters of Paul and wrongly added thrones, dominions, powers, principalities, and virtues to the more familiar list of seraphim, cherubim, archangels, and angels.

I was stunned to learn that there are those today who will argue about these classifications just as strenuously as divines in the Middle Ages argued about the number of angels that can fit on the head of a pin.

Have you read the Book of Enoch, a noncanonical work that has now been dated to at least the second century BC, since fragments of it were unearthed with the Dead Sea Scrolls at Qumran? The early Church fathers accepted the once-lost book as holy Scripture, and it is hard to dismiss the belief that Jesus must have read it as well, as it is so prominent among the scrolls of the Essenes. It is still part of the official canon of the Ethiopian Coptic Church. Why is it important? The Book of Enoch is replete with angels, including the names of the leaders of the fallen rebels, who "saw that the daughters of men were fair, and they took to wife such of them as they chose." It is for that sin, according to Enoch, and the subsequent births of sinful "giants in the earth," that the angels were cast down. The Old Testament bears no reference to a battle in heaven.

None of that was known to John Milton, of course, and it is odd to find even scholarly works on angels that refer to his poetic imagination in *Paradise Lost* as a primary source for our presumed knowledge of angels. I have spoken with ministers who hopelessly confuse *Paradise Lost* with the Bible and relate with passion the awesome struggle between the two factions of heavenly hosts. Yet the only mention in the Bible of such a battle lies in the scant description of *Revelation 12:7-9* with no detail to support either Milton or the ministers.

If you are not Catholic or Eastern Orthodox, you will probably know nothing of the Book of Tobit, but it remains in the canon of those churches, and Hebrew fragments of that book were also found in one of the caves at Qumran in 1955. The entire book is filled with the presence of the angel Raphael as he assists Tobit and his son Tobias.

And so I continued to read about angels at the university as the days and the weeks passed, both the primary works and the commentaries. One reference led to another and yet another. There was no end. Ambrose, Augustine, Jerome, Aquinas, Scotus, The Zohar, Kaballah, Swedenborg, Steiner ...

Yes, there were bits and pieces that flew off the page directly into my mind and stuck there at that time. Ambrose, for example: "We should pray to the angels who are given to us as guardians." And Augustine: "Every visible thing in this world is put in the charge of an angel." And even Jesus in *Matthew 18:10:* "See that you do not despise one of these little ones; for I tell you that in heaven their angels always behold the face of my Father who is in heaven."

And yet somehow it was the simple contemporary stories, the new testaments to apparent encounters with angels that affected me most profoundly. I found myself engrossed in the hesitant recollections of farmers, housewives, and solid citizens throughout the United States who had kept the stories to themselves out of fear of ridicule and yet had pondered them in their hearts until such time as they could relate them to sympathetic researchers who would not abuse their trust. What do we make of these strangers who appear in the midst of snowstorms and save stranded motorists, or who protect children from certain death, or who lay their hands on the sick in hospitals, or who lift the drowning from the water, or who guide the family from a burning house, or who perform all manner of miracles and then disappear? Are all of the people who report such things struggling at the far end of sanity?

I would have thought so in times past. No longer.

There was one uncontested bit of information that appeared in every treatise on angels—the derivation of the word itself: from Latin *angelus* and from Greek *angelos*, meaning literally "messenger."

The stories, both in the religious texts and in the personal narratives, indicated that these spiritual beings, if real, conveyed messages directly from God and that they also were entrusted with direct intercession in the lives of human beings—often the two were the same thing.

My mind kept returning to "messenger" and "message," until I finally remembered what Jimmy had said: *But as I'm talking to the operator and giving her the message, I hear the sirens and I look up and there's the ambulance and a police car both. It all happened so fast, you know. It don't make sense, really.*

It didn't make sense. How could the emergency vehicles have arrived before the messages were delivered on the cell phones? But what doesn't make sense is always a good place to start when someone is trying to learn something new, and the police department is always a good place to start when the subject is 911 calls.

Actually, those calls are sometimes routed through emergency operators at fire departments or elsewhere in a city's emergency management system. Not in Indianapolis, though, where the system is smooth and reliable through the police department, and I knew the operator supervisor. Written transcripts of all calls were held on file indefinitely, and audio recordings were kept for a minimum of one year.

Even though it was my own case, Maggie made me fill out three pages of paperwork in order to read the transcript and listen to the tape. Yes, they had the call on file. With the date of the accident, approximate time, and my own name cited afterward as the injured party on the scene, it was not difficult to trace. There was also a notation on the side indicating that two other calls had been initiated but dropped as vehicles arrived at the accident site.

The transcript was brief and to the point:

Operator: This is the 911 emergency operator.

Caller: There has been a traffic accident between a moving van and an SUV on State Road 37 near West Southport Road. One man is seriously injured and requires immediate treatment.

Operator: May I have your name please?

Caller: Hurry! (Caller terminated conversation. No telephone number appeared on ID trace. Location and number of caller unknown.)

Maggie helped me find the call on the cassette, and both of us listened to the brief exchange. The difference between the words on the page and the passionate message in the voice of the caller was startling. I had never before heard such peremptory urgency in anyone's voice. Yet the voice itself was crystalline clear, unwavering, and decidedly feminine. It was the undertone of unquestioned authority that struck us both with such raw force. The imperative power of *"Hurry!"* on the tape had us both reaching instinctively for the phone on the table, and both of us slowly pulled our hands back and laughed nervously while looking uncomfortably into each other's eyes.

"Now I understand," Maggie said slowly. "It was *you*, and I'm glad the operator acted as she did. But I didn't understand until now why this call was acted on at all. Usually, if the caller fails to give a name or number or any other required information, and we cannot reconnect, then we don't move on it immediately. You would be surprised, I'm afraid, at the number of fake calls that we receive. Jake, I almost swung into action myself just now on a call that was made nearly eight months ago. What's going on? Our system not only failed to pick up a Caller ID, but it seemed to go dead completely during the call. All we have is the recording. Who is she?"

"I wish I knew," I said. "The truth is, I saw a woman at the scene, but nobody else did. The first two men to reach me said that I was dead. One of them says that the ambulance arrived before he could even call in the accident. Let me see the transcript again."

Maggie pushed the document across the table. I looked at the boxes at the top—date, time, caller, etc.

"May I have a copy of this, Maggie?" I asked.

"Sure," she said. "Let me know if you learn who she is. I'm not certain that I'd like to talk with her, but I would like to know how she developed that voice."

She got up and took the document to the copier in the hallway. I called to her from the table in the reading room. "Thanks again, Maggie. I owe you twice on this one." My thoughts were swirling around another document though.

When I got home, I took the file out of the cabinet and placed the police report on the center of my desk. I put the transcript alongside it. Police report: *Time of accident: appx. 6:15 p.m.* Telephone transcript: *Time of call: 5:59 p.m.*

* * *

How did I feel in those days? You should know that I had never been very religious before the accident and that I had never even considered the possibility that angels might really exist. I can't tell you that I was completely convinced even after the evidence began to mount that I had truly encountered a supernatural reality that had broken through into my everyday existence. That was part of the problem, you see. All of us long for proof of God's existence, proof that there is an afterlife, and proof that our lives and our suffering are meaningful. There are times for all of us when we feel absolutely certain about God, afterlife, and ultimate meaning behind human existence but then the everyday grabs us by the throat and pulls us down into worrying about our jobs, our families, our bills, and even the state of our digestion and imperfections in our skin. The certainty disappears, and we shift back into body awareness and the everyday world and the odd self-hypnosis that convinces all of us that death will never come, certainly no time soon, certainly not until we are old and wasted and longing for it.

Oh, I was not oblivious to the cracks in normal reality that were opening up all around me, far from it. I knew that I was obsessed with proving the validity of both my memory and my experience. The further I probed, the more certain I became that mistakes had been made. She should not have looked into my astral eyes and therefore proven that she could see me in spirit. She should have known that I was an artist who could recreate her image. She should have known about my contacts in the police department and my ability to trace the call that was logged before the accident. I had an unimaginably rare opportunity to prove to myself and the world that our supernatural longings are all based in reality, and I would use that opportunity and the mistakes that were made to lighten the unspeakable load of death that we have always carried on our shoulders and struggled with in our minds.

No, I was not a character in *The X-Files* who continues to disbelieve in the reality of the occult even after it is proven to him week after week, or a character in a horror movie who discounts all of the signs of the monster until it devours him. Nevertheless, the power of the everyday is almost invincible, and perhaps it has been designed that way in order to ensure that we take life seriously and continue to play our parts in the grand play with earnest passion. I could not completely shake the thought, for example, that my doctor was right and that my mental faculties were still fragile and likely to mislead me. Moreover, I truly loved Allison, and there were wedding plans to finalize and a precious relationship to nurture. My hardheaded lawyer father added to the mix by flooding me with details about the settlement, investments, taxes, and a host of other legal issues. There were also friends and unfinished responsibilities with the police department and the desire to paint and household matters and all of the other demands on my time and my energy and my shaky mind. The everyday is so powerful, you see, and I almost succumbed to it and what I knew as normal and the sense of reality shared by most of us on the planet.

But only almost. I had my trump cards—the painting and the soul-piercing eyes in the painting. And now I had a soul-shattering voice to go with it. I told my doctor that I would continue to check in with him faithfully. I told Allison that I loved her deeply, and I asked for and received her continued patience and understanding. I told my father to handle as much as he could on his own, and I asked that one hundred thousand dollars be placed in my checking account. I sent an email message to my friends, resigned from my job at the police department, and devoted myself to the one task ahead.

Then I set out to find her.

* * *

How would you begin? I sent letters to the many living authors of books devoted to descriptions of angelic encounters. I told them my story in outline and asked for their advice in contacting angelic beings. Most never answered. In fact, it is unlikely that the letters ever penetrated the walls erected by publishers, agents, secretaries, and others. The two who did respond advised me on meditation and visualization techniques.

I continued my research at the university, and I read through the Bible intensively. However, there was nothing in any of the texts about actually summoning angels. Oddly enough, though, there were countless incantations and techniques for summoning demons, as if they were somehow more inclined to accept the invitation. No, angels were sent on special missions by God, and guardian angels appeared in times of mortal danger. They were not likely to pop in for a chat.

And then I heard about the angel festivals and conventions. Spurred on by the television series *Touched by an Angel,* they had sprung up all over the country. I attended three of them—in Nashville, Phoenix, and Los Angeles, in that order. Suddenly, interest in angels seemed to be skyrocketing. A Gallup poll showed that about eighty percent of Americans believed in their existence. And why not? I thought. If I am well on my way to believing, why shouldn't others also believe? Perhaps the incidence of intervention is far greater than anyone supposes. Perhaps everyone truly has a guardian angel, and the world is now awakening to that fact. Perhaps my task will be much easier than I had dreamed.

I placed the painting carefully in its travel case, printed five hundred copies of the sketch in flyer form, packed my bags and the flyers, along with my banner, and began my journey, traveling first-class air for the first time in my life.

Nashville, Tennessee—capitol of the state, home of the Grand Ole Opry, and the country music center of America. The festival itself was being held in one wing of the Nashville Convention Center, where I dutifully set up my small booth with the painting displayed handsomely on an easel beside me and the flyers stacked on the cloth-covered table in front of me. I stretched the white silk banner with gold fringe behind me between two flag stands provided by the convention center. Its message was simple enough: "HAVE YOU MET THIS ANGEL?" Then I placed two clipboards between the two stacks of leaflets. Each clipboard held a sign-in sheet with the same "HAVE YOU MET THIS ANGEL?" at the top and space provided for up to twenty people to provide their names, addresses, and telephone numbers. It was a start.

Strangely enough, I didn't even feel sheepish about it. In fact, in the beginning, I felt as if I were returning home, the prodigal son surrounded by his people at last. I may be crazy, I reasoned, but, Lord help me, I am no crazier than the thousands streaming through here. It was a madhouse, no doubt, in more ways than one, but the inmates were happy, sincere people who had either actually been touched by an angel, so they said, or were honestly looking forward to the experience with humility in their hearts and passion in their souls. I sat on one of two chairs behind the table, along with the other exhibitors and purveyors of angelic wares, as the doors opened and the masses began to enter. I should not have been surprised, I suppose, but the sheer numbers and eagerness of the faithful amazed me, as if we were offering big-screen television sets for fifty dollars "while they last" instead of a rather suspect glimpse into heaven.

Nevertheless, the crowd flowed into the hall and through the stalls like a tsunami spilling through the streets of a city. I knew that the painting would draw some interest, yet I was far from prepared to deal with the heap of humanity deposited before me as the great wave settled and gradually began to recede.

Too late, I realized that I needed a sound system in order to compete with the rumble of the human tide and the electronic speakers springing to life all around me. I stood up and did the best I could.

"Ladies and gentlemen," I shouted. "I need your help. Has anyone else ever met this angel?"

The response was uncoordinated babble. I quickly picked up one of the stacks of flyers and began to pass them out to the extended hands while trying to shout my story in the least offensive and most comprehensible way possible. I know that I failed. The crowd quickly dispersed, leaving a remnant of some ten souls staring at the painting as the deafening noise in the hall around us continued unabated.

"Who do yuh think she is then?" asked an elderly gentleman in overalls standing directly in front of me.

"I believe she is an angel," I shouted into his right ear. "I believe she saved my life."

"Ah caint read the writin' at the bottom uh this here paper," he said.

"It says to contact me at the address or phone number listed if you have ever seen this woman—or angel—before. My name is Jake Daniels."

"Pleased to meet yuh," he said. "Ah'm Earl Dawkins." We shook hands. He kept gazing back and forth between the image that he held in his hand and the much larger color portrait on the easel. As he did so, I passed out the flyer to the three or four others who were not already holding it. Other questions arose. They were nice people. Nobody laughed.

"And what's this other thing?" Mr. Dawkins asked a few minutes later as he pointed to the clipboard.

"Well, that's really for people to leave their contact information for me if I'm not at the booth and they think that they recognize the woman. Those people should leave their names, addresses, and phone numbers so that I can contact them later."

"Oh," he said, as I turned back to the others.

The first group moved on and others took their places. Even Mr. Dawkins left after about fifteen minutes of staring at the painting. He smiled at me as he moved away slowly and said in his slow drawl, "A real angel."

There were plenty more like him: decent, hard-working people who believed in angels or at least wanted to find something to help them counter their disbelief. And there were others, of course, who seemed to merge together after a while as they passed by my booth: middle-aged flower children, all in white with gold crosses; teenagers hooked on *Touched by an Angel;* the devout elderly sensing mortality breathing down their necks; and the hucksters, most of them so obvious that it was painful to watch them. The latter were the most frequent speakers or performers on the huge stage at one end of the hall. Almost all of them were selling something. They were the money-changers at the temple, transforming piety into the coins that you could almost hear clinking in their pockets as they walked by. Some were selling their books, others their audio and video tapes, still others their retreats and techniques guaranteed to bring the enrollees into direct contact with their personal angels—unless their hearts were impure, of course, in which case the advanced course was definitely required.

Even the music from the loudspeakers around the hall that wafted through the atmosphere whenever the stage was bare seemed to sound more like dollar bills inserted into a wallet than the flutter of angel wings.

And yet whenever "Angels Among Us" by the group Alabama began to flow through those same loudspeakers, a hush would fall upon the hall as everyone began to reconnect with the real thing that had brought them there:

> *Oh, I believe there are angels among us*
> *Sent down to us from somewhere up above.*
> *They come to you and me in our darkest hours*
> *To show us how to live,*
> *To teach us how to give,*
> *To guide us with a light of love.*

Yes, the faces looked different then, and a softness smothered the clink of coins, and the possibility of the truly miraculous began to shine through the merchandising and the hucksterism:

> *They wear so many faces,*
> *Show up in the strangest places,*
> *Grace us with their mercy*
> *In our time of need.*

And who was to say at that moment that an angel might not already be at that strange place wearing the face of a tired waitress, say, who might just brush up against you and cure your eczema or flash the warm smile that turns you away from the drug overdose?

On the second evening of the festival, I felt the need to break away from its single focus and clear my head. I reserved a ticket in the afternoon for the Grand Ole Opry, handed the painting to security for safekeeping, and took a cab that evening to the performance at the Grand Ole Opry House across the river. I didn't really care who was performing. I just needed a respite.

I also should have known better, as whatever was driving me was not about to lift the pressure. I noticed a poster for the Nashville Angels Band even before I reached the ticket counters. When I did have my ticket in hand, I could not overlook the main attraction spelled out in large type—"Honky Tonk Angels." When I really looked around for the first time in the huge lobby, the signs for Honky Tonk Angels jumped out at me everywhere. Sitting in the cab thinking about why I was in Nashville as we approached the theater, I never noticed the sign blazing on the marquee until after the show. I actually laughed out loud in the lobby to the surprise of several people standing near me before I began to look for my seat.

For all I know to this day, the Opry may have arranged the production purposely to coincide with the festival. It didn't matter. Bathed in the glow of synchronicity, I took my seat and enjoyed the show. I learned not only that "It Wasn't God Who Made Honky Tonk Angels," but also what it is that angels do:

> *That's what angels do; that's what love is for:*
> *Points you to a window when you can't find a door.*
> *When you're all out of faith and it's more than you can take,*
> *You're not strong enough; you need someone to pull you*
>   *through.*
> *That's what angels do.*

Somehow, "That's What Angels Do" resonated within me. You know what it's like when you hear a song on the car radio that just exactly fits your situation at the moment? I can't even say to you honestly that I am a big fan of country music. It was the atmosphere, of course, the festival itself combined with the odd coincidence of country rhythms driving home the angel imagery. Anyway, I kept thinking about my angel pointing at the truck as it crossed the centerline and warning me at the last instant before certain death, and I knew for certain that I had not been spiritually strong enough to pull my spirit back into my body. *She* had saved me. Why?

The next day was the wind-up of the festival. I felt energized, as if the homespun music had cut through the artifice of the festival and the synchronicity of the events had validated my search. I noticed that more people had signed the sheets on the clipboards in my absence. Even those who stopped to chat about the painting or to pick up a flyer—more out of a wish to retain the image than to help me, I'm sure—seemed more genuine and more credible. One gray-haired woman in particular, around fifty or so, spoke unusually clearly and directly about her experience with that indefinable ring of truth in her voice that almost compels your acceptance.

"I have never met her," she said, referring to the painting, "but I recognize the power in her eyes. There is no way for them to disguise that."

"You said 'them.' Who are 'they'?" I asked.

"Oh, you must know yourself," she said, "since you obviously have been with this one long enough to capture the eyes. They're the guardians, of course—real angels, I think, who step in from time to time and alter things. I don't believe they undermine free will, mind you, but instead they make sure that it's honored by cancelling out the accidents that would claim certain souls before their time. That's what I think."

"And why do you think that? What happened?" I asked.

"Mister, I've met them twice," she said firmly. "I wasn't sure the first time, but there is no way to forget those eyes. So the second time I knew. Look, my husband and I were driving at night, coming home from a visit to my mother, who lived in a farming community about a hundred miles out of Nashville. The blizzard came out of nowhere before we could reach the main road. The car slid into a ditch, and the engine died. There was nobody else on the road. After half an hour, we were freezing, no matter how close we held each other. It was dark, and the wind was blowing the snow around fiercely, drifting it up around the car. Charlie's eyes were closed, and I felt myself sinking into sleep. And then two men yanked open Charlie's door and pulled him out of the car. You tell me how they could do that—the snow was up to the window. They stood him up on the snow-covered road and shook him. Then one of them reached in for me and pulled me out. The snow was swirling around us like crazy and the wind was whistling. The next thing I really remember, we were in some kind of tractor with an enclosed cab, all squeezed in there together, the four of us, moving slowly but steadily. Then I saw some lights through the windshield wipers and the blowing snow, and it was a gas station with a little diner attached to it. They stopped and let us out, but then I turned to the one who helped me down from the cab and lifted my hand to his face to thank him and the hood of his parka slid back a little and I could see his eyes with that sparkling fire in them—the same as in your picture. Then he pulled the hood forward and pointed toward the diner. The people inside rushed to help us when they saw us stumbling through the door."

"And why do you think they were angels," I asked. "Why couldn't they have been just good-hearted farmers who saw the car in the ditch and saved the two people inside?"

"Well, first," she said, "what would two farmers be doing out on a tractor in the middle of the night in the middle of a blizzard? Second, they never said a word. Isn't that strange? Most important, though, I asked the cook right away to take some of the hot soup that they were offering to us out to the two men in the tractor. He nodded, poured some of that life-giving soup into a thermos, then threw on a heavy coat and fur hat, one of those with the earmuffs built in, and plunged out into the night. He was back in a couple of minutes, though, still carrying the thermos, his coat and hat covered with snow. 'There's no tractor and no men out there,' he said. 'And I tell you what, you two been through hell in that storm, so just rest now and warm up. Ma'am, I followed your footprints, and they're fillin' up fast, but they stop at the road, and there ain't no tractor tracks out there, no tracks at all. The snow on that road is deep and smooth—no tracks.'"

She paused and stared at the painting.

"Well, Charlie never remembered any of it after we woke up the next day, still inside that diner. I did, though, and I'll never forget those eyes. We got home through people's kindness the next day, but it took us almost a week to get our car back."

"And the second time?" I asked with real interest.

"I don't want to bore you, Mister," she said, still staring at the painting.

"No, no, please … I really want to know."

"Well," she began slowly. "It still hurts when I think about it. The dog's barking woke me in the middle of the night. There was smoke rising up the stairs and already streaming into our bedroom. I tried to wake up Charlie, but he wouldn't move. I kept shaking him until I heard the voice at the door behind me: 'You must leave now. Your husband has left the body behind.' I turned to see the figure of a woman standing in the doorway, much like the woman in your painting. It was the sparkling eyes again, though, that seized me, the eyes and the voice. 'Do not be afraid,' she said, and, strangely, I wasn't afraid, even though the house was on fire and I was talking with an unknown woman in my bedroom in the middle of the night. She pointed to the window and said, 'You cannot use the stairs. Leave through the window now. Your husband's body will not suffer.' That window had been stuck for years, but it shot up as soon as I touched it. I climbed out on the roof in my nightgown and dropped to the ground after hanging on to the gutter. I wasn't hurt at all. The fire engines arrived shortly after that. Most of the house was gutted, but Charlie wasn't burned at all. They told me later that he had died of a heart attack."

She still stared at the painting. "Poor Charlie," she said. "Why me? Why was I saved twice? What do they want from me?"

After a minute or two of silence, she filled out one of the information sheets. "You can reach me at that address and number if you want to," she said. "But there's not much more I can tell you. There was no woman's body found in the house, of course. That was not a woman. I don't tell people about it usually, but you're here and this seems like the right place. I hope it helps. God bless you."

She put down the pen and walked away. I gathered up the sheets without really looking at them and began to dismantle my booth. The sound of Alabama filtered through the voices and the clamor in the hall:

> *They wear so many faces,*
> *Show up in the strangest places,*
> *Grace us with their mercy*
> *In our time of need.*

* * *

Phoenix was a disappointment—oh, not the city itself, which was surprising in its size and rhythm, a pulsating oasis metropolis in the middle of an unforgiving desert. Did you know that Phoenix is the fifth largest city in the country? Few people do. What I did know was that the very name of the city appealed to the sense of mystery that was consuming me. I had risen like a phoenix myself from the ashes of my own death. I had actually experienced resurrection, for I knew that I truly had died in the accident. The eyewitnesses had told me so, and my own spirit hovering above my body had confirmed their testimony. In Phoenix, then, why should I not find confirmation of her existence and testimony from others about her presence?

Yet somehow my experiences in Nashville had dulled that very sense of mystery. The more adept I became in probing it, the farther away I seemed to slip from it. Oh, I learned from my mistakes in Nashville, and I erected a larger booth at the Phoenix

Convention Center, complete with sound system and a private cubicle for discussion with those who seemed genuine to me. My introductions were smoother, and I could explain my own experience with the angel more glibly, and people came and filled out the forms and told me their stories. Maybe it was predictable, but the more I told the story, the more the magic wore off it, and the more I began to wonder myself whether the most compelling experience of my life might actually have been merely the hallucinations of a gravely injured man.

There was also the western feel of it, the cowboy hats and the Mexican overlay, which impinged on my ability to relate the atmosphere to what I had experienced in Indiana. That was my own shortcoming, I know, but I felt it nevertheless. The crowds were heavy, and, if anything, the sincerity of the participants was more obvious than I had sensed in Nashville. But, despite the enthusiasm of the visitors and the many "angel stores" and the Hispanic name Angel that I saw on business fronts and billboards around the city, I found myself slipping into spiritual apathy and self-doubt in Phoenix, as if the heat and the dryness outside the conference hall had sapped the strength from the mythical bird and left it covered in ashes.

And then there was Los Angeles.

I couldn't explain the difference to myself in the beginning. Humidity replaced dryness, of course. Inline skates replaced cowboy boots. The sheer size of the stretched-out city left an impression of its own. It was the raw vitality of the city and its countless suburbs that struck me most as I arrived. The bustle and the energy of the crowds at the airport were different, the controlled chaos of the freeways was exciting in a hair-raising kind of way, and the characters walking the streets near the Los Angeles Convention Center exuded a different kind of manic freedom. The convention hall itself was bursting with noise and excitement. Yet there was something else in the air, something that I had not felt before, an expectation that bordered on near certainty of … what?

The atmosphere simply felt *right*. How could it not, actually? Los Angeles, the City of Angels. What could be more auspicious? My own sound system competed strongly with all of the others, and it seemed that multitudes had descended upon my booth to stare at the portrait and relate their tales of angelic contact. The sweet smell of marijuana drifted heavily in the air. I began to feel euphoric. The feeling persisted throughout the day and into the evening. As I lay in bed on Friday night at the conference hotel, my mind raced through the events of the day and all the way back to the accident. Suddenly, I realized that the images in my mind had become sharply defined in radiant colors. I knew instantly that I was asleep and dreaming, but the knowledge did not wake me, and soon I lost the awareness in the light of the blazing images. She was staring directly at me, her eyes burning into me, her blond hair flowing behind her like flames—and then she spoke with intense urgency: *"Holy Angels! Holy Angels in the Valley of Gabriel!"*

I awoke in the middle of the night trembling in awe and fear, the image of her and the words as clear in my mind as if she had just been standing three feet in front of me in my hotel room. *Holy Angels! Holy Angels in the Valley of Gabriel!* What in the world did that mean? What out of the world did that mean?

* * *

So I began a search within a search, as wheels within wheels turned in my mind. I felt certain that the dream was far more than a dream. The colors and the intensity were unlike anything I had ever experienced before. I sensed that I could paint her again from memory, but this time from the memory of a dream alone as she looked into my eyes and spoke directly to me. How is it possible to remember dreams anyway, when there is no sensory input from the outside world and therefore nothing to imprint on the brain as a memory? In this case, I *knew* somehow that my poor brain could not have generated the glory of the experience and the lasting power of it. The voice was identical to that on the 911 tape, and the effect was the same, as I felt compelled to understand the message, even though it made no sense at all to me.

Holy Angels? Holy Moly! I had to laugh just to maintain some semblance of sanity. Yes, I believed in the angel and my own preservation at her hands. But was I now to be conversing in my dreams with holy beings? I had somehow moved from buried memories to dream memories, and my hold on "reality" seemed ever more tenuous. And yet … and yet … the power of the voice and the flashing eyes spoke to me at a level far beyond words and even beyond the meaning of communication as I had known it. I searched.

And I found. The very first entry listed under "Valley of Gabriel" on my laptop in the hotel room that same night was the definition of San Gabriel Valley: "… one of the principal valleys of Southern California. It lies to the east of Los Angeles, to the north of the Puente Hills, to the south of the San Gabriel Mountains, and to the west of the Inland Empire." I had no idea what the "Inland Empire" might be, but the linkage of Gabriel to Los Angeles seemed in my strung-out state to be more than simple coincidence. Was it not fitting and ordained that I should encounter the Holy Angel Gabriel in the valley that bore his name in the land of the Angels? On the other hand, I soon learned that San Gabriel Valley is huge, let alone the County of Los Angeles. Just how might a stranger in a strange land go about arranging a meeting with Archangel Gabriel, even if an invitation has been issued?

I didn't know either—but I spent a lot of time thinking about it. My discussions at the conference hall the next day all seemed of secondary importance or worse, and I just could not concentrate on the stories lavished upon me. My frustration reached the breaking point shortly after lunch. I returned to the hotel room and my laptop.

Without hesitation, I typed into the search engine "Holy Angels in San Gabriel Valley," pressed "Enter," and looked again at the very first entry: "Holy Angels Church," Arcadia, San Gabriel Valley. It jumped out at me in red letters, and I knew from the feel of it that it was right and that my invitation now included an address—and a telephone number. I wrote down both on the hotel pad next to the phone and called the church. A pleasant voice informed me that there would be a service at five that afternoon. I lay back on the bed and drifted into a restless sleep, all thought of the conference oddly distant and inconsequential.

A mighty wind filled the hall and disciples praised the Lord and prophesied in strange languages and each looked at each and saw a tongue of flame above the heads of the others and the multitude gathered around them in amazement as they heard the languages of their native lands flowing from the mouths of the blessed and ....

And I awoke with a heavy head and confused thoughts of Pentecost and other dreams that preceded the last one. One glance at my watch shocked me out of my drowsiness, as it was 4:45 and I had planned to leave the hotel no later than 4:15, not knowing how long a taxi might take to Arcadia. I quickly threw cold water on my face in the bathroom, slung my sport coat over my shoulder, and headed for the elevators. There was a taxi stand at the large front entrance, and the bellman quickly placed me in the first one in line. I still felt groggy, and I realized that I had left the address and phone number on the pad next to the pad.

"Do you know the Holy Angels Catholic Church in the San Gabriel Valley?" I asked the driver from the back seat as the taxi began to roll forward.

"No," he said, "but I can call it in and get the directions. It'll just take a second." He pulled to the curb along the circular driveway and rang the dispatcher. We were on our way again in less than a minute. "Lean back and relax," he said. "It's not such a long ride."

"Just get me there," I answered. "I've got an important appointment. I wouldn't miss it if my life depended on it—and maybe it does."

He looked at me a bit oddly in the mirror, but then pulled smoothly into traffic and headed east. I took his advice and relaxed, with the drowsiness seeping back into me heavily. It must be all the travel, the mental pressure, the deep dreaming of the night before, I thought to myself. I remember jerking my head up from my chest twice before finally giving in to it and sinking into the blackness.

"Wake up, buddy," he was saying loudly. "We're here." I surfaced from the depths, blinked in the sunlight, and saw that we were parked in front of a church. I paid the smiling cabbie and stumbled out of the vehicle. It was quiet outside the church, no singing, no organ music, no voice thundering to the rafters filled with the threat of damnation. I glanced at my watch as I walked to the double doors at the front entrance: 5:20 p.m.

Yet, as I walked through one of the front doors and stood inside the shaded anteroom, I felt an enormous energy somehow emanating from beyond the new double doors in front of me, much the way firemen must know that a fire is blazing on the other side of a closed door in a burning building. I opened one of the doors and stepped inside a large vaulted structure blazing with light and immediately felt the power of the priest's words filling the space and the hearts of the hundreds of worshippers spread out before me in the countless rows of pews. He gesticulated rapidly as the words boomed forth and echoed off the walls around me, and I felt the spirit of the Lord expanding within me as I sat toward the back and basked in the love that surrounded me and the congregation, most of whom gesticulated in turn and praised the Lord in response to the words of the priest:

"... and rise up as one holy being and praise the works of our Creator. Be not afraid of those who disbelieve, of those who smite you and mock you. Yea, even those who imprison you shall have no power over you. Did not the Sadducees imprison Peter and John? But at night an angel of the Lord opened the prison doors and brought them out and said, 'Go and stand in the temple and speak to the people all the words of this Life.' And this I also do, as I enjoin all of you to show by your works that you have understood the words of the Lord and that He is Himself the very Word of God and the Creator of all that is and was and ever will be. Let the words live within you and let them go forth and be multiplied in the glory of the Word and of God Almighty. May His holy angels guide you and protect you in this Life and ...."

And the words rolled into me and through me and the gesticulations of the priest reached fever point as the Spirit filled the cavernous room and hurled itself into the hearts of the worshippers, who raised their hands with their fingers twitching and opened their hearts completely to Life and the Lord, Life in the Lord, and the Lord of Life Himself.

I closed my eyes and marveled at the sudden silence as the priest descended from the pulpit and moved in front of the great altar to prepare the Eucharist. I am not a Catholic, and I must admit that the fervor of both the priest and the congregation had startled me at first, as the sermon and the responses had been much more intense and passionate than I had expected. The quiet and the coolness of the church as I sat with my eyes closed in peaceful contemplation matched my preconceptions of a Catholic church much more closely. When I opened them again, the faithful were filing in front of the altar and accepting the Host upon their tongues as they knelt in humility and gratitude. The flickering candles above them appeared for all the world like tongues of flame suspended over their heads. Never before had I felt such kinship with my fellow beings, truly my brothers and sisters, as they accepted God into their bodies in recognition of His place in their souls. Words again crackled in the air, but in more subdued fashion as the congregants moved to the front and then back to their seats at the end of their pilgrimage. I closed my eyes again and floated in the serene quiet and holiness of my surroundings.

Time passed. I have no idea how much. The shuffling of feet moving past me toward the door roused me and signaled the end of the mass and a genuinely moving experience. I arose and merged into the line. The priest stood at the side of the main entrance, and I thanked him for the power of the sermon and the intensity of love that I had felt within his church. My own passion seemed to demand my own gesticulation for emphasis. We spoke for at least a minute, and I'm afraid that I held up the line. He thanked me for coming and said that he hoped that I would return soon. Outside the church, I asked one of the congregants about finding a taxi, and he directed me to a stand only some three blocks away. I returned to the hotel, pondering the experience and trying to decipher the meaning of it. Yes, I had been moved and uplifted at the Holy Angels Church. Yes, the priest had actually referred to an angel releasing the apostles from prison. But was that *it*, after all? Had my "invitation" led me to transitory transcendence and permanent frustration in my search for the meaning of my own resurrection?

The next morning, early, I called the church and learned from the recording that mass would be held at 11 a.m. I explained to one of the managers at the conference hall that I planned to close my booth and fly back to Indiana. I stored the gear and the painting in my hotel room, folded one of the flyers and placed it in my coat pocket, and again descended in the elevator to the front entrance and made my way to the taxi stand. This time, I carried the note with the address of Holy Angels Church in Arcadia and handed it to the driver. He said it would be no problem. Traffic was light. I felt fresh and alert as we sped toward the church. I hadn't even thought to ask anyone about angels the day before. There really had been no opportunity anyway. And I had felt so hazy on top of everything else. There was something missing, I thought. There had to be something more. Or was I merely fanta-sizing and exaggerating my own importance?

Something was missing, all right—the church. The cabbie insisted that we were parked in front of the Holy Angels Church in Arcadia and that there was only one Holy Angels Church in Arcadia. I insisted just as emphatically and even more loudly that I knew the Holy Angels Church in Arcadia and that the church he was pointing to was certainly not it.

"Wait here!" I said roughly.

"I'm not going anywhere, buddy—and you better not either!" he shouted at my back as I walked toward the church. People were streaming toward the small church with a beautiful bell tower to the side, and I noticed with some annoyance that the sign planted tastefully in front of it did say "Holy Angels Church."

"Excuse me, sir," I said politely to a white-haired gentleman approaching the front entrance. "I'm new in town and really don't know my way around. Are we in Arcadia?"

"Why, yes," he replied, in a bemused way.

"And is this the only Holy Angels Church in Arcadia?"

"It's certainly the only one that I know of," he said, "and I've lived here forty years now. I don't mean to be rude, but I have to join my wife inside."

"Of course," I said, beginning to understand myself the full definition of bemusement.

I followed him inside, arousing his concern, I think. Fortunately, a priest in vestments was standing just inside the door.

"Pardon me, Father," I said, "but I am really turned around here. Is this the only Holy Angels Church in Arcadia?"

"Yes, it is," he said with a smile, "and you are very welcome indeed."

At that moment, it suddenly dawned on me that I had told the other cabbie to look for the Holy Angels Church in the San Gabriel Valley, not Arcadia.

"Father, do you know whether there is another Holy Angels Church in the San Gabriel Valley?"

"Why yes," he replied. "There is one in Vernon, not far at all from here."

"That's got to be it!" I said excitedly. "Thank you so much."

I shook his hand and started walking quickly toward the taxi. The priest stuck his arm outside the door and waved at me. I think he shouted "Are you sure . . ." about something as I climbed in the back seat, but I had already closed the door, and I waved back.

"Let's go," I said to the driver. "It was my mistake, and I apologize. The church I'm looking for, with the same name, seems to be in Vernon. Can you confirm that?"

A quick check of the yellow pages, and we were on our way. This time, I watched the streets carefully, and familiarity grew to certainty as we passed the taxi stand. The next three blocks were like signposts in my memory and then there it was—a beautiful white stone church with a black slate steeple atop a bell tower built into the entryway. Again, there was no sound emanating from the church, but rather a sense of great serenity and inner peace. I paid the relieved driver and again stepped through the outer doors and ... into emptiness. The second set of doors was wide open, and the church empty inside, the only light streaming in through the stained-glass windows. I walked slowly down the center aisle, remembering the priest and his passionate sermon, envisioning again the congregants on their knees in front of the altar, yearning for the power that had transported me the night before, but finding only silence and emptiness inside the church and within my spirit. I stopped at the first step leading to the altar and knelt reverently.

A door some thirty feet to the right opened wide.

The priest wore his white clerical collar and black suit. He looked at me, smiled broadly, and began to gesticulate as he walked toward me. He continued to move his hands and fingers quickly as he approached. His lips were moving, but there was no sound at all in the church, only my own heavy intake of breath as I tried to understand what was happening. He stood directly in front of me.

"I said, 'It is good to see you so soon, my son.'" The words flowed from his mouth finally, but his fingers continued to move in what now seemed to be signs of madness rather than sweeping gestures underlining his oratory.

He looked at me oddly.

"Father, what are you doing with your fingers?" I asked.

He moved his hands and fingers in response for several seconds. Then he said, "You really don't understand the signing, do you?"

"No, not at all," I said after a pause. "Why are you using sign language?"

"It's American Sign Language, to be exact," he replied, "and you were using it yourself yesterday as you left the church. Are you feeling all right, son? You don't look at all well."

I also didn't feel at all well. I was confused, deeply so.

"Come with me," he said, leading me by the arm toward the door from which he had emerged. The door led into a hallway with offices.

"Normally, the church would be full for Sunday mass right now," he said, "but we have changed the schedule in order to prepare for Pentecost next week. The normal mass will take place this evening."

We walked into a room that was clearly his own office, as he sat down behind a large desk and motioned for me to sit in one of the two chairs in front of him—the empty one.

He signed to the young woman seated next to me and spoke the words aloud simultaneously and slowly so that I might understand.

"This gentleman appears to be the man you are seeking," he said. "He sat at the back of the church during the mass, and his eyes were often closed. We spoke together at the door as he left. His eyes were shining, and he spoke from his heart about my own words and the love that he felt within the church and the congregation. His signing was perfect. Today he says that he has no knowledge of signing."

The woman had not stopped staring at me since I walked into the office. She continued to look at me as she signed her response to the priest.

"I will need to know something more myself about you, my son, before I can understand this," the priest said to me as he continued to sign so that the woman might also understand. "Look at the church letterhead … and the top of the flyer here … and my card."

He passed the materials to me. I looked at each one in turn as the words pummeled me: Holy Angels Catholic Church of the Deaf. All of this can be checked, by the way. It can all be checked.

"But I don't know sign language," I insisted. "I have no knowledge whatsoever of sign language."

"And yet you followed my sermon with no difficulty and spoke to me afterward in perfect American Sign Language. How do you explain that?"

"I can't!"

"Well, perhaps *she* can," he said, nodding his head to the young woman and smiling at her. "She arrived here no more than twenty minutes before you did—no appointment, no advance notice. She is lucky I was here, and so are you, I believe … if there really is any luck involved. Her name is Teresa. She was not here yesterday, but she had an oddly clear dream about the church last night. She says that she was standing outside the church in her dream when a powerful wind swept down upon her and pushed her inside the building, where she saw me and my parishioners in worship with tongues of flame above our heads. She says that an angel appeared above the altar and spoke to her, even though she was born deaf, mind you. She was frightened, and she brought her fear with her today. We were praying together when you arrived. The angel's words were ... No, she should tell you herself. Please repeat the words, Teresa."

She signed slowly and the priest translated as he had before, equally slowly: "*Seek the man who finds the sign within the signs. He must go and stand at the temple and speak to the people all the words of this Life. You will know him, for he will close his eyes in order to see and close his ears in order to hear. For lo, Ariel Angel is a real angel. A real angel.*

The priest thanked Teresa and turned back to me. "I thought that the upcoming Pentecost must have stimulated her dream, and that it was only a dream, although it was interesting to me that some of the words spoken by her angel also appeared in the text of my sermon. Then I thought about you, because I was intrigued by the stranger last night in a church for the deaf who kept his eyes closed for so long. That doesn't happen often in this church. And as I was thinking about you, I heard steps through the crack in the outer door approaching the altar. And here you are, my son, and now it is your turn to tell us who and what you are."

I did so very willingly, as I knew full well that I had found the sign within the signs, and that I knew the name of the angel, and that I knew where to find her. I also knew what it meant to speak in tongues, even when the tongue is not involved. When I showed Teresa the image on the flyer, she burst into tears and continued to sob for several minutes. We promised to remain in contact with each other—a promise that I have kept and the reason that I know that Teresa had suffered her own near-death experience when she was struck by a bus and escaped with minor bruises. At that time, though, I suddenly grew anxious to leave. I thanked them both profusely for helping with the certitude that I had so badly needed, and I swore to the priest that I would return to discuss the matter in much greater depth with his superiors. I gave him all of my contact information. We parted.

As soon as I reached the hotel, I booked a ticket to fly to Nashville the next morning. Ariel Angel—a real angel.

It was the slowness and the deliberateness of the priest's translation of the angel's name, you see. I had heard it before, but I had misunderstood. As soon as he said "Ariel Angel" in a slow drawl to make certain that I could follow, my mind flashed back to an elderly man in overalls, a man named Earl Dawkins, who had stared so long and hard at the painting in Nashville and had said "a real angel," or so I had thought, as he slowly walked away from the booth. No, it suddenly became crystal clear to me that he had said "Ariel Angel" in the same slow drawl. The two pronunciations were identical, and the conviction was doubly underlined by my experiences in the church. I now *knew* that the angel was real, that the dreams were more than dreams, both my own and Teresa's, and that the name was Ariel.

I had to find Dawkins. Don't ask me how I knew for sure. My intuition was sure, and by that point I had learned to trust my intuition—and to believe that intuition is much more than we usually imagine. The image of Dawkins was in my head, and I found his name and address back at the hotel at the top of the first sheet from the first clipboard that I had used in Nashville. Clearly, he had not simply stared at the painting the entire time. Ariel Angel.

At first, I simply lost myself in the beauty of the name and the intense satisfaction derived from the successful completion of a quest. She was real. Speaking in tongues was real. Divine communication through dreams was real. My life, all of our lives were real—they had purpose and solemnity and majesty, after all. God Himself was *real*.

And then I began to be troubled yet again. Ariel? Wasn't that the name of a sprite in a Shakespearean play that I had never quite understood in high school? Ariel? Wasn't she the mermaid in a Disney film? Wasn't that a wine, an Israeli politician? Why Ariel? Why not a holy name that no one had ever heard before?

I returned to the Internet and forgot about sleep that night. And I learned about the angel Ariel by delving into a mass of information filled with contradictions, legends, Judeo-Christian apocrypha, and New Age mysticism. Was the angel male, female, or both? Was it truly an angel, or rather a demon? Are Ariel and Uriel, the "Flame of God," the same? There were far more questions than answers, and the "answers" required far more suspension of disbelief than I was willing to summon.

Nevertheless, an angel named Ariel had entered my life, had indeed saved my life, and now, so I believed, was guiding me both to her and to my very purpose in being alive. What were my options? Should I perhaps stay in Los Angeles and devote myself to Catholicism and the examination of miraculous events? Should I fear demonic possession and return instead to my home in Indianapolis and surely a good and happy life with Allison? Or should I follow the trail wherever it might lead me in the hope of finding the actual answers to existence that all of us seek? I wrestled with these and other thoughts throughout the night. And in the morning, I summoned all the power of intuition that I could muster and wrote down on the pad of hotel note paper what I believed "felt" right about Ariel:

1. Ariel is female.
2. She is an angel of healing.
3. She controls the elements, particularly the wind.
4. She may be an archangel.
5. She may be a guardian angel.

You can do the research yourself. I would expect your results to be different, particularly if the whole concept of angels is alien or utterly foolish to you. As for me, I had felt the wind, I had felt the healing, I had felt the power of the Holy Spirit upon me in the church to which she had directed me, and I had gazed directly into her eyes. I packed my gear and left L.A. on the early nonstop flight to Nashville.

* * *

I had an address for Earl Dawkins, but no telephone number. He had scrawled a dash in the column where the number should have been. It was a rural address, and even the manager at the rental car desk had trouble locating it for me. The best we could do was to approximate where the county road hit the state road. Then, I would be on my own. That was fine, though. There are always gas stations and country stores and good people who know their neighbors far better than city folk can manage with theirs.

In fact, it all went smoothly, except for the storm.

Earl was well known in the area. He was an itinerant preacher, famous for his appearances at revival meetings. The people at the store where I stopped to inquire all knew him as Earnest Earl, and they took pleasure in telling me about him and providing the final directions to his small farm. One even joked, "Hey, and he'll cure yur lumbago for yuh, too, if only yuh ask."

It was late afternoon when I drove up the hard dirt driveway. There were dark clouds in the sky, and, as I got out of the car, thick drops of rain began to thud quickly around me. By the time I reached the porch of the white wood-frame house, the rain was heavy and the wind had picked up noticeably. The door opened on the second knock.

Earl looked at me with interest but no surprise. "She said yuh were comin'," he said slowly. "Get yursef in now. Yur wet, son."

There was a fire burning in the stone fireplace in the simple living room. Earl sat down in one of the rocking chairs facing the fireplace, and he motioned for me to sit in the other one. "Yur the first one to sit thar since mah wife died," he remarked.

We sat there in silence for the next five minutes or so. That can sometimes be excruciating—but not with Earl. He was perfectly relaxed, and it was clear he was thinking about how to begin.

"Well," he said finally. "I imagine our stories are quite similar."

The change in his accent and wording was startling to me. I jerked my head away from the fire to stare at him. He was gazing at the flames without blinking.

"I died from a fall off a cliff not far from here about twenty years ago—that is, I should have died from a fall not far from here twenty years ago. I was about forty feet up. The ledge crumbled. I went down head first toward the rocks below. There was a thick, heavy bush down there a few feet to the side. I can still see it. There was no way I could land in it, though. I was going to miss it by about four feet. Then the gust of wind hit me—a strong gust, mind you—and I went headfirst into the bush. When I came to, I had a lump on my head and scratches all over me. But I was alive—not even a broken bone. The dreams started coming a few weeks later. Then I saw her in one very clear, colorful dream, standing off to the side, her blonde hair blowing in the wind as I fell. The very next night, just as the ledge crumbled and I began to fall again, she floated next to me and said so clearly that I can never forget it: 'Exodus 4:10-12.' Well, I woke with a start, and I got out my Bible, and I read the passage, and I saw that I was to speak for the Lord. I could never speak in front of people before. Yet I went to the camp meeting on Sunday, and I listened to the preacher shouting hellfire, and I knew something was wrong. And suddenly, suddenly I felt the Holy Spirit descend upon me, and I fell into a kind of trance—and so did the preacher. At the moment I began to speak from the crowd, he stopped speaking entirely. He just stood there, struck dumb, as I walked up on the stage, and began to preach the true gospel of Jesus Christ: love, mercy, and compassion. It takes hate to wish the fires of hell upon anyone, or even to describe them, and He was not about hate. I had never verbalized that to myself before, but suddenly the words of love and forgiveness came pouring out of me in an irresistible torrent that could not be stopped or even slowed. Oh, and the crowd, my Lord Almighty, they were rapt and transfixed, and when the Spirit finally lifted up from me, I stood there trembling and in a sweat, and the people surged forward and fell to their knees in front of me and asked for forgiveness. And I blessed them in the name of the Lord and walked among them and touched those that were afflicted and they were healed—all except for the preacher, who had suffered a stroke and would never speak again."

Then he closed his eyes and lowered his chin slowly to his chest. I waited five minutes.

"Earl," I said. "Earl, are you all right?"

"The Spirit is draining from me, son," he replied slowly, his eyes still closed. "She revealed herself to me later as the Angel Ariel. She sets things right, you know. She said the Spirit had to descend upon me before we could actually meet. She's waiting for you outside now."

"What?"

"Go out the back door … and walk to the middle … of the field. My energy is … leaving." His whole body relaxed, although I could still see the slow rise and fall of his chest as he slumped in his chair in front of the fire.

Lightning flashed in the distance, and the few lights that had been burning in the house shut off immediately. My boyhood scout training kicked in automatically as I counted off eight seconds before the thunder came rumbling through the old structure. Then I walked into the kitchen and stared at the back door off the screened-in porch for several seconds. Lightning flashed again, and I could see the field clearly in front of me through the thin wire mesh of the screened door. It was a cornfield, freshly harvested, with scattered stalks lying on the ground or bent down close to it. The field rose to a small knoll, and I knew without a doubt that the top of the knoll was also the center of the field. I would be by far the tallest point on that field. I counted seven seconds before the thunder cracked.

Yes, I admit to more than a little hesitation as I stood in front of the fragile porch door and felt the wind-driven rain pelting me through the screen. The thought of Ariel as a demon also swept through my mind. Why be saved just to be destroyed, though? Why fear the triumph of love over hate?

I pushed through the spring-loaded door and let it slam behind me. I was already drenched. I had to lean into the wind in order to move forward. It was maybe a hundred yards to the top of the knoll in good weather, but in that storm and the churning mud the distance had quadrupled. The time between the lightning flashes and the crashing thunder claps dropped steadily as I struggled forward into the wind—six seconds, five, four, three— until suddenly the lightning bolts seemed to be striking simultaneously all around me and hissing filled the air along with the thunder. The earth shook. I stood on the knoll with the rain beating down upon me and striking me horizontally as the wind shrieked and the lightning pounded, and I raised my arms above me as words from my childhood began to flow from my mouth even though I could not hear them myself in the roar of the storm: "Even though I walk through the valley of the shadow of death, I fear no evil; for thou art with me."

All of the hair on my body stiffened, hissing erupted above me, and the light blinded me. And there was no rain, no wind, no lightning strike, just light, brilliant white light that gradually softened so that I could see the radiant figure at the center of it. The blonde hair flowed behind her, even though I felt no wind. She wore a dazzling long white gown. There were no wings.

"May peace be with you," she said in the same peremptory tones that I had heard on the tape recording and yet somehow mercifully softened. *"Now and forever."*

The same glowing, blue-laser eyes gazed into mine—but this time into eyes of the flesh.

"The Holy Spirit is with you," she said. *"You can perceive me safely."* Then she bowed her head.

I stood there transfixed—and utterly stunned, in so many different ways. To this day, I have no idea how many times angels have appeared before humans. The occasions that are recorded are few, but the reality may be endless. To compound the inexpressible honor and joy of her presence with a bow of the head was incomprehensible to me. I began to drop to my knees.

"No!" she said forcefully and without hesitation. *"This belongs only to God. I am His messenger. You will understand in time."*

"What am I to do?" I finally managed to stammer.

"You have received the message. Now the power of your body and spirit must grow so that you may fulfill the task. You must also remember what you have forgotten. It is time to meet Raphael. You will be guided."

"And what of you?" I asked.

"I am with you always," she said. *"Seek the Azeri."*

"But there is so much I need to ask!" I blurted.

"Prepare yourself, Jacob! It is not for me to relieve the pain."

The light around her suddenly flared and erupted into the sun itself. The lightning bolt struck.

CHAPTER III

NEW ROME

*O*nce more, I climbed slowly out of the darkness and awoke in pain. I was bandaged heavily on my right side, particularly on the upper thigh. Earl Dawkins sat on a wooden stool next to the bed. "Not near as bad as she might look," he drawled. "Yuh got burns on that side uh yuh. Yur thigh's been ripped a bit. Ah laid my hands on yuh, and ah used the ointment. Yur gonna be fine."

Under other circumstances, I surely would not have shared in Earl's confidence, but it was difficult not to believe in his medical skill given what I had just experienced and what I now knew about him. "Yuh bin out fur near a day," he said.

I soon learned from Earl that he had found me lying on the knoll after the storm had passed. He had slept through most of it, but he was "told" that he should look for me in the field. He loaded me into a small trailer pulled by his tractor and hauled me back to his house. I was moaning and delirious, he said. In any case, he had stripped away the ruined clothes, cleaned and bound the wounds, and somehow got me into a bed. He had worked hard. I owed Earl Dawkins more than I could repay. And I learned that I respected him more than I could say.

"When the Spirit comes," he said, "ah know ah talk diff'rent. Ah'm still me, tho'. But ah know that the talk and the healin' come from God, not from me."

I healed very fast, much too fast, actually, as I could practically see the burned skin peeling off and the pink new skin rising to replace it. Strangely, too, whenever I thought of Raphael and what he might be, the skin seemed to tighten and the pain lessen. The gash in my thigh had uncovered the bone, according to Earl, but, by the time I saw it for the first time, the wound had closed with no sign of infection or even serious trauma.

By that time, you have to understand, though, that I had no more doubts about the angels and miracles. There comes a point when the rational mind has to concede that "rationality" can be a synonym for "ignorance," whether that occurs in an examination of quantum physics or in a conversation with an angelic being in the middle of an electrical storm. I had been struck by lightning, and my body was totally healed in three days. Well, I had also died in a car accident, hadn't I? I could sign fluently under the influence of the Holy Spirit, couldn't I? I had spoken face to face with an angel of God, hadn't I?

So be it.

Thoughts rushed through my mind in the two days that I spent with Earl after I regained consciousness. He cared for me, fed me, and helped me as I first hobbled around the house. He also gave me time to myself, as he tended the chores necessary to life on a small farm. I needed that time.

I would lie on the bed and listen to the words of Ariel repeat themselves in my mind. There was no difficulty in that, as the entire experience had been imprinted in me, as if I could press an invisible replay button through an act of will and simply relive the encounter endlessly.

"You have received the message. Now the power of your body and spirit must grow so that you may fulfill the task. You must also remem-

ber what you have forgotten. It is time to meet Raphael. You will be guided."

The "message" and the "task" had to lie in the words of Teresa, I decided: *"He must go and stand at the temple and speak to the people all the words of this Life."*

Unfortunately, that made very little sense to me. I certainly felt prepared to meet Raphael, or so I thought, but I had no idea who or what he was at that point. I took some comfort in thinking that I would be guided, but I also had no real understanding of what that meant. And then I would go back to the "message" and the "task" as if my mind were stuck in a closed loop.

The thought then struck me for the first time that I may have misunderstood from the beginning. I had assumed that she had made a mistake in gazing into my disembodied eyes at the scene of the accident and allowing me to capture both her image and the memory of the encounter. I had thought that I was pursuing her in order to confirm my sanity and to prove to my fellow humans that there is a divine purpose. But what if she had been pursuing me all along, preparing me step by step to learn how to fulfill a task? Can angels make mistakes? Who or what is *the Azeri*? What had I forgotten?

On the last evening before I returned to Nashville and the flight back to Indianapolis, I sat again in front of the fire with Earl Dawkins. I had related my own escape from death to him and described the journey that had led me to him for the second time. I had already told him about my encounter with Ariel shortly after regaining consciousness, but I went through it one more time. "The Lord works in mysterious ways," he said slowly and portentously. But then he added with a smile, "Or so it seems to those with no understandin' uh the mystery."

We stared at the fire together for some time. Then he began to speak again, slowly and precisely. "I feel the Spirit descendin' on ..."

His head slumped forward and then jerked back abruptly. He turned his head to look at me in the chair next to him. His eyes bored into mine. They did not blink.

"Afterwards, Jesus returned to Jerusalem for one of the religious holidays," intoned the sonorous voice rising from Earl's chest. "Inside the city, near the Sheep Gate, was Bethesda Pool, with five covered platforms or porches surrounding it. Crowds of sick folks—lame, blind, or with paralyzed limbs—lay on the platforms (waiting for a certain movement of the water, for an angel of the Lord came from time to time and disturbed the water, and the first person to step down into it afterwards was healed).

"Get ready for the journey and good success to you both. Blessed art thou, O God, with every pure and holy blessing. Let thy saints and all thy creatures bless thee; let all thy angels and thy chosen people bless thee for ever. Blessed art thou, because thou hast made me glad. It has not happened to me as I expected; but thou hast treated us according to thy great mercy. It is good to guard the secret of a king, but glorious to reveal the works of God. Ye must go and stand in the temple and speak to the people all the words of this Life."

Earl then fell silent, and his head again slumped onto his chest. He slept for about an hour in that position.

I left the next morning in the rental car for Nashville International Airport and caught a one-way flight to Indianapolis by way of Chicago. By then, I counted Earl Dawkins as one of my closest friends, certainly as one who understood my state of mind and inner emotions better than anyone else could have at that time.

The weeks that followed constituted a period of consolidation. I called Allison immediately from the airport—my loving, patient Allison—and assured her that I was fine. She spent the night with me and all of the next several days. I didn't tell her everything at that point. It would not have helped. I talked with my parents also and told them that I was happy and healthy. I spoke on the phone several times with Father Mark, the priest from Vernon, who also became my friend and advisor. He was anxious for me to meet with his superiors. I asked for his indulgence and for his prayers, and then I told him about Earl Dawkins and the encounter with Ariel. He did not know how to respond.

There is a strange paradox upon the earth. The very people who live their lives according to belief in miracles and the divine are usually unprepared to credit miracles and divine action when they actually occur in their everyday lives. And those who do not believe in the reality or even the possibility of spiritual immanence will probably not perceive it. Perhaps there is simply too much false testimony, too many unbalanced people, too much wishful thinking. Or perhaps there is something more fundamental at work—perhaps we could not function as we should or go about our Father's business and our own if we expected divine intervention to resolve all of our problems. Doubt may be a necessary component of human existence, the anchor that ties us to human life and the earth and allows us to participate fully in the lessons presented to us. Most of us have no trouble identifying with the disciple Thomas.

In any case, even Father Mark's faith was tested by my description of a face-to-face meeting with an angel. He needed proof, and I could not blame him, but I was also in no position to arrange an introduction. I still did not know why I had been chosen.

But I no longer had any doubts. In fact, I wrote down what I believed to be true, what I *knew* to be true, and I repeated it to myself often as a kind of credo that would sustain me in the years to come. I repeat it here:

1. I am not insane.
2. Angels exist.
3. I have died and returned.
4. There are others like me.
5. I have a divine task to fulfill.

I spent considerable time answering calls and letters from people who had met with me at the conventions or merely picked up one of the flyers and decided at last that they would tell their stories. Most were not persuasive, but several were highly provocative and paralleled my own experience, particularly in regard to brushes with death and the unexpected presence of helpful strangers who disappeared before identifying themselves.

It will not surprise you to know that I returned frequently to the library at Butler University and read everything I could find on Raphael and Azeri. As you might guess, my research on Raphael uncovered the archangel and the Renaissance painter, and little else. It also remained possible that Raphael might be a human being who would lead me to further revelation. I doubted that Raffaello Santi (or perhaps Sanzio), who had died in Rome in 1520 at the age of thirty-seven after establishing himself as one of the greatest artists of all time, would be visiting me any time soon. Nevertheless, I had learned not to reject anything at that point. I had experienced my own spirit in an astral body and met directly with a holy angel. There was no particular reason why I should not meet with Raffaello if heaven willed it. I even imagined at one point that he would be sent to instruct me in my art and that my "task" would be to compensate for his short life by painting further works of the Holy Family and choirs of angels under his tutelage. Please understand that all limitations on my former modes of thinking were rapidly vanishing in the light of angelic intercession.

Nevertheless, my thoughts were far more focused on Archangel Raphael as the most likely and appropriate subject of Ariel's reference to an upcoming "meeting," and I cannot say that I was completely pleased with such thoughts. After all, I had nearly been blasted to bits during my encounter with Ariel, and I suspected that she was a guardian angel, rather than an archangel. Frankly, I was afraid that the Raphael to whom she referred might indeed be the archangel revered by many

Christians, Jews, and Muslims. The Holy Spirit might be with me, as Ariel had said, but the genuine awe and joy that I had felt in her presence had been mixed generously with fear, and I could scarcely imagine standing in the presence of a more powerful being without trembling.

In any case, I read everything that I could find about Archangel Raphael and archangels in general. I learned with relief that his name stemmed from the Hebrew for "God Heals" or "God Has Healed." I discovered that he is only mentioned by name in Scripture in the Book of Tobit, which, I remind you, resides in the canon of Catholics and Eastern Orthodox Christians, but not in that of the Protestant faiths. I found Tobit in a copy of the Apocrypha, for I was neither Catholic nor Orthodox, and read through it eagerly, discovering that Raphael had disguised himself as a human in order to protect Tobit's son and to instruct him in the ways of heaven. "I am Raphael," he said, as he revealed himself at last, "one of the seven holy angels who present the prayers of the saints and enter into the presence of the Holy One … Do not be afraid; you will be safe. But praise God forever. For I did not come as a favor on my part, but by the will of our God."

I was surprised to learn that Raphael was in fact one and the same as the Muslim angel Israfel. According to the Hadith, the body of traditions relating to Muhammad and his companions, Israfel will blow a sacred horn twice to signal the end of days and the judgment of all souls. Edgar Allan Poe quoted from the Hadith in describing the angel's musical power in his poem "Israfel":

> In Heaven a spirit doth dwell
>   "Whose heart-strings are a lute";
> None sing so wildly well
> As the angel Israfel,
> And the giddy stars (so legends tell),
> Ceasing their hymns, attend the spell
>   Of his voice, all mute.

The more I read, the less fearsome he seemed. Mystic traditions identified him as the angel of prayer, love, joy, and light, as well as science, knowledge, and healing. And yet he was also an archangel, if real, and his power and majesty beyond all human comprehension. My fear did not suddenly disappear, far from it.

And what of the other archangels? The word *archangel* means "primary messenger." Their names all end in "el," meaning "in God." There are seven in the Judeo-Christian tradition, almost always including Michael, Gabriel, Raphael, and Uriel, with the other three shifting among Anael, Chamuel, Haniel, Jophiel, Oriphiel, Phanuel, Raguel, Remiel, Samael, Sariel, Zachariel, and Zadkiel. Eastern Orthodox believers count them in the thousands, although Barachiel, Jegudiel, and Selaphiel stand out among them. Islamic traditions include many names not found elsewhere. Cabalistic tradition adds Metatron and Sandalphon to the list, both of whom are said to be former human beings—Enoch and Elijah respectively—whom God raised to the level of archangels. And occultists name still others.

Enough? Yes, I do remember all of those names and much more from that period of study. There is a reason for that, as you will learn. I tried very hard to prepare myself for the meeting to come, no matter what form "Raphael" might assume. My body seemed to pulse with a newfound energy, and my mind crackled with thoughts and perceptions that were new to me. There were also odd fragments of memories that I could not link together, although I felt an urgency in them that troubled me.

And yet I still had to deal with the wild card in all of this: "*Seek the Azeri*." How could I seek something that made absolutely no sense to me? What was an Azeri?

The answer seemed to be close at hand at first—Webster's Dictionary. *Azeri* was listed as a shortened version of *Azerbaijani*—"a member of a Turkic-speaking people of Azerbaijan and northwest Iran," as well as "the Turkic language of the Azerbaijanis." The major difficulty, of course, was that I had no knowledge whatsoever of Azerbaijan, its people, its language, or anything else concerning the country. I had to look it up in an atlas to discover that it was a small Central Asian country on the Caspian Sea bordered by Iran to the south and Georgia to the north in the Caucasus. I could find no conceivable connection to me in the dictionary definition of *Azeri*.

Worse still, I discovered that *Azeri* lay only two words below *Azazel* in my dictionary, and I had encountered that fearsome name before in my study of Raphael and the archangels. In fact, it was Raphael, according to the Book of Enoch, who cast Azazel out of heaven after it was found that he had corrupted mankind by teaching them how to make both weapons and jewelry: "And again the Lord said to Raphael: 'Bind Azazel hand and foot, and cast him into the darkness and split open the desert, which is in Dudael, and cast him in … The whole earth has been corrupted through the works that were taught by Azazel: to him ascribe all sin.'"

Most disturbingly, referring to the sacred Torah text of *Leviticus 16*, the dictionary described Azazel as "an evil spirit of the wilderness to which a scapegoat was sent by the ancient Hebrews in a ritual of atonement." Not altogether free of my concern that Ariel herself might yet prove to be a demon, and well aware that so many religions recount the transformation of angels into demons when they challenged God, I was not pleased to think that I might become a scapegoat in a ritual of atonement. Had I offended God by pursuing His angels and presuming to seek out knowledge not intended for me? Why the peculiar juxtaposition of Azeri and Azazel? Why the direct connection between Raphael and Azazel?

I know that I was overwrought and reaching for fatal meanings and occult connections at every turn. But how would you respond to a real encounter with a real angel at a point in your life when all of your former beliefs and comforts had already been shattered by signs and wonders? I returned to my credo and repeated the key sentences in my head as if they were talismanic: I am not insane. Angels exist. I have died and returned. There are others like me. I have a divine task to fulfill.

And I added: I shall trust in the love, mercy, and compassion of God. I can do no other.

I continued to search for other meanings for *Azeri*. And I found none.

Finally, truly exhausted by the research and the tension building within me in recognition of the momentous but murky "meeting" to come, I discovered the one certain and obvious way to find release, spiritual comfort, and the answers to all of my questions.

How can it be any clearer? And yet I and so many others have still missed it time and time again. Are all of us so submerged in our petty lives that we simply cannot rise above the waters of the everyday long enough to hear the message being shouted into our ears from all directions? "He who has ears to hear, let him hear."

I was sitting in the great room at the lake with Allison, turning over everything in my mind that I had learned about Raphael the Angel, Raphael the Painter, Azerbaijan, Azeris, Azazel, Ariel, and archangels, when I heard her say to me softly from the sofa across from my desk, "Jake, you can't go on like this. *We* can't go on like this."

I looked up from the books and documents scattered across my desk and gazed at the beautiful woman with her legs tucked beneath her as she leaned back with her head propped up on her elbow and stared directly into my eyes. There was no doubt that I loved her, and there was equally no doubt that I had been unfair to her. Frankly, I had feared that she would doubt my sanity completely if I told her everything that had happened to me. Would you believe your wife if she told you that she had just met with an angel? On the other hand, she had been more supportive than I probably deserved as I traveled around the country in pursuit of understanding and perhaps a wraith existing only in my imagination.

I took a chance, as I must have known would be the case all along. You cannot hide your innermost thoughts and most precious experiences from someone you claim to love without hollowing out the relationship—and, in the end, yourself. I let it all flow out, directly from my heart: The Holy Angels Catholic Church of the Deaf, Father Mark and Teresa, Earl Dawkins, Ariel, Raphael, Azeri, Azazel, etc., and then I waited for her response.

She rose from the sofa, walked over to me behind the desk, and sat on my lap. "I love you," she said. "For better or worse, for richer or poorer, in sickness and in health, I will always love you." She bent her head to mine, and we kissed for a long time and held each other even longer.

"Jake," she said, "I need to be a part of this. I need to know that it is real or that you are having delusions—one or the other. If you love me and you want me, then I am going to be with you through all of this—but I need to know. Please tell me: How can I reach Father Mark?"

The unaccustomed lines in her forehead relaxed when I handed her his card and the flyer from the church. Her hands were sweaty. "Call him," I said. "Use the phone in the studio for privacy. It's two hours earlier in California. Take your time, sweetheart. I love you, too, very much."

It was then, while she made the call, that I fumbled through the bookcases looking for the Bible that my aunt had given me when I was in high school in the hope that I would focus less on basketball and cheerleaders and more on things of the spirit. The phrase *Seek and ye shall find* kept running through my head. *Seek and ye shall find*. And then came *Seek the Azeri*. I found the Bible and began leafing through the New Testament quickly, focusing on the words in red, as I knew that it was the Nazarene who had spoken the words now rushing through my head. "*Seek and ye shall find*" even seemed to apply to my search for the passage itself, as I felt driven to find the words that were repeating themselves with ever greater power in my head. My finger rushed up and down the lines in a way that now reminds me of another finger in an ancient tale of prophecy and then it stopped, cold, for there was the passage and the wisdom that I had sought:

> And I tell you, Ask and it will be given you; seek,
> and you will find; knock, and it will be opened to
> you. For every one who asks receives, and he who
> seeks finds, and to him who knocks it will be opened.
> What father among you, if his son asks for an egg,
> will give him a scorpion? If you then, who are evil,
> know how to give gifts to your children, how much
> more will the heavenly Father give the Holy Spirit to
> those who ask him!

The invitation is so clear! Why does anyone ever hesitate? Why had I been so deeply troubled, so consumed with doubts, and yet had not even bothered to ask for guidance about angels from the One who had sent them. Angels are *messengers*. They *deliver* messages; they *do not write them* themselves.

So I did what I should have done from the time I first awoke in the hospital, and probably should have done many years before that: I prayed deeply. Not that I was any good at it. To be honest, I felt foolish at first. I dropped to my knees with the Bible still in my hands, closed my eyes, and bent my head. The first thing that occurred to me was this: "Now I lay me down to sleep, I pray the Lord my soul to keep. If I should …" It had been a very long time.

I shook my head, and then I asked and I sought and I knocked as simply and honestly and humbly as I could manage.

"Father," I began. "You know how weak and ignorant I am. You know my heart better than I do. Please forgive me for everything that I have done that has displeased You. Please help me believe in You. Please help me find the truth in all of the religions that claim to speak for You. Please give me the courage to face the angels or demons that you may place in my path. Please give me the strength to fulfill the tasks that You have set for me. Please help me understand what is Your will and assist me in doing Your will, not mine. Thank You for giving me my life and preserving it. Thank You for sending the Holy Spirit to me. Please send the Holy Spirit to me whenever I need it to fulfill Your wishes. All of this I pray in Your name and obedience to Your will and Your design. Amen."

I lifted my head and slowly opened my eyes, fully expecting the room to be filled with radiant light and perhaps a choir of angels singing to me from the ceiling. Instead, there was nothing unusual, just the same room and the same twilight and the same stillness. We poor humans. I had just tried so hard to bare my soul to God Himself, and what did I find? Instead of holy serenity, the words of one of my favorite songs by Bob Dylan kept running through my mind: "Knock, knock, knocking on heaven's door ...." Why were such crazy beings created?

As I struggled to free my mind from the song, Allison opened the door from the studio and walked directly toward me. She put her head on my chest and hugged me tightly. Then she looked up into my eyes and said, "I'm ready for anything now."

That night the dreams began.

* * *

Most dreams are disjointed. They are fragments that join other fragments as the brain refreshes itself by discharging the detritus of unimportant sense impressions that have accumulated during the day. Sometimes we have recurring dreams or long, coherent dreams that can even pick up again where they left off if we have been lightly awakened and return to sleep. Those are the Freudian dreams that help us work our way through deep-seated problems that we would rather not face when we are awake. And then, on rare occasions for most of us, there are dreams that are not even self-generated. I know this to be true. These are the dreams in deep and remarkable color that dreamers never forget—the dreams of precognition or glimpses of the future, the visitations by deceased loved ones, the lightning strikes of inspiration that solve the scientific puzzle or provide the missing notes of music. We all have them, and we are all reluctant to talk about them, because they are too private and too important to us. We could not bear to have them doubted or belittled. Ariel had already appeared to me in one such dream, but something had clearly shifted in me once I had met her face to face.

Allison and I fell asleep in each other's arms that night. She told me as we lay entangled lovingly together that she was both awed and frightened by the implications of my experiences, and I confessed to her that I felt much the same. She asked if I had prayed for guidance, and I described the scene in the great room while she was talking with Father Mark. We both laughed softly and nervously as I told her about the persistence of "Knock, knock, knocking, on heaven's door," and then we fell asleep.

The archangel Raphael was even more magnificent and awe-inspiring than I had expected. And yet I felt no fear in the dream. He was beautiful rather than fearsome. He appeared to be a young man of 25 with dark, curly hair. He wore a golden robe. The brilliant radiance that flowed from him exuded love and understanding without in any way subtracting from the undeniable power and authority that pulsed within him. Like Ariel, he had no wings. His blue eyes sparkled and glowed like hers. Unlike Ariel, he did something that immediately relieved the tension: He smiled at me warmly and bowed his head toward me.

"I am Raphael," he said. "I could appear with wings, of course, but there is little need now."

"Where are we?" I asked.

"*We are at a place that your spirit can reach without difficulty. You have been here many times before without remembering. This time, you will remember.*"

"What am I to do?" I asked.

"*There is much that you must learn and much that you must convey,*" he said. "*Your power will grow. The Azeri shall be your teacher in the body. I shall be your teacher in the spirit. I shall make myself known to you in visions; I shall speak with you in dreams. You shall meet the Azeri at the School of the Jesuits in the City of New Rome.*"

Raphael looked directly into my eyes as he spoke, unblinking, unhurried, unmoving.

"How will I know that this is not just a dream?" I asked.

"*Read Daniel 10:12,*" he answered. "*Memorize all of the words and all of the texts that come to you from above. There shall come a time when you must write them down from memory alone. May peace be with you, Jacob. You are greatly beloved.*"

He smiled again, bowed his head slowly, and disappeared instantaneously. I awoke just as fast. Allison was sleeping gently at my side. I remembered every word. I found that my ability to recall conversations and written texts had somehow been vastly heightened. At first, I thought that I was kidding myself, but every word of the dream conversation was burned into my mind, and I discovered that I could relive every other conversation that I had experienced since I awoke in the hospital word for word simply by recalling the event. I suddenly seemed to have a photographic memory for every text and every conversation—a talent that I checked again and again afterward until I was satisfied that it was real. To give you a minor example, I read the text of Poe's "Israfel" only once during my research on Raphael, but I wrote it down in its entirety a few pages ago, and you know that I have had no access to books of any kind. You can check its accuracy easily.

At any rate, I climbed out of bed quietly in order not to awaken Allison, even though my heart was pounding at that point. I walked into the great room and retrieved the Bible from where I had placed it in the bookcase. I had no memory of ever reading through the Book of Daniel before, although I certainly remembered the stories of Daniel in the lion's den and the three young men in the fiery furnace. I checked the index, since I had no idea where Daniel was located in the Bible, and I leafed my way to *Daniel 10:10-12* and read the passage out loud:

> *And behold, a hand touched me and set me trembling*
> *on my hands and knees. And he said to me, "O*
> *Daniel, man greatly beloved, give heed to the words*
> *that I speak to you, and stand upright, for now I*
> *have been sent to you." While he was speaking this*
> *word to me, I stood up trembling. Then he said to*
> *me, "Fear not, Daniel, for from the first day that you*
> *set your mind to understand and humbled yourself*
> *before God, your words have been heard, and I have*
> *come because of your words."*

I closed the book gently and walked slowly back to the bedroom still holding it in my hand. I set it down on the bedside table and climbed back under the covers with Allison. I hugged her gently, and she curled up in my arms with a light purring sound. It had begun.

* * *

The next morning, we began to puzzle out the meaning of the "School of the Jesuits in the City of New Rome"—or, more accurately, we *tried* to puzzle out the meaning. In fact, we hit a series of dead ends. The atlas told me that New Rome was a small town in Ohio. The encyclopedia advised that New Rome was the name that Emperor Constantine gave to the capital of the Eastern Roman Empire on the site of ancient Byzantium—before the inhabitants changed it to Constantinople in his honor. Travel literature insisted that New Rome referred to the upscale areas in contemporary Rome, Italy.

New Rome of west central Ohio in Franklin County, located on the west side of metropolitan Columbus, was incorporated as a village in 1947, even though it had fewer than sixty residents. It became nationally famous as the worst speed trap in the country. There would be no School of the Jesuits there, unless the angel had referred to the pack of lawyers trying to defend the thousands of motorists trapped each year by the sudden drop of the speed limit to 10 mph. Somehow I had not detected any sense of humor in the angels thus far.

Constantinople had become Istanbul to the Turks, of course, after they conquered it in the fifteenth century, and then they insisted on the name to the rest of the world in the early twentieth century with the founding of the new Republic of Turkey. I thought there were real possibilities there, as the New Rome of A.D. 330 was certainly linked to the old Rome and the early Christian Church. The First Council of Nicaea was held just a few miles away. The beloved Pope John XXIII served as Apostolic Delegate in the city in the late thirties and early forties and saved many Jews from the Holocaust. Religious references kept piling up around us in my study. Turkey was the site of the seven Christian churches of Asia and the homeland of Saint Paul. Istanbul welcomed the Jews fleeing from the Inquisition in Spain and Portugal in 1492, and their descendants live in the city to this day. The Muslim caliphate was located in Istanbul in the person of the Sultan. The Prophet Muhammad's most revered personal belongings are housed at the Topkapi Museum, because the city was the capital of the Ottoman Empire, and all of the greatest treasures in the Ottoman lands flowed to the Sultan.

Nevertheless, we could find absolutely no mention of a School of the Jesuits in Constantine's "New Rome." Sadly, we learned the opposite—that the Turkish state controls religious affairs and does not permit Christian denominations to operate their own schools in Turkey today.

That left Rome, Italy—certainly not the best definition of New Rome at first blush, but by far the most likely possibility for meeting the mysterious Azeri, or so it seemed to us at the time. After all, Rome is the "holy city," and modern Rome might well be termed the "New Rome" by beings who could easily recall the Old Rome of two thousand years ago. I completely discounted the notion of New Rome referring to the latest "in" areas of upscale Rome, as I rather suspected that those who congregated there appeared so slim in the travel magazines because of their concern about one day having to pass through the eye of a needle.

The main factor, though, that argued so heavily in favor of Rome itself was the compelling information derived from the Internet about "Pontifical Gregorian University." A simple search for Jesuit universities revealed immediately that Gregorian University in Rome is not only the most famous of all Jesuit universities, but it is indeed the very first, founded some four hundred-fifty years ago by Saint Ignatius Loyola himself, the founder of the Jesuit order. With three thousand students from over one hundred-thirty countries, what better site could there be for meeting with a man designated by angels who would guide me in my appointed task to "stand in the temple and speak to the people all the words of this Life"? I would happily become a student of the Azeri myself, if necessary, and proclaim whatever Gospel was appointed to me, for I had lost all doubt and inhibition by then, as well as all false modesty, for I truly believed that I had been chosen by God to perform this great but as yet unknown work. You will probably want to note that, won't you?

It made no difference that I was not a Catholic. The realization had been growing in me for some time that God is not interested in labels and that the names of religions and denominations are not engraved on the human heart. Allison and I read with fascination all of the information that we could gather on Gregorian University and Rome itself. I had been there once before on a summer tour of Rome and Florence with fellow art students arranged by the University of Indiana. Those four weeks of immersion in the Italian masters had confirmed in me the rightness of my decision to become a painter, and even my father had to concede upon my return that his rearguard action on behalf of the law had failed. My passport was still barely valid.

Ah, Rome! There is no end to its beauties, both architectural and female, and sometimes both at the same time. Those were unforgettable weeks. This time, though, it would be quite different. My second trip might well expunge the sins of my first. This time, I would visit the churches to seek out the indelible spiritual meaning within their walls rather than the beautiful art and artifice upon their walls, and the same would be true of my dealings with people.

I yearned to explore the Piazza della Pilotta and all of the buildings and alleyways and traditions, both sacred and secular, that would define for me the great Gregorian University, named after Pope Gregory XIII, who had personally lifted up the modest "Roman College" established by Saint Ignatius at the base of the Capitoline Hill, transferred it to new and spacious buildings near the Via del Corso, and confirmed it as a "Pontifical" institution under the tutelage of all subsequent popes. I ached to drown myself in the glories of the Vatican, uncertain whether to give myself up more fully to the inspiration of the Fisherman or that of Michelangelo. I longed to discover the one "temple" where I would deliver my message among the countless ancient and modern temples that dot the map of Rome. I ordered my tickets from Indianapolis to Rome by way of New York with Allison's heartfelt blessing.

That night, finally cognizant of the heavenly power granted to all of us—"knock and it will be opened to you"—I prayed fervently for a vision of New Rome that would guide me in my search for the Azeri. And I drifted off to sleep.

Raphael and I glided side by side through the night air swiftly and smoothly. The thick white plumage of his wings reflected the moonlight much like the sea reflecting sunlight on a cloudless, dazzling day.

"Why do you have wings this time?" I asked.

"I thought it would soothe you in this situation," he replied calmly. *"Turn your head and look at your own."*

I did so and simply accepted the fact of my own beautiful, white, feathered wings. Nothing seemed unnatural in the dream state.

"All realms are controlled by thought alone," he continued. *"All energy arises from thought, and all mass is energy shaped by thought. The same is true in your waking realm, but the process is so much slower there that you are usually not aware of it. Here, if you wish to have wings, you have wings in the same instant. On earth, the same wish required many thousands of years for fulfillment."*

I can't say that I really understood what he said, but it made perfect sense to me in the dream.

"Now look below," he said. *"New Rome."*

Paris may enjoy the sobriquet "City of Light," but I am sure that it looks wan in comparison to the light show that erupted below us in that instant, as New Rome seemed to spread out its own dazzling wings in honor of our approach. Gleaming white buildings with massive pillars stood everywhere in the center of the city. The fabled river snaked through it on its way to the sea. A great white obelisk marked the triumph of one of the bold military conquerors of its storied past. We swooped down to a brilliantly lit domed temple with a pond shimmering in the moonlight before it. We walked alone inside it and viewed the massive statue of one of the rulers standing proudly beneath the dome with words of greatness carved into the marble surrounding him. Then we rose silently into the sky again and flew effortlessly to the west as the outlines of a great university grew ever plainer. It was built above the river in red brick. It was clearly not Gregorian University, and I was grateful to the angel for correcting my mistake. We circled over the expanse of buildings and green spaces below three times.

"The city and the school are one," he said. *"Here you will find the Azeri."*

Then we reversed our course and flew quickly to a massive white temple surrounded by 35 magnificent pillars and streaming light from all directions. The angel and I drifted slowly onto the wide and steep front steps and began to climb toward the inner sanctum. There were people there, even in the middle of the night, but it was clear that they could not see us. Finally, as we entered the temple together, we could see the great white statue of the fallen warrior as he sat impassively and stared out across the water at the obelisk and into the hearts of his countrymen. And at last I knew exactly where I had to go to find the Azeri.

The next morning, I cancelled my flight to Rome and booked a direct flight to Washington, D.C.

* * *

Washington. George Washington. George's Town. Georgetown. It was not at all difficult to make the connections— once I knew what they were. But isn't that the way it is with all mysteries? There is nothing to the magic trick—once the trick is known. There is nothing to Rubik's Cube—once the method is known. Yet it was finally dawning on me that I was not supposed to take the shortcuts. How can learning take place if the answers are all provided without benefit of effort? Where is the discovery and respect for the mystery if we only parrot the answers or practice the techniques without earning our understanding? The angels were not deficient in English. I was deficient in understanding. "He who has ears to hear, let him hear." And I was being taught to correct my deficiencies. Take nothing for granted, they were saying. Study and learn, they were saying. You have a divine task to accomplish, they were saying, but you are not yet ready to accomplish it.

So why was Washington, D.C., being labeled New Rome? A quick stop at the Butler University library before I left Indianapolis began to open my eyes. Scholars and commentators of all political stripes had been comparing the United States to Rome for years without my knowledge. I was stunned to find that the Founding Fathers had found direct and conscious inspiration for the new country in the history and traditions of Rome. The very idea of the Senate, for example, stemmed directly from the Romans. The new country adopted the eagle as national symbol—arrows, olive branches, and all—from Rome. After leading the Continental Army and then serving as President for two terms, George Washington consciously emulated the citizen warrior Cincinattus in returning to his farm after the challenge was completed. The architecture of Washington, D.C., is both Roman and Greek, with Roman gods and goddesses sitting and standing in places of honor throughout the city. The architect and urban planner Pierre Charles L'Enfant designed major areas of the new city, including the central mall, in imitation of the Roman forum.

The list of physical similarities goes on, but it is the global reach of the United States that has attracted even more comparisons to imperial Rome, with military power as the prime example. The United States does have military garrisons spread across the world and does seem to be guarding the frontiers against attacks by modern barbarians. Beyond that, American popular culture, lifestyle, and fashion have spread around the world. The Internet has extended the reach of its influence, and English is now the closest to a world language that man has ever known—unless the story of the Tower of Babel is true.

I had known about Georgetown University primarily from basketball, although I had also heard that it was one of the finer universities in the country, with a School of Foreign Service second to none. Founded in 1789, the school is the oldest Catholic and Jesuit university in the United States. It is indeed the "School of the Jesuits in the City of New Rome."

I landed at Reagan National Airport on a Saturday afternoon, rented a car, and drove to the Marriott Hotel in Rosslyn, Virginia, just across the Potomac from Georgetown University via Key Bridge. I did not intend to walk into the office of the provost on Monday morning and boldly ask him to introduce me to the Azeri. No, I had a plan, tenuous though it may have been. I felt certain that the Azeri, whoever he or she was, had to be involved with religion. Otherwise, why had I been led to the "School of the Jesuits," and how could the Azeri be my spiritual guide during waking hours as a mere layman?

After checking in at the hotel and quickly getting myself organized, I walked across Key Bridge on a fine spring afternoon and up a series of steep steps in order to reach a street that would take me to the main administration building. Several friendly people, most of them students, directed me along the way, and I finally entered the right building in the late afternoon. A kind office manager who was working late on Saturday gave me a map and marked the primary home of the Department of Theology on it, handing me a list of faculty members at the department and courses for that semester in the bargain. I thanked her profusely and walked out into the spring sunshine feeling good about myself and my foresight.

Looking up into the deep blue spring sky and the chirping birds flitting back and forth over the open green, I suddenly found myself within the memory of circling over the campus three times at night with the angel Raphael. The phrase "bird's eye view" flashed through my mind, and I realized that in my mind I was literally looking down again at the very spot where I was then standing. I could see myself standing there, superimposed on the crystal clear memory of the view from my flight, with my spirit once again looking down at my own body. Am I completely out of my mind? I thought. Flying overhead with the angel Raphael?

There is a mechanism, I think, that protects us from being overwhelmed by the numinous—a word I picked up from the Azeri, by the way. I am now thirty-three years old, nearly thirty-four. I could not have written this when I was thirty. There is ample testimony in the holy texts of the dangers encountered by humans in contact with the divine, as many have been "blasted" by the experience. I think of the poor Israelite who laid his hand upon the Ark of the Covenant in order to steady it and fell dead immediately afterward. Or Lot's wife turned into a pillar of salt. And even Moses could not look directly at God, *"for man shall not see me and live."* It is not without reason that the angels so often declare *"Fear not!"* before the humans in front of them run as fast as they can from holiness. Yet the doubt protects us, I think. We cannot bear the full impact of what the evidence keeps telling us must be true, and we are left with what is both a prayer and a cry of what is nearly despair: "I believe, O Lord! Help me with mine unbelief."

So my thoughts returned to where I stood on the open green, and I breathed deeply of the fresh spring air, and I thanked God for my life and for the task ahead of me, although surely I was unworthy of it. Then I sat on a vacant wooden bench across from the administration building and began to work my way down through the extensive list of faculty members within the Department of Theology. There were nearly fifty names on the list, including all of the visiting and adjunct professors. I was certain that one of them would jump out at me, that something close to Azeri would grab my attention. In fact, there was nothing even remotely similar. I went through the list three times, so certain was I that my intuition had taken me to the right department.

Then I began to examine the list of courses. "The Problem of God" would have been my first choice as a student, and I noted that it was a required course in the core curriculum anyway, although I doubted that the problem had been solved. "Truth, Illusion, and Salvation" also seemed to fit my situation well. But then I found my eyes being drawn back repeatedly to "Islamic Religious Thought and Practice" for no particular reason. I would scan up and down the pages, finding such intriguing titles as "Religion and Public Policy" or "Christian Mysticism," both of which piqued my personal interest, but then I would be drawn back to "Islamic Religious Thought and Practice." I couldn't shake it, so I decided not to try any longer. I circled the title with my pen, folded all of the sheets together, and put them in my pocket. I enjoyed the walk back to the hotel, ate a modest dinner in the hotel, and got a good night's sleep.

Sunday was a glorious day filled with sunshine and the eternal optimism that spring brings to all of us by jolting our hormonal systems and preparing us to go forth and multiply. That thought elicited the incongruous image of a legion of fourth graders bursting out of schools everywhere with their math books in one hand and pencil and paper in the other. God works in mysterious ways, as do the minds that He has given us.

The beautiful but ephemeral cherry blossoms had long since vanished from the tidal basin, but I walked there anyway, strolling first through Georgetown and then past the State Department and down to the Lincoln Memorial, where I lingered in awe of the great man who still serves as the conscience of our nation, partly in the present and partly in my dream again, before I set off across the Great Mall and slowly approached the Jefferson Memorial.

It was JFK who said at a dinner with his top advisors that there had not been so much brainpower concentrated at a table in the White House since Thomas Jefferson dined alone. I had never been to the Jefferson Memorial before, but I had always felt that Washington, Lincoln, and Jefferson somehow represented the ideal body, heart, and mind of the Republic, in that order—

physical strength, moral strength, and intellectual strength. And what of the soul? I soon learned to my surprise that it may also be encapsulated within the Jefferson Memorial, the last of the three great presidential memorials located on or adjacent to the National Mall and dedicated as recently as 1943.

As I stood finally at the top of the white marble steps and began to see the huge bronze statue inside, I was unprepared for the true memorial to both the man and the source of his inspiration inscribed on the walls inside. It is God who infuses every word of the man who wrote the Declaration of Independence. It is those words and the spirit that dictated them that create the sense of reverence in the Jefferson Memorial: "I have sworn upon the altar of God eternal hostility against every form of tyranny over the mind of man. … Almighty God hath created the mind free … God who gave us life gave us liberty … Can the liberties of a nation be secure when we have removed a conviction that these liberties are the gift of God? … We hold these truths to be self-evident, that all men are created equal, that they are endowed by their Creator with certain inalienable rights, among these are life, liberty, and the pursuit of happiness."

In truth, then, the Jefferson Memorial is a genuine temple, modeled after the Pantheon in Rome, that enshrines not only Jefferson himself but also the fact that the United States is a nation whose creators honored their own Creator. Is it any wonder that the sentence "In God we trust" is engraved on the money of the country just as clearly as it was engraved on the hearts of the men who gave it birth?

I was determined to do exactly the same—trust in God and whatever purpose had been prepared for me. As I strolled slowly back across the Mall, I heard singing in the distance near the Lincoln Memorial. A black church choir in gold and purple robes had gathered at the steps and was singing spirituals. I could hear the last few phrases of "Swing Low, Sweet Chariot" as I drew near. There was a pause of a few minutes as they rearranged themselves on the steps, but, just as I reached the near end of the reflecting pool, they began again, with a rising power that stopped me in my tracks and stopped all conversation in the growing crowd:

> *Mine eyes have seen the glory of the coming of the*
> *Lord:*
> *He is trampling out the vintage where the grapes of*
> *wrath are stored;*
> *He hath loosed the fateful lightning of his terrible*
> *swift sword:*
> *His truth is marching on.*
> *Glory, glory, hallelujah!*
> *Glory, glory, hallelujah!*
> *Glory, glory, hallelujah!*
> *His truth is marching on.*

I realized that there would never be a better moment for walking in my life, so I strode off in cadence with the song in the direction of Georgetown up past the State Department. I could barely hear the last stanza and chorus before the thunderous applause began:

> *He is coming like the glory of the morning on the*
> *wave,*
> *He is Wisdom to the mighty, He is Succor to the*
> *Brave,*
> *So the world shall be his footstool, and the soul of*
> *Time his slave,*
> *Our God is marching on.*

The chorus kept ringing in my ears as I continued the walk that had become a march toward whatever destiny lay before me. I thought of the fateful lightning in Tennessee. I thought of the glory that I had already seen with my own eyes. I thought of New Rome and the new Eden envisioned by the Founding Fathers. I thought of ancient Rome and of two thousand years of history since a birth in Bethlehem. I thought of the return of the Jews to the land that had been promised to them. I thought of tortured Jerusalem and the three great religions under one God that cherish the same place on earth but not each other. I thought of the divine task that I was destined to fulfill. Glory, glory, hallelujah! And I kept marching on.

* * *

The next morning, I arrived at the administrative offices of the Department of Theology in building New North at 9 a.m. with a spring in my step and a song in my heart—actually in my head, as the strains of "Glory, glory, hallelujah!" kept running through it. There had been no evening visitation in my dreams, only restful and refreshing sleep. I felt strongly that I had been led to the right spot and that the Azeri would soon be guiding me toward my purpose in life.

"Good morning," I said cheerfully to the attractive young lady typing at a desk behind the counter dividing the public from academic officialdom. "I wonder if you can help me."

"Of course," she said with a smile, as she lifted her fingers from the keyboard and turned in my direction.

"I need to meet with an instructor or professor in the Department whose name is Azeri or something very close to that."

"That doesn't sound at all familiar," she said, "but let me check the updated faculty roster. Maybe that's someone new or slated for next semester."

She drew out a file from a nearby cabinet and carefully checked it while standing in front of me on the other side of the counter.

"No, I'm very sorry," she said finally. "We have no one of that name here. But if you give me your name and a contact number,

I can check more thoroughly with the department head. You may be looking for a graduate student who is helping out part-time, for example."

I gave her the information and started to leave when the thought finally struck me. "Oh, there is one other possibility," I said. "Who is teaching the course 'Islamic Religious Thought and Practice'?"

"Let me see," she said slowly, reaching for another folder and beginning to scan through the documents inside. "Oh, yes, here it is. That's Professor Tobias. His office is down the hall and to the right, Room 156. I don't know if he's there now, but you can certainly check."

I thanked her warmly, and she repaid me with another friendly smile. I walked out of the office just as several students were walking in, and I noticed that the hallway was suddenly becoming crowded with students and faculty. I weaved my way down the hall and turned right, carefully checking the numbers above the doors as I worked my way to Room 156. I saw an elderly gentleman with sparse white hair unlock the door to an office about twenty feet in front of me and close the door behind him. When I reached the door, I also saw the number 156 above it. I knocked.

He opened the door and squinted at me momentarily. "My office hours are posted," he said quietly.

"Yes, sir," I said quickly. "I apologize for disturbing you, but I thought that you might be able to help me find the Azeri, or, excuse me, someone named Azeri or something very close to that."

"Do you have anything against Azeris?" he asked with obvious interest and a hint of concern in his voice.

"No, no, not at all," I said, suddenly remembering that Azeris were the people of Azerbaijan. "My advisor told me to contact what I thought was Professor Azeri in regard to my field of study."

"Well, then," he said with a bit of relief in his voice. "I believe you are referring to Professor Azarias in the Department of Arabic and Islamic Studies. We are colleagues, in fact. I have learned a great deal from him, but he will be returning to Baku shortly, unfortunately. He is an Azeri, you see. And I thought that there was a bit of condescension in your voice when you inquired about 'the Azeri.' You will find him in Poulton Hall. Give him best wishes from John Tobias."

"Thank you, sir, I will," I replied.

I imposed on the young woman in the administrative office one more time by asking for directions to Poulton Hall and then set off briskly on the sidewalk outside—too briskly, actually, as I realized once again that I was marching to the tune in my head. I slowed my pace and enjoyed the balmy weather.

At Poulton Hall, the earlier scene repeated itself up to the point when the receptionist said, "Why, of course. Professor Azarias has his office in Room 235. I don't see a class on his schedule now. Go up the stairs and turn left."

I climbed the stairs with enormous anticipation, turned left, and walked down the hall. The door to Room 235 was open. I leaned into the room and knocked on the open door. "Professor Azarias?" I asked hesitantly.

The man at the paper-strewn desk turned his swivel chair in my direction slowly. Silence ensued. We looked at each other closely. He was a tall, well-built man of perhaps sixty, with thick brown curly hair just starting to turn gray hanging down to the top of his shoulders. He wore a white dress shirt and pleated light brown trousers. His blue eyes bored into mine as he somewhat incongruously munched on a fish sandwich. The paper that the sandwich had been wrapped in was spread out over many of the academic documents on the desk. Finally, he nodded to me, pointed to his full mouth, and waved me over toward the chair at the side of his desk.

"Professor Azarias," I repeated as I sat down. "I would like to introduce myself to you. My name is—"

He waved me into silence with one hand as he placed the remainder of the sandwich on the paper with the other, withdrew a white napkin from the brown paper bag next to his chair, and dabbed at his mouth quickly before tossing the napkin back into the bag and swallowing mightily for the last time.

"I know who you are, Jacob," he said in a husky, accented voice that I could never have placed had I not known that he was "the Azeri." "We know someone in common," he continued matter-of-factly. "I knew that you were coming, and now I welcome you." He stood up and motioned for me to do the same. A bear hug followed, and I was glad that I had stayed in shape.

"This person that we know," I said as we sat down again facing each other, "has friends in high places, does he not?"

"Oh, yes, that is true," he said. "And he has a way of challenging you, as if he alters your dreams, is that not the case?"

"Yes," I responded. "And he appears young. He might almost be a boy, wouldn't you say?"

"No, Jacob! I would not say that," he responded with force. "Do not let appearances deceive you. The beings that we are discussing are nearly omnipotent, and they could turn you into dust in an instant. I repeat: Do not let appearances deceive you. You will know one day how to distinguish appearance from reality, and on that day your way of thinking will change, and you will be close to your goal."

I was taken aback by the strength in his voice and demeanor. He clearly was not to be a kindly and fragile mentor.

"Now," he said, passing a piece of paper from the desk to me, "read this passage and tell me where it is found in the Bible."

The passage was short, and I read through it quickly:

> *"Jesus, son of Mary," said the disciples, "can your*
> *Lord send down to us from heaven a table spread*
> *with food?"*

*He replied: "Have fear of God, if you are true
believers."*

*"We wish to eat of it," they said, "so that we may
reassure our hearts and know that what you said to
us is true, and that we may be witnesses of it."*

*"Lord," said Jesus, son of Mary, "send down to us
from heaven a table spread with food, that it may
mark a feast for the first of us and the last of us: a
sign from You. Give us our sustenance; You are the
best provider."*

*God replied: "I am sending one to you. But whoever
of you disbelieves hereafter shall be punished as no
man will ever be punished."*

Frankly, I had no idea where the passage was from. I could not
remember reading it in the Bible. "I don't recognize it," I said. "It
could be anywhere in the New Testament. Or perhaps in the
Apocrypha."

"It is from the Quran," he said. "Both Jesus and Mary are
revered in the Quran. Jesus is described as a 'holy son' and 'a sign
to mankind and a blessing from Ourself.' It is said of Mary in the
Quran, in the words of the Angels: 'God has chosen you. He has
made you pure and exalted you above womankind.'"

The professor stood up and spoke with passion in his voice,
and I was beginning to think that he only had one mode of
speech.

"You will learn two things from me," he said loudly. "The first
is the nature of the angels. The second and far more important is
that Christians, Jews, and Muslims all serve the same God, and
that indeed all peoples everywhere who pray with love, mercy,
and compassion in their hearts speak to the same God and receive
His blessings. There is no God but God."

I also stood, gazed into his penetrating eyes, and held out my hand to him. He grasped my forearm, and I his, and we stood that way for at least ten seconds without speaking. Thus began my association with the Azeri.

He had earned an international reputation from his base in Baku as an expert in angelology. There seemed to be nothing about angels, no source of any kind, that he had not already examined and critiqued in a professional journal or religious forum, in several different languages. His English was impeccable, for example, although his native language was certainly Azeri, a form of Turkish. He was a Muslim from a country slightly smaller than Maine with a population approaching nine million people, about ninety-five percent of whom are also Muslim. It is a country transformed in our time by its oil resources, but its rich history includes connections with Alexander the Great, Romans, Parthians, Byzantines, Seljuk Turks, Tamerlane, Ottoman Turks, Persians, Russians, Soviets, and many others.

We did not have much time. Azarias had agreed to teach as an adjunct professor at Georgetown for the spring semester only. They were happy to have him, and I heard repeatedly from other faculty members that he had brought a new spirit of ecumenism on campus among the three great religions of "the Book." According to Muslims, the gospel given to the people of the earth by the Prophet Muhammad, as revealed to him by the Angel Gabriel, speaks very clearly of the linkages among Jews, Christians, and Muslims, as all three religions are based upon holy books prepared or conveyed in their time by prophets sent directly to mankind from God—Moses, Jesus, and Muhammad. The campus was astir with stories, particularly among the theology students, about fierce and passionate debates on points of doctrine between Azarias and his brilliant Jesuit friends and colleagues that lasted until daybreak and beyond. Not a single story spoke of an Azarias defeat.

When I first met him, there were only four weeks remaining before his return to his native country. I moved into an apartment in Ballston, Virginia, from where I could jump on to the Metro and get off at Rosslyn or the Foggy Bottom Station in D.C. and walk to the university. Or some days I would remember that I was a wealthy man and simply catch a cab. He set aside half an hour each day for our sessions, and sometimes I would sit in on his seminars. He convinced the university that I was helping him with a book, and no one minded our talks together or my presence on campus.

He chose not to raise the subject of Raphael again while we were in Washington, and I was quite certain that his other colleagues at Georgetown knew nothing of the apparent "inside" knowledge that informed his scholarly work. There were similarities, though, in his approach to my education and the information that I was receiving in dreams at night. Both Azarias and Raphael gave me subjects to research, usually religious passages from holy texts, but also related worldly topics and even works of art.

For example, Azarias once asked me to read in the "al-Imran" and "Maryam" sections of the Quran about the Annunciation, or the announcement to Mary by an angel of the incarnation of Jesus—the angel identified as Gabriel in *Luke 1:26.* There are two versions in the Quran, attesting to the great reverence of both Mary and Jesus in Islam:

al-Imran

And remember the angels' words to Mary. They said: "God has chosen you.

He has made you above womankind. Mary, be obedient to your Lord; bow down and worship with the worshippers."

85

This is an account of a divine secret. We reveal it to you. You were not present when they argued about her.

The angels said to Mary: "God bids you rejoice in a Word from Him. His name is the Messiah, Jesus son of Mary. He shall be noble in this world and in the world to come, and shall be one of those who are favored. He shall preach to men in his cradle and in the prime of manhood, and shall lead a righteous life."

"Lord," she said, "how can I bear a child when no man has touched me?"

He replied: "Even thus. God creates whom He will. When he decrees a thing, He need only say: 'Be,' and it is. He will instruct him in the Scriptures and in wisdom, in the Torah and in the Gospel, and send him forth as an apostle to the Israelites."

Maryam

And you [Muhammad] shall recount in the Book [Quran] the story of Mary: how she left her people and betook herself to a solitary place to the east.

We sent to her Our spirit in the semblance of a full-grown man. And when she saw him, she said: "May the Merciful defend me from you! If you fear the Lord, [leave me and go your way]."

"I am but your Lord's emissary," he replied, "and have come to give you a holy son."

"How shall I bear a child," she answered, "when I have neither been touched by any man nor ever been unchaste?"

"Thus did your Lord speak," he replied. "'That is easy enough for Me. He shall be a sign to mankind and a blessing from Ourself. Our decree shall come to pass.'"

As you can see, I know the passages well, and I was struck somehow by the fact that Muslims believe that Gabriel dictated the Quran to Muhammad and that Christians believe that Gabriel delivered the message to Mary that she would be the mother of a son conceived by the Holy Spirit. In any case, I absorbed the lesson easily enough that Islam has adopted many of the same passages found in the New Testament and holds both Mother and Son in the highest reverence.

That same night, after I had read repeatedly through the two Quran passages, a wingless Raphael again appeared to me in a crystal clear dream in radiant colors. His laser-blue eyes stared straight into my mind.

"The Annunciation," he said. *"There are two paintings entitled 'Annunciation' attributed to Leonardo, one in the Louvre and one in the Uffizi. Which one did he actually paint? Look at the angel and look at Mary. He who has eyes to see, let him see."*

Then I awoke suddenly, as I always did in those days after the dream visitations. I could think of nothing but the Annunciation, with Azarias pushing its significance in my waking hours and Raphael forcing my attention to it at night. I had seen the work in the Uffizi Gallery in Florence, but I could not begin to remember its details. I had never been to Paris, let alone the Louvre. I could not sleep again, so I took out the Bible and read through *Luke 1: 26-56,* comparing the description of the Annunciation there to those in the Quran, and then I tried desperately to picture the painting in the Uffizi. I failed.

When I arrived at the university at midmorning the next day, I fought to suppress the yawning attacks that had begun over breakfast. Professor Azarias was waiting for me in his office.

"You look tired," he said. "Was the homework too much for you?" he added with a wry smile.

"No, it was the dream work," I replied. "How many of your students have to work as hard in their dreams as they do in their waking hours?"

"Not many," he agreed, "but then not many of them have been given your chance at advanced placement either. So tell me: What has your after-hours tutor been demanding of you?"

I explained about the two paintings of the Annunciation thought to have been produced by Leonardo—and the fact that I could not remember the one and had never seen the other.

"I can remedy that," he said. "I have illustrations of both in this book about the works of Leonardo." He got up from his chair and retrieved a large book filled with magnificent illustrations of all of the artistic works of daVinci.

"Has it never occurred to you that Leonardo might be more than a genius?" he asked. "How could one man have demonstrated so much greatness in so many fields? Is it not reasonable to think, knowing what you now know, that others may have been aided in their lifetimes as well? In any case, Jacob, look at the two paintings. Better yet, photocopy them and then place one above the other. They are on separate pages in the book."

I did as he proposed and looked back and forth at the two images. In both works, an angel kneels before Mary in a garden with his right hand raised. However, even at first glance, the painting from the Uffizi looks more like the work of Leonardo. The use of shadow is in his style, and the attention to detail is far more marked. The image of Mary is also more noble and compelling. The painting lacks the maturity of his best work, with some apparent mishandling of perspective, but the contrast to me with the painting in the Louvre was still quite noticeable.

"I believe that the Uffizi version is by Leonardo," I said finally. "Let's start with the 'Leonardesque' shadow effect—"

"Let's not," Azarias interrupted. "You have chosen correctly, but not for the right reasons. Let's stipulate that Leonardo was a master painter and that you can see his genius in the work, even though he was only twenty years old when he painted it. The work in the Louvre was actually painted by Lorenzo di Credi, but this will not be proven for several more years. Did your tutor not tell you to look for something else?"

I thought for a few seconds and then realized that he was right. I had been told very clearly to *"Look at the angel and look at Mary."*

"Yes," I said. "I'm still so sleepy that I forgot. Let me concentrate on the two figures in each painting."

"As you do so, Jacob, do not get lost in the surface qualities. You must learn to see through surfaces at the reality that rests behind them. Remember that I have charged you with distinguishing appearance from reality. You do not yet realize that nearly everything that you can perceive is a symbol for something else and that almost nothing is what it appears to be. Remember that I have stressed this to you. Now, look beyond the paint and the brush strokes and the artifice of the master painter and delve into his mind instead. Try to penetrate the thoughts in his mind as he created, for it is thoughts that create reality, here and elsewhere."

I did what he said. I forgot about the art, the mastery of the painting medium, and simply looked at the subjects and the objects, all of which, according to Azarias, were symbols of something else. The basic layout was the same: a walled garden with trees beyond the walls, a winged and robed angel on bended knee with head bowed and right arm outstretched and right hand lifted, a piece of furniture separating the angel from Mary, and Mary herself receiving the angel with grace and humility. And then I saw it! The Mary in the Louvre version bows her own head and crosses her arms across her chest on bended knee in deference to the angel. The Mary from the Uffizi sits regally with head upright and raises her left hand in greeting to the angel. The position of the angels is virtually identical, but the two Marys are strikingly different. Why? What was the difference in the minds of the two artists as they contemplated the composition of their works—and as they decided on depicting the posture of Mary for countless generations to come? If Azarias was right, Leonardo benefited not only from a greater mastery of art but also from far deeper knowledge of the scene that he was painting.

"I think I see it," I said. "Leonardo's Mary is far more regal and commanding. She does not bow to the angel. The Mary from the Louvre—di Credi's Mary—seems to be on an equal if not lesser footing with the angel; they bow to each other. That seems to be appropriate at first glance, as the angel of God bows to the Holy Mother and she in turn bows to the messenger of God, but I sense now that such a scene is not appropriate."

"NO!" Azarias thundered. "It is *not* appropriate. It is in fact *forbidden* for angels to accept the obeisance of men. The angel will always bow first or nod first, out of respect for the being created in God's image and that actually shares in the creative powers of God. You have no idea how the angels stand in awe of mankind! They cannot create. Their thoughts are attuned only to the thoughts of God. They deliver messages; they cannot create them. When they see humans for the first time, they actually see the power and image of God, and they must bow in reverence. And, Jacob, Jacob, they feel such enormous pity for creatures so powerful that they can actually choose not to do God's will and therefore bring such horrible suffering upon themselves. The guardian angels are assigned to protect men from themselves. Everything is designed to protect men from themselves. They live in a universe of incredibly dense matter, so their random, uncontrolled thoughts do not materialize instantly and bring horror upon themselves and others. It is only when humans bring their thoughts into alignment with God of their own free will that they can then make full use of their creative power in realms of attenuated matter. Begin now to understand this, Jacob, as Leonardo understood it."

I was awestruck myself, both at the vehemence in his voice and at the knowledge that he was imparting. I certainly in no way compared myself to Leonardo, quite the contrary. I had been content to make a living as an artist, and the only piece that I had ever created with stunning power in it was the portrait of Ariel, and the credit for that, I was quite certain, really belonged to Ariel. Was I now being told that Leonardo's extraordinary gifts could be traced to angelic assistance? And how in the world did Azarias, the Azeri, know of such things?

"Professor," I said. "Forgive me, but I need a little more information now. What is the source of your knowledge on these matters?"

"I thought that you understood that, Jacob," he replied with some puzzlement. "You of all people should know that angels exist. Is it any wonder that others may have the same contact? I have been in direct communication myself with the holy angels for quite some time. They inform all of my knowledge about them, as they will inform all of your knowledge in due time. Do you doubt this?"

"No, no, I don't," I said slowly. "I … I am just still … having some trouble understanding why *I* have been chosen, and why *you* have been chosen, for that matter."

"Jacob," he said without the least sign of condescension, "you already know why you have been chosen: You have a divine task to fulfill. It should not surprise you to know that I also have a divine task to fulfill—in fact, more than one. That is why I have been here in Washington, D.C., in the very heart of the New Roman Empire. You will learn that the very language of the empire bears secrets for all of mankind, and that what happens here affects all of mankind, whether the citizens of this country understand that or not. Trust me for a while longer—and trust certainly in the visions that you receive at night."

"But, Professor," I nearly implored, "I still have no idea what my task may be. I am gathering information at every turn, and I know that my memory has progressed to the point of near total recall. I am astounded by this and deeply grateful, believe me, but I simply don't know what my goal may be."

There was a lengthy pause in our conversation while he simply stared fixedly out the window and up at the sky. Then he closed his eyes and turned in his chair to face me directly. He resumed at the instant he opened his eyes.

"There is a reason why you cannot yet know the nature of your task, just as there are reasons why most humans cannot yet know the secrets of their existence. Only believe me for now when I tell you that you would not be able to fulfill your task in the way that you yourself would wish it if you knew what it was before the time allotted. You will know at the point that the wall disappears in your mind just before it disappears in your reality. This is all that I can say."

Another conundrum. Another answer without an answer. At least he did not say, "He who has ears to hear, let him hear." My ears were functioning quite well, and my mind was not far behind, thank you, because it was finally clear to me that I was not meant to understand at that point. I was meant to have faith in the process itself, the process of living and learning, the process of submission to a higher power, and the process of truly meaning "Your will, not mine."

As I struggled with those thoughts and the frustrations that arose from them despite my best efforts, Azarias then struck me metaphorically between the eyes. "I am returning to Baku in exactly one week," he said, "and you are coming with me."

I was stunned. I had never considered that I might have to continue my "apprenticeship" in Azerbaijan.

"You will need a visa, which I can acquire for you here at the embassy. You will need to pack well with two heavy suitcases, your briefcase, and your laptop. You will need to see your fiancée and settle your other affairs as quickly as possible. I cannot tell you how long we will be, but I do know that we must also visit other countries in the region. There may be danger. Has your faith prepared you for this, Jacob? Are you ready to face your destiny without fear and perhaps your death without regret should God require it of you?"

I had no ready answers for those questions. Intellectually, I could have said "yes," but emotionally and physically, I was not at all certain. I valued my life, and it was growing ever clearer to me that I was far from reaching the point where I could give it up without hesitation, trusting only in the wisdom and mercy of an unseen God. Somehow, the existence of angels had not yet proven to me beyond all doubt the immortality of my own soul, despite my own disembodied experience. I wish I could say that it was otherwise. I was, in fact, still all-too human and still all-too limited. I prayed every day, and I prayed that my prayers would be heard. Oh, Lord, I believe. Help me with my disbelief.

Nevertheless, I did as he said. I gave him my passport, paid the remaining rent, began to pack what I had and buy what I needed, and arranged for Allison to spend the last week with me. And I continued to experience the visitations of Raphael in my dreams almost every night. The messages in that last week were shorter, though, and quite specific. Usually, they were simply references to biblical passages that I had to look up the next day. Some were clearly linked to the existence and importance of angels, but others made little sense to me.

In one dream, for example, he looked straight at me and said, *"Zechariah 4-6."* I took the passage as confirmation of other angelic messages delivered in sleep.

In another such message, Raphael intoned *"Genesis 18."* After reading through it the next day, it seemed to me that I was being advised again about appearance and reality, since Abraham first mistook the three angels of God as mere men.

In yet another, Raphael used his finger to write the following on a wall in letters and numbers burning with scorching fire: *Mark 16:17-18*. The passage contained the last message of Jesus to his disciples after the Resurrection, and, at first, I thought that it also referred to me, but I could not reconcile my puny self with the powers proclaimed there, as you will see if you take the time to read it.

Finally, he pronounced *"Leviticus 16"* with great intensity, but it was only a description of the ancient tradition of scapegoats and the purification rites that followed.

My sessions with the Azeri grew shorter as the time for our departure approached. "We will have plenty of time together later, Jacob," he said. "Allow me to attend to other business here."

Allison curled up in my arms at night in that last week, and we spoke fervently about our love and our plans for the future. I shared everything with her about my stay in Washington. We visited the Jefferson and Lincoln memorials together, and I traced for her the exact pattern of my dream flight overhead. We walked across the Georgetown University campus frequently and ate almost every night in a different cozy restaurant in Georgetown itself. I introduced her to Professor Azarias, and he charmed her thoroughly with an old world bow and congratulations on our coming marriage. As hectic as it was with all of the preparations for an open-ended trip to Azerbaijan and perhaps the region around it, that week was still one of the happiest of my life.

Then, as strange and unexpected as it may have been, I found myself kissing a very tearful Allison as Professor Azarias and I boarded a British Airways flight at Dulles Airport for the journey to Baku by way of London that would take us some twenty hours to complete.

I used much of that time to read the section on Azerbaijan in a book that I had bought on Central Asia. I had never really studied ancient history, other than the usual smattering of knowledge about Alexander and the rise of the Greeks, followed by the rise and eventual fall of the Romans. The book told me that the country occupies territory that had been part of the ancient Median Empire, whose inhabitants were the famous Medes, neighbors of the Persians, the forebears of contemporary Iranians. Little is known about the culture of the Medes, other than the fact that Zoroastrianism was the primary religion. I began to be truly interested in all of this when I learned that the priestly caste of the period was called the Magi—suddenly a term familiar to me and a possible connection to the purpose of my trip.

My attention was then riveted on the derivation of the name *Azerbaijan*, as scholars believe that it stems from *Atropates*, a satrap of Persia under the Achaemenid Empire who was reinstated as the satrap of Media under Alexander the Great after his conquest of the region. *Atropates*, which means "protected by fire" in Old Persian, is believed by etymologists to have its roots in Zoroastrianism, specifically the "Frawardin Yasht" or "Hymn to the Guardian Angels," one of the religion's sacred texts. Do not misunderstand me here. None of these names, except for Alexander, had any more meaning for me then than they have for you now. I did have an advantage over you, though, in that I could remember absolutely everything I read by that point. Oh, the knowledge was not sitting there in the front of my brain all the time, overwhelming me with intellectual input, but I could call it up, much the same way that you can access information from your computer. I began to believe that the change in my powers of memory could be traced directly to the lightning strike, which must have activated neural pathways that simply had not existed before. That thought led to another that would repeat itself throughout my trials: We are not wise enough creatures to recognize that ultimate good rises up from our pain and distress. We are caught in the excruciating present because of our failure to understand the illusion of time, whereas we should be moving freely throughout the so-called past, present, and future.

At that moment, I was struck by the juxtaposition in the book of both the "Hymn to the Guardian Angels" and the mention of the Magi. I felt—I believed—that these must be omens of success.

I continued to absorb the often bitter history of a region ravaged by conquerors from every direction and ruled by countless dynasties that rose and fell with disturbing regularity. Some fifteen hundred years after the high point of the Achaemenid Empire, the Seljuk Turks established their dominance in the area that became Azerbaijan, only to be subjugated by Tamerlane and later by a series of Iranian rulers. Eventually, after two Russo-Persian Wars, a number of nominally independent *khanates* were merged into the Russian Empire, which itself collapsed in World War I, allowing for Azerbaijan to band together with Armenia and Georgia to form the short-lived Transcaucasian Democratic Federative Republic. Azerbaijan declared independence in 1918 but was invaded once more and conquered by the Soviet Red army in 1920 and found itself in 1940 to be a full constituent state of the Soviet Union. In 1990, the country announced its sovereignty, and, with the collapse of the former Soviet Union, Azerbaijan declared its independence in 1991. Military coups and political corruption, as well as bitter combat with Armenia over the disputed territory of Nagorno-Karabakh, marred the infancy of the new republic, and it was to this hotbed of conspiracy and bloody political rivalry reflecting the long and internecine history of the region that the British Airways jet in which I found myself was hurtling through the stratosphere.

Somehow the earlier omens had lost much of their luster by the time the plane settled to earth at the Bina International Airport of Baku.

CHAPTER IV

RAPHAEL

*P*rofessor Azarias was in full control. I was a master of ignorance at that time, with no knowledge of the city, language,
customs, Islam, and practically anything else, or so it seemed
upon arrival. He led us past passport control to a bank outlet for
currency exchange and then to the baggage area through an
incredible cacophony of shouts, unintelligible voices, loudspeaker announcements, and the pleading of dozens of would-be
baggage carriers. He was unfailingly polite but also firm in reject-
ing unwanted offers. He was a big man with an aura of authority
about him, and no one ever approached him a second time once
he had said "No." No one stopped us at Customs or even bothered to look at us as we walked behind the man he had selected
to load and push our baggage cart out to the waiting throng of
taxi drivers, all of whom seemed to be simultaneously declaring
cheaper prices and better service than the others. Azarias chose
the driver of a small van and the crowd melted away.

The drive to Baku State University was uneventful in one way,
but my senses were battered into full submission in the course of
the trip. There was no air-conditioning in the van, and the full
impact of the burgeoning city's aromatic and auditory vitality
swept through the open windows and into my being in a tsunami
of culture shock as my eyes tried to transmit exotic images to a

brain on sensory overload. Azarias contented himself with talking in friendly fashion to the driver and glancing over at me periodically with a knowing grin.

Darwin would have nodded knowingly—but at a safe distance—at the traffic conditions, in which two lanes miraculously transformed themselves into four and where red lights had the same effect on men as red capes on bulls. Our driver had obviously learned in his short life (with a likely short future) that the best way to escape calamitous conditions was to speed his way through them. Azarias chatted calmly and smiled.

There was one moment of grace as the van became totally boxed in at an intersection and had to stop despite the protestations of its valiant engine and the outraged manhood of our driver. Pedestrians poured into the street all around us and weaved through the blocked vehicles—working men, head-scarved women, and children of all ages with no more fear or concern than the driver had demonstrated. Then I began to hear the call to prayer sounding from a loudspeaker mounted on a minaret next to a mosque about a block ahead of us. Within seconds, the call was echoed by another, slightly different, magnified voice behind us, and soon there were so many electronically enhanced calls to prayer in the holy language of Arabic rising from minarets in all corners of the city that it seemed as if a massive holy choir was raising its voice to the heavens in supplication and submission to the one God, no matter what name for Him is used. I lowered my head and joined the choir in silence.

The van finally stopped at a modern four-level apartment house near the university, and the driver helped us carry the luggage up to a surprisingly spacious and comfortable second-floor apartment—home for Azarias in Baku and home base for me indefinitely. It occurred to me as we walked into the apartment that I could no longer think of Azarias as "the Azeri," as I would be living in a country where the term would be meaningless.

Somehow, we never got beyond the one name of Azarias, but we did become friends, even if the mentor-student relationship was still clearly defined. He still insisted that I focus intensely on the symbolic meaning of all things and penetrating beyond surface characteristics in order to discover the hidden reality obscured by our physical senses. Beyond that, my tasks were specific and simple. I was to roam the city in the mornings and learn about daily life in a Muslim society. And I was to study the life and works of the poet Rumi in English translation at the university in the afternoon. Over dinner, we would discuss my findings on both scores—and also the messages that I once again began to receive at night from Raphael. An outside observer would probably have been appalled by the ease and near nonchalance with which we discussed the workings in my life of an archangel. Nevertheless, that is the way it was.

I was far more perplexed by his insistence that I devote so much time to Jalal al-Din Rumi, the great poet of Muslim mysticism who lived most of his life in Turkey but wrote in Persian. "It is deeply important for you and for the world," he said, without elaborating. "You will understand when the time comes."

Regardless of heavy jet lag, I began my tour of the city by bus, foot, and taxi on the day after arrival, armed with a map, a guide book, a phrase book, several suggestions by Azarias, and optimism that probably bordered on idiocy. I found the city to be less exotic than I had expected. Most of the people wore western clothes. Yes, newly built mosques were everywhere, a reflection of the earlier suppression of religion by the Soviets, but Islam did not seem to be the driving force that I had expected upon arrival in a country where some ninety-five percent of the people were Muslims. A little reflection, mixed with conversations with foreigners, revealed to me that the Soviets had done their work all too well and that the people might call themselves Muslims but were still learning how to be Muslims. It is no surprise, however, that the people were returning enthusiastically to their religious roots, as my guide book revealed to me that the very name *Baku* probably means "Mount of God" and may find its roots in Zoroastrianism—and perhaps beyond, as *Baga* means God in Sanskrit.

On that first day of exploration, I headed straight for the Inner City with its magnificent protective walls and towers. There I saw more people in traditional dress, with most of the men wearing the round lambskin *papah* hat and many of the women in long, pleated skirts. All of the women, regardless of age, had their heads covered in scarves or cloths that covered both their heads and shoulders. I strolled through narrow alleyways and on cobbled streets, absorbing the sounds and sights and both the obvious and subtle variations in the way that life is lived in a foreign country in the vague hope that knowledge and understanding might also waft themselves into my consciousness along with the odors of grilled goat and lamb and the pungent smell of cabbage, which seemed to be one of the remaining Russian legacies.

I passed the fabled Maiden's Tower, where legend has it that a young woman threw herself from the heights to the rocks below in order to avoid marrying a man she did not love. I walked around the magnificent Palace of the Shirvanshahs and inside an ancient caravansary. Time passed much too fast, and I found myself by mid-afternoon back at the university, where I located Professor Azarias's office with some difficulty, a bit of comical sign-language, and the blessed arrival of an English-speaking student. Azarias took me to the library and procured a card for me that granted permanent access and allowed me to check out books. I discovered with pleasure that many of the books on Rumi were in English, including several different translations of his most important works. My studies began.

And time passed. I was surprised and relieved at first to find that so many signs in Baku were posted in both Azeri and English. Some of the store signs were only in English, as if to give them a special shopper's cachet. Although many, if not most,

Azeris clearly could speak Russian, they seemed reluctant to use the language. Moreover, the oil and gas boom had attracted hordes of foreign investors and oil workers, and English had become the preferred common language. There were also many Turkish investors and contractors who profited from the closeness of Turkish and Azeri, but, still, English had established a strong foothold in the expatriate community and become an entry point for me in the city.

At first, the sight of men kissing each other on the cheeks in greeting and farewell struck me as odd and vaguely distasteful, but the genuine affection between friends and family members that the custom conveyed soon won me over. There seemed to be a greater warmth among the people on the streets than I had experienced in my home country, and certainly the sincere hospitality offered to strangers went far beyond my own experience in the United States. I was always recognized as a foreigner and always offered black tea whenever I entered a shop or office.

In short, my forays into the streets and lifestyle of Baku served to enhance the very ability that Azarias had been demanding of me—to see beyond the superficial and into the heart of the matter, including the hearts of people. Differences in clothing, language, food, traditions, religion—none of these seemed important any longer. Smiles are universal, of course, even when the teeth that seem essential to them are missing, and I found smiles wherever I went. The warmth of friendship that I encountered and particularly the close family ties that were so obvious among Azarias's colleagues and even in small family-run shops was palpable and affecting. Children were spoiled in a positive way, for example, as they were touched and kissed with pride and affection by parents, grandparents, aunts, uncles, and others.

The sense that the entire country was somehow a great family struck me most forcibly on one particularly memorable day. It was a Friday morning about six weeks after our arrival, the weather was fine, a bit humid but not really hot, and I had begun to feel at home among the Azeris. I was strolling down a rather wide avenue when I heard the first call to prayer in front of me. About a block away, I could see men streaming through an archway that led to a large mosque. I quickened my step a bit and then joined the gradually declining flow into a courtyard beyond the archway. Men were washing their hands and feet at spigots near the entryway of the mosque clearly designed for the purpose, while others were simply removing their shoes in front of the thick curtain that covered the entrance and hurrying inside. I felt swept along both by the stream of men anxious to enter the mosque and by an immense and spontaneous sense of curiosity. I removed my shoes and carried them past the curtain, as I had seen most of the others doing.

I found myself inside a great vaulted space beneath a tiled dome with light streaming through high windows above us. There was a huge circular wooden chandelier suspended from the ceiling only a few feet above the heads of many of the worshippers, who had arrayed themselves on places marked on the main green carpet as they bowed in prayer toward Mecca and then stood erect for several seconds before bowing again. I placed my shoes in a rack near the entrance and watched other men situate themselves on the carpet. I was fascinated to see that whenever one man filled an empty space in a row in front of him, another would immediately step forward to fill his vacated space. It was as if they were all highly trained soldiers who moved forward in the ranks to replace their fallen comrades before the phalanx could be broken.

An older man around sixty moved forward from my side toward one of the last rows, as the mosque was reaching its capacity. When he reached his place, he bent forward with his hands on his knees in preparation for kneeling but suddenly stopped, tilted his head back toward me, and motioned for me to join him with his right hand. I looked around to be sure that he meant me, but I was alone by that point. I turned back, and he was still motioning toward me, this time a little more urgently. I moved forward and stood at the space on his right side. Just then, a voice began to intone from a loudspeaker mounted on one of the columns of the mosque. I had no idea what it meant, but I felt a tug on the left sleeve of my shirt. The older gentlemen motioned for me to kneel as he bent down on his knees, and then I noticed that all of the men were kneeling. The voice from the loudspeaker continued to intone in a language completely unknown to me, and I looked up to see that a turbaned cleric was sitting on an elevated platform and speaking into a microphone. The men around me lowered their foreheads to the floor, and I did the same. As everyone began to rise, I followed suit. We did this three times, and I dutifully copied all of the movements. The gentleman to my left looked over at me once and smiled. The last time we stood, I saw that the men had all cupped their hands with their palms up in front of them with their heads bowed as the cleric spoke somberly into the microphone. Suddenly the older gentleman turned his head on his neck in my direction, and I thought that I had somehow disgraced myself until I noticed that all of the men had turned their heads to the right. My friend signaled that I should do the same. As soon as I had turned my head to the right, all of the men turned their heads to the left, and I immediately did the same. It began to dawn on me that the cupped hands had received the word of God and that the men were perhaps recognizing that God is everywhere, in all directions. Then everyone sat and listened to the sermon of the cleric. This time, I could tell that he spoke Azeri, although the words flew over my head, both figuratively and literally. As the sermon ended, the men again got on their knees and bowed their heads to the floor. I could hear many of them praying quietly. I also prayed, asking God for love, mercy, and compassion.

When I heard the soft rustling at my side that indicated that my friend was rising, I did the same. Again he smiled and then led me by the elbow back toward the entrance. As hundreds of men began to file past us, many of them staring at me oddly, he looked in my eyes, smiled, and put his right hand on my left shoulder. He said something like "cardash." I returned the smile and put my right hand on his left shoulder. "Cardash," I said, hoping that we had not insulted each other and that he was not carrying a knife. He nodded his head and then turned to retrieve his shoes, which he carried outside with him. I gathered mine up as well and took them beyond the curtain to the carpeted area outside, where everyone was putting them on again. He left without turning around. By the time my shoes were on, he had disappeared in the crowd.

When I told Azarias that evening about my experience in the mosque, I asked him at the end what "cardash" might mean.

"Brother," he said. "*Qardas* means 'brother.'"

That night, Raphael appeared in my dreams. *"Luke 10:29-37. Read and remember!"*

In some ways, mundanely, it seemed as if Raphael and Azarias had consciously assumed good cop/bad cop guises. I knew that both of them intended for me to prepare myself for a divine task, but Azarias had always been the gruff one, while Raphael still reminded me somehow of a gentle youth, despite the unimaginable power at his disposal. Yet the tables had turned somewhat in Baku, as Azarias became friendlier in his own element and Raphael was becoming more insistent in the dream state.

"There is little time remaining," he would say. *"You have so much to learn."*

Finally, one week before the calamity, Raphael actually bellowed at me in a way that brought instant fear: *"Zoroastrianism. Ahura Mazda and Angra Mainya. Know that Ahriman did not exist before the advent of humankind. The time is near. Call upon Rumi."*

The truth is that I knew nothing about Zoroastrianism. I cannot deny it. Ahura Mazda and Angra Mainya meant nothing to me. When I awoke the next morning, Azarias reminded me that Baku and Azerbaijan were situated in a region associated with

Zoroastrianism, and that the religion was still being practiced there, along with much larger communities in India, Iran, and Pakistan. I spent the day at the university library reading about the religion. Thus spake Zarathustra:

> *Now will I speak out: At the beginning of life*
> *The holier Mentality said to the opposing Mentality,*
>   *Who was more hostile,*
> *"Neither our thoughts, doctrines, plans,*
> *Beliefs, utterances, deeds,*
> *Individualities, nor souls agree."*

In essence, Ahura Mazda is the god of light and positive action, and Angra Mainya is the god of darkness and evil, and they and their followers are constantly fighting with each other. Angra Mainya eventually evolved into Ahriman, or the Devil. Every action of every human counts in this ongoing war, and the outcome of this great battle will be determined by the weight of good versus evil actions. I simply did not have enough time to study the religion with the care that it deserves. Scholars trace both Manichaeism and Mithraism to Zoroastrianism, and even postulate that the Chinese concept of yin and yang descended from it.

But how could a Persian poet of divine love who lived in Turkey have any role to play in any of this? In fact, Rumi had become quite important to me. All those weeks of study had revealed to me a man of extraordinary love and artistic achievement, as well as the founder of one of the great Sufi mystic orders and someone truly to be admired and emulated, regardless of personal religious belief. It is known that he was born on September 30, 1207, in the city of Balkh in what is today Afghanistan. His real name was Muhammad Jalal al-Din. He became known as Rumi after settling in Konya, Turkey, in an area long known as the domain of the Byzantines, who were the descendants of the Romans who transferred the capital of the

Roman Empire to Byzantium in A.D. 330 under the Emperor Constantine, although the people of the great new city quickly named it Constantinople, rather than New Rome, as I have already described. In an odd linguistic shift, Rome became Rum, and Rum eventually became synonymous with Greece as the Byzantines gradually lost touch with their roots in Italy and grew ever closer to the Greeks. Jalal al-Din became one of those living in the Greek lands: a Rumi.

His father was a renowned Islamic scholar and mystic who moved the family from Balkh just in time to escape its conquest by Genghis Khan. They wandered through Baghdad, Mecca, Damascus, Malatya, Erzincan, and Karaman, and finally settled in Konya, the capital of the Seljuk Turks. Rumi trained in religion and Islamic law under his father and then under several other teachers after his father's death, spending several years in Damascus in the process. After returning to Konya and spending forty days and nights alone in a meditation room, he was ready to begin his spiritual mission in the world. As he later said, "I was raw; I am now cooked and burned."

Around that time he was given the special name Mevlana, or Mawlana, meaning "our Master" or "His Excellency," an honorific title of respect for a great teacher, but eventually claimed by Rumi distinctively for himself and for the order of whirling dervishes that he established.

I had been looking for love, mercy, and compassion in religion, and I found it in the Sufi writings of Rumi, as I had found it in Jesus before him. I had been looking for tolerance of other people and other religions, and I found it in Rumi, as I had found it in Jesus. If I had learned anything at that point in my life, it was that love, mercy, and compassion are the cornerstones of genuine closeness to God. If a religion does not contain them, if a religion does not profess them and practice them, then it is a false religion that only pretends to have knowledge of God. "If you want to live," Rumi writes, "then die in love. Die in love if you want to remain alive."

His call to people of all faiths to join him in the love of God soon burned itself into my own consciousness, and I could not free myself from it:

> Come, come, come, come again,
> If you are Christian, Jew, even atheist.
> Our place is not a place of despair.
> Even if you break your oath a hundred times, come
>   again.

So yes, I had found the beauty of religious love and tolerance in Muslim Rumi, but I still was lost in regard to any connection with Zoroastrianism or, God forbid, with any encounter with Ahriman.

On August 7, I had been in Baku for exactly nine weeks. I had called Allison and my parents frequently. My father had no idea what I was doing, and he had trouble containing his frustration. Nevertheless, he was proud of his investments, as the money kept flowing in. I tried to pretend that I was interested for his sake. Money meant absolutely nothing to me. That is easy to say when you have more than you can spend, I know, but the thought of money in comparison to the wonders that I was experiencing was embarrassing to me and even shameful.

I was troubled on that particular morning, as Raphael had appeared during the night with an unusually serious and even solemn expression on his glorious face. *"Remember Rumi,"* he had said. *"Release your own anger and remember these words of Rumi: 'Sometimes, even the angels envy our purity. Sometimes, Satan witnesses our fearlessness and runs away. This body of clay of ours has undertaken God's trust. God save our nimbleness; may God preserve our power and performance.' Remember!"*

I spent the day at the university library, studying as much as I could about both Rumi and Zoroastrianism. Exhausted, finally, I returned to the apartment in the late afternoon to find Azarias with the same solemn expression on his face that Raphael had presented to me in the dream.

"There is bad news," he said. "The American embassies in Kenya and Tanzania have been bombed. There is heavy loss of life. Islamic terrorists are suspected."

I was stunned. Azarias had a television in the apartment, but no cable, so I could not watch any of the international stations. I thanked him and quickly hailed a cab to the Absheron Hotel, where I could watch the news on CNN in the bar, which was packed when I got there with other expatriates doing exactly the same thing. There was strong speculation about al-Qaida and Osama bin Laden, names that I remembered only vaguely from an attack on the World Trade Center in New York City a few years before, as well as a disjointed so-called *fatwa* that had been issued earlier in the year calling for Muslims to kill all Americans and Jews wherever they could be found anywhere in the world. The level of raw hate dripping from that peculiar document had been sickening, but I could not imagine at the time that anyone would take it seriously. Suddenly the names were popping up again on the television screen. As the reporting continued, and it became clear that well over two hundred people had been murdered in the twin bombings, most of them Kenyans but quite a few Americans also among the dead, I no longer felt stunned but rather intensely angry at the viciousness of the attacks, presumably in the name of Islam, a religion I had grown to respect since meeting Azarias.

I watched the news coverage well into the evening and returned to the apartment seething with anger and disbelief. Allah the merciful? Allah the compassionate? What kind of people could murder innocents in the name of their religion, actually believing that God would reward them for the slaughter of women and children? I knew, of course, that wars had been fought in the name of religion for thousands of years and that bloody sectarian violence in Northern Ireland and elsewhere in the West had not entirely disappeared. Those conflicts in the modern era, however, had basically demonstrated the use of religion as an excuse for achieving political aims through violence. I was hard put to remember anyone claiming that God not only approved but encouraged the random murder of innocent civilians in His name—until then. If the bombing attack on the twin towers had succeeded, thousands would have died, instead of the six who had lost their lives so senselessly.

I raged at the murderous barbarians and the religion that placed such a low value on human life, and Azarias allowed me to vent until I finally stood wordlessly in the center of his living room with my fists clenched.

"They do not understand the words of the Prophet," he said evenly. "They have been seduced by a violent interpretation of Islam known as Wahhabiism. You must understand, Jacob, that no religion has been passed down through the centuries without error. There are no exceptions. Did you know that there are two stories of the creation in Genesis? They cannot both be right. Some words of all of the prophets have been both misunderstood and improperly transcribed or translated. Other words in the holy books have actually been added to the texts centuries afterward by men wishing to persuade others of their political views. Many of the commentaries in all of the religions are completely misguided and represent the words of angry men rather than the original religious leaders. Do you really believe, for example, that Jesus said '*I have not come to bring peace but a sword*'? No, but he did say about false prophets, '*By their acts shall you know them,*' and I tell you that by their real words shall you know the true prophets, for they shall speak of love, mercy, and compassion, not of hate, violence, and killing. The true words of Jesus are these: '*Put your sword back into its place; for all who take the sword will perish by the sword.*'"

Once again, I was taken aback by the confidence with which Azarias spoke of things about which no man could ever really know. "By what authority," I started to say, "can you speak of—"

"You shall soon know by what authority I speak," he interrupted. "But now the time has come for which you have been preparing. We leave tomorrow for Turkey and the home of Rumi. It is imperative that you understand the truth of Islam and the love of God that stands at its center. I promise you that your anger will melt away in the heat of His love."

My fists unclenched, but I still stood there speechless, stunned both by his assertion that all of the holiest texts were corrupted and the announcement of our departure. "But Azarias," I implored, "there is so much more that I need to know."

"For now, Jacob," he said, "prepare for the journey and trust in God." Then he turned and walked toward his own bedroom. After a few seconds, I gathered myself together and walked into mine in order to pack.

* * *

Konya today has a population approaching 1.5 million. Much of it has become modernized as a result of an economic boom in the Anatolian heartland among small and medium-sized businesses, most of them owned by devout and conservative Muslims. The city is filled with mosques, including magnificent structures from the Seljuk period, which began some nine hundred years ago. Archaeologists affirm that habitations on the site go back five thousand years, long before the rule of the ancient Hittites, only some thirty-five hundred years ago. Its history somewhat parallels that of Baku, with the various conquerors streaming through on their way either to historical glory or oblivion. The New Testament tells us that Paul and Barnabas preached there at least three times when it was known as Iconium in Asia Minor. It was conquered by the Ottoman Turks in 1420 and made a provincial capital in 1453 with the final victory of the Ottomans over the Byzantines and the sack of Constantinople in 1453. It remains an important provincial capital in the Republic of Turkey today.

For me, though, the prime importance of Konya was its distinction as the home and burial place of Mevlana Celaleddin Rumi and the center of the Mevlevi Sufi order of whirling dervishes.

* * *

Our travel itinerary was decidedly odd and did nothing to improve my mood, darkened first by the attacks on our embassies in Africa and blackened further by our rushed departure from Baku. For some reason, Azarias booked us on a roundabout route with connections in Baghdad and Damascus, before we landed at a small airport in Malatya, Turkey. From there, we transferred to a touring bus that drove through the heart of dusty Anatolia through Karaman before depositing us at the bus station in Konya. The exhausting trip took a full day and a half. By the time we reached Konya, I was drenched in the lemon cologne that the bus attendant periodically sprinkled on the passengers in order to keep the sweating odors to a minimum presumably or perhaps to embalm the corpses of any of the passengers who might have died on the trip, as the attendant didn't hesitate to sprinkle even those who were sleeping or otherwise unconscious.

"Why, Azarias?" I had asked. "Why such an incredible route? Why did we not fly to Istanbul and then straight to Konya? What is this all about?"

"You need to experience the landscapes and absorb the feel of the region. Otherwise, our journey will be for nothing. Do you know anything about sympathetic magic?"

"No," I had answered, as my head grazed the ceiling of the bus after a particularly heavy bump in the road.

"I didn't think so. It could have been worse." Then he nodded his head and fell asleep.

Nevertheless, my spirits quickly revived in Konya. There was something in the hot, dry air that seemed enormously refreshing—and familiar—to me. Azarias also seemed to be in his element, although he never really seemed out of his element. He chatted easily with the driver as we retrieved our luggage and then again with our taxi driver as we headed toward a modest hotel near the Mevlana Museum. After a shower and change of clothes, we headed directly to the museum, I as usual following behind without really knowing what to expect.

We entered a wide courtyard paved in marble with a washing fountain in the center and passed by a number of small domed structures that Azarias explained to me were dervish cells. We walked through a gateway and into a small, richly decorated room, before then passing through a silver door and into what I soon discovered was the burial chamber that contained the remains of many of the most revered figures of the Mevlevi Sufi order, including Mevlana himself. Pausing only briefly to pay his respects, Azarias quickly moved into the great Ritual Hall, now just another part of the museum housing the musical instruments and special clothing used in the whirling ceremonies. An old gentleman with a white beard came running from a corner of the hall as soon as he saw Azarias and embraced him strongly. They began to speak immediately and forcefully together with the old gentleman's eyes widening more and more as the fast-moving conversation continued. He swept his right arm around the entire hall in a manic gesture while repeating several times something that sounded like "yasak." Suddenly he grew very still and simply stared into the eyes of Azarias, who continued to speak in a low, measured tone. Finally they kissed each other on both cheeks, and Azarias turned to leave the hall. His friend simply stood there and stared at his back without saying another word as Azarias walked through the doorway. I hurried to catch up.

"What was that all about?" I asked as I reached his side.

"He will be arranging a ceremony for us tonight, quite a special ceremony. We should return now to the hotel and rest."

There was a kiosk just inside the gate lined with guidebooks in all major languages. I begged Azarias's indulgence and took a couple of minutes to select a small collection of Rumi's poems and a guidebook to the Mevlana Museum, both in English. We then made our way to the hotel, where Azarias chatted amiably with the desk clerk while he retrieved our keys.

"I'll meet you in the lobby at seven sharp," he said to me while handing me my key, and then he walked off to his room.

"You speak English then," the clerk said from behind the counter.

"Yes," I said, turning in his direction. "I'm an American."

"I thought you were both Turkish."

"Could you not tell from his language that he is Azeri?" I asked.

"My friend," he said. "I know a little Azeri. He spoke only Turkish, and perfect Turkish, too."

I checked my watch when I got to my room: five o'clock. I tried to nap but could not. I picked up the guidebook and sat down in the one easy chair in the room to read. The museum is open daily from 9 a.m. to 6 p.m., it said. I was able to retrace our steps easily. The gateway had been the Tomb Gate, as it led first into the Tilavet Room, where the Quran was continually read aloud before the complex became a museum, and then into the mausoleum. Apart from Mevlana/Rumi himself, the mausoleum held the remains of his father, wife, and children, along with many of their descendants and some of the faithful spiritual guides who had accompanied the family from as far back as Balkh. As I had easily surmised, Rumi's own grave lies under the green dome, and his cenotaph is richly adorned with gold and gold cloth.

The great Ritual Hall is called the Semahane from the "Sema" or dance of the Sufi dervishes. It was closed to further dancing by the decree of the young Republic in 1925 that legally banned every Sufi lodge or "tekke" throughout the country. Nevertheless, the government relented in 1954 and allowed the whirling dances to be performed again for tourists at special sites in Konya and Istanbul. The location in Konya was a converted basketball court, but, according to the guidebook, the strange locale could not detract from the mystic beauty of the entranced dancers as their movements guided them toward oneness with God.

I set down the guidebook and picked up the small collection of Rumi's writings. Many I had read before, but some I had not. I was surprised, but should not have been, to discover that the same poems appeared quite different according to the English translator. I thought of Azarias's words about the corruption of holy texts as I read a different version of one of the most famous of Rumi's poems:

> *Come! Come whoever you are.*
> *It doesn't matter if you are an unbeliever.*
> *It doesn't matter if you have fallen a thousand times.*
> *Come! Come whoever you are,*
> *For this is not the door of hopelessness.*
> *Come, just as you are!*

Then I read what Rumi had to say about the Prophet, and I was deeply happy and relieved to find what I knew must lie at the heart of Islam, rather than the random butchery of those who murdered in the name of God:

> *Our Prophet's way is love.*
> *We are the sons of Love; our mother is Love.*

Finally, I read an excerpt that struck so deeply inside of me that I grew intensely drowsy and knew that I was about to sleep:

> *At every instant and from every side resounds the*
> *   call of Love:*
> *We are going to sky—who wants to come with us?*

> *We have gone to heaven, we have been the friends of*
>   *the angels,*
> *And now we will go back there, for there is our*
>   *country.*

My eyes closed.

"Do not fear the swift rising of spirit," said Raphael, as we stood face to face, he dressed in blazing armor and carrying a flaming sword and I totally naked. *"I shall be there, as shall Ariel and others. Do not fear the attack of the demon, for I shall be by your side. You have been prepared to defeat pain. You will be prepared to defeat evil. Rest now. May the Holy Spirit be with you."*

Only the repeated pounding at the door could have roused me from such intense slumber. I could barely say to Azarias on the other side of the door, "Yes, I'm coming." I looked blearily at my watch and saw that it was 7:10 p.m. I almost tumbled to the floor when I first tried to stand. I had never felt so weak before. It was as if I had forgotten how to operate a vehicle and I was experimenting with the controls.

"Wake, Jacob, wake!" shouted Azarias at the door.

"I'm coming!" I said more loudly. By the time I reached the door and unlocked it, I could almost move normally.

"We must walk quickly now," he said. "We are late. How do you feel?"

"Very strange," I said.

"You went farther this time than you have gone before. That was to prepare you for what is coming next."

"Where are we going?" I asked.

"Back to the Mevlana Museum."

"But it closed at six," I said.

"It will be open for us, Jacob. It will truly be open for the first time in 73 years."

Here is the point where you will want to take out your highlighter, if it is not already in your hand. The material up to now has probably been psychotic enough from your perspective. But now we jump to another level. It is all true, though, regardless of your belief. The truth has a refreshing way of ignoring belief, opinion, and pretense.

When Azarias and I reached the gate of the museum, it was clearly closed for further business. Nevertheless, the guard opened the side door and allowed us through after only a few seconds of conversation with Azarias. The grounds were completely deserted. We walked directly to the outer door of the Semahane, upon which Azarias knocked twice, paused briefly, and knocked twice again. The old gentleman in the white beard opened the door. Dressed in a red cloak, he beamed broadly, and ushered us in. The room had been transformed. The candlelight alone would have sufficed for the transformation, but the display cases had been moved from sight, and there was no longer any sense that the space had served as a museum only three hours earlier.

I saw that six musicians dressed in black cloaks were seated cross-legged on cushions with their backs to the wall on my right and their instruments resting in their laps. To my left, there was a red sheepskin stretched on the floor, and in the center of the hall there rested four white sheepskins in a small circle. Three tall young men dressed in black cloaks and odd cylindrical brownish hats were standing to the side on my left with their heads bent and their arms crossed in front of them with hands resting on their opposite shoulders. Two men were standing directly across from me next to several pieces of clothing stretched out carefully on a small table beside them. They looked questioningly at Azarias, who turned to me.

"Let the Holy Spirit guide you," he said softly, and then he motioned me toward the table.

There are times in all of our lives when we simply know that something is *right*, without knowing how or why it should be so. Perhaps as you read this you are already aware of the sacred whirling dance and the forms that provide the structure for at least the possibility of reaching genuine union with God. I was not, but my ignorance could not deflect the sense of *rightness* in the entire candlelit scene laid out before me. I crossed over to the table feeling the same sense of distortion in reality that I had experienced upon awaking in the hotel room just a short time before. I know that I stood there expectantly as the men removed my clothing and replaced it with a white shirt and long white skirt covered by a short white coat. They then covered me in a black cloak and placed one of the strange hats on my head. The word *sikke* flashed into my mind. Then they escorted me across the room to join the three young men. I remembered my experience in the mosque, and I assumed the same position with my head bent and my arms across my chest.

The rest is like a poorly remembered dream. I believe now that my spirit was already preparing to leave my body at that early stage of the ceremony.

This is what I do remember: We sat together on the white skins, and the old man, now wearing a hat similar to ours, began to bow to those in the room. When he sat down, someone recited a poem, and I knew with no understanding of either Persian or Turkish that it was Rumi's praise of God and the Prophet. A drum was struck, and then the cry of a reed flute pierced the air with such shocking and inexpressible beauty that I began to tremble uncontrollably. The "*ney*," I thought. Music began to fill the hall, and all of us stood and walked together in a circle behind the old man—no, the "*Shaikh*," I suddenly knew with certainty. We walked and bowed, and walked and bowed some more, and suddenly the four of us threw off our cloaks, and truly I felt as if I were discarding my body itself and beginning to move only in spirit.

The next thing I remember is the actual whirling. How or when it began I cannot say. I do not even know whether my eyes were open or closed. I only know that my right arm was outstretched with my palm up and left arm outstretched with my palm down, and I was cross-stepping foot over foot without thinking and whirling counter clockwise around the room behind and in front of my brothers at the same time. The word *kardesh* flashed into my mind, and I knew that I had heard it before or something like it, but it seemed so long ago that I could not place it. And I began to see in my mind the earth spinning on its axis and then the earth spinning around the sun and the sun spinning with the galaxy and the galaxy spinning around other galaxies and then electrons spinning around atoms; and suddenly I became aware of the great cycles of death and rebirth and the seasons of earth and the very circulation of my blood; and the awareness grew within me in a place beyond normal thought that all such cycles were not only realities of their own, but also symbols of much greater realities and that everything that could be perceived or imagined was also a symbol of something beyond perception and imagination; and at that point I heard a buzzing within my head and felt an odd but not unpleasant pressure at the top of my skull and suddenly *suddenly* ... I was rushing through blackness at incomprehensible speed, and Raphael should not have been concerned as there was no fear, only delight in the high-toned singing without words around me and the presence of Ariel whispering comfort, and the certainty beyond mere knowledge that everything *everything* consists of thought and that we are nothing more than thoughts of God and nothing less than thoughts of God with our own thoughts assuming their own realities in an endless process of creation stemming from LIGHT BLINDING LIGHT AND LOVE LOVE LOVE EVERLASTING LOVE LIGHT—

* * *

"Where ... where ... am I?" I asked blearily, only half-conscious at best. I ached in every muscle. I had trouble opening my eyes, and I felt very cold.

"We are on the Sinai Peninsula in the Desert of Paran," responded a familiar voice. "How do you feel?"

"Not good at all," I said.

"Yet you are certainly alive, are you not?" asked Azarias.

I forced my eyes to open wider. I found that I was lying on a cot inside a large tent. A blanket covered me. I lifted the blanket and sat up slowly on the edge of the cot. I was fully dressed in some kind of khaki clothing. Azarias sat on another cot across from me and stared into my eyes. He then closed his eyes and bowed his head briefly. I could see through the flap of the tent that dawn was breaking.

"I seem to be," I said, "but my body aches, and I have no recollection of coming with you to the Sinai, of all places."

"You should know that two sons of Aaron died when they approached too closely to the Lord. You should also know that even Moses could not look upon God's face and live. You were in the spirit when you approached, and you have survived. I honor you, Jacob. What do you remember?"

Konya! The Mevlana Museum. The dancing. The rushing through darkness. The Light! And the overpowering majesty of Love that filled me to the point of ecstasy magnified beyond comprehension. And then …

And then I could not remember anything.

"I know your thoughts, Jacob. I have tended you for three days. The others were sorely frightened, for your face was white and glowing as you whirled without pause, even when the music and singing stopped and the ceremony ended. The Shaikh led everyone in prayer until your body finally collapsed in the middle of the hall. Know this: God is infinite potential, infinite possibility, the spirit that underlines all thoughts and all existence. The human brain cannot encompass infinity. It explodes under the pressure of input that it cannot contain. Massive strokes always occur. Even in the spirit realms, I AM THAT I AM can only be approached through holy grace that cannot be explained in words. You will not be able to remember in this life, but you will carry the sense of the miracle within you forever. You will also carry the power that may lift you to physical awareness of Raphael."

"Azarias, I'm having trouble understanding any of this. I feel a strange warmth around my heart, not pain at all, but something more like a pulsing of energy, but the rest of my body is aching, I have a headache, and what do you mean you know my thoughts?"

"Your body was pushed to its farthest limits, you were gone for a long time in your terms, and you are about to learn much that has been hidden from you. In a few minutes, Jacob, you will meet an immensely powerful demon."

"What?" I shouted.

"Look to your right, Jacob. There is a cobra coiled and ready to strike at the entrance to the tent."

I turned my head slowly as if in a trance and was shocked to see the cobra weaving its head beyond the insect netting at the entrance.

"Go and pick it up," he said firmly.

I turned my head back again to look at Azarias in wonderment and fear. How could he be asking me to handle a cobra? I knew nothing about snakes, except that I had no fondness for them.

"*Mark 16:17-18!*" he said with passion. "You have read it, and you can recite it from memory. Just where do you think these powers of recall have come from, Jacob? Recite the passage!"

And he was right, of course. As soon as I thought of *Mark 16:17-18*, I knew it word for word, and I repeated it to him: "*And these signs will accompany those who believe: in my name they will cast out demons; they will speak in new tongues; they will pick up serpents, and if they drink any deadly thing, it will not hurt them; they will lay their hands on the sick, and they will recover.*"

"How can you of all people not believe, Jacob? You are now in a state of grace, but this will dissipate quickly in the dense matter of this realm. Look in the mirror."

He grasped a shaving mirror propped up on a small table next to his cot and held it up to me. I looked and jerked back momentarily and then looked again. My skin was as white as snow, and it seemed to be radiating energy similar to sparks from a campfire.

"Now pick up the cobra!" he repeated forcefully. "It is a creature of God and subject to the love of God. Direct thoughts of love to it, genuine thoughts of love as you recognize its beauty and its place in creation. Yes, it could kill you, but it will not, if your belief in the power of love is greater than your fear. Time is short now. Go!"

Something moved inside me at that moment. It was the odd pulsing warmth around my heart, I think, that somehow shifted. As I looked at the snake again, I could see its intense beauty and marvel at the absolutely perfect design of the creature. I did not need to concentrate on loving it, as a rush of appreciation for a fellow being and its place on the earth flowed out of me spontaneously and enveloped the snake. I walked over to it, unzipped the netting, stepped out of the tent, and simply bent down and picked it up in both hands. Its head weaved in front of mine, and its tongue shot out of its mouth and touched my lips. Bless you, o creature of beauty, I said silently, and then I placed it gently on the ground in front of me. It slithered away immediately.

"Well done," Azarias said from inside the tent. "Now sit down again across from me. The demon approaches, and there is more that you must know. No matter what happens, remember that you are in a state of grace. You may not remember it, but you were speaking Turkish, a new tongue, at the Semahane. You have just picked up a deadly serpent, and you have the power to cast out and defeat demons."

I quickly sat down across from him again as he continued talking.

"Know this now, Jacob. The Zoroastrians and those who followed their dualistic beliefs in God and Satan were wrong. There is only one God, only one I AM THAT I AM. In the original creation, there was never a Satan, an Ahriman, a Devil, or whatever name has been given to the essence of evil by men. It is men who have created such beings. Remember that God has given mankind the power of creation and that all thought carries within it the seeds of actual materialization in this realm. This takes time here in order to prevent instant materialization and utter chaos. Yet time indeed has passed, thousands upon thousands of years of superstition, fear, bloodshed, torture and all the rest, and the thoughts connected to all of these have been growing and solidifying, and the shadowy manifestations have become more real than you know."

I listened intently with a growing chill in my spine.

"So the Zoroastrians and Manicheans and the rest were wrong in the beginning, but now they are partially right. The demonic beings are helpless against God, but that is certainly not the case in regard to men, their own unwitting creators. A terrible loop has come into being, in which the demons incite further evil among those inclined to evil, and those in turn reinforce the reality of the demons through their own demonic thoughts. O, children should never be told that there are no monsters, because there are those who take the innocents from their beds at night and mutilate and kill them. There are those who torture with pleasure and laugh at the screams of their victims. There are those who rape and maim and kill with no compunction—and these things are growing on the earth. Your task is related to the effort to break the chain and restore humaneness to humanity. Know this too, Jacob. All humans are spirit souls in temporary bodies that allow them to function and create in this dense realm. When they leave their bodies, they return to the lighter realms and their sins and pain are obliterated in the presence of God's love. But the demons are without souls, and they cannot depart from the dense realm. There is the possibility that they will control it entirely one day and that the magnificence of human creation will be lost and therefore God's creation stained. Have you understood me?"

"I think so," I said. "Yes, but all of this is too vast. How can you and I—individual men—have any impact on all of this?"

"It is men who have created the problem, and it must be men who resolve it, for God has granted men creative power and free will unending. Men must never forget, however, that as thoughts and extensions of God themselves, they share in his unlimited power and being. The angels are also engaged. Do you hear the buzzing?"

There was a vague droning in the air outside the tent.

"Azazel approaches."

"Azarias, no!" I shouted in terror. "I know about Azazel. If he is real, no mere human can fight such a demon. You must know that!"

"What I know, Jacob, is that you must face him in order to understand your task. You have no choice. Now listen carefully: Demons have been constituted from thoughts of hatred and evil. You must project thoughts of overpowering love in order to survive one. It is something like matter and antimatter. One cancels the other. If the demon wishes to survive, then it must either flee the source of the love or exterminate it."

For the first time in a long while, I began to have thoughts again of being sacrificed to the demons. What did I really know of Azarias, anyway? He had always appeared to know much more than any human could possibly have learned in one lifetime. What he said next only heightened my worst fears.

"You were told to read *Leviticus 16*. That means you will know about the tradition of scapegoating among the Israelites. But know this also Jacob: The tradition did not begin with the Israelites. Peoples of the region sent goat sacrifices to the Se'irim goat demons long before the arrival of the Israelites. They forced young girls to copulate with goats in order to appease the demons. Understand then the thousands of years during which the demons have been able to take their hideous forms. And, lo, the king of these monsters is Azazel, to whom the Israelites specifically sent the goats that bore the sins of the tribes upon their heads. Try to imagine the countless generations of sinners who have transferred their sins to the heads of the goats that have been devoured by Azazel and then try to imagine the hideous condition of Azazel, who now bears all of those sins upon his own head. I say to you, Jacob, that the cobra was truly a snowflake in comparison to what you now face. You can well be killed this day and your soul tainted by the indescribable evil of Azazel. You can be one more sacrifice—or you can resist and send the same love to the monster that you sent to the cobra. If your will and your belief and your love are strong enough, then you can stand against him and prevail, even if it means your own death. Otherwise, may God have mercy on you."

As you might imagine, there was nothing really to say. I was too much in shock. I had not anticipated my own death immediately after the most profound experience that any human being can ever have. I believed that I was still in a state of grace. I could *feel* it—and even see it in the mirror. But how could I withstand the *real* attack of one of the most powerful demons ever imagined in the tortured minds of men for thousands of years? And what if I had been intended as the scapegoat all along?

"Go to the center of the circle of stones that I have placed outside the tent. They will not stop him, but they can slow him. Concentrate on love, mercy, and compassion, Jacob, for these are the cornerstones of the universe. Do not listen to the demon. Try not to look at it directly. Love it, if you can, as the very expression of the mind of man, who himself springs from the mind of God. I shall stand with you. God bless you and keep you. Now go!"

The horribly irritating buzzing filled the air. As I exited the tent, I could see a massive but shapeless brown and black mass slouching toward us less than fifty yards away. I ran to the circle of rocks and stood in the center. Azarias stood behind me. As the demon grew closer, I could see that the buzzing arose from the thousands and perhaps millions of flies that swarmed around it. Then the stench reached us. I tied a handkerchief quickly around my head to cover my nose and protect my mouth from the flies, but it was useless against both the sickening odors and the insects. At about twenty yards distance, apart from the whirring flies that surrounded its mass, I could see that the entire surface of its body was writhing in a strange and undulating fashion. Then it became clear as it continued to lumber forward that the writhing reflected the twisting and turning of millions upon millions of maggots that feasted on the vomit and filth that dripped from the demon's body. I could not take my eyes away from it despite the warning of Azarias. All of the impurities and treachery and lies and betrayals and murders and sadism and pederasty and obscenities and degradation of countless generations of men and women had been absorbed into the stinking, hideous mass of the creature. Despite my utter revulsion, I felt a sense of pity for the living creature in front of me whose existence was so inconceivably vile. At that instant, the demon stopped about ten yards from the rocks at the top of the circle and groaned loudly. Then I could see that it had been crawling on all fours as it began to stand erect and reveal the four limbs covered with filth and twisting maggots as the flies continued to swarm around it.

I can only guess at its final height, fifteen feet perhaps. My pity had quickly turned to terror, despite my best efforts. The demon then began to wipe away the brownish slime covering its head with both hands, so that features finally appeared. It continued to wipe away furiously until it had uncovered the iciest and cruelest eyes imaginable. Then it vomited in our direction for several seconds as it cleared its loathsome throat.

"**I am Azazel**," it said finally in a surprisingly high and cackling voice that reminded me of my worst nightmares about witches as a child. "**Kneel before me and live.**"

Try as I might, I could not summon love for the vile being. Even my sense of pity had been crushed under the enormity of the evil that faced me. I could think of only one thing to say.

"Get thee behind me, Satan!"

The demon cackled in response before saying with infinite coldness, "**That place is taken. Now kneel or die in a way that will shrivel what is left of your soul.**"

Azarias then spoke in a language and a tone completely unknown to me. I understood nothing.

Azazel cackled even more loudly. "**This moment is mine. This goat is mine. It has been given to me. And I am stronger than before. Even Raphael knows this!**"

It moved forward and started to step across the stones, but it seemed to be pressing against an invisible wall that denied it entry.

"**Such things mean nothing!**" it shrieked. Then its foot began to cross the rocks, as if a hole had been opened in the protective wall.

Azarias made no move. So I was to be the scapegoat after all. Once my death seemed assured, I found that my courage returned. Despite the horror, it occurred to me that I could not die in a better way than fighting against evil in the name of God.

"I abjure thee in the name of God to be gone, unclean spirit!" I shouted.

The demon's leg pierced the protective barrier, and the rest of its hideous body followed. It stood no more than ten feet from me. The flies enveloped all three of us. The unbearable stench filled the air.

"**I piss on the name of God!**" it roared. "**Kneel!**"

At that moment, a stream of steaming hot piss came shooting from its groin and splashed on to my right foot. First, there was only numbness, but when I looked at my foot, I could see that the top half of my boot and my foot itself had been instantaneously eaten away by the liquid. Then the excruciating pain struck, and I collapsed on to my right knee.

"**The goat knows its master!**" shrieked Azazel.

The top half of my right foot was gone, and I could not use it to help me stand, but I used my hands and my left foot to press myself upward again. I stood before the demon as the loathsome acidic piss continued to burn into my right foot.

From out of nowhere, I remembered Rumi. I raised my right arm into the air and said to the beast while the flies flew in and out of my mouth, "Be not without love that you may not die. Die with love, that you may stay alive."

A huge groan rose from its stinking mouth, and the demon staggered backward. The movement that followed was preternaturally fast and brutal, as a huge claw attached to its right arm swept through the air and sliced my arm in half. The sound of my forearm hitting the ground sickened me. Blood spurted from the stub, and I knew that I could no longer stand. Yet I would certainly not kneel. I shifted my weight and pushed with my left foot so that I fell directly backwards onto my back. My head rested on Azarias's feet. Azazel moved forward and towered over both of us.

"**Die, stupid goat!**" it roared. "**Now I feed on you.**"

As it bent its head downward, I could see the long fangs dripping excrement for the first time. Terror filled me—raw, chilling terror. I could hardly breathe. But something in my soul simply refused to allow the fear to cancel out the love of God.

"May God forgive you and love you," I said with my last breath.

"**May God and love be damned!**" it roared as it thrust its head and terrible jaws toward my helpless, bleeding body.

Roaring fire suddenly burst forth from behind and above me as I braced for the vile puncturing of the fangs into my flesh. At first, I didn't understand. The pillar of flame shot straight upward, rising directly out of Azarias's body. I could still see his face above me in the flame for an instant before the great thunderclap struck. The force of the wind pushed Azazel backward. He stared in anger and shrieked in frustration. Lying on my back and looking upward, I could at last see the gleaming armor and the huge sword of Raphael, both of which shone so brightly that my eyes burned painfully. He was at least three times larger than I had ever seen him in my dreams.

"He gave you your chance, Azazel," Raphael boomed. "'Be not without love that you may not die.' You ignored him, and you have sinned against the Holy Spirit and God Himself. Did Jesus not say that 'whoever blasphemes against the Holy Spirit never has forgiveness but is guilty of an eternal sin'? Your time is over and your last chance wasted."

Raphael swung his sword and Azazel exploded into tiny pieces upon impact, all of them burning swiftly and vanishing into nothingness as I watched. Not a single fly remained in the air. And I fell into painful and nauseating darkness.

* * *

"'Die with love that you may stay alive.' Rumi was right, wasn't he?"

I could say that it was a dream, but from that point onward I knew beyond all doubt that such "dreams" were more real and meaningful than anything in my waking life. Raphael sat across from me in his usual stature without armor and sword in what appeared to be a Renaissance villa in Tuscany on a late summer afternoon.

"I cannot always appear as you see me now," he said. "In order to be near you longer and train you properly without overwhelming and harming your physical body, I needed to assume the form of Azarias. You should read the Book of Tobit again."

"Where are we?" I said.

"In a place created by my namesake from memory, a place that is now just as 'real' as the original. His creative talent has expanded far beyond the greatness that he displayed on earth."

"What is my task, Raphael?"

"The answer has already been given. Do not forget the walls. In the meantime, you are preparing to fulfill the task. You have learned determination and the power of love. You have received the Holy Spirit. You have faced the most fearsome evil. You have even been in the presence of God. I envy your purity, Jacob. Mine was given to me, for which I am eternally grateful. You have earned yours, and the new energy and power that flows within you now will allow you to be in the presence of Gabriel and to hear the truth of all things, for he is the messenger of truth and understanding. Do you have questions?"

Did I have questions? I was filled with questions, but my questions always seemed to elicit unintelligible answers, such as the mystery of my task: You will know at the point that the wall disappears in your mind just before it disappears in your reality?

"Yes, what has happened to Azarias?"

"He is simply one of my projections, a thought form that allows me to pursue my work among humans. You will not meet with him directly again, for there is no longer a need."

"Will I be maimed for the rest of my life?"

"Would it make any difference to the power of your heart and spirit?"

"In all honesty, I don't know," I said. "I hope not."

"Know that there are many who suffer far greater physical wounds and handicaps, Jacob, and yet please God all the more because of their faith and their works."

"I know that to be true," I said. "But I do not yet know it of myself."

"Your body has been restored and enhanced," he said. *"Yet, the trace of acid that remains in your foot will burn to remind you of the presence of evil in the world. God bless you, Jacob."*

"God bless us all," I said. "All creatures, all things, all of creation. Why did you wait so long before acting, Raphael?"

"The Holy Spirit was with you. You needed to draw upon it and send a blessing to the demon even though it was about to kill you. There was a small chance that you might have failed and died. It was a test of your free will and your ability to align yourself with the Holy Spirit. You have done well, far better than you know. Now close your eyes. Your body needs rest."

I awoke lying within the ring of stones. There was no sign that my arm had ever been touched or that my right foot had ever been all but obliterated. It ached slightly. As I limped toward the tent, a jeep with two men in it pulled up on the other side.

"Are you Jake Daniels?" the driver asked.

"Yes," I said.

"Professor Azarias sent us. We're supposed to help you pack up and take you to Amman. Here are your plane tickets to Indianapolis via London and New York. I can never figure him out, can you? He always pops up without warning and gets people moving. Anyway, did you find what you were looking for out here? This is one barren area."

"Yes, it's not fit for man or beast," I said. "It can test a man's faith to be out here alone. Thanks for your help in any case. I'll be glad to get moving."

This should give you far more than you need already. Oh, but there is more—so much more.

CHAPTER V

GABRIEL

So let us recapitulate. I have told you about extensive contact with angels and one loathsome, terrifying demon. I have also said to you that I may actually have been in the presence of God. And you, of course, think that I am completely insane. But then I have to remind you that every recorded religion contains descriptions of angels and their contacts with human beings. The Old Testament is filled with such descriptions, as early as Genesis and as late as Daniel. The angel Gabriel announced the incarnation of Jesus to Mary. An angel opened the door of a prison for Peter and John. Some six hundred years later, Gabriel dictated the Quran to Muhammad. Some twelve hundred years after that, the angel Moroni gave the Book of Mormon to Joseph Smith. Apart from that and many more doctrinal examples, countless stories by lesser known individuals and those totally unknown to you affirm direct angelic contact—and even contact with God Himself. Do you wish to deny the story of Moses? Or perhaps the efficacy of prayer? Or shall we just stipulate that the Mormons are insane for actually believing the story of Joseph Smith? Or shall we expand that a bit and declare all Christians insane for actually believing in the story of Jesus, and all Muslims insane for actually believing in the words of Muhammad, and all Jews insane for actually believing in the Torah, and all other believers ranging from Hindus to Baha'is insane for actually believing in divinity and the reality of contact with divinity? If so, you may be left with five percent or so of the world's population that shares your view—temporarily, at least, since that view will seem pretty silly to them in a remarkably short time. O foolish men, and slow of heart to believe all that the prophets have spoken!

Regardless of your belief, my examiner and keeper, this is what happened next.

I returned to Indianapolis safely and directly into the arms of Allison, who was as awed and frightened as I had been when I told her what had happened. Whether it was the strain of the separation or the near fatal outcome in the desert, both of us decided almost simultaneously to move up our marriage date. We chose September 29 for no particular reason, except for the fact that the minister was free and we needed a minimum of six weeks to complete all of the arrangements for our small wedding. It was a busy period for both of us, since Allison had chosen to keep her job at the elementary school for at least one more year, and I had gone back into research mode to learn as much as I could about Archangel Gabriel, all while both of us happily worked on the marriage arrangements.

I spoke at length on several occasions with Father Mark, who grew ever more anxious to arrange a meeting with his Bishop. I also remained in contact with Teresa and sent a rather long letter to Earl Dawkins. There was a health scare with my mother, who was diagnosed with a breast tumor. I flew to Chicago immediately to be with her and my father even before the results of the malignancy test were known. I felt such incredible love for my mother as we embraced on the doorstep of her home and the warmth flowed between us. The results were inconclusive, and they tested again—or rather, they tried to test again, as they could find no trace of the tumor. So much was *right* in my life at that time.

Do not misunderstand me here. I returned to my former life with gratitude and happiness, but clearly I was not the person that I had been before. The emotional power that I had felt practically churning in my chest after the experience at the Semahane appeared to be permanent, and I knew that I had the ability to project it toward others with important consequences. Moreover, if anything, my powers of memory had actually increased since my experience in the desert. I simply had total recall at my command of everything that I read and everything that I heard. This had been disconcerting at first, but I had learned to control it, as if I were truly an organic computer whose information had to be consciously accessed rather than streaming across the screen at all times. My "training" seemed to have been as much physical somehow as mental and spiritual. I also had come to understand that each angelic meeting was designed in part to prepare me for the next one at a progressively higher and more glorified level, for the inconceivably charged presence of the higher angels could as easily destroy me as bless me without proper protection.

At the same time, I was most definitely still a human being with all of the needs and the failings that all of us share. I was a human being in the process of being prepared for a special task, and whatever it was, the conviction was growing in me that it involved enhanced ability to love and to remember.

I returned to my carrel at the Butler library and began my research on Gabriel, perhaps the best known of the seven archangels because of his association with the last days and the proverbial blowing of his horn to announce them. His name means the "Power of God." Mystics have also called him the "Angel of Life." He is revered in Islam under the name of Jibril, because he revealed the Quran to Muhammad. He first appears by name in the Old Testament in the Book of Daniel. Many Jews also believe that it was Gabriel who told Noah to gather the animals in the Ark and who stayed Abraham's hand when he was about to stab Isaac. Both the Quran and New Testament agree that it was Gabriel who appeared before Mary in the "Annunciation." It was also Gabriel who announced to Zechariah that Saint Elizabeth would give birth to John the Baptist, a bit of biblical lore that I now view with enormous interest. It has been said that Gabriel is the coordinator of all of the angelic orders. All traditions consider him to be a master communicator who conveys important and usually good news to mankind.

I could find nothing anywhere of a fearful nature in Gabriel, other than vague and unpersuasive allusions to him as the angel of death, perhaps because of the association with the end of days.

I prayed for guidance in regard to the meeting with Gabriel. Three nights in a row, I received a crisp message from Raphael in my dreams advising patience and urging that I read *Daniel 9:21- 23*. The passage follows:

> *While I was speaking in prayer, the man Gabriel, whom I had seen in the vision at the first, came to me in swift flight at the time of the evening sacrifice. He came and he said to me, "O Daniel, I have now come out to give you wisdom and understanding. At the beginning of your supplications a word went forth, and I have come to tell it to you, for you are greatly beloved; therefore, consider the word and understand the vision ..."*

I knew by then that my "training" or initiation or whatever it was involved progressively more important or powerful entities. I had never heard of Ariel as a heavenly angel before my accident, and I had known little more about Raphael even after the accident, but my experience in the desert had provided me with ample evidence of his unimaginable power. Gabriel was an entirely different story. His presence and his messages had changed the course of human existence more than once, and I suspected that most of his earthly activities had not even been recorded. Not only is he listed as one of the seven archangels, and stands as only one of three mentioned by name in the Bible, but The Book of Enoch declares that he sits on the left hand of God.

How could I possibly stand before such a being? Then I remembered the words of Azarias/Raphael: *"It is in fact* **forbidden** *for angels to accept the obeisance of men. The angel will always bow first or nod first out of respect for the being created in God's image and that actually shares in the creative powers of God. You have no idea how the angels stand in awe of mankind! They cannot create. Their thoughts are attuned only to the thoughts of God. They deliver messages; they cannot create them. When they see humans for the first time, they actually see the power and image of God, and they must bow in reverence."*

And had Raphael not said of Gabriel, *"... the new energy and power that flows within you now will allow you to be in the presence of Gabriel and to hear the truth of all things, for he is the messenger of truth and understanding"*? I slowly realized the enormity of the experience that was about to unfold. I had already been blessed by the divine beyond comprehension. And now was I really to hear *"the truth of all things"*? Why had I been chosen? What was my task? And why did the odd fragments of memories or dreams of another time and place seem to be increasing?

In the meantime, my relationship with Allison had grown so intense that it was actually physically painful for both of us. My capacity for love had been vastly expanded, and I was not yet able to control the power of my projection of that love. It was one thing for the power of love to impede the forward movement of a demon, but another entirely for it to discomfort my beloved. Our physical love for each other, stimulated and sustained by our emotional love, was so powerful that we were completely exhausted for hours afterward and sometimes for an entire day. The first time after my return was a joyful revelation for both of us, as every nerve ending seemed to be sending off sparks, but the fierceness of our longing for each other was actually difficult to bear. Both of us felt a compelling need for marriage to sanction and bless and even moderate the intensity of every touch between us.

* * *

The first contact with Gabriel was not announced in advance, but I at least had a few seconds of warning.

The sun was glinting brightly off the placid blue waters of the lake on a Sunday afternoon—so brightly, in fact, that I had to shield my eyes against the glare as I looked out over the water. Oddly, the intense light seemed to be moving rapidly in my direction, as if a giant mirror were being carried by a speedboat directly toward my house or the sun itself were moving much too fast across the sky.

"Honey," I said to Allison, who was puttering in the adjoining kitchen, "come look at this."

She took the few steps into the great room that allowed her to look out over the lake with me and almost immediately threw her hands over her eyes and cried out in pain.

I turned immediately to help her. She was clearly hurting. "What's the matter?" I asked anxiously.

"My eyes," she whimpered. "They're burning, and I can't see!"

Tears were streaming down both of her cheeks.

Then I heard the voice in my mind. *"She has not yet been prepared, Jacob. Take her into your studio. She will be fine."*

"Come with me, my love," I said. "Gabriel is approaching. He just spoke to me. The light is coming from him. He said you will be fine."

She nodded her understanding, and I led her into the studio, closed the door, and held her close. "I love you," I said. "Don't leave this room. I'll come for you afterward. He said that you haven't been prepared sufficiently for his presence." I kissed her and gently seated her on the easy chair that I had used for thinking out approaches to my paintings. I kissed her again. "This won't happen again, love," I said.

When I opened the door, the entire great room was engulfed in brilliant white light. As my eyes slowly adjusted to the overwhelming radiance, I could see a magnificent male figure in a light blue tunic standing at the center of the light in the center of my great room. His blue eyes sparkled and radiated still more light. He slowly knelt on one knee and bent his head.

I remembered the words of Azarias/Raphael about the relationship of angels to human beings and fought off my own desperate compulsion to kneel and declare my unworthiness.

I was also stunned by the number of glowing white wings that fluttered with his every movement. It slowly dawned on me that the intense radiance streaming from him that so overshadowed what I had experienced with Ariel and Raphael stemmed in large part from the literally hundreds of wings that appeared to reflect and magnify any and all light to an astonishing degree.

He stood and spoke in a deep, rumbling voice: "*Fear not, Jacob, for from the first day that you set your mind to understand and humbled yourself before God, your words have been heard, and I have come because of your words, to the very place of your humility. Your words are strong, Jacob: 'Please help me find the truth in all of the religions that claim to speak for You. Please give me the courage to face the angels or demons that you may place in my path. Please give me the strength to fulfill the tasks that You have set for me. Please help me understand what is Your will and assist me in doing Your will, not mine.' Your task requires the strength of your words, and I am here to strengthen them more with the power of truth.*"

"You honor me, Gabriel," I said, my voice quavering, "with your presence and your words. Please help me be worthy of both."

"*Every choice and every decision changes the individual and the world itself, Jacob, in very real and fundamental ways that human scientists are only now beginning to understand, but are you aware of how the process has been accelerated with you? You could not have met me in this fashion only a short time ago."*

"I know about the physical changes, at least some of them, Gabriel, and I know that my awareness and understanding of the numinous have deepened. Allison has not been prepared for your presence, though. Will she be all right?"

"Yes, Jacob," he responded kindly. *"There will be no lasting physical harm. Trust me when I tell you that we can do nothing by accident. Unlike you, the angelic hosts act only under direction. There are no mistakes. The possible consequences of our acts are known. Allison's last doubt has now been shaken, and it will disappear on the day of your wedding. She has feared for you, Jacob."*

"Thank you," I said with relief. "There is still so much that I do not know, that I cannot know."

"It may not comfort you to hear that there are some things that even I do not know, Jacob, but I shall share with you those things that I do know. We shall meet here on three occasions after you see me on the day of your wedding. You may ask questions that I must answer as best I can. Choose wisely, as you will know better than I what it is that mankind needs to hear in its suffering."

"Did no one else see you as you approached the house?" I asked.

"There were many who saw the light glinting off the water, and they either shielded their eyes or turned away to protect them. Humans on Earth almost always see what they expect to see. Farewell, Jacob."

He then knelt again on one knee and bowed his head slightly. The radiance dimmed slowly at first and then rapidly vanished, leaving me standing alone in the great room with a mixture of awe and relief flooding through me before I moved quickly into the studio. Allison was still sitting in the easy chair with her eyes closed.

"I'm so sorry, love. He said you will be fine. Can you open your eyes?"

"Let me try again," she said.

She gradually opened her eyes. The tearing had stopped.

"I can see better now," she said, "but my eyes still ache a little."

"Close them again," I said, as I bent down slowly. I kissed both eyelids and settled on my knees next to the chair with my arms around her. "Ariel said that I could perceive her safely after the Holy Spirit had touched me in California. Gabriel said that he would somehow be at our wedding and I assume in a safe way. There is just so much I don't know. I'm so sorry, my love."

She opened her eyes again and placed her hand on my cheek. "It's going to be all right," she said. "My eyes are feeling much better now. I also feel better in my heart somehow, because I've been tormented by doubt. I could hear part of the conversation, Jake, and I could see the incredible light flowing from under the door when I first tried to open my eyes. Please forgive me for ever doubting you. I trusted Father Mark, but I just couldn't quite allow myself to accept the consequences of what you and he have said. I still feel overwhelmed."

"I have been through the same process, sweetheart. It is one thing to *believe* casually in the divine, but it is very different to encounter its reality in our personal lives. I think that we are programmed that way so that we do not focus constantly on the other world and lose sight of this one, where we are supposed to be learning how to create responsibly."

So now you can add Gabriel to your list of hallucinations. I caution you, though, not to lose sight of reality yourself. Remember—much of this can be checked. I won't bore you with the preparations for the wedding and the household events over the next three weeks or so. There is only one more thing that you should know before we get to the meat of the matter—and that occurred at the wedding itself.

We held it outdoors at the lake, both of us wanting to pledge ourselves to each other in the midst of nature. We had set up a platform and a flower-covered archway that opened directly onto the blue water of the lake. We stood there together with the minister as we clasped our hands together and said our vows before our families and closest friends. The day had been disappointingly overcast, but as the minister completed the fateful words "What God has joined together let no man put asunder," a bright ray of sunshine broke through the clouds and appeared to center itself on the platform, flooding all of us with light to the appreciative gasps and nervous laughter of the guests. I felt an intense warmth around my heart, and I could see from Allison's odd expression that she was experiencing the same sensation. When the minister then pronounced us husband and wife, my father released a single white dove that rose slowly into the sky above the lake. Suddenly the sun broke out from behind the clouds in force, and the light glinted heavily off the wings of the dove and even more brightly off the water below. All of the guests smiled and applauded as they followed the flight of the dove as it rose ever higher and farther out over the lake. Eventually, they had to shield their eyes or turn away entirely as the fierce sunlight and its reflection off the water became too much to bear. Allison and I continued to watch, however, as the dove flew into the outstretched hands of the winged figure in the blue tunic just before the sun faded behind another cloud.

"Was that ... ?" she asked haltingly.

"Yes," I said. "And your eyes?"

"They're fine," she said. "Everything is fine."

And it was.

* * *

All right. You will be among the first to learn what I have learned and probably one of the last to accept it.

We returned to Bermuda for one week on our honeymoon in recognition of the life-changing event there. It was a time of unbroken bliss, for which I will always be grateful. On the last night, Gabriel appeared to me in a "dream."

"The time has arrived," he said. *"Prepare yourself."*

"Can Allison be with me when you come?" I asked.

"It would still not be good for her," he replied. *"She has not been prepared as thoroughly as you have been. Look to yourself now, Jacob."*

We arrived at our home on the lake early the next evening. We had agreed that she would retire to the studio at the first sign of a visitation. Nothing happened, however, and we slept peacefully together throughout the night. The next morning, we sipped our coffee together in the great room as we looked out over the lake and talked both about Bermuda and the sessions to come with Gabriel. The light breeze that had been blowing across the lake stopped abruptly, along with the birdsong that had welcomed in the new day. The reflection of the sun on the lake began to intensify.

"He's coming, love," I said.

She gazed at the steadily growing light without pain. "I wish I could be with you—and with him," she said with sadness. "But I do understand. I feel something odd around my heart even now. I love you."

No more than five seconds after she closed the door to the studio behind her, the great room filled with dazzling luminescence, and Gabriel stood before me in such magnificence that I staggered backwards, even though I had known what to expect.

"Let us begin," he said. *"Know that nothing is what it seems to be on the surface. You think that you have a body, and therefore you do. You think that your spirit is encased in the body, and therefore it is. But nothing truly exists except intention and thought. The stuff of all existence is creative energy flowing from the thoughts of God. Your scientists now understand that once the smallest particle is reached that what lies beyond is pure energy. In fact, there are no particles, only energy waves that have condensed temporarily into matter under the power of intention. All of existence is an interconnected web of energy waves*

flowing from God with infinite potential for creative form under the direction of intention and thought. We are made from the thoughts of God, as is everything else. I cannot create, because my thoughts and my intentions are one with God's, and I can only glorify what already exists. You can and do and must create, because your awareness has been separated from God's. You share in God's creative power and therefore constantly extend the parameters and glories of existence. But such great freedom carries with it great responsibilities and great dangers, as you and all human souls can choose not to love, something that is inconceivable to me and my kind and brings us great sorrow and pity, for you and your creations must then be produced and shaped in a special environment that cannot contaminate the rest of existence.

"Know, Jacob, that all of the sacred texts and all of the divine myths and legends have been corrupted or misinterpreted. There is no guilt in this. The human brain is a receptor device that resonates with the energy waves on this plane and provides the illusion of mass and stability that you and all human souls accept as reality while on this plane. The capacity of the human brain is limited and cannot encompass all of the information encoded in the energy fields. Information on this plane is therefore always limited and incomplete at best. Your brain has now been altered so that it can record with absolute clarity everything that you 'hear' and 'see.' Nevertheless, whatever you may write or tell others will be changed and corrupted by time, errors of transmission, and conscious manipulation of the information by others with their own goals and intentions. This is the case with all sacred texts.

"Knowing this, you may not be as surprised to learn that the 'fallen angels' are not angels at all but actually you and the other human souls. Angels cannot rebel or do anything counter to God's intentions. Human souls can, however, and, as their creations departed ever more widely from God's intentions, they moved farther and farther away from God's presence. You can imagine, if you wish, a fall away from the light and into ever deeper levels of darkness. You exist at this moment at the eighth level of separation from God. It is not easy or pleasing for angels and others to attune themselves to this level. Energy waves here and the

mass that they produce are extremely dense and compacted. Therefore, creative power has been slowed and limited. Thoughts and intentions will eventually materialize on this plane, but the slowness of the process in comparison to the higher levels prevents constant catastrophe. Nevertheless, human thoughts and intentions devoid of love have gradually created such monstrous effects as the demon Azazel. Beauty and love do exist on the earth plane, and humanity has created works of magnificence, but it is constantly at war with itself and the consequences of evil intentions.

"Know, Jacob, that God has not and never will abandon humankind. Help is always at hand. Prayer is always answered. Holy beings are sent. Angels are sent. The Holy Spirit is always here. Everything is done to assist, except for removing free will and the power to create, for this would destroy God's own creation rather than expand it. The authentic messages in the holy texts given to mankind are short. God is Spirit. Would he concern Himself with meat sacrifice and ask that His worshippers "burn the fat for a pleasing odor to the Lord"? Would He list pages upon pages of dietary restrictions for those who love Him? Or would the real message not rather be: 'Do you not see that whatever goes into a man from outside cannot defile him, since it enters not his heart but his stomach and then passes on? What comes out of a man is what defiles a man. For from within, out of the heart of a man, come evil thoughts, fornication, theft, murder, adultery, coveting, wickedness, deceit, licentiousness, envy, slander, pride, foolishness. All these evil things come from within, and they defile a man.' The primary message of Moses, which has not been changed by time, lies in the Ten Commandments. The primary message of Jesus, as he himself declared it, is short and simple: 'You shall love the Lord your God with all your heart, and with all your soul, and with all your mind. This is the great and first commandment. And a second is like it. You shall love your neighbor as yourself. On these two commandments depend all the law and the prophets.' The primary message of Buddha is even shorter: 'Work out your salvation with diligence.' The new gospel is shorter still: 'Love, mercy, compassion.'

"Yet the messages are never heeded, for humankind chooses by acts of free will to walk a path toward misery. How simple the message: 'Thou shalt not kill.' How tortured the excuses: 'But of course that cannot refer to self-defense. That cannot refer to infidels. That cannot refer to just wars. That cannot refer to execution of the wicked. That cannot refer to animals.' The commandment is clear! 'Thou shalt not kill.' Period. There are no exceptions. And the only people on earth who observe the commandment are the Jains, who have won great favor with God because of their righteousness. The same is true of every commandment. They are all broken all the time. Jacob, man is not made for the law; the law is made for man. All of the genuine messages from the divine sphere are meant to guide and help humankind in its struggles to use its creative powers meaningfully and productively, as well as to work its way back from the dense levels to the divine sphere where it began. They are not restrictions, but rather practical guidelines pointing the way to salvation.

"Now the message is reduced to its simplest form: 'Love, mercy, compassion.' Without these, human souls can never return. Without these, faith is meaningless. Without these, any religion is false. Without these, more and more Azazels shall be born.

"Know all these things, Jacob. Contemplate them."

I noticed before he ended that the movement of his lips and the words that I heard were somehow not completely aligned. Yes, there was perfect synchronization, but I realized that I was not actually hearing the words through my ears but rather directly inside my brain without the mediation of the auditory canal. The difference in actual speed would have been negligible in the extreme, but the *immediacy* of the communication was different and striking nevertheless.

"The physical changes are continuing, Jacob," he said, without moving his lips. *"Do not fear them. Do you have questions?"*

"I am filled with questions, Gabriel," I responded, "but I need some time to contemplate what you have already said, as you suggest. Thank you, Gabriel."

"There is only One to thank, Jacob, and He knows what is in your heart."

The intense radiance faded and disappeared. I closed my eyes and fell on my knees to give thanks to God. When I opened them again, the light was normal, and Allison stood in the doorway to the studio.

"I heard nothing," she said, "although a dazzling radiance streamed beneath the door. Am I allowed to know what was said?"

I repeated everything into a tape recorder word for word, and Allison then typed the session into my computer. Neither of us spoke for a while after that. We hugged each other silently, and I kissed her on the forehead.

Later we discussed the message thoroughly and tried to determine what was expected of me. It seemed so far in the past, but it had been less than a year since the first message had been delivered to me via Teresa: *He must go and stand in the temple and speak to the people all the words of this Life.* What temple? Whose life? It seemed clear that I was to convey important information to "the people," perhaps the very information that Gabriel was conveying to me, but I still had no idea about the process or the details of my task.

* * *

The next morning, at exactly the same time, the process with Gabriel repeated itself. The reflected light upon the lake began to glow and shimmer more intensely, Allison left the room, and I waited no more than five seconds for his arrival.

"May peace be with you, Jacob," he began.

"And with you, Gabriel," I replied.

"Know this well, Jacob: Nothing is what it seems to be at this level of your existence. However, in His compassion for human souls, God has filled this level of reality with signs and wonders pointing to the higher

worlds and how to return to them. He who has eyes, let him see. He who has ears, let him hear. Many of these signs have been found and appreciated, yet many have not. Think only of death and rebirth and how this pattern recurs everywhere and in everything. Think of the famous caterpillar and butterfly. This is to remind you that there is no end to existence, only change in form. You are a spirit, or wave energy with unique imprinted information, if you will, that moves freely between this world and the one at the next higher plane. At that level, you will still be aware of physical form that appears solid to you, including your astral body, but that will change as you continue to climb. You visit the next level now in your dreams and on other occasions often unknown to you. The human brain cannot retain memories of nonphysical existence, or what you conceive as nonphysical. To know the things of the spirit, rely on the spirit, not the brain. Use what you know as intuition. Use the brain to explore this world, but use the spirit to find the others. Render unto the earthly Caesar what is of the earth, but render unto God what is His beyond the earth.

*"Whatever you perceive with the senses has two levels, the ordinary and the transcendent. The ordinary may be magnificent in your terms, but know that you and other humans have created it. The transcendent signifies creation beyond the human. No matter how much your thoughts and intent may shape the energy that is available to you, that energy is and always will be a part of God, and it will proclaim itself as such from behind whatever form it has taken. You have already been advised: '*You must learn to see through surfaces at the reality that rests behind them.'* Consider the lilies, how they grow; they neither toil nor spin, yet I tell you even Solomon in all his glory was not arrayed like one of these. Consider the ravens: they neither sow nor reap, they have neither storehouse nor barn, and yet God feeds them. The way has been shown.*

"Zen Buddhists know that words are only symbols for the objects that they represent. Therefore they dispense with words and encounter the objects directly. The wisest among them also know that the objects themselves are only symbols for the transcendence that they seek behind

the illusion of reality. Yet words do matter, because they, too, can be both ordinary and transcendent: In the beginning was the Word, and the Word was with God, and the Word was God. Know that special messages have been relayed through words not only to the people who lived in the times of the prophets who spoke them, but also to the people who would come later. There are codes and messages in the Torah and other sacred texts, for example, that are only now being discovered.

"Language in your world is converging for the first time in many thousands of years. English has become the world language. This is not accidental. There are passages in the New Testament translated into modern languages that transcend time, and there are important messages hidden in the English words of today. Consider the parable of the silver talents, in which the departing master gives to one servant five talents for safekeeping, to another two, and to the last servant only one. Upon his return, he praises the first two servants for using and doubling their talents and berates the last servant for burying the money in fear that he might lose it. In the time of Jesus, the word 'talent' referred to money and only to money. The parable only flowered into its full meaning many centuries later when 'talent' began to signify 'ability' rather than 'money.' This also is not accidental. The message was directed at future generations, and the evolution of the message was itself the message.

"Consider the very word for humankind—'Man.' In the recent past, no message could be found in it. Today, if you examine 'Man' from all angles, you quickly discover 'Nam.' This is not frivolous. Man has indeed reversed his initial orientation and evolved into Nam, now a symbol for protracted and bloody war with neither a clear justification nor a clear resolution. Man is at war with himself and not understanding why, because of the accumulation of unloving thoughts and intentions. This pattern is rapidly congealing. Love, mercy, and compassion must become both the conscious and unconscious guideposts for human development, lest this magnificent and noble branch of creation find itself at a literal dead end.

"You will learn that even the tetragrammaton bears a message for mankind. You will learn that the extent of man's creative power has reached far beyond your imagination. For now, contemplate these things; allow them to reach beyond your physical understanding and into your spirit, where they will be magnified and returned into the physical plane with ever greater power."

What do you say to "the messenger of truth and understanding"? What can you say to a nearly omnipotent being who may sit on the left hand of God? You want to worship such a being, but you know that it would be sacrilege to do so. You know that the messages have been vastly simplified to fit your limited intellectual capacity. You know that the very descent into the abyss of existence eight levels removed from God must be unimaginably tortured and disgusting. And even so, you know that God has not abandoned you and all other human souls, for the proof of it stands in front of you and actually speaks to *you.* What do you say?

"Know, Jacob," he continued, *"that only energy exists, that you and I and all things consist of information-laden energy waves flowing and swirling in an unending sea of interaction that is as close as I can come on this plane to describing the glory of God. Thought and intention cause some of the waves to coalesce into particles that form what we perceive as matter, yet the particles are still only energy waves in a different phase that will lose their 'mass' when the intention changes. All thought and intention originate from God. God's thoughts, however, are limitlessly creative in their power to cause the waves to coalesce into particles. If it is His intention that those particles and the waves that create them should also carry the properties of thought and intention, then the process of creation can continue infinitely, even though ultimately everything still is a part of God. I can change my shape at will, just as you can change the persona that you present to your world, depending on whether those you are dealing with are relatives, friends, competitors, strangers, colleagues, or all other possibilities. The process is the same; only the speed and effect on this plane are different.*

"God has countless personae through which He interacts with His creation, but no single one can or should be termed God. You and I are among those personae, but we are not God, just as the projection that showed his back to Moses was not 'God,' yet you and I and he all share in the essence of God.

"The human brain cannot contain the data of infinite creation, nor can it even process the concept of infinity. Therefore, it cannot know God, except as He chooses to reveal Himself in a form that can be perceived and partially understood. Spirit can survive the encounter with infinity, but it immediately becomes one with it and loses its power to exercise individual thought and intent, until God wills that it again detach itself.

"This is the fundamental nature of reality in the simplest form of expression within my ability to communicate with you. Do not mistake the necessary simplicity of the message, however, as a sign that the totality of creation is in any way simple or even comprehensible. Neither of these is true. You need only one example to begin to understand.

"I have told you that the myth of the fallen angels actually refers to the fall of human souls as they steadily distanced themselves from God through the abuse of their creative power. Know, Jacob, that this did not happen quickly. Unmeasured time has been required for the descent to the eighth level of removal from God. Their acts of creation have continued throughout that time—and with vast impact before they removed themselves too far from the divine center. You imagine that God created the universe in which you find yourself and that it is infinite. I tell you that much of this universe has been created by human souls before they lost their way and that creation is continuing here, but you can only begin to understand the true majesty of creation when you realize that your universe is only one in an infinite number of universes. Your scientists are surprised that the conditions for life in this universe seem so precariously balanced, that the physical laws are just exactly right to support your form of physical life—without realizing that it is humans that have helped create these conditions, not the other way around. Do you have questions?"

"Yes," I said. "How is it possible for humans to have such immeasurable power and yet be confined on this small planet, a speck in one galaxy that is itself a speck in a universe that is also a speck?"

"Many are in the process of returning to the higher realms. Many more are in the level above this one. All of those at this level rise to the next frequently but cannot retain the memory in their physical brains. All of those at this level find themselves here as a consequence of their own decisions and their own creative acts. What you think of as death will take them again to the next level. The construction of much of this universe was accomplished by human souls at higher levels before many of them became trapped in the dense matter of their own careless creation. All continue to create with every decision they make and every act of intention. Thoughts and intentions on the earth spread throughout this universe and affect areas and beings far from the earth. At higher levels, such intentions spread into countless universes."

"I have enormous difficulty understanding this," I said.

"I know that, Jacob. All human spirits at this level fail to understand the meaning of God and His creation, precisely because they have belittled themselves by falling so far and therefore belittle the very essence of reality by postulating a single universe and God as an old man living in the clouds. What I have told you is only the beginning. Know, Jacob, that every decision made by every being of sufficient awareness alters the nature of their reality, as the intent of the decision collapses some waves into particles and allows others to continue untouched. Nevertheless, since there was a choice, the possibility of another option has affected those waves connected to that possibility, and an alternate reality is born. In effect, new universes within the larger universe split off constantly as a necessary by-product of conscious choice. Every universe carries infinite universes within it, and the original universes themselves are infinite. You cannot understand this in your current condition, but you can understand that love, mercy, and compassion are the cornerstones of God's own intent and therefore pervade all of creation.

Conscious focus upon these three elements of existence will lead back to the higher planes and help bring salvation to this universe."

Gabriel bowed his head as before, and the radiance began to dim. I could repeat all of his words without hesitation or mistake, but the full meaning of them certainly eluded me.

"You look strange somehow, Jake," Allison said as she walked toward me. "What happened?"

"I think that Gabriel was trying to explain infinity to me," I answered, "but I find myself infinitely confused, and I can't decide whether that means success or not."

We looked at each other for a moment, and then both of us started laughing, at first mildly and then uncontrollably as our laughter fed on our mutual spasms and rocked both of us wildly. Soon we were both sitting on the floor gasping for breath, with the spasms gradually decreasing like the aftershocks of an earthquake. Finally we simply looked into each other's eyes and hugged.

Later, I again repeated every word into a recorder, and Allison again transcribed the session into my computer and then transferred both of the sessions onto a disc. Whether we were truly the appropriate vessels for such information or not, we wanted to be sure that the words would not end with us. Then we walked around the lake hand in hand and found it lovely beyond description. What must the other planes be like if this miserable, corrupted one still retains such beauty?

* * *

On the third day, a surprise occurred. The process unfolded as before, yet …

"Tell Allison to enter the room and not to fear," Gabriel said.

I stared at him in wonder for a few seconds and then walked across the room to open the door into the studio. Gabriel's radiance filled it immediately, but Allison did not close her eyes or even blink.

"What ...?" she began to ask from the easy chair where she was sitting.

"He asks that you join us and not to be afraid. I know nothing beyond that, my love."

Allison stood immediately, and we walked back into the brilliant radiance holding hands.

"The Holy Spirit is with you," he said to her. *"Your body has adjusted. It is fitting that the two of you, man and woman, should pose your questions together."*

In fact, Allison and I had been discussing the questions for days, but neither of us had expected that she would be part of the discussion. We had both assumed that there was physical danger for her in the presence of Gabriel. That was apparently no longer the case. Nevertheless, Allison was clearly in deep awe of the glorious being at the center of the blazing light. We sat closely together on the sofa.

"We thank you, Gabriel," I said with intense humility. "You have already answered part of our first question, but it is so important to humankind and so often discussed that we feel the need to ask for more information. What is the reason for the existence of pain and suffering? Even if we ourselves have created evil upon the earth, how can God in his infinite mercy and compassion allow innocents to suffer such torment, to include torture and the cruelest butchery. How can this be allowed?"

"None of this comes directly from God," he began. *"You know now, Jacob, that such acts are allowed in this universe as a necessary consequence of free will and the descent of human spirits into selfish and loveless acts. Creation here is human, but certainly not all of it is harmful to the spirit, far from it. Nevertheless, terrible pain and horrific acts do exist. Much of the suffering has been freely chosen at the next level by human spirits in advance of incarnation on earth as a means of spiritual advancement or as a means of fully understanding the consequences of*

their earlier thoughtless and loveless acts. There are former rulers, for example, who believed in their hearts that they were serving the interests of humankind when they issued orders that led directly to the slaughter of innocents. Only by experiencing such slaughter themselves can they fully understand their errors and learn to practice creation with love and compassion. Similarly, some suffering is direct recompense for suffering caused to others, so that forgiveness and mercy may flow more freely. Some of the suffering is actually assumed by advanced spirits who have returned from higher levels to serve as examples for humankind. Much of the suffering in all of its forms is accepted by human souls as a means of providing opportunities for others to manifest love, mercy, and compassion in their quest to return to the higher levels. In no case can freely chosen suffering be considered evil. You have suffered greatly in the physical body, Jacob, but you accepted this freely as a way of preparation for your task in this life, so that you might address the problems of humankind with full understanding and compassion."

"What is my task, Gabriel?" I blurted out without thinking.

"And is that really to be one of your questions on behalf of humankind, Jacob?"

I realized immediately that such selfishness was unforgivable. "No," I said. "Forgive me."

"It is not for me to forgive. Forgive yourself, Jacob, and use the forgiveness to rid yourself of your remaining selfishness. Your time approaches. But first know, Jacob, that there is more in answer to your question, for now there is evil in your world, as you have seen with Azazel. Such beings have no souls, but they do possess the same freedom of will as their human creators. Since they are themselves the results of evil thoughts and intentions, they can do no other than continue to foster evil. Therefore the victims of such beings or of their followers do not grow spiritually from their pain and suffering, but must instead be cleansed of the contamination at the next level after their 'deaths.' The followers and perpetrators of such evil must themselves be cleansed in order to retain any hope of return to God. This evil grows on the earth. It can only be removed by the power of the Holy Spirit, which in turn is

invoked by love, mercy, and compassion. You are now connected to the Holy Spirit, and you have the power to bring others to it in order to effect a cleansing here on earth. Know, Jacob, that you are not alone in this, as many others have also been chosen, now as in the past.

"*The outcome in this universe is not certain, as the permutations in the sea of creation are endless. There are those on earth who know of the destruction of Azazel and who now seek to prevent further loss of their power. They will be drawn to you eventually.*"

Gabriel then looked directly into Allison's eyes as if willing her to ask a question of her own. She paused only momentarily.

"What is the nature of time, Gabriel?" she asked suddenly. "We sense that our experience of time must be an illusion, but we cannot reach beyond the illusion. What is time?"

"*In the most fundamental sense,*" he began, "*everything exists simultaneously. Every instant is coexistent with every other, and always will be. The illusion of progression is created by spiritual consciousness that shifts its focus from one coexistent instant to another. Let me explain this by means of music. All the notes of a composition lie on a page or pages at the same time, all of them ready to be brought into being by the musician as his focus shifts from one note to the next. The sound of a single note carries within it no meaning, no progression, no life. As each note is struck in turn, the awareness of the musician jumps from one to the next to the next and unites them in his consciousness in order to experience the meaning, the progression, and the life of the composition. The same is true with reading, as consciousness unites the individual letters that by themselves mean nothing but seen together as awareness unites them are filled with living meaning. Consider also the individual frames of movie film, the 'instants' that by themselves are still and lifeless and even bear the name of 'stills.' As the projector rolls the film, awareness jumps from one frame to the next at great speed, and it both perceives and creates the illusion of life arising from a collection of single frames.*

"*In each case, the notes and the letters and the frames represent individual instants that all exist simultaneously with all of the other* instants in the composition, book, or film. When awareness moves on, the composition, the book, and the film remain, all existent in the same instant. Nothing is lost, and nothing is added. It is only awareness that has come and gone.

"Know, Allison, that all of creation exists in a single instant, and every action in every life in every world becomes possible because God is the musician and the reader and the viewer, and His awareness moves from one point to the next and the next and allows His creations to express life and meaning.

"Imagine, if you can, that each frame of creation is represented by the tip of a cone similar to those in soundproof rooms and that the bases of these cones of existence are touching and that the cones stretch across a plane infinitely in all directions, all existing at the same instant, all of them bearing the potential for life and meaning within themselves, but all of them static until awareness begins to move across their tips. Now know that God's own awareness is partly realized within the awareness of all sentient beings, and that all sentient beings move their awareness from point to point across the field of existence as they play the compositions of their lives. Every instant is coexistent, yet the symphony of life in all its variations is played triumphantly and endlessly. Human awareness creates its own reality as it makes its way from point to point, all the touching cones practically identical like adjacent frames of film, yet every decision changing the direction that awareness will take from point to point as it moves across the field. Every possibility and every potential exist simultaneously along the field of existence, but thought and intention shift the awareness so that one line is taken and others abandoned. God is aware of every possible end point of every 'life' but does not decide which of those points will be reached or how. That is the meaning of free will. At the same time, there are definite probabilities in every life that become sharpened with every decision. It is possible to look ahead at every life according to the path that is being followed through the field of existence. Unexpected shifts can and do occur, but the probabilities of such shifts are known and can be predicted with a high degree of accuracy.

"All of this is altered as the soul advances through the higher levels of existence in its return to God, but the principle is similar. Have you followed me in this?"

"I think so," she said, although I was not at all certain that I had. "But you said that future events can be predicted with high levels of probability," she continued. "If this is so, how can that be reconciled with free will?"

"No decisions are forced or preordained, Allison. However, every lifetime can be traced across the field of existence, and the pattern of decisions in a given lifetime can be traced to the threshold of the next decision, which can then be predicted with great accuracy. For example, the demon Azazel would certainly have killed Jacob if he had not found it in his heart to bless the loathsome creature. However, we expected such a blessing, and it drew forth the blasphemous curse from Azazel that justified his destruction by Raphael.

"Everything I have told you and much more has already been revealed and distorted or lost on many occasions. I know that you have been preserving my words. Protect them if you can from those who would destroy them, for they are now gathering against the two of you, as your own intentions are felt by others whose lines of existence are running close to yours. They will soon attack. You have both been provided with certain protections, and you, Jacob, possess more power than you yet understand. You must love your enemies, for there is no other way to drain the energy from their hatred.

"Remember: If all else is lost, the central revelation must be preserved—Love, Mercy, and Compassion. With these three alone, the direction of this universe can be reversed, and human creation can achieve the place first intended for it. Otherwise, it will sink further and further into the darkness.

"You are never alone. Those you have already met watch you. You will soon meet with one greater than I. For now, contemplate my words and all that you have seen and learned since your reacceptance of the body. May peace be with you."

"And with you, Gabriel," we said simultaneously.

Frankly, at that point, we had no real idea what to expect. We were receiving important information for the enlightenment of humankind, even though we ourselves truly did not understand all of it. At the same time, it sounded as if there were terrible times ahead, and that we would meet with at least one more incomprehensibly powerful being, whether angelic or otherwise. Yes, certainly I know how all of this will sound to someone who has not experienced it. On the other hand, I subscribe to the proposition that truth remains truth regardless of anyone else's ill-informed opinion or limited ability to perceive it. I am not dealing in opinions or interpretations of reality here. I am only telling you what happened, even though I realize that your own opinion has other consequences.

Allison remarked that there was something odd in the way that she had "heard" Gabriel's words, as if they were resonating directly in her brain rather than being channeled through her auditory canal. I explained that I also received the messages in that way, even though Gabriel's lips were moving and sounds were being produced. Clearly, physical changes were also occurring in her.

She and I followed our customary procedure of taping and then transcribing my verbatim reconstruction of the discussion into the computer. We had never asked about taping Gabriel directly, because I assumed, and I believe correctly, that both the radiance that streamed from him and the telepathic element of his conversation would render any recording useless. Ariel was clearly in a different category, and she had used the police emergency line to convey her message.

We could not then imagine who would attack us or how or when. Are you now thinking perhaps "paranoid schizophrenic"? If you have a sense of humor, do you muse that even paranoiacs can have real enemies?

We stayed up late into the night discussing the sessions and what they might mean to us personally and to the world at large.

If the information were meant for humankind, as certainly appeared to be the case, how was I to disseminate it? I thought of Earl Dawkins, and said as much to Allison, for he was a man who surely was spreading the true word of God in the back country of Tennessee and perhaps elsewhere as far as I knew. How many others were there? Were we supposed to know each other?

Allison and I assured each other that we could not be experiencing identical and simultaneous delusions. Yes, the everyday still tried desperately to intrude and to convince us that such things cannot happen in a suburb of Indianapolis, Indiana, regardless of all of the evidence to the contrary. Of course, you do not yet accept that evidence, do you? Have you started to check some of the details?

Both of us grew tired early, and we went to bed around 9:30 p.m. Yet I couldn't fall asleep, and I soon discovered that Allison had the same problem. We knew things by then. I mean we *knew* them—that God is real and omnipresent, that angels and demons are real, that the human soul is real and everlasting, that humans possess the divine creative force and have created a universe with it, however misguidedly. Even so, the everyday continued to operate, and the demands of the body in this world were not voided by the possession of such knowledge. We still ate and drank, eliminated, slept, worried, shaved, plucked, brushed our teeth, and all the rest. And on that particular night, the worry seemed to have the upper hand on sleep. We talked and talked.

The smoke alarm shrieked. I had no idea how long we had been asleep or when we had actually managed the feat. The house should have been dark, but I could see the dancing shadows on the wall of the great room from our bed—and then I smelled the smoke.

"What's happening?" Allison asked in a daze.

I was already on my feet. I pulled on my pants, grabbed my wallet, and headed for the great room. "Get up!" I shouted. "There's a fire!"

As I reached the doorway of the bedroom, I could see that flames were leaping in my studio, where the painting of Ariel sat on the main easel, and that black smoke was pouring from the doorway out of the studio. Movement at my desk then caught my eye. A black-robed figure was lighting papers on top of my desk, papers that I knew immediately would be the transcripts of our meetings with Gabriel. The drawers of the filing cabinet had all been opened and ransacked. A second hooded figure to my left near the front door was sloshing gasoline from a can into the great room. He looked up to see me standing in the doorway and then threw the can directly at me.

"Get out *now*," he shouted to the man near the desk. I blocked the can with the bedroom door, but gasoline spilled all around me. Allison was already coughing from the smoke, and I knew that when the flames hit the gasoline in the great room that the entire room would explode in flame and suck all of the remaining air into itself.

I slammed the door closed and ran immediately to the low bedroom window, an old-fashioned and fragile wooden-framed affair that slid up and down with a latch in the middle. As I freed the latch and started to pull the window upward, it slammed down again hard onto the sill. Two big men in the same black robes were pushing down on it from the outside. Smoke started to fill the room. Allison slumped to the floor, and my throat began to burn. I grabbed a wooden chair at the side of the bed, moved back to the door, and charged ahead straight at the window with the legs of the chair pointing toward the glass and the seat serving as a shield. The chair and I both plunged through the window and bowled over both of the men. I kicked one in the throat hard, and he crumpled to the ground, gurgling. The other was rising when I hit him with an uppercut that knocked him over backwards and sent a shock of pain through my fist. A huge whooshing sound was followed by the front windows exploding in flame, and the entire great room became a roaring furnace.

Somehow, the bedroom door held, although the room was filled with smoke, and the door was burning. I took a deep breath and climbed back into the room. Allison was lying on the floor in front of the bed, unconscious and still. I lifted her quickly into my arms and carried her through the window just as the door gave way and a blast of hot air and flame knocked us several feet forward. My own body had protected Allison, but I could feel that the back of my clothes and my hair were on fire. I rolled in the grass and the earth and beat at my hair until I was sure that the flames had been stifled. Then I returned to Allison, bending close to check her pulse and her breathing. I could detect neither.

I heard the shuffling of feet in front of me. There were at least ten black-robed and hooded figures moving slowly in my direction no more than twenty feet away. My right foot ached horribly, and I thought for an instant that it must have been injured in my plunge through the window or the blast afterward from the bedroom, but then I remembered the words of Raphael after the encounter with the demon. Why had it not warned me earlier?

The black figures stopped about ten feet away from us. One of them took a final step forward.

"Do not expect mercy from us," he said in a low, rumbling voice. "You did not show any mercy to them." He pointed behind me, and I saw for the first time that the two men at the window were both burning steadily and intensely. Neither one moved within the flames.

"They killed themselves," I said. "They set the fire and tried to burn us alive. The fire chose them instead of us. Whether you espouse mercy or not, I pray that God will have mercy on their souls."

The leader spat heavily on the ground. "Do not speak of God in our presence, fool!" he shouted. "There is no God. There are only the nature spirits and the Great Mother. And, of course," he added, "our Lord Satan, who rules the earth with the Great Mother and commands the powers of the Universe. You pathetic fool! Did you truly imagine that you could harm Azazel and walk away untouched? Our master Satan has told us of the enchantment wielded against Azazel, who yet walks the earth despite your cunning. Prepare yourself to join the woman in everlasting flame, worm."

Those were his words—a bit overdramatic and stilted aren't they? I had concluded that they were deluded cretins, and I began to project the power of love surrounding my heart toward all of them. They stumbled backward as I bent down to start CPR urgently on Allison. Then the crashing of trees and heavy thumping on the ground announced that something else was approaching, something massive and terrifying. The rank of robed figures split in the middle and stepped to both sides as a ghastly vision pounded forward out of the darkness.

CHAPTER VI

MICHAEL

I stared in terrible fear at the bone-chilling personification of evil itself, exactly as he has been depicted by artists for centuries, complete with horns, cloven hooves, and all the rest of it. Standing at least fifteen feet tall, he was hideously naked, displaying the massive organs of a giant goat, his skin a gleaming black with reddish highlights on his face and scattered about his body. I fought back the terror rising in me with thoughts of love and all of the preparation that the angels themselves had bestowed upon me—as I continued the chest compressions on Allison, who had still not moved in any way.

"**That will not help her,**" he said suddenly in a loud but sibilant and utterly chilling voice. "**Nor can anyone help you.**"

Then I felt a sudden pressure inside my head, as if someone were actually pushing on the surface of my brain. It lasted about ten seconds.

The horrible voice then sounded inside my head. The creature's lips were not moving.

"**You have been protected. You are much farther along than I expected, but not yet so far that I cannot destroy you. That need not happen, Jacob, for they have told you lies, you know. Behold!**"

The demon spread his arms, and it was as if a giant film screen had opened up in the space next to him. Three-dimensional aerial views of the most beautiful places on the planet appeared before me in gleaming color—the Hawaiian islands, the lagoons of New Caledonia, the Austrian alps, Bermuda, Normandy, Norwegian fjords, Rocky Mountain lakes and valleys, the Socotra Archipelago, Big Sur, and so much more. One scene followed another in seemingly endless succession, and then the "screen" vanished abruptly, and I was back in semidarkness with the flickering light of the flames casting odd shadows on the demon and his followers, who seemed to be utterly frozen in place.

"**You see!**" he shouted in triumph. "**The earth is no place of degradation far removed from the glories of creation. They have lied to you. They envy you, Jacob. They envy me. This is our world. Behold what I offer you!**"

The bold aerial views again appeared before me, this time of the world's greatest cities—New York, Paris, Rome, London, Madrid, Tokyo, Istanbul, Moscow, Beijing—cities and wealth and power beyond imagination.

"**All these I will give you, if you will fall down and worship me**," he said with chilling intensity, staring directly into my eyes.

Oddly, the more he showed me of the earth and its great cities, the less otherworldly and terrifying he appeared to be. My fear began to ease, and my disgust to grow.

"Who and what are you?" I asked with as much calmness as I could muster. "On what authority do you presume to offer me the earth?"

At first, he simply stared menacingly into my eyes, and then I felt the strange pressure inside my head again as he tried to probe my thoughts. His whole massive body began to tremble, as if a tremor from the earth had passed through his feet and up toward his head and out into the sky above him.

"**I am Ahriman!**" he bellowed. "**I am the equal and more of Ahura Mazda and the ruler of this planet, you insect. Do you** not know your Lord? Do you not feel the power that rages through my veins and strikes terror in the hearts of humans? The Great Ones long before you bowed to me and worshipped my glory before they could even see me. Then men began to call me Satan, and they shaped me with their thoughts so that I might appear to them as I appear to you now. You think me evil, yet everything I have ever thought or done has sprung first from the mind of Man. I am You! We have inherited the earth together, not the meek, who lie as pebbles beneath our feet. You created me in your own image, and now I create you in mine. Did you not kill those two men in cold blood? Now fall on your knees and worship me—or die, fool!"

I cannot fully explain what happened next, nor do I expect you to believe me, not yet anyway. That, too, will come. I only know that the warm areas around my heart began to pulsate, and the loathing that I felt for the demon and the abomination of its acts upon the earth somehow began to soften into pity for the tortured souls that had created it in the first place out of their ignorance and their separation from God. The utter horror and unspeakable degradation experienced by humans radiated from the demon in sickening waves that threatened to drown my newfound courage in a spasm of vomit before I could act on it.

Instead, a new voice somehow boomed out of my very soul.

"LIAR! LIAR! You rule *nothing*!" I shouted. "You have no soul. The souls of humans leave the earth and pass where you cannot go. The beauty that yet remains on this planet flows from the grace of God, not from you. You are only a projection of what is worst in humans, and you cannot touch what is best in us. I did not kill those men—they died from their own act of destruction. *You* fear *me* because of the obliteration of Azazel. You know that if he can be obliterated, then so can you. You lied to those men about Azazel, because you fear what they might do when they learn that demons are not immortal, even one who calls himself

Satan. Repent while you can and hope to live a little longer—or die yourself, fool!"

At that instant, the earth shook, vomit spewed from the mouth of the demon in all directions, and the black-robed men, no longer rigid as statues, began to charge as one with hideous cries rising from their mouths and daggers gleaming in their hands as the fire continued to blaze behind me. I summoned every last flicker of love that I could muster for the spark of God that animates all creatures and projected it toward them with my gratitude to the Almighty for the life that he had given to me and for my time on earth with Allison, for I knew that I must surely die in the face of Satan himself.

Again, the men froze in front of me, some of them appearing to defy the laws of gravity, as they leaned forward on one foot in their zeal to kill me and serve their master and yet did not fall or move in any way.

At first, Satan seemed to gape in disbelief, as if he himself had somehow frozen them as before. When he finally accepted that I had apparently managed the same feat, he bellowed in a fiery rage and leaped toward me in one standing bound, spreading his dark and baleful wings as he floated above me and prepared to rip me to shreds with the glistening talons on his misshapen and grotesque hands.

I closed my eyes and prayed quickly, "Your will, Lord, not mine." Then I tensed every muscle in expectation of the slashing horror to follow.

Nothing happened.

Or at least I felt nothing. My first thought was that I had been killed so quickly that I must again be floating out of my body—until I heard the voice at my side.

"Vicious looking creature, isn't he?"

I opened my eyes and turned my head to the right and blinding radiance. There stood a wingless man not three feet away from me, about my height, bathed totally in impossibly white light, completely nude, exuding an aura of power and justice so overwhelming that it removed any thought of lewdness or incongruity in his lack of clothing or covering. You, of course, are free to read more meaning into this somewhat unexpected detail than it deserves. His laser-blue eyes shone intensely.

"What a waste of creativity," he said, as he looked over my head.

I looked upward myself—and reflexively lifted my arms above me to ward off the horror that floated there, unmoving and silent, its mouth spread wide with fangs exposed, claws extended toward my face, and the coldest eyes conceivable staring into the void.

"Yet it was all foreseen," he continued, shifting his blinding gaze back to me. *"With the knowledge of good and evil came the concept of evil and with the concept came the thoughts that generated the intentions, and the acts that followed reinforced the thoughts that eventually created this thing that plagues your kind to this day. What a waste."*

"Who are you? What happened?" I stammered.

"I am Michael, Jacob. It is my honor to meet you here." He knelt and bowed his head with a fluidity and grace that I had never before seen or imagined.

"No!" I said. "I do not—I cannot—deserve this."

"You have no idea yet what you may deserve, my friend. That is what is so delightful about you. Do you know that angels cannot feel pain? That we have no experience of doubt? That we cannot create? Ponder these things and then perhaps we can discuss which of us is more deserving of honor."

He then turned his eyes and attention back to the ghastly figure hovering motionless above us. *"What do you want to do with him?"* he asked.

"Please tell me first what has happened to him," I said.

"Nothing at all—yet. We have just stepped out of his time reference. That is all. Now tell me what you would like for me to do with him."

"Can you remove him from the mind of Man?" I asked weakly.

"No, that I cannot do," he replied. *"The thoughts of Man are inviolate, for that is the precondition of free will and the creation that stems from it. There is a temporary amnesia imposed on human souls when they function on the earth, but no thought is ever lost permanently. The only way to remove satanic impulses is to align yourself with God's intentions. That is accomplished for us through grace at the very heart of our being, but you must choose it and act upon it both consciously and unconsciously. No one will ever tell you that it is easy, for it is not. Nevertheless, it must be accomplished in order for Man's creation to proceed without the weight of self-destruction."*

"Can you destroy him?"

"I can destroy this one, but another will arise and another and another, until the cycle of evil action stemming from evil intention is broken through the power of love, mercy, and compassion. Are you at least beginning to understand what your task may be?"

"I know that I must proclaim this message somehow in a temple. I know that a wall will disappear in my mind just before it disappears in reality. I know only this much, Michael, and even that is unclear to me."

"What do you want to do with the men in robes?" he asked.

"Spare them, Michael, for truly they know not what they do. They have been seduced by the demon and their own devilish thoughts. Two have already died."

"You speak well. Those two are already repenting the waste of their lives," he said. *"They are forgiven. Let us convince the others not to waste what God has given them. Are you content that the demon should live?"*

I did not know how to reply. How could anyone not wish for the end of Satan? And yet, is he or his manifestation not also part of Man's own creation and therefore also part of God's?

"I am in conflict over this," I said honestly.

"And yet I am not," he replied simply. *"I also have divine tasks, Jacob, and the negation of such demons is one of them. I feel no joy or sorrow in this, as my own commandments are clear. Humankind cannot*

advance as it should while such creatures hold sway over the earth. I remove them, but only temporarily. You must keep them from reconstituting by altering the way that humans think. This one at least can serve a good purpose for the first time in its existence."

I am deeply ashamed to admit it, but only then did my attention fully return to Allison. "Will she recover?" I asked in desperation as I bent down to her and cradled her head in my arms.

"Your power grows stronger, Jacob. You have already restored her body, but her soul cannot yet return. Lift her and carry her to the side, as the lesson is about to begin."

Sheltered by the trees, we stood together with Allison in my arms about thirty feet from the spot over which Satan hovered. Michael's radiance dimmed dramatically. Suddenly the heads of the men began to move, and their eyes all turned to the frozen figure hanging in midair, while their own bodies remained locked in stasis. Just as suddenly, Satan landed heavily on the earth, slashing the air in front of him with his clawed hands, snapping his jaws, and flapping his wings wildly while his eerily high-pitched cackle rang through the forest and out across the lake. Several seconds passed before he actually noticed that there was nothing either in front of or under him.

"Now," said Michael, *"his own evil intentions and the inherent malice that drives him will destroy him—this time. I have made him believe that his own body is actually you, and he will mete out the bloody violence upon himself that he had intended for you."*

The monster's head moved from side to side, as he tried to orient himself and make sense of his situation. The men began to shout from behind him.

"Free us, Master! Free us!"

"Silence, fools!" he roared in reply. **"I must kill him now before he destroys all of us and all that we have built together. He grows much too strong."**

In the silence that followed, Satan scanned the area immediately in front of him and to the sides. Then his eyes suddenly focused upon his own abdomen.

"**So!**" he shouted in triumph. "**Now you wish to embrace my beauty. Now you wish to call me Lord. Now is too late, fool!**"

He plunged his deadly claws into his abdomen and ripped and slashed at the phantom that hugged him until the black liquid inside him began to flow from his body in torrents and solid masses slipped from the gaping holes onto the earth in front of him.

"Stop it, Master!" his followers screamed as they saw the earth in front of him turn black in the flickering firelight. "There's no one there. You're killing yourself!"

"**Too late! Too late! Now his body lies before me. Now have I conquered him at last. Now he dies before even knowing who he is. Now ... now...**"

He slumped heavily onto his knees and stared dumbly in front of him. His eyelids flickered.

"*Now, Jacob,*" said Michael. "*Now walk in front of him and then address the men after the flames strike.*"

I strode in front of the monster, still holding Allison in my arms.

The cold, dimming eyes managed to look into mine. "No, no," he groaned in agony and disbelief.

"Yes," I said loudly, so that the men could hear without effort. "Yes, now you have chosen to kneel at last. Now evil turns upon itself as it always must. Now you serve as a lasting example of self-deception to the men whose hearts you have blackened. Now you die kneeling before the two whom you sought to corrupt and bring to death."

The stream of black gore that still flowed from inside his massive frame had nearly reached the burning cottage. It looked so much like thick crude oil that I stepped several steps backward with my thoughts on the flames that Michael had mentioned. The fluid erupted into a foul, smoking fire that followed the rivulet back to its source and exploded inside Satan's body with acetylene-like flames shooting into the sky. His burning head and torso crumpled forward onto the ground with a thud that punctuated his demise and brought shrieks of disbelief from the mouths of his otherwise paralyzed followers.

"Address the men directly." I heard the words clearly inside my head, but I was certain that the others could not. What would be appropriate? I suddenly thought of Earl Dawkins and the Holy Spirit that spoke through him. I lay Allison's body upon the ground gently at a safe distance from the sizzling hulk that had been Satan/Ahriman and approached the wide-eyed men with confidence.

"This was no divine creature. This was no Prince of the Earth. There is no God but God, and He asks only love, mercy, and compassion from you—not hate, cruelty, and violence. If I, a man, can so easily destroy that thing that turns to glowing ashes before you, think what your Heavenly Father can do to or for you if He should wish it. Speak to the others. Tell them what you have seen. Ask for forgiveness from God. Return to the holy Scriptures. You have little time left to you. Go, brothers, and sin no more."

As my arm swept through the air, the paralysis lifted (thanks to Michael probably), and the men tumbled forward with the return of the laws of inertia. They clambered upright, dropped their daggers, and backed away cautiously toward the forest before turning and running.

Michael then stepped into view.

"Why did you give the credit to me?" I asked him. "Would it not have been infinitely more impressive and life-changing for you, an angel of God, to have appeared before them and destroyed the demon?"

"Probably so, Jacob, but is it not infinitely more devastating for Satan and those who worship him to appear to be defeated by a single

human being rather than an archangel? Quickly now—we must see to the woman."

I ran to Allison and sank to my knees next to her, finally giving her my full attention, and feeling sick for not having done more to protect her.

"You did all that you could," he said, standing above her and gazing intently at her still form. *"In fact, you have even reanimated her body. But it is not for you to recall her soul. This, too, may come. Know, Jacob, that you have been subjected to trials and changes that began on this plane with your conscious experience outside your body. You have accomplished much, and you have grown greatly in spirit. Even the amnesia that every soul must experience on this plane in order to profit from its lessons is beginning to lift from you gradually. Your tasks are daunting. You will be asked to unite the future with the past as you move forward in the present. You know that all time is coexistent, but the spirit moves through and among the instants of time and creates endless patterns of meaning within the fabric of existence. Your own pattern is far more complex than you can yet fathom."*

He also knelt next to Allison and placed his hand on her heart.

"Her body must be kept alive until you are truly strong enough to protect her soul from harm. Arrange for a place of security and sanctity for her body until you are conscious of your task and complete in your own being. She will lie under my protection. I must go for now. Use your dreams. Follow your intuition. Seek out the others. And, Jacob, come to me at Mont Saint-Michel on October 16. Mont Saint-Michel. Be well, Jacob."

One instant he was there in shining glory, and the next simply gone—no fading of light, no heat shimmers in the air, nothing. Then I heard the sirens and saw the approaching headlights. At least one of my neighbors had stayed up late enough to see the flames. Mentally I thanked whoever he had been for the act of kindness and wished nevertheless that he had minded his own business. How was I to explain the presence of two corpses and a smoking mass of putrid demon flesh?

* * *

The firemen got to work on the blaze, although the cabin had already collapsed in on itself. Fortunately, the flames had not spread to the nearby forest. One of them quickly examined Allison and determined that she was breathing. I saw another on the radio with an odd look on his face as he stared at the corpses. An ambulance and two police cruisers quickly followed. The officers would not allow me to accompany her in the ambulance. I sat on the backseat of one of the cruisers with my feet on the ground outside the open door. One of the officers knelt in front of me copying out information from my driver's license and then asked questions with notebook in hand while another stood upright and kept the door open. Two others knelt over the bodies in the distance, while the rotating headlights of the cruisers added a surreal quality to the scene. Surreal? Yes, I know. That is not a word that I should be using in this narrative, is it? To you, everything I have told you must seem surreal.

I told them the truth. I just did not tell them all of it. Two black-robed men had set fire to the house with gasoline cans while my wife and I were in bed. I fought my way through the window and subdued them. I had then carried my unconscious wife out of the burning cabin and encountered more of them. They seemed to hold the charred mass over there in awe. They were moving in with knives drawn when something seemed to stop them. They fled into the forest about the time that the fire engines had arrived. In my concern for my wife and the rhythm of the CPR, I had not even noticed that the two men had caught fire until it was too late to help them. No, I had no idea who they were. No, I had no reason to believe that there was anything human in the ash heap.

The policeman who had been standing at the door walked over to the heap. The white-hot flames had truly reduced the demon to ash. He bent over the ground a few feet away and then walked to the side a short distance and bent over again. He stood there several seconds with his hand on his chin staring at the ground in the firelight before returning to the car.

"There are knives on the ground over here," he said to his partner. One of the other officers joined us as he was speaking. "Those two over there were both carrying knives," he said. "I.D. too—charred but legible. I just called it in. Records on both of them, one of them for arson."

They all turned to look at me. "I think we can take you to join your wife now," said the one who was kneeling as he closed the notebook. He handed me back my driver's license. "You won't be able to leave town for a while. We will have more questions for you tomorrow. You had better contact your insurance company too. Do you have a place to stay?"

I thanked them for their help and advised them that I had worked for the department for several years as a sketch artist and that the chief could vouch for me. They looked at each other briefly, and the two who had been interrogating me slid into the cruiser quickly and drove me to the hospital.

I knew what to expect, of course. Allison was in deep coma. She had suffocated in the smoke. My CPR and perhaps something else had restarted her heart and returned her lungs to something approximating normal function. I accepted that the oxygen that they must have given her in the ambulance and the ongoing emergency treatment at the hospital had played their own roles in the survival of her body. I nodded politely and somberly as the doctor explained that the earlier lack of oxygen to the brain had caused the coma and almost certain brain damage, but I knew from Michael that her soul had left her body and that our chance for happiness on the earth depended on my ability to keep her body alive until the time for her soul to return had been fulfilled. Our roles had been reversed. Therefore a man leaves his father and his mother and cleaves to his wife, and they become one flesh.

The newspapers were filled with the story for days afterward. The hints of a satanic ritual at the scene and the likelihood of attempted human sacrifice were not far from the truth, of course. The police even traced the dead men through their friends to a vaguely defined blood cult with covens scattered throughout the country apparently. No arrests were ever made, however, and there were rumors that some defining event had shattered the unity of the group.

Police forensics had called in zoologists from Purdue University to help identify the remnants found within the ash heap—bits of bone and teeth, pieces of horn, and shards of hooves apparently. Even they were puzzled by the DNA results, and their best guess remained that several different animals had been slaughtered and cremated together, including at least one exotic goat and perhaps a water buffalo. No zoo reported missing animals.

Why me? It was known that I had become "obsessed" with angels and had attended so-called angel conventions on numerous occasions. Could the culprits have been so deluded as to take such things seriously? The *Indianapolis Star* ran a series on "Angels in America." I declined the interview.

I stayed at a small hotel near the hospital and spent several days in the beginning sitting next to Allison's bed and watching the slow rise and fall of her chest. My father and mother drove down from Chicago on the second full day after the attack. Dad and I set to work on the insurance and the re-creation of the paperwork that so often defines human existence in modern society. I had lost everything, of course, in the fire, including the painting of Ariel and the tapes and notes from the sessions with Gabriel. My father was far more worried about bankbooks, checks, deeds, and all the rest of it. I pretended for his sake that such things were important to me. To have explained why they were not would have caused him far greater worries—worries similar to yours, I'm sure. The truth shall set you free, don't you know? In my case, that will be literally true, as the wall in my mind is beginning to crumble as I look at the stack of paper in front of me. That, too, you will understand in time. Let us first complete the work though.

After one month, with my affairs back in order, and no sign of improvement from Allison, I had her removed from the hospital to a "place of security and sanctity," somewhat to the consternation of her doctor, until I proved to him that I was, in fact, a multimillionaire with the ability and connections to care for my own wife. Father Mark proved invaluable to me in this enterprise, not for the first or last time. I also bought and furnished a small apartment in Indianapolis, knowing that I would be returning there often.

And then? And then I resumed my quest to "seek out the others," to locate those who had survived certain death and returned to their lives with altered minds and new visions of their own existence and the way that life on earth ought to be. I had ten months before my appointment on the coast of France.

I returned to Los Angeles.

* * *

More properly said, I returned to Father Mark and the Holy Angels Catholic Church of the Deaf—and to Teresa. Why had Ariel chosen her to deliver an important message to me at a time when apparently I was not able to receive it directly? What was the connection between Teresa and me?

The flight was uneventful, and I was finally able to direct the cab to the right church. I had called ahead, of course, and Father Mark was waiting for me in his office. I thanked him again for his help with Allison and then got to the meat of the matter.

"Father, I need to meet again with Teresa. She has already been the key to my search, and I believe that there is something more that unites us."

"That can easily be arranged, Jake," he said, "but please tell me now, in detail, what has happened to you."

I had given him the broad picture over the phone, including the news of the attack by the satanic cult, yet I had been hesitant to mention the actual angels and demons that had inserted themselves into my life. Or had I summoned them somehow, all of them? Regardless, it finally occurred to me that if anyone could ever believe the entire story, then it had to be Father Mark, who had at least witnessed some of it himself. Moreover, as I sat across from him in his office and absorbed the quiet serenity of the church, Ariel's words as conveyed by Teresa came back to me strongly: *"He must go and stand at the temple and speak to the people all the words of this Life."* Was this the temple and Father Mark the first among the people outside of Allison to hear the words of my life? I told him everything—well, almost everything. I knew that the death of Satan, however temporary, would be too much, and so he remained Ahriman. I also sloughed over the identification of Azarias with Raphael in order not to compromise the likely ongoing work of the scholar, whose words I remembered so clearly: *It should not surprise you to know that I also have a divine task to fulfill—in fact, more than one. That is why I have been here in Washington, D.C., in the very heart of the New Roman Empire.* He listened patiently, wide-eyed and fascinated for over an hour.

"Jake," he said, "you have just described what every person of religion wants to hear and wants to believe. If all of this is true, then you give all of us renewed hope and renewed faith in the grace of God and life everlasting and the triumph of good over evil. You cannot keep this to yourself."

"Nor do I intend to, Father," I replied, "but it is clear that more lies ahead. I am to meet Michael again. I am to preserve Allison's body and prepare the way for her return. I am to reach a point where the wall in my mind collapses just before the wall in reality falls. I am to accomplish a divine task that must be of untold importance. I am somehow to unite the past and the future. Much of this I do not yet understand, but I do know that I am being shaped both physically and spiritually in order to accomplish all of it."

"Please allow me to inform my superiors of the miracles that you have described."

"Of course, you may, Father, but why would they believe you?" I asked.

He stared at me in silence for several seconds.

"But I have told them already, as you know," he said finally, "about the speaking in tongues and the vision of Teresa, and the Bishop and others are excited about meeting you and examining these things. Why would they not believe?"

"Blessed are those who have not seen and yet believe, Father, for they are blessed few. There will be those who question your memory of my night in the church and those who will believe that I do know how to sign. And others will say that Teresa's dream was only that—a dream. Let me show you something that should convince the hardest skeptic—and yet will not. Hand me any volume in your bookcase."

He wasted no time in selecting a thick book and handing it to me. It was entitled *The Lives of the Saints.* "Now name a page between one and five hundred," I said.

"Two hundred and forty-three," he replied.

I quickly flipped the pages to two hundred and forty-three. "Give me a few seconds please to read it," I said. It did take only a few seconds, as my ability to read quickly had also increased dramatically. Then I handed the book back to him and recited the words on the page quickly, confidently, and correctly.

"Father, I can read the entire book and recite *all* of it back to you in the same way. I can also recite our conversation back to you from the time I entered your office without the slightest mistake—both voices and even the pauses between the words. I have been changing in so many ways since we last met. I have been subjected to physical, mental, and spiritual trials that I would

have considered unimaginable before. I believe that I have actually been in the presence of God. I know that I have been
instructed and protected by his holy angels and that I have faced
two of the most ghastly demons ever to step out of the collective
nightmares of humankind and survived. Nevertheless, if I should
repeat the feat with the book before the Bishop, he will be compelled not only by the skepticism that is his by human birthright
on the earth but also by the very dictates of his Church to seek a
rational explanation for my 'talent.' There will be serious and sincere scientists who will label me an 'idiot savant' or perhaps more
kindly as a high-grade autistic, even though my talent is new and
can be proven so. No one in authority really wants the established
order to be dramatically overthrown, even if that is what they
profess to long for. Surely, the Catholic Church and all Christian
faiths long for the return of the Messiah, yet I tell you that the religious authorities of Jesus' time professed the same longing and
refused to accept Him. The religious authorities today claim that
all of God's truth lies in the Bible, yet it has been hammered into
my head that the Christian Scriptures—and indeed all scriptures—are filled with hearsay, emendations, faulty translations,
lost passages, and outright falsehoods. Why would anyone wish
to claim that God has already explained everything that there is
to know? Why is it suggested to us that prophecy is dead? Why
does any of this even matter, frankly, since Jesus has already
given us the entire Gospel in one short passage that no one ever
lives up to anyway? *'You shall love the Lord your God with all your
heart, and with all your soul, and with all your mind. This is the great
and first commandment. And a second is like it. You shall love your
neighbor as yourself. On these two commandments depend all the law
and the prophets.'* But I tell you that we must live up to it in order
to rid our minds and our planet of the evil intent that now per-
vades both. The message now is so simple that it cannot be misunderstood—or neglected without penalty: Love, Mercy, and
Compassion. In some way, the transmission of that message is to

be my mission, and I cannot allow the mildly curious or actively resistant to prevent me from fulfilling it!"

Father Mark was clearly taken aback and perhaps even a bit frightened at my outburst.

"Jake," he said hesitantly. "You *have* changed, my friend, perhaps even more than you realize."

"Forgive me, Father. I did not mean to startle you. When I speak of these things, the area around my heart grows warm, and energy suffuses me."

"Yes, but there is more. Let me turn off the lights."

He switched off his desk lamp and crossed the room in order to flick the switch for the overhead light. There was no window in the room, and the door was closed, yet the room was not really dark.

"It's subsiding now," he said. "Look at your hands."

An aura of light surrounded them.

"My face?"

"The same," he said. "Let us see the Bishop."

* * *

His office was quite different, as you might expect. It was located in one large corner on the second floor of a brick building nearly adjacent to a cathedral. The walls were paneled in richly worked wood, and there were large windows that allowed sunlight to stream into the space when the curtains were open. One of the windows looked out on to the cathedral.

Father Mark had told me that Teresa would be there as well, along with at least two members of the Bishop's staff. Nevertheless, I felt a surge of warmth and happiness when I saw her sitting on an easy chair in front of the Bishop's massive desk upon our arrival. She, too, had changed. If there was no visible aura around her, then there was at least a presence and a self-assurance that I did not remember from our first meeting.

A young priest had ushered us into the office, and I barely had time to shake her hand and tell her through the beauty of Father Mark's fingers how happy I was to see her again when the Bishop and a second priest entered the office to greet us.

I was truly happy to meet the Bishop, a mature man of indeterminate age with lightly graying hair. His handshake was firm, and his smile genuine. He was as tall as I and seemingly as fit. He radiated a robust physical energy and real human warmth and concern could be sensed in both the timbre of his voice and his steady gaze. He wore a suit and collar.

"I thank you all for coming," he said, after shaking everyone's hand and quickly accepting the homage of both Teresa and Father Mark. "Let us sit at the table." He waved us gently toward a lustrously finished and rather massive wooden table with six matching chairs in one corner of the room, directing Teresa and Father Mark to one side of the table and the priest who entered with him to the end seat next to Father Mark.

"Please sit on my right hand, Mr. Daniels," he said. He took the end seat to my left, and the first priest, apparently an aide, sat to my right. I smiled at Teresa across the table from me.

"This is not a formal inquiry, or an interrogation of any kind," he said, while looking back and forth at me and Teresa. Father Mark's fingers moved swiftly for Teresa's benefit. "With your permission, though, I would like for Father Sweeney to take notes of our conversation." Teresa and I both looked at the priest at the other end of the table and nodded our assent. He withdrew a notebook and pen from his pocket.

"Mr. Daniels, I am aware of the terrible incident with the sect in Indianapolis. Please accept my condolences on the harm done to your wife. It has been an honor for us to assist. And I wish to thank you for the donation on behalf of the Church. I also know of the car accident that nearly killed you. And Father Mark has told me of the events at his church and of the vision experienced by Teresa that has apparently been of great importance to you. I wish very much to know more about you and your experiences. Why should a young painter and police sketch artist be singled out for such ... unusual events?"

"Grace, Your Excellency. It has been grace that saved me from death in the first place and grace that preserved me in the attack on my home. And the angels, Your Excellency. Most definitely, the angels."

The Bishop stared into my eyes, and just the slightest change in the set of his mouth and the way that he then shifted his gaze to the table revealed for the first time a sense of pity.

"Mr. Daniels," he began. "I know that you have been through a—"

"Please forgive me, Your Excellency," I interrupted. "Before we go further, I must demonstrate something for you, as I know full well that what I say to you will strain your belief beyond the breaking point. Will you allow me to proceed with the demonstration?"

"Yes, Mr. Daniels, please proceed."

A massive bookcase filled with heavily bound volumes covered one entire wall of the office. "Please select one of the books in English, open it to any page, and then hand it to me."

The Bishop rose and did as I requested, again taking his seat next to me afterward. I read both of the open pages quickly without even looking at the title of the book, handed the volume back to him, and repeated the text back to him as he followed the recitation word for word with his eyes.

"Is it correct, Your Excellency?" asked Father Sweeney, who spoke for the first time.

"Yes, it is," he replied slowly. "Word for word, without error."

"There are others with photographic memories, Your Excellency," Sweeney continued. "Such things are known."

"But this ability is new to me," I interjected. "The angels have told me that it is related to my mission."

"And how can we know the truth of either of those statements, Mr. Daniels?" Sweeney asked.

"You cannot, not yet anyway," I said. "Your Excellency, I can also repeat verbatim every conversation that I hear. Listen, please." I then recited every word that had been spoken in the room from the time that the Bishop entered.

"That is impressive, Mr. Daniels," said the Bishop.

"And yet really more of the same," added Sweeney, who was beginning to get on my nerves.

"Are you the Devil's advocate then?" I asked.

"Something like that," he replied.

I looked at Father Mark, who nodded almost imperceptibly.

Then I stood up from the table and walked to the center of the room, turning to face the Bishop. "Please stand, Your Excellency," I said.

He did so, with his fingertips still touching the table.

"Your Excellency, I am going to project the power of love toward you. I know it as a physical energy that gathers around my heart as I concentrate on love for all of God's creatures and the whole of His creation. I can use it as a defense against the dark powers. With you, I expect that you will feel an emotional warmth and increased appreciation for the beauty in all things. If you don't mind, I will also turn off the lights and close the curtains."

"This is too much, Your Excellency!" burst out Sweeney, rising to his feet. "What have we to do with such parlor tricks?"

"Sit, Father Sweeney," said the Bishop. "What have we to do with anything that is more important than testing the possibility of new miracles upon the earth? Have you forgotten Teresa and the connection between them?"

I returned to the center of the room and faced the Bishop.

"Tell me if there is discomfort," I said, "and I will stop immediately."

I projected an enormous sense of love toward the Bishop and all of the good works done throughout the world in the name of Christianity, despite all of the evil that had also been enacted in its name and all of the false prophets and hypocritical priests and ministers that had sullied their oaths and compromised their relationship to God.

The Bishop suddenly lifted both hands to his heart and fell backward against his chair, landing heavily on it and nearly tipping it over. The priest who had sat next to me leaped to his feet and pushed aside my chair in his rush to aid the older man, while Sweeny looked on in horror.

"Stop it! Stop it!" Sweeney shouted finally.

The Bishop raised one hand and said weakly, "No. No, this is not pain. This is love as we are intended to feel it. Sweet Mother of God, look at the crucifix." He pointed toward the wall, where a small carved wooden crucifix with Jesus hanging upon it rested in utter simplicity and glory. Tears streamed down the Bishop's face as he stared at the carving, a gift, I learned later, from his mother when he was a seminarian.

Sweeney turned his eyes from the crucifix back to me. "You will stop whatever you are doing, now!" he shouted.

My intention was simply to soften the man's heart and allow him to feel the same renewed sense of grace and beauty that were reflected so clearly in the Bishop's tears. As soon as I projected the same sense of love in his direction, however, he was lifted from his chair and slammed against the wall, his feet dangling several inches above the floor and his arms outstretched on each side in frightful imitation of the man on the cross not three feet away from him.

I was as much surprised and disturbed as anyone, until I saw the look of fear and hatred in his eyes. I felt myself tugged into them as he struggled and flailed against the invisible spikes that held him to the wall. "Help me! Help me!" he screamed.

And then I was somehow inside a holographic scene in sharp color and three dimensions. Sweeney was taking off his cassock in a small room and speaking to a curly-haired altar boy in front of him. "You know that God wants us to love each other," he said. "He wants us to help each other and bring each other joy. Now you are old enough to experience the secret of physical love and how it brings us closer to each other and to God." He continued to strip away his clothing. "Now I want you to hold something for me, as I will hold something for you, and we can together feel the joy of love rising within us." As he stepped out of his shorts, the same tug pulled on me in reverse, and I found myself back in the Bishop's office as Sweeney squirmed on the wall.

As I started to walk toward him, the other priest pointed at me in shock and said haltingly, "Your Excellency . . . he . . . he glows."

I looked at my hands and knew that it was true. Father Mark looked at me and smiled wanly, shifting his gaze back and forth between me and the struggling Sweeney. Teresa seemed preternaturally calm in the midst of the uproar, as if she had foreseen it all. The Bishop crossed himself and addressed me softly.

"Release him, please."

"Your Excellency," I said. "The man is a pedophile. He has forsworn his vows, and he has brought pain and misery to many. When he admits this to you, I will release him."

"Don't listen to him!" shouted Sweeney. "He is the Devil!"

"Lucky for you," I said. "There no longer is a Devil."

I stepped directly in front of him and posed a simple question. "Your God, your God, why hast thou forsaken Him?"

His eyes grew wide, and then they snapped shut and he bent his head and groaned. "The pain," he wheezed. "The spikes in my wrists and feet."

"You feel only the pain of your own guilt," I said. "I projected love, only pure love, not the false love of your own guilty and destructive pleasure. Confess this now or be consumed in the guilt of blasted childhoods and ruined lives."

He continued to groan until at last he shouted with fervor, "Father, forgive me, for I have sinned against Thee and Thy Church and all of Thy saints. I tried to resist the lust but could not. Forgive me. Forgive me, Jesus, My Lord. Forgive my trespasses as I forgive those who trespass against me. Please bring me peace. Please bring peace to the boys. Please forgive me, my Lord and God. Forgive me." With that, he simply hung his head and wept uncontrollably.

I don't really know what happened next. I remember that I felt a surge of pity for the man, and I heard in my mind the words of Raphael in the guise of Azarias about the angels: *"And, Jacob, Jacob, they feel such enormous pity for creatures so powerful that they can actually choose not to do God's will and therefore bring such horrible suffering upon themselves."*

Love the sinner, not the sin. I felt a rush of love pour out of me for the man who had struggled against his own worst nature and lost—but not forever and not beyond redemption. I actually tried to contain the love in the fear that he would be tormented even more, but I saw to my own relief that Sweeney slid down the wall and collapsed in a heap beneath the crucifix.

All of us remained motionless in stunned silence for several seconds.

"See to him," said the Bishop finally to the other priest. "Take him into the cathedral and allow him to pray. Then take his confession. His duties here are suspended. Report back to me this evening." The priest and I lifted Sweeney on to his feet and steadied him. I opened the door, and the two of them slowly left the room with Sweeney's arm over the shoulder of the other priest, who held him about the waist. I closed the door behind them.

"I think that we can dispense with accusations of parlor tricks, Mr. Daniels," the Bishop said quietly. "Now please tell me what has happened to you and try to explain to me what you have become."

I related a shorter version of my experiences that lasted about twenty minutes, as Father Mark worked his magic with Teresa, who nodded and occasionally asked for clarification with her own signing.

"There is much more that I could add, Your Excellency, but that should provide you with enough background to draw some conclusions yourself. As to what I am becoming, I cannot really tell you. For the first time, today, and with no awareness of what I was doing exactly, I was able to look into another person's mind. I am still learning to control the power around my heart. I do not consciously memorize anything—the information is simply there for me to draw upon. The angels have said that humankind is in a fallen state and that our own misguided thoughts and intentions have created demons and other evil manifestations. Am I evolving with their help into what humans are supposed to be or what they once were before the Fall? I do not know. But the conviction is growing in me that I am to spread the message that Love, Mercy, and Compassion are the cornerstones of God's creation and that all of us must focus our thoughts and intent upon them in order to avoid disaster here on the earth."

The Bishop stared at the table in front of him before he spoke again. Then he looked up and into my eyes.

"Mr. Daniels, you will understand that I am overwhelmed by what you have said and by what I have seen this day. You will understand that even better when I tell you that the focus of our discussion today was to have been Teresa, not you."

It was my turn to be surprised.

"You see," he continued, "Teresa has been performing, for lack of a better word, what I believe we must call 'miracles.' I wanted to learn more about your first encounter with her in order to question her further. Now I realize that these 'miracles' may very well be reduced to insignificance in comparison to what you have told me and demonstrated before my own eyes. I actually thought that she may have been the source of your ability to sign at the Holy Angels Church of the Deaf."

* * *

The Bishop then said that he was genuinely too shaken to continue, both by the overpowering sense of love and beauty that had filled his chest and by the uncanny spectacle of Father Sweeney pinned to the wall and his subsequent confession of mortal sin. He begged our indulgence and asked that we allow him to pray in private. We honored his wishes, of course, and agreed to meet with him again the next afternoon. Father Mark drove Teresa and me back to the church, and the three of us joined together once again in his office after barely speaking a word in the car.

Father Mark began with a wry smile. "You were more than convincing, Jake." His fingers moved as always as he talked for Teresa's benefit.

"We shall see tomorrow, Father. For now, I wish very much to speak with Teresa."

She nodded immediately and smiled. Her fingers then moved rapidly, and Father Mark translated at the same pace.

"I saw you glowing in the same way in a dream last week," she said. "I saw you lift a Roman centurion onto a cross, and I did not understand the meaning. Now I do. I have seen you often in my dreams."

"I believe that we have the same guardian angel, Teresa," I began. "I believe that is why she contacted me through you at a point when I could not yet communicate with her clearly. When did you begin to have such dreams?"

"When I left the hospital after the bus accident," she said. "The time in the street doesn't count, I think, because that wasn't really a dream."

"I don't really follow you, Teresa."

"I'm sorry," she said. "I forget sometimes what I have told different people. The bus wasn't really going that fast. It had stopped to take on passengers near the corner. I was going to cross in the same direction that it was heading, but the light turned yellow that way and so I turned to my left to save time and cross that way first, but the driver had started on green and was going through on yellow. I didn't see him until the last instant. The horn blared, and then I was standing next to the bus looking at a body lying in front of it. I really didn't know that it was mine until several moments had passed. In fact, it seemed as if everyone was moving in slow motion. I felt so good, so free somehow, as if I had been caged for a long time. The body reminded me of the space suits that I had seen on television. I had no need for it once I was out of it, and I felt no attachment to it. I started to rise above the gathering crowd, and I felt such warmth and love enveloping me, and then everything froze and she was floating next to me ... and she said, and I remember this so clearly, she said, 'This is not your time, Teresa. Your work lies ahead of you.' And the next thing I remember is waking up in a hospital bed with a huge bandage on my head and a broken leg. They said that an ambulance had been returning to the hospital and that the medics had gotten to me almost immediately and stabilized me in the ambulance. They said that I had no pulse at first. But I really don't think that counts as a dream, do you?"

"No, Teresa," I said. "That does not count as a dream."

"But then I did start to see her in dreams after I left the hospital, and then I had the beautiful dream in color about you and the angel in the church and the message that I remembered so clearly. And I came to see Father Mark and then you stepped into the office and you showed me her picture. I felt so happy, Mr. Daniels, not just for you, but for me, too, because then I knew it was real and that death is not to be feared. And so I went to see my grandmother the very next day in Anaheim because she was dying of liver cancer and I wanted to tell her not to be afraid because I had already died and returned. And she really wasn't paying attention to me, because of the drugs, I think, so I just hugged her and told her that I loved her and that everything would be all right and not to be afraid. And her body gave a jerk after a while and she opened her eyes and said to me, 'What are you doing to me, child? The heat. I feel the heat.' And then she closed her eyes and slept with a quiet smile on her face. I told Mama what had happened and she thanked me for thinking of my *abuelita*. And then *Abuelita* felt so much better that she went for a check-up at the hospital a few days later, and they tested and retested her and they couldn't find any cancer. And other people heard about this, and they started coming to me, and that is the way it is today, Mr. Daniels. My life is good, and I am happy to see you."

She smiled beautifully, and I felt the warmth of it suffuse me. Then I turned to Father Mark and posed the obvious question.

"Why did you not tell me about this before, Father?" I asked.

"I promised the Bishop that I would not tell anyone, Jake," he replied softly. "There have been complaints about practicing medicine without a license, and the medical investigations of the healings are continuing. But, Jake, the healings are real. I have seen them. Teresa gives credit every day to Jesus Christ Our Savior and the Holy Mother for the works—and the angel, of course, who she believes was sent to her by Christ. I also believe that everything you have told me about your own life since I saw you last is real. I do, Jake. And I give thanks to the Lord myself every day for the chance to bear witness to the wonders that are occurring among us. Yet there is one thing that troubles me in your case."

He paused and seemed to search for the proper words.

"Please. You can say anything to me, Father. You have no idea what a comfort you are to me. I have never even told my parents about these things. Frankly, they would think me insane. My wife is in coma. You are one of the very few people who knows and believes. Please say whatever is on your mind."

"Then tell me, Jake, please. Why do you not speak of Jesus? Why do the angels speak to you of God and the Holy Spirit but not of the Son?"

"The angels speak of Jesus with holy reverence," I said, looking first at him and then at Teresa and knowing that his question arose from his very soul and that the structure of their entire lives depended at least in part upon my answer. "They repeat His words, and they praise Him for His love and His truth and for the Gospel that he brought to Humankind. More, I do not know, Father. He has not appeared to me. He has not spoken to me. This I do know: The angels insist that many of the details of the Scriptures are unreliable. They also insist that we look beyond the surface levels of the Scriptures and our lives alike in order to seek the symbolic and more penetrating truths. They give praise to the founders of all religions if the principles at their most fundamental levels are Love, Mercy, and Compassion. I have to tell you that I have even less understanding of the Holy Spirit, even though I have felt its power and its reality. But what is it—an entity in itself, a projection of God's presence? Nor could I ever understand the concept of the Trinity or even the need for the concept in Christianity. Can we not simply honor the anguish of the man on the cross who asks, *'My God, My God, why hast Thou forsaken me?'* and then celebrate His victory as He *'was taken up into heaven, and sat down at the right hand of God'*? Yet I do not wish to shake your faith, even if I could. I honor it, Father, as I honor you, and you, Teresa, and all people of good will who find their own way to God's truths. I can best show my own reverence for Jesus by following what I now believe to have been not only accurately recorded throughout the centuries but which contains all of His message that is essential to us: *'You shall love the Lord your God with all your heart, and with all your soul, and with all your mind. This is the great and first commandment. And a second is like it. You shall love your neighbor as yourself. On these two commandments depend all the law and the prophets.'* Theological argument beyond that is speculation and doctrinal reaching by people who were not witness to the events, including Paul. Forgive me, Father, if I have offended you in any way. I have pondered this question myself, and I can only tell you the truth as I know it."

"You need no forgiveness from me, Jake," he said. "Let us pray in Jesus' name and give thanks to God for the glory that now attends us."

And we did.

* * *

The Bishop had fully recovered. We all sat again at the heavy table, with a different priest sitting in Father Sweeney's place, pen and notebook in hand.

"Thank you for coming again today," the Bishop said, looking at each of us in turn and settling his gaze on me. "I wish to begin by offering a prayer of thanksgiving as well as a request for divine guidance—and protection."

I could not really blame him, I suppose. The new priest looked at me with undisguised suspicion as we bowed our heads and shared in the invocation. Afterward, he got to the point—several points.

"Father Sweeney is resigning from the priesthood. He actually thanks you, Mr. Daniels, for helping him with that decision. He is also seeking both psychological and spiritual guidance, and he will receive both. I have spoken by phone with the Cardinal and with the Vatican at his request. I am to advise you, Mr. Daniels, of several things. First, regardless of the unexpected outcome of his participation yesterday, Father Sweeney was correct in saying that astounding feats of memory have been thoroughly documented by science. Such spectacular demonstrations as your own yesterday cannot by themselves be credited as evidence of divine intervention. Similarly, although I have expressed my reluctance to tell you this, there are examples of bioluminescence in the animal world that would appear little short of miraculous to the uninitiated. My colleague Father Martin, who will be taking notes of today's session, is an expert on poltergeist phenomena. He has, in addition, performed several exorcisms. I have myself witnessed objects flying off of shelves when I was a young priest examining strange events at the house of a young couple with a twelve-year-old daughter. When we noticed that the phenomena always occurred when the daughter was present, we determined that the inner turbulence of her physical maturation process was somehow responsible for the physical manifestations, in line with other poltergeist research. Within one year—and another year, of course, of her experience with the physical changes of adolescence—all such phenomena ceased permanently. But, as I mentioned, Father Martin knows much more about these things than do I, even though we both freely admit that no one fully understands them. Father Martin, would you comment on the boy, please."

"Yes, of course, Your Excellency," he began. "Two years ago, Mr. Daniels, I participated in an exorcism involving a ten-year-old boy. We do not do such things lightly—please believe me. However, when his language in English became so unspeakably vile and he began speaking in tongues that we were able to identify as precursors of modern Semitic languages, we agreed to perform the ceremonies in the hope that we could relieve the boy of the symptoms—and, in the worst case, to drive out an actual demon that may have possessed him. Unfortunately, the Church records contain far more cases of this kind than the public generally realizes. In the midst of our efforts on the second day, the boy, red-faced with screaming and sacrilegious oaths, simply shot off the floor and actually flew towards the door of his room some fifteen feet away, where he proceeded to pound upon it and actually smash through the wood before the three of us, all grown men, were able to subdue him. I was there. I witnessed it. I was a part of it. It has been hypothesized that muscles can contract and then release enormous kinetic energy under compulsion of extreme stress or emotional duress. There are many documented cases of ordinary people, particularly women, who have lifted automobiles or other equally heavy objects in order to free children or other loved ones trapped beneath them. Is this an explanation for the flight of the boy? Many would say so, but those many would not include any of us who were in the room. You will understand that there are those who were not in this room yesterday and who now know of your self-described encounters with demons who fear that you may also be infected. You should know that His Excellency is not one of them. Nor obviously is Father Mark or Teresa. I am here as a neutral observer."

"Thank you, Father Martin," said the Bishop. "You have probably said more than our colleagues would have wished in regard to my own position, yet I am personally grateful to you for having done so. Mr. Daniels, you are not a Catholic, are you?"

"No, Your Excellency, I am not. I was brought up by my mother as a Methodist, but I must admit to you that I have not been a particularly religious person—that is, not until some two years ago, when I first left my body and encountered the angel Ariel."

"And how can you be sure that she was an angel and not a demon?"

"Because she is the same angel who has guided Teresa and a preacher in Tennessee and very likely a host of others throughout the world, Your Excellency. Moreover, she directed me to Raphael, and from him to Gabriel, and from him to Michael. They all speak of God's love for humankind and of Love, Mercy, and Compassion as the cornerstones of existence. They have also destroyed two loathsome demons in my presence. These are God's angels, Your Excellency, Messengers of the Almighty, certainly not His enemies, or ours."

"And why have they chosen you, Mr. Daniels?" asked Father Martin. "Why a painter from Indianapolis?

"I do not know the answer to that, Your Excellency. I have wondered about it often. I cannot and do not in any way compare myself to those in the past who are now revered. But, if the various Scriptures are correct, why should God choose a shepherd from Midian who committed a cold-blooded and calculated murder to be the savior of His chosen people? Why a carpenter from Nazareth? Why a merchant from Mecca? Why a farm boy from Palmyra? Or should you deny the Scriptures, and, if so, where do you begin and where do you end, and why? I can tell you, though, what I believe has happened to Teresa and me and many others. I believe that those who have survived their own deaths have existed for a time in a place between worlds, and that, when they return, they bring back with them some of the knowledge and the power of that other world. They also no longer fear death, and they wish to help others. And as we speak about this, suddenly I know where I can find them. I thank you for this, Your Excellency, for I have been wandering without direction until now."

"Do you care to explain that further, Mr. Daniels?"

"No, not now, not yet."

"Can you truly look into my mind?" asked Father Martin.

"Probably, yes, although this is new to me, and I do not wish to experiment on others."

"Yet I give you permission to do so with me. I need to confirm that this is true—that you looked into Father Sweeney's mind and found the dark secrets festering there. My powers of concentration are good. I will focus upon a memory that is important to me. Will you do this for me?"

I did not have time to answer. Suddenly, I was again inside a colorful hologram. I saw a much younger Father Martin in blue jeans sitting beneath a tree with spreading branches on a bright sunny day and an attractive young woman perhaps in her late

teens speaking to him and handing him a ring. "I do understand," she said, "and I do love you, Roger. It is your sincerity
and the love of God that flows within you that makes me love
you, I think. It hurts. It hurts badly in one way, but my respect for
you only grows in another. Please keep this ring for me and let it
be a symbol of our own love as you follow the greater one." He
took the ring, and the two held each other closely, and tears began
to flow, and it was much too personal for me to be there, and …

I snapped back into the Bishop's office. The echo of "Will you
do this for me?" still rang in my mind.

"She was very lovely," I said. "She understood your choice,
although it was very hard for her, and she gave you the ring. You
are a true man of God, Roger, and I, too, respect your choice and
your sincerity."

"Thank you, Mr. Daniels," he said quietly, "and is the process
really so fast then?"

"I seem somehow to exist within the memory and out of time.
I don't really understand it either."

"Are you then agreed?" the Bishop inquired of Father Martin.

"Yes," he answered. "The abilities are real, and I sense no evil
intent of any kind here. I actually agree with Father Sweeney."

"What do you mean?" I asked.

"He says that you are a man of God. He says that if he has any
hope of salvation, then it will be because of you."

That was unexpected. I still had so much to learn.

"Teresa," said the Bishop, looking at her intently and then
pausing. "What do you feel when you conduct the healings?"

She lifted her eyes from Father Mark's fingers almost immediately and then began to sign herself while returning the Bishop's
gaze.

"There is a warmth that begins in my heart and then flows
through my fingers," she answered through Father Mark. "I
didn't notice it much with my *abuelita*, because I thought it was
just the warmth of my love for her. But now, with the others, the

MESSENGERS

complete strangers, I feel it just as much, and I don't know why, but I feel that I love them too. Is it bad to feel such love for strangers, Your Excellency? I am sometimes concerned by the closeness of it, the intimacy."

"No, Teresa. It is not bad. I very much doubt that you are capable of doing anything bad. As Mr. Daniels has reminded us, Jesus tells us very clearly to do exactly as you are doing: *You shall love your neighbor as yourself.* Tell me now, Teresa. This power to heal—where does it come from?"

"Oh, from the angel, Your Excellency, and through her from Christ and the Holy Mother. This I know. And I tell those I help to give thanks to Christ and the Holy Mother, because they are doing the healing, not me.

"And why do you think that the angel that comes to you in your dreams is the same angel that has helped Mr. Daniels?"

"Oh, he showed me the drawing of her that he had made himself, Your Excellency. It was her exact image. There is no mistaking her—particularly her eyes—once you have seen her. And it is certain that the message was for him. Father Mark knows this also."

"And do you affirm, Mr. Daniels," he said, returning to me, "that the angels actually appear to be male and female, rather than neuter?"

"Yes, I do, Your Excellency. Certainly, in the case of Michael, he has left nothing to the imagination."

The Bishop raised his eyebrows markedly, and I could do no other but smile.

"Actually, that is neither here nor there," he said, snorting slightly. "I must learn to suppress my own curiosity. You should both know that the medical reports that we are receiving confirm the total disappearance of cancer in five of the patients seen by Teresa, including her grandmother. There are also two cases of renewed sight in the formerly blind, both patients having lost their sight through years of macular degeneration, and there are yet other reports of similar miraculous healings. A representative of the Vatican has been in Los Angeles for the last three months examining these events. The Pope is personally engaged. When we combine what we know to be true about Teresa with what we are gradually beginning to believe is true about you, Mr. Daniels, then there is little doubt but that we are witnessing the intervention of the divine upon the earth. I personally can only welcome such evidence, as it merely confirms what our religion has been affirming as the truth for the last two thousand years and more. There are others, however, who choose to insist that direct contact with the divine can only occur in the hereafter, not in the here and now. This puzzles me no end but does not really surprise me, for a variety of reasons that I will not get into now. As a good Catholic, Teresa has agreed to work with my office and representatives of both the Cardinal and the Vatican as we continue to explore the meaning of these events. You, on the other hand, Mr. Daniels, apparently happy heathen as you are, remain a … *puzzlement* to us, shall we say. Far be it from me to question God's choice of servants, particularly since the parable of the Samaritan has always been particularly meaningful to me. Tell me, please: Will you also cooperate with our more formalized inquiry as it proceeds?"

"Your Excellency, it is my genuine pleasure to meet you and your staff, and I count Father Mark and Teresa as my friends. Please understand, though, that the angels have said to me very clearly that I have a divine task to perform. They have never told me exactly what that task may be, but the knowledge grows in me that I am being trained to disseminate a new and simple gospel that in no way conflicts with the one by which you live. I have also been given information by Gabriel that by rights belongs to humankind, not just to me. This, too, I must somehow make available to everyone. As you know, my wife lies in coma. Whatever part of my life that is not demanded by God belongs to her. These are and must be my priorities. I pledge to you that I will always remain in contact with Father Mark if I can and with you directly on occasion if I have your permission—and your direct phone line."

"Both are yours, of course," he said. "Beyond this, with the concurrence that I have received from Father Martin, who is in fact the representative of the Vatican about whom I spoke, I am authorized to offer you the support of the Church with your own tasks as you proceed. It is our hope that you will in fact remain in very close contact with us and that some members of the Church might even share in the events that you are experiencing."

"Trust me, Your Excellency, when I tell you that I would not have chosen for myself, let alone anyone else, some of the things that I have experienced, including terror and pain beyond measure. You should also know that physical proximity to the angels brings its own problems and that special preparation by the Holy Spirit seems to be required for it. I now trust in the angels completely, however, and I have been given abilities to help ward off whatever new dangers may arise."

"How can we help you?" asked Father Martin.

"In two ways," I replied. "First, I would much appreciate it if you could provide me with a list of the most effective volunteer relief organizations in Los Angeles, those that provide direct assistance to the poorest of the poor and the sickest of the sick. If you can recommend me to their directors, so much the better. Second, I need special access to the main chapel of Mont Saint-Michel on the evening of October 16."

* * *

I had finally understood, with great clarity, as I spoke about those who had encountered angelic beings in the space between the two worlds and felt the direct power of God's love that they would inevitably seek to help others upon their return. They would have no fear of death or concern about their own safety in the most miserable circumstances. They would indeed have become *bodhisattvas* who had returned to the earth to help others in their suffering, even if they had not made that decision consciously in the higher planes. The sense of love that they had encountered required that it be so.

My own experience had been different. There had been no conversation in the between world—the *bardo* of the Tibetans perhaps—and no one had told me that my time had not yet come. I had only been out of my body long enough to see Ariel look into my astral eyes, and I was convinced that she had made a mistake in doing that. I pursued her until she finally allowed me to establish contact in the middle of a lightning storm that almost killed me again. I did not feel any new sense of love for humankind when I awoke in the hospital after the car accident. I felt sick and miserable, and I had more than I could handle in trying to cope with the pain. Why then did I find myself as an apparent student of the most majestic angels in the collective memory of humankind in preparation for what seemed destined to become an act of divine importance? My experiences had left me with no room for doubt about the reality of the situation—although you will not and cannot share that certainty, not yet anyway, no, not yet.

I had learned to trust in divine providence. That was enough for me, as how many other people had ever been able to say that with honesty? How many others had stood in the presence of angels and faced the ancient enemies with their help and survived? How many others had actually been in or near the presence of God, even if I could not remember it? What extraordinary megalomania, wouldn't you say? Well, you would be wrong. No, I was humbled to the point of despair, as I knew that I could not be worthy of any of it, yet I had to pretend that I was and keep responding to the challenges placed in front of me. I was reluctant to use the new abilities that had been given to me, as I could not control them completely and could not comprehend their full meaning.

Then I began to visit the shelters and the soup kitchens and meet the true saints and chosen people. I had been right, you see. The Bishop's office had arranged introductions for me with the directors of several of the most successful but highly demanding volunteer relief organizations in the City of the Angels. They were good people, but they were paid and paid well, as were the supervisors in the aid centers and some other members of their staffs. It was the volunteers, the ones who gave of their time and themselves, without receiving financial recompense of any kind, who interested me most.

No, they were not all survivors of near-death experiences, not by a long shot—but some of them were. And nearly all of them shared a belief in a higher power and in another life to come. They were not selfishly trying to ensure a comfortable spot for themselves in that next life, quite the contrary. They all felt that they were not doing enough in this one to help relieve the suffering that surrounds all of us when we open our eyes and allow ourselves to see it. They all felt vaguely ashamed that their efforts were "insignificant" or "poor" in some way. And they were not kidding or fishing for compliments, none of them.

So, yes, I went to the shelters and the kitchens, many of them in poor repair and all of them in poor neighborhoods. I was introduced to the supervisors and social workers as a researcher on volunteerism in the United States, an explanation that had the advantage of being true, as far as it went. They were happy to assist, particularly as it meant that I would also be lending a hand with the work as I gathered my data about the workers. And, of course, I really did gather data about them, because I was searching for those who had decided to devote themselves to the welfare of others as a result of some life-changing experience, preferably a near-death experience.

In the course of more than six months' work, I talked at some length with more than two hundred different people, most of them either volunteers or part-time employees who were not doing the work for the sake of the low wages. In fact, the work could be profoundly distasteful at times. There were street people with filthy bodies, open sores, and loose bowels who fouled the sheets and the very air around them. There were those infested with lice and fleas, and many who had found their way to the streets from mental institutions that had not found a way to help them.

I explained to all of the workers at some point in our conversations that my own life had been profoundly changed by a near-death experience involving an angel and that I felt a need to devote myself to God's work, providing an opening for anyone with a similar experience to reveal it to me. Of those two hundred or so people, twenty of them confirmed similar experiences with me. Are you surprised?

You should not be.

Yes, ten percent is high for the population at large. I expected to find a higher percentage involved with volunteerism and social work. Let us be conservative then and say that the figure for the entire population is only one percent, or roughly three million people in the United States alone. Can you grasp the fact that three million people spread across this country have died, however briefly, encountered the divine, and returned to help their fellow humans? All right, then, if you are unimpressed with my sample and/or my math, cut that figure down to one tenth of one percent and try to work with three hundred thousand people instead. The point is that there is a large substratum of your fellow humans doing God's work all around you under the conscious or subconscious guidance of angels without your knowledge or your notice. Add to this figure the number of genuinely religious people in the country who are running their own charities and social programs through their churches, synagogues, mosques and other places of worship and you begin perhaps to grasp the enormity of the power and impact of the supernatural in our everyday lives.

If you are still resisting the reality of it, then let me give you something else to ponder as you consider the relevance of all this to my own case. Of those who did not confirm a near-death experience similar to my own, almost all of them—with the exception, in fact, of only two people, both of whom were unusually reticent in general—*did confirm* some other supernatural occurrence in their own lives or in the lives of someone close to them. You can check this yourself at any time with anybody. I have confirmed it and reconfirmed it over the last two years. Sit over drinks with a friend, if you wish, and pose the question, or start reminiscing with relatives, or remark upon an odd occurrence with colleagues at work—the precise circumstances make no difference. The point is this, the crucial point that is almost always laughed off or quickly forgotten: everyone will bring up his own personal experience with the supernatural when given the opportunity in an atmosphere of trust. This is universally true of everyone who has reached the age of forty and most people younger than that, even though a few "hard-headed" souls will have to be cajoled into relating their own experience. And then eventually there will be silence and a few reflective "hmms," and then someone will change the subject, and the everyday reasserts itself.

You know this to be true. You will have experienced it yourself.

How then—unless you are an atheist so blinded by your own "religious" faith that you have closed your mind to the world around you—how then can you believe that I am the one who is insane here? Is everyone insane except you? That sounds very much like insanity to me.

When I returned to Indianapolis after six months in Los Angeles in preparation for my trip to France, I visited three similar shelters in the city just to determine in a small way whether there might be regional differences in regard to those who worked there. The shelters were smaller and cleaner, but the volunteers were much the same—good, idealistic people who wanted to help other people for a variety of reasons. Two of them had undergone near-death experiences. I did not visit the churches in that period. I already knew about Teresa and Earl, and I was certain that many others who had experienced contact with divinity would also have turned to their places of worship with new eyes and new fervor to help their fellows—and perhaps new abilities.

Do not misunderstand me here. I did not spend over six straight months in Los Angeles, and neither did I devote myself entirely to the volunteer organizations and my search for others who had shared my experience or something resembling it. In fact, I returned frequently to Indianapolis and to Allison's refuge in Indiana in order to be with her and confirm the health of her body. After the third month, the doctors began to wonder why there was no loss of muscle tone or deterioration of any kind in her vital signs, let alone the facts that she had developed no bed sores and could breathe easily without artificial assistance. She was simply a new kind of coma patient for them, yet the private medical staff that I had assembled was also influenced by the site that I had selected for her care with the help of Father Mark and others in the Catholic Church. No, I cannot tell you now where she is located, but that time will come.

There were also countless details of everyday life that demanded attention, even though my father was dutifully attending to most financial and legal matters. The money, in fact, kept growing astonishingly from the investments, due in part, I was sure, from his undoubted expertise, but also very likely for reasons that he could not yet comprehend. He and my mother also looked in frequently on Allison, who was an only child whose parents had died together years before in a private plane crash. Still, she had many friends and other relatives who wished to visit her while she lay in coma, as the story of the attack had been reported so widely. We advised them of the need for security in light of the ongoing threat of further attacks, and they honored our wishes to delay their visits indefinitely, particularly, I think, since they could not have communicated with her in any case. My parents, too, had become deeply alarmed by the attack and the harm to Allison, and they generally heeded my warning to them to keep a lower profile themselves and to protect the secret of her location, as I suspected that whatever network that connected the demons and led their followers to me in the first place would not have been totally disrupted by the loss, temporary or otherwise, of Ahriman/Satan.

In addition, I continued my research in the Bible and other holy texts on archangels and Michael in particular, both in Los Angeles at facilities provided by the Bishop and in Indianapolis at my carrel in the library of Butler University. Actually, I should not have mentioned that, but I do not think that it will help you much in any case.

The information, speculation, whatever it may be, on Michael is particularly voluminous. I had already reached a point, though, where my own personal experience was of far greater consequence than any material that I could find in books and manuscripts. Nevertheless, a quick summary may be useful to you.

In large part because he is mentioned as the leader of the angelic hosts against Satan and his minions in *Revelation 12:7,* Michael is usually considered to be the most powerful of all the angels, the very commander of the army of God. This is repeated in the Essene text "War of the Sons of Light Against the Sons of Darkness." His very name is said to mean "God's Likeness." I can affirm to you that the sense of power that I felt emanating from him was limitless. And yet, somehow, I had felt more at ease and comfortable with him than all of the other angels.

Catholics refer to him as Saint Michael the Archangel, although there is no indication or belief that he was ever human.

Nevertheless, rabbinic tradition has established particularly close ties between Michael and the human race. Many traditions relate that he was the first of the angels to bow down before humanity. He is said to be the protector of Israel (and later the champion of Christians and the patron saint of knights and warriors). He is spoken of as the teacher of Moses and the mentor and patron of Adam. Some believe that he continued to watch over the first family after the Fall, that he taught Adam how to farm, and that he convinced God after Adam's death to forgive his soul for the great sin of disobedience that led to the loss of Eden.

It is written that Michael has four great tasks in regard to humanity: (a) to champion God's people; (b) to fight against Satan; (c) to rescue the souls of the faithful; and (d) to accompany the souls to heaven for judgment, as with Adam.

The Christian faiths have ascribed powers of healing to him over the centuries, and several healing springs have been associated with him, complete with legends of his physical visitations. In fact, his apparitions have become the basis for several special feasts and religious ceremonies. Until 1960, the Catholic Church celebrated a feast in honor of the "Apparition of Saint Michael" that dated back to a military victory attributed to his intercession by the Lombards in A.D. 663. The most famous of his appearances, though, is said to have been in 708 before Saint Aubert, the Bishop of Avranches, in Normandy. Saint Aubert declined his request to build a church on the famous granite tidal islet until Michael convinced him by burning a hole in his head with his finger. (Biblical scholars may recall that Michael is mentioned by name in the Book of Daniel, in which a disembodied finger writes upon the wall before King Belshazzar.)

The first church at Mont Saint-Michel was dedicated on October 16, 710, although the Feast of Saint Michael associated with the dedication has been celebrated ever since on October 18. There is clearly confusion about the date, as October 16 still is celebrated by some as one of his feast days. There is no confusion about Michaelmas on September 29 in England and other countries, as it is still considered a day of hospitality and obligation for settling financial accounts. Other feast days associated with Michael include May 8, September 6, and November 8.

In sum, Michael is the supreme angel in most religious traditions and is even thought to be equated with Jesus or Adam in some. Islam regards him somewhat differently, as the second in rank after Gabriel, who after all delivered the Quran to Muhammad and was predicted by the Prophet to be the first to pray for him after his death.

My nighttime hours were filled with dreams, almost all of them meaningful. My conversations continued with Raphael and Gabriel, who offered continual encouragement and praise for my progress in becoming someone or something that I already was in some unfathomable way but had forgotten. Always, just as I began to approach the mystery consciously in my dreams, both of them would smile and fade away. Ariel appeared only rarely, as she advised me that she was always with me. It was Michael who dominated my dreams—and Allison. She assured me that she was secure and even joyful and that she only needed my presence to be complete. She praised me for the care given to her body, and she informed me that she, too, was learning to reconnect somehow with things long past and forgotten. The amnesia in her case was not even lifted on the astral level, although her spiritual knowledge was greatly enhanced, and she had long since made contact with her parents and others close to her who had "died." Perhaps more importantly, she assured me that Michael was watching over her closely in "heaven."

Yes, the progression of angels had led me at last to Michael, the supreme and nearly omnipotent archangel, as if my spiritual energy had been boosted progressively to the point where I could encounter him successfully and without physical harm. I knew full well that he could appear in any guise and project any level of power. Raphael's transformation from the seemingly human

Azarias to a gigantic holy warrior had left no room for doubt. Yet he appeared to me in my dreams as he had at the cabin—wingless, smiling, open-eyed, and completely nude. He was surprisingly congenial and completely relaxed in my presence, far more so than the other angels, as if we were old friends on a fishing trip together.

"Why can you not simply tell me what this is all about, Michael?" I had asked in one of the "dream" encounters. "What has been happening to me and why?"

"You are regaining the knowledge and abilities that rightfully belong to you," he replied.

"Why are you devoting so much effort to me?" I asked in all sincerity.

"Let's say that you represent a unique project of a kind, my friend, and that what happens to you is important to me and also to the One who sent me."

"And how is it that we are friends, anyway? Can a man and an angel be friends?"

"Quite remarkable, isn't it?" he answered. *"I bow to you in awe, and you are rightly wary of the power that God has given me, yet we are close. Memories should be returning to you."*

"Only flashes of some other place," I said. "A tropical area at times ... a vast plain at others ... sometimes you are there. I can't put it all together."

"You will one day, and, when you do, the barrier will lift, and past and future can be united. I will stand with you on that day. In the meantime, our appointment approaches. We meet in the chapel after eleven at night, thanks to the Bishop."

There were many such "dreams," and I knew that information was being relayed to me at levels beyond my consciousness. I concentrated on Raphael's injunction through the medium of Azarias: *"You must learn to see through surfaces at the reality that rests behind them. Remember that I have charged you with distinguishing appearance from reality. You do not yet realize that nearly every-*

thing that you can perceive is a symbol for something else and that almost nothing is what it appears to be. Remember that I have stressed this to you."

I was always so close to uniting my daily consciousness with the vastly greater knowledge that lay somewhere in subconscious or superconscious levels just beyond my grasp. It was intensely frustrating, yet exhilarating also, to know that answers would be forthcoming at some point, but not yet ... not yet. Perhaps only Tantalus could have understood, as he stretched out his hand toward the fruit.

* * *

I left for Paris from Indianapolis on a Continental flight via New York City on October 14, flying first-class, arriving on the morning of October 15 at Charles de Gaulle Airport and almost immediately stepping into a rented Mercedes. I wanted to be as relaxed and alert as possible for the encounter the next day, and there are some things that money *can* provide. The drive to and through Normandy was a pure delight, just as charming and beautiful as I had imagined. Normandy itself always affects Americans in the same way: The beauty of the landscape mingles with thoughts of the horrific sacrifices made on the beaches below the coastal cliffs to create a mood of thoughtful contemplation mixed with gratitude for those who fought and defeated the Nazi regime.

My own thoughts were conflicted, though, as I tried to reconcile the blood and death in what everyone agrees was a truly "just war" with the simple injunction "Thou shalt not kill" and the instinctively difficult one, "Turn the other cheek." I knew full well that I could take the life of a man on the verge of machine-gunning a group of children, whether in wartime or civilian life, as I could certainly justify to myself the loss of one twisted life in order to save many innocent ones. Yet once the injunction is broken, regardless of the circumstances, where does one draw the line morally? At what point does an individual decide that someone must die to prevent the *hypothetical* or even *likely* loss of innocent life in the future? At what point does a regime cross the line into corruption when it orders a deadly attack against those who *might* kill its people? Did the destruction of Hiroshima and Nagasaki save more lives than it cost? Almost certainly. Almost? Was I really certain in the first place that the machine gunner would pull the trigger? Would revenge be justification enough for his death afterward if he had pulled the trigger? Gabriel had said that there is never justification for killing.

There are some places on the earth that exceed the promises of the travel posters and the guidebooks. Mont Saint-Michel is one of them. It is, of course, the Mount of Saint Michael, a rocky islet about one kilometer from the mainland, one kilometer in diameter, and about eighty meters high. It is connected to the mainland by a causeway today, but many unsuspecting or unbelieving visitors in the past thought that they could easily outpace the tide on foot if they were caught on the tidal plain, only to be swept to their deaths by the rampaging water or sucked down into the shifting holes of quicksand that dot the surface of the plain. The sight of the abbey church rising above the isolated rock is spectacular whether the tide is out or in, but most visitors prefer the vision of Mont Saint-Michel as a true island when the tide is high and the water laps hungrily at its base.

I checked into my modest but cheery hotel about two kilometers from the island after a good five-hour drive, settled quickly into the room, and then walked to Mont Saint-Michel.

After reading as much as I could about the magnificent site in general, I had assumed that the meeting would be held in the abbey church on the site where Saint Aubert had originally established an oratory chapel shortly after Michael's friendly persuasion in the year 708. Arrangements had been made for me to meet with one of the Benedictine monks at noon on the 16th and then to be alone in the church from 11 p.m. until midnight. The order had been established there in 1017, but shut down in 1800. The mixed Gothic and Romanesque abbey church had been completed in 1520 and repaired frequently since then. The fortress itself had long since become a military stronghold, and it was later used as a prison until the French government declared it a national monument. In 1966, however, monks and nuns began to return and conduct services once again in the Abbey Church. The last entrance for tourists would be at 5 p.m., and the church would be cleared by 6 p.m. on the 16th.

Even though I had slept comfortably on the plane, the jet lag was beginning to affect me as I crossed over the causeway, marveling at the strength and symmetry of the merger of man and nature that rose before me, with the spire of the abbey church reaching for and perhaps literally touching heaven, yet with its base firmly planted in the great mud flats that surrounded it. The tourists would be speaking of the legend of Michael's appearance there before Saint Aubert nearly thirteen hundred years in the past, while I would be concentrating on the reality of his appearance there the next evening.

And tourists there were, in abundance, both on the causeway and inside the walls. As I passed first through the Boulevard Gate and then the King's Gate on my way to the Grand Rue that led to the Church, I succeeded—but only barely—in shutting out the noise of the crowd and the omnipresent souvenir shops by focusing on the stone walls and cobblestones that spoke to me of age and grandeur, of the great and successful defense against English invaders during the Hundred Years' War, of the piety and religious fervor that had motivated so many who had lived and died there, and of the Archangel Michael, who had invested one of mankind's treasures with both his name and his spirit.

I strolled upward, pausing frequently to absorb the atmosphere of the town and the inner walls, until I found myself almost unexpectedly in front of the abbey and the great church that surmounted the rock. I entered as a tourist, paying for my ticket, and exploring the colonnaded monks' quarters, the "hall of the knights," and at last the church itself with its Gothic and Romanesque arches and columns in stone rising above and around me in an atmosphere of solid and unshakeable faith.

Michael himself, or at least artists' renderings of him in both stone and oils, was a decidedly martial figure standing astride Satan and leading the angelic hosts in battle. I could not argue, of course, with the defeat of Satan, nor even with the emphasis on military prowess, as Mont Saint-Michel itself has stood for centuries as an undefeated monument to faith and courage in the face of the enemy. And perhaps that was his intention all along, or that of the One who had sent him to Saint Aubert, as I had to remind myself continually that angels are messengers, not agents of free will. Nevertheless, Michael's gilded likeness stood protectively at the top of the church spire and appeared to gaze out in pride over his domain.

By then, the combination of the jet lag, the long drive, and the steep climb to the church had taken their physical toll. I sat in one of the wooden pews before the altar and prayed in gratitude and thanksgiving for all that had been given and revealed to me. Thine will, not mine.

Then I left the church and began the downward climb, the energy draining from me with each step, until I again reached the causeway and slowly trudged back to the hotel and dreamless sleep in my room.

I awoke early the next morning, famished, as I had not even eaten dinner before collapsing into slumber on the bed, barely able to remove most of my clothes. After a fast shower and change of clothes, several visits to the breakfast buffet table satisfied me finally, and I again joined the stream of tourists that was beginning to flow across the causeway as inexorably as the tides that made it necessary. This time, I explored the lower reaches of the island and the town, using my guidebook to identify such landmarks as Saint Aubert's Chapel, a tiny structure at the base of the mount said to have been built by the Bishop in 708 after his encounter with Michael, as well as the Tiphaine Lodge built by the commanding general of the French army in 1365 for his wife, and the fascinating history museum, before joining young Brother Henri, or Henry, as he insisted that I call him in his impeccable English, at the entrance to the church.

Preparations had already begun for the Feast of Saint Michael at the church on October 18, and I thanked him for taking the time to meet with me as we strolled through the abbey. His robe and sandals only added to the atmosphere.

"There is no need to thank me," he said. "The request came from the Cardinal directly. Your purpose must be serious, Mr. Daniels. It is an honor for me to assist."

"I would like to be completely alone in the church from about 10:30 tonight, Henry. Can you ensure that will happen?"

"You may rely on me," he said. "I will not let either you or the Cardinal down. All entrances will be locked, and I will stand outside the front door myself after you have entered. May I ask a question, Mr. Daniels?"

"Of course," I said.

"Are you on a pilgrimage?"

"Yes, Henry, I believe I am," I said. "I believe that I have been on the wrong path for a very long time and that now I am returning to what God had intended for me."

"Are you Roman Catholic?" he asked.

"No, I am not," I answered. "Yet I can tell you that Saint Michael means as much to me as I'm sure he does to you. I believe in God and His angels, Henry, and I believe that He calls all of humankind to Him, not just those of a single faith. In fact, I do not just believe, Henry. I *know* that God and his angels exist."

"Your faith is strong."

"If you insist," I said. "And what has brought you to the Benedictine Order?"

He looked at me without answering for several seconds. "Fair enough," he said finally. "I usually don't talk about it much. There are two stories, you see. The first one is true but far from complete. I was a good student at the lycée, and I had a talent for languages, partly because my mother was British and I grew up bilingual, but I was orphaned at the age of seventeen. I was lost, really lost, and then I linked up with a kind of gang in Paris that moved up quickly from petty theft to actually breaking into shops at night. We got caught, of course, and I was on my way to juvenile prison when a friend of my father, a priest, interceded with the court and convinced them to release me into his custody. I was still a very angry young man, but the priest reintroduced me to the church and then to the order. I saw them helping people, people like me actually, and then I joined. That was eight years ago, and I have never regretted it. That's the story that I tell most people when they ask. The real story, the story behind the story, is that I had a vision, Mr. Daniels. I don't know what else to call it. I was attending Sunday mass, and the priest was speaking about original sin and explaining that all men are born into sin because of Adam's transgression and that only the grace of God through Jesus the Son can erase that sin. He was continuing to expand on that theme as I looked at the crucifix above the altar and wondered whether I, too, could really be forgiven for my theft and loss of faith after the death of my parents, when the cross seemed to gleam much more brightly and suddenly I heard a voice in my head, saying, 'Forgiveness is for everyone, for all the Sons and Daughters of Adam in their struggles and their misery as they join in God's creation.' It was something like that. Maybe a few words are wrong, but it was very much like that, and I felt that my own misery had lifted and that I had been forgiven. It is very hard to describe that feeling to you, but I wanted to share it and somehow needed to share it. I joined the order shortly afterward."

"You're a good man, Henry," I said after a few seconds of silence between us.

"I'm not quite certain why I told you all that," he said quietly.

"Perhaps because I have had visions of my own," I said. "Perhaps because a new day is coming for all of us, and you and I and others have already been given glimpses of it. It is an honor for me to know you, Henry."

"Thank you, Mr. Daniels. I'll be standing at the same spot tonight to let you in. The church will be empty. I promise."

We shook hands and I left, wandering by myself back down into the town, and stopping to buy one item at one of the many stores—a flashlight.

* * *

Henry was true to his word, as I knew that he would be. He opened the door to the church for me at exactly 10:30 p.m. It was lit, but only dimly in key areas. No one else was there. I had spent most of the afternoon and early evening back in my hotel room reviewing in my mind all that had occurred since the car accident some two years earlier. I knew that the angels that I had encountered were still watching me in some way, particularly Ariel, who did indeed appear to be my guardian angel. But I also knew that the stage had been deliberately set for Michael and that I had evolved spiritually at least in part in order to be safe in his presence. I considered praying for guidance in the church, but realized quickly that the appointment with Michael was designed exactly to provide me with such guidance. Then I remembered: *"Your Father knows what you need before you ask him. Pray then like this: Our Father who art in heaven, hallowed be thy name, thy kingdom come, thy will be done, on earth as it is in heaven. Give us this day our daily bread, and forgive us our debts, as we have also forgiven our debtors; and lead us not into temptation, but deliver us from evil, for thine is the kingdom and the power and the glory forever."* And that was my prayer.

I sat in the first pew directly in front of the altar, and I waited—and waited. As the minute hand on my watch crossed 11:15, I began to grow ever more concerned. What had I forgotten? What had I done wrong? I replayed the last conversation with Michael in my mind: *"In the meantime, our appointment approaches. We meet in the chapel after eleven at night, thanks to the Bishop."*

I suddenly realized that "the Bishop" might not have referred to the one in California who had been instrumental in granting me access to the abbey church at night, but rather to Saint Aubert, who had established the small oratory chapel on the same site so many years ago. Yet, even so, I should have been in the right place. I went to the front door and knocked loudly for Henry to open it.

"Henry," I nearly shouted, "what do the monks call this structure?"

"Why, the abbey church, Mr. Daniels. You know that. A few refer to it as a chapel, but for most of us it is far more than that."

"And is there any other chapel, undoubtedly a smaller one, anywhere in the abbey?"

"No, but there is, of course, the small Saint Aubert chapel outside the walls, but it would be dangerous to reach it now because of the incoming tide."

Thanks to the Bishop! Of course! I thought. I had seen the small chapel myself that very morning when the tide was out.

"Henry," I said, "we must go to that chapel. I apologize to you for the terrible inconvenience, but I need to be there before midnight. Today is the 16th. I must reach it immediately!"

"Mr. Daniels, I must warn you strongly against it. The water has already reached the base, and the fog has arrived with it. This is not a child's game."

"No, Henry, it is not," I said. "It is extremely important to me—and to the Cardinal, I might add—for me to reach that chapel quickly, regardless of the fog or the tide. Can you help me get there?"

"No, Monsieur. For your own sake, I will not."

"I understand, Henry, but I have no more time to waste. God bless you."

I took the flashlight out of my pocket and switched it on and began the steep descent down the staircase to the Grande Rue. The few lights that were still on helped enormously, but I was not so much worried about the walk through the town as I was about what might lie outside the gates. No more than five minutes after I had begun, I heard the flapping sandals behind me.

"You are crazy, Mr. Daniels," he said, slightly out of breath, "but I cannot allow even a crazy man to go down there by himself. I think the Cardinal would not be pleased by your death. I know the chapel well, but I do not have the key. Follow me closely. The danger is very real, and I think you may change your mind once you see it."

We walked quickly but as carefully as possible down the twisting street and to the outer gate. I had seen the chapel from above in the daylight situated on rocks above the mud flats but had not visited it. Even with the help of a bright half moon above us, I could not see it from the top of the stone steps leading down to the base of the island through the deepening fog, although I could hear the water lapping at the rocks below us.

"You cannot still wish to do this, can you, Mr. Daniels? The water has surely covered the sand by now, and the way is slippery and sometimes unpleasant even in the daylight and at low tide."

"Henry, you need not come with me any further," I said. "For me, this is a spiritual quest. I know it all seems very strange to you, but this is something that I must do. It is not something that you must do. Thank you for helping me this far."

I started down the steps, trusting once again in the guidance of the angels and what I believed was the unlikelihood of my death after so much training at their hands. Again, Henry followed, believing in … what? His duty to the Cardinal, his reverence for life, his vows?

"Please give me the flashlight and follow close behind me—and kiss your shoes good-bye," he said.

Water covered the sand below, and both water and sand tugged at our feet mercilessly as we reached the bottom and leaned against the rocks whenever we could and tried to see through the fog with the pitiful help of the flashlight. The water was cold and the fog dank. I slipped twice and fell to my knees, grasping for rock and fighting against the pull of the tide as it rolled mercilessly past the islet and on toward the shore beyond. I was soaked and cold and somehow *exhilarated* as we struggled together toward the invisible chapel somewhere in front of us perched on the rocks that had sustained it against tide and storm for twelve hundred years.

Henry turned his head back toward me and shouted, "You are crazy, you know!"

"And so are you, my friend, for being out here with me!" I shouted back at him.

The water seemed to be growing deeper, and the wind had started to blow. And then it all happened very fast.

Henry sank in front of me. Whether the sand had given way or he had slipped on a rock—I couldn't tell. I only knew that he had collapsed heavily and had slipped beneath the water. The flashlight was gone. The fog swirled in the wind as I dropped to one knee in the water and groped for him. He wasn't there. I ripped off my worthless shoes and dove into the deeper water. The current hit me immediately and yanked me to the left. I surfaced but couldn't see anything. Suddenly a blaze of light erupted behind me, and I could see his body lying face down in the water in front of me. I swam hard—two, three, four fast strokes and I had him by the hair. I yanked his face back out of the water and kicked as hard as I could toward the base of the mount and pulled with my free arm against the current. At least I could see where I was going, as the brilliant light illuminated the entire area, despite the fog. My feet touched the bottom easily on one of the kicks, but I couldn't yet stand against the tide and shifting sand and didn't even try. I kept stroking and kicking as hard as I could and focused on keeping Henry's face out of the water until I found myself on my knees dragging him by his arms and cowl into a sitting position next to me against the rocks. There was a gash on his forehead.

We had been swept back toward the stone steps where we had started. Brilliant light was streaming from Saint Aubert's Chapel from one small window on its side, as if a new and powerful lighthouse had just been erected there. I knew that I could lift Henry onto my shoulders in a fireman's carry and leave him higher up on the steps until my return from the meeting with Michael. Yet he looked in bad shape, and I wasn't entirely certain that he was still alive. I knelt in front of him, pulled his right arm over my shoulder with my right hand, propped him up enough to slide my left arm through his legs, and then managed to shift his weight enough on to both of my shoulders so that I could stand up, barely. He was not a big man, but I was already exhausted, and the dead weight and soaked robe constituted a very heavy burden. I set off soaked and barefoot in the only direction that might ensure his survival—or lead to both of our deaths.

Our one advantage was the light. I knew that it had to be streaming from Michael. It was too brilliant to be anything else. Yet the light did nothing to stem the sucking of the sand and the swirling water or cause the rocks to be anything but slippery and treacherous as I slogged ahead. Words from the past entered my mind: "The light shines in the darkness, and the darkness has not overcome it." Nor would I allow it to overcome me and the burden that I carried.

"He's not heavy; he's my brother" entered my mind, and I smiled wryly, as I wished it were true. Then I remembered that

Henry was, in fact, a brother, a member of the Benedictine brotherhood, and, in fact, my *own* brother—a man. I sloshed ahead.

Still more words from the past flowed into my mind: "My yoke is easy, and my burden is light." Then somehow the weight actually did seem to lift, and I made even greater headway, until I reached the spot where Henry had fallen. Was there quicksand in front of us? The water was at my knees, and I had no way of knowing. I did not dare move toward the water, and a boulder stood to the side, the very rock upon which he had probably struck his head. I moved forward cautiously and felt with the toes of one foot the upward jutting rock beneath the water that must have tripped him. Over the stone, slowly, move ahead, move forward toward the light.

Then the words to a popular song began to run through my head, and I wondered why it had not occurred to me consciously before: "Michael, row the boat ashore." I shouted "Hallelujah!" madly into the wind and bent my head forward against it, grasping Henry fiercely with both hands, readjusting the weight on my shoulders, digging my toes deeply into the sand, and slowly, slowly, inexorably drawing closer to the light, and at last actually standing on the stone steps that led up to the chapel, as the water lapped at my feet and tried one last time to add me to its long list of hapless victims.

I carried Henry up the rough-hewn steps to the door of the chapel, which swung open as I approached it. The light burst through the opening, and there at the center of it, sitting on a wooden bench and gazing at me calmly, was Michael.

"Stretch him out on his back on the floor," he said.

I knelt down on one knee and gently moved Henry from my shoulder onto the stone floor, cradling his head with my hand.

"Look at your watch," he said.

It was one minute to midnight.

"There were some who thought you wouldn't make it. I thought otherwise. In fact, if you had hesitated for even a second before diving after

219

him, you would not have made it—and neither would he. As it is, he will be fine."

At that moment, Henry coughed, and water ran out of his mouth.

"Am I still being tested then?" I asked with frustration and anger rising in my voice.

"By the way," he said, ignoring my question and my anger, *"I didn't save him just now. You did."*

"What do you mean?" I asked.

"I mean that you brought his dying body to shore, that the movement of his body on your shoulders helped clear his lungs, that the burst of brotherhood from your own body warmed his blood, and that you set him down right in the middle of the healing light. He will awaken at dawn. You rowed the boat, Jacob, not me. Well done."

I didn't know what to say. I just kept looking back and forth between Michael and the now peacefully breathing Henry, who was somehow completely dry. Only then did I notice that I, too, was dry and warm.

The adrenaline still flowed heavily in my veins, though, and I had not yet relaxed, even in the midst of Michael's radiance. "You knew that all this would happen?"

"There was a very high probability, Jacob, that you would prove yourself to be the man you were intended to be."

"So this was a kind of test, then?"

"Yes," he said. *"And the last one, actually. You are ready to fulfill your task, although the time has not yet arrived."*

It was a combination of things, I'm sure—the adrenaline, the brush with death, the accumulated frustration of not knowing what my task might be, and probably much more besides. In any case, I erupted.

"Michael! God be praised—please tell me *now* what I am supposed to *do!*" I shouted in exasperation. "And why are you sitting there stark naked anyway?"

We looked at each other for a few seconds, and then both of us burst out in the loudest, most energetic, soul-refreshing laughter that I have ever experienced, before or since. Do angels laugh? Yes, I am here to tell you that they do, or at least Michael did. I suspect that we give them a great deal to laugh about, and that it is far more likely that they are rolling around in heaven laughing than gently plucking the strings of harps. In any case, our laughter swelled and rolled and echoed off the walls in a timeless and infinitely cleansing way that left me weak and exhausted afterward and even Michael holding his ribs.

"Well," he said finally, still shaking slightly, "*I was hoping you wouldn't notice.*" And then the laughter exploded again, and both of us were slapping our knees and shaking uncontrollably. Even Henry's face had relaxed into a gentle smile.

Eventually, we calmed down enough for him to say, "*Well, call me sentimental, my friend. You can also call me the messenger and tester that I am. And you can call me the one who is here to provide some more information to you that will be important to the fulfillment of your task. If it is any consolation to you, Jacob, then know that you will understand everything just before the task is fulfilled and your amnesia breaks.*"

"Oh, yes," I said. "The wall in my mind will fall and then the wall in reality. But this means nothing to me in my present reality."

"*The amnesia **will** break,*" he said. "*Have you not yet appreciated what that means, my friend? Do you have any idea how few humans have ever walked the earth with their knowledge of the higher planes intact, and what an incredible gift this is from God Himself?*"

At that moment, finally, the full significance of what Michael and the other angels had been telling me actually penetrated my poor earthly brain. Whatever it was that I might accomplish would occur simultaneously or nearly so with a vast revelation that would leave me in possession of divine knowledge while still in human form. Gabriel and Raphael had already provided revelations, but my physical brain had not been able to absorb all of the meaning that they had tried to convey to me. I felt completely humbled—and ashamed. How could I have been so bold as to question Michael and God through him? I bent my head and began to weep in shame.

"*Actually, that doesn't really become you,*" said Michael. "*I liked you better when you were laughing. Don't you know that you have a bold spirit, and that it was God's intention for you to be created that way? Now listen to me closely, old friend, for this is the last time that you will receive direct revelation in physical form. The whole intention, after all, is for humans to create for themselves and bear responsibility for whatever they create. But you and your fellows have gotten so far off track with the demons and such that you need a little respectful nudging.*"

I remember so clearly thinking that Michael was not at all what I had expected from the inconceivably powerful commander of God's army. My spiritual energy and knowledge had been boosted vastly by the other angels to enable me to survive in his presence, yet he was by far the most "human" of all the angels.

"*Yes,*" he said, clearly having read my mind with ease. "*That is true. It was a bit of a concern early on, but I have expressed infinite gratitude to God for allowing this to happen. I have been with the human race from the beginning, you see.*"

I raised my head and stared into his laser-blue eyes.

"*You know that all knowledge exists in multiple layers, just as there are seven 'heavens' through which souls must pass in order to return to God. Each of those 'heavens' represents a different layer of spiritual meaning and of the very stuff of creation. In one way, we are sitting here in Saint Aubert's Chapel, but in another and far more fundamental and important way we are thoughts in the consciousness of God. Hold the awareness of multiple layers of meaning and existence in your mind as we look at the beginning of your race together.*

"Know, Jacob, that much of Genesis is true, although its symbolic levels have been largely misunderstood, and some parts have been lost and other parts falsely added. Nevertheless, it is no accident that it remains as a guide to both surface and esoteric knowledge among many of the great religions.

"In the beginning, the earth and the universe that you know had been created largely by human souls themselves when they still existed in the presence of God. However, their continuing creation and manipulation of energy into matter eventually led to selfish intentions that contradicted the intentions of God and led to their fall away from God and eventual capture in the densest levels of matter.

"Your scientists are correct in tracing the evolution on the earth of the physical form that was to receive the souls of humans. The souls of Adam and Eve did indeed occupy such forms when they were sent to earth to change the direction of human development, and they were located in a special area of the earth that has become known as Eden. But they were not the only humans on the earth, nor was Eden the whole of the earth. Has it never bothered you to read that Cain feared death at the hands of other men and dwelt in the land of Nod, east of Eden, and married a woman from there?

"These were the fallen souls that had lost their way from God and could only return to the first plane beyond it at their 'deaths' in preparation for a new attempt to reverse the corrupted direction of life upon the earth. God had pity upon them and sent the souls of Adam and Eve to serve as models of godliness for them on the earth and to help change the evil thoughts and intentions that had begun to create the demons that only encouraged further evil and a spiral farther away from God. I was sent to watch them and protect them as they matured in knowledge and spirit in their new environment—and to teach them the gift of farming intended for all of mankind.

"Their primary task was to wean the others away from blood and killing. At that time, men were hunters who traveled in bands to slay large beasts. The killing and the blood coarsened them, and the weapons they had created for their hunts became the tools of war and bloodshed

among them. It was foreseen that agriculture could replace the hunts and remove the focus upon blood, which had already led to human sacrifice under the encouragement of the demons, which arose themselves from men's own bloody thoughts and became the dark 'gods' that they turned to for help in finding their prey.

"God's commandment was clear to the two in Eden: 'Behold, I have given you every plant yielding seed which is upon the face of all the earth, and every tree with seed in its fruit; to you it shall be for food. And to every beast of the earth, and to every bird of the air, and to every thing that creeps upon the earth, everything that has the breath of life, I have given every green plant for food.'

"The 'forbidden fruit' was not fruit at all or any kind of plant life— it was blood, for it would be their task by their example with the superior physical and mental gifts that God had given them to change the course of human life on earth. Humans had steeped themselves in blood, first among the animals and then among themselves. They worshipped bloody imaginary 'gods' and sacrificed first animals and then fellow humans in blood ceremonies stemming originally from their hunts and later from their jealousies and hatred of their own kind.

"And, yes, there was an early form of Satan that had already arisen from the blood ceremonies and the depths of men's conscious and unconscious thoughts and intentions, and he knew that he and his kind would soon disappear from the earth if the experiment were to succeed and the lust for blood were to disappear. He waited with cunning until my awareness appeared to shift to other realms, and then he stood before them in Eden and revealed to them by the same visual imagery that you experienced at the cottage the other parts of the earth, where men and women feasted on meat and wore as clothing the skins of the beasts that they had killed.

"It was a test intended by God to determine whether even new and superior human souls could withstand the temptations and excesses of free will on the corrupted earth at such a far remove from His own continual presence. They failed.

"Or so it seemed. I found them weeping over the skinned carcasses with the skins arranged upon their bodies still dripping blood. 'We could not eat of it,' she said. Yet blood had entered Eden, and the lion could no longer lie down with the lamb, and the place of glory began to shrivel and the icy winds entered and they shivered for the first time.

"'You must leave,' I said, 'for you have chosen to disobey the Lord, and now much is lost because of your action.'

"And Adam spoke to me thus: 'Michael, how can we act against the blood and the corruption if we know nothing of it? And what of this strange being that showed us the things that had been hidden from us? Must we not know our enemies in order to defeat them? Is it God's will to keep us in ignorance and then punish us for our acts of ignorance? We could not eat of the meat. Yea, did we already repent in deep sorrow of the death of the beast before you found us.'

"'Yet have blood and death entered Eden because of your action. Go and be ignorant no more. Till the soil and multiply this knowledge upon the earth, though your days be long and hard and you feel the pain that has been kept from you until now.'

"And they left, Jacob. Hand in hand, they walked out of Eden and into a world howling with rage and pain and lust for blood. And it was God's will that I watch over them. And I sought out and slew the first Satan, as I have slain many since, for they are soulless beings filled only with evil and hatred for all that is good.

"The gift of agriculture spread, and the hunting groups disbanded, and the seeds of agriculture grew more than crops alone, as communities arose and towns began to take shape. Yet the killing kept pace, as the warrior bands reconstituted themselves like Satan himself in times of war and conflict. And Adam and Eve could not stay immune from it, as their own son Cain tasted the meat and lusted for it, not wanting to remain in the fields. When Abel burned one of his flock that had fallen from a cliff rather than prepare it for food, Cain erupted against him and slew him in anger with a stone, splattering his blood upon his own forehead. Thus did the first sons depart from the parents. Yet the pair lived *on and on in youth and superior gifts, for they were a new lineage sent by God to change the direction of humankind.*

"And I pitied them, Jacob—and admired them. They kept to the ways of God, and their spirit spread, along with the farming, as they radiated love in ways unknown to the others. Their love and their knowledge multiplied, as did their family, and true religion was born on the earth, though it soon evolved into misunderstanding and superstition after their deaths. I accompanied their souls to the Most High, where they remained without judgment.

"The Torah preserved the spirit of their existence and that of their descendants and many of the actual events, as well as symbolic wisdom that remains important today. Eve handing the fruit to Adam represents human progress on earth from hunting and gathering to agrarian life, as well as the female need for roots and community in raising families. The conflict between herding and farming that has often raged on earth was clearly defined in the altered story of Cain and Abel.

"You know now that the sacred texts are distorted. One of the gifts to humankind was the injunction not to eat meat and the blood that flows from it. The warnings were clear:

Thou shalt not kill.

It shall be a perpetual statute for your generations throughout all your dwellings, that you eat neither fat nor blood.

He who slaughters an ox is like he who kills a man.

"Yet the central injunction against blood and killing became lost in tortured dietary laws. The taking of life becomes easy when it begins with animals, and without the killing of animals, the killing of human by human would not have begun. And so many diseases reside in the blood, diseases known then and diseases known only now.

"Read the texts, however distorted. Look for the signs. There are codes and messages not yet deciphered in the multiple layers of the Torah. God has no name, other than 'I AM THAT I AM' as revealed by Moses. Yet he is given one in the text that your scholars in this time of English dominance now accept as Yahweh. What does it mean read back-

*wards except a repetition of His central commandment to pursue agri-
culture and use the cutting tools for crops rather than bloodshed?"*

Suddenly I was able to blink and look away from his eyes, and
I was far from certain that his lips had even been moving. The last
bit of information seemed so outlandish to me that I was ready to
object, when it occurred to me: Outlandish? What could possibly
be more outlandish than a sentimental, naked archangel in the
middle of the night at the base of Mont Saint-Michel with an
unconscious monk lying on the floor of a structure built eight
hundred years ago by a bishop with a hole burned into his head
by the very same archangel?

*"There are more things in heaven and earth than are dreamt of in
your philosophy, Jacob,"* he said with a smile in response to my
reverie.

With that familiar reminder of my own utter insignificance
and ignorance, I knew that it would be true insanity not to believe
every word that one of the most powerful beings in existence was
uttering or conveying in my presence. Oh, *you* are free, of course,
to continue to consider it insanity—for a short while yet. But I
could not and would not. And I vowed on the spot to become the
vegetarian that I had always somehow wanted to be.

"How could all of this have been lost, Michael?" I asked.

*"I am speaking of events that go back more than ten thousand years
in your time,"* he said. *"It is a miracle that anything has survived, so
do not be surprised by the distortions that have occurred."*

"Why then has the message not been reinforced?"

This time Michael stared at me with amazement in his eyes,
and I quickly realized that I had said something remarkably stupid.

"Let me take that back," I said. "I know that it has been reinforced time and time again. The question should be: Why has
humankind failed to heed the message?"

*"You had me worried, my friend. These are the words of Jesus: 'Woe
to you, scribes and Pharisees, hypocrites! For you build the tombs of the*

prophets and adorn the monuments of the righteous, saying, "If we had lived in the days of our fathers, we would not have taken part with them in shedding the blood of the prophets." ... Therefore I send you prophets and wise men and scribes, some of whom you will kill and crucify ...' So many prophets and wise men have been sent, Jacob. So many have been killed. What could be simpler than 'Thou shalt not kill'? What could be more direct than the Ten Commandments? Let us simplify the simple and say instead, 'Love God, and love your neighbor as yourself.' Since this, too, is so complicated, let us now say, 'Love, Mercy, Compassion.'"

He paused for a few seconds, never taking his eyes from mine.

"Why has humankind failed to heed the message?" he repeated. *"They are so caught up in their own illusion of reality that they do not understand why they are here and where they originated. The amnesia in the body necessary to profit from experience on the earth has been too complete with many of them, and they do not feel the longing toward their Creator that sets humans on the path to righteousness. The demons have grown powerful, and their influence is great. The inviolability of free will necessitates the option of departing from God's intentions. These and other factors are all part of the answer. Yet the time now draws near when all of human creation will lie at fatal risk, for God himself will be invoked as the agent of hate and evil in a time when irretrievable destruction is possible. Thoughts and intentions must be changed and focused upon love instead of hate and destruction. I will do my part in neutralizing the demons, and you will do yours in changing the thoughts. You have less than two of your years in which to complete your preparations, Jacob. You now have the abilities and the intentions that you need, and you must use the time available to you to perfect your use of them."*

Once again, though, I could not fathom why I would be in any way joined together with Archangel Michael in an effort to change the course of humankind. That made no sense. Yes, the angels had arranged matters so that I was "protected" and obviously capable of feats beyond those of most—if not all other—humans. But I remained very much a man, with a man's emotions, misgivings, and certainly failings. I had been truly blessed by God in the first place in surviving the accident. I had been doubly and triply blessed by the teachings and protections of Raphael and Gabriel, and now I apparently stood with Michael on the brink of a great effort to save humankind from itself before the fruit of its creation imploded under the weight of its hateful thoughts and intentions—and the encouragement of real, live demons. Why me? Was I supposed to stand on the sidelines and sketch the more spectacular events of Armageddon perhaps?

Michael interrupted my strange and specious train of thought. *"I actually wish that I could tell you that right now, Jacob, and you should know that it is more than odd for an angel to wish anything, since we are already totally at one with everything that is. Nevertheless, I feel what must be very much akin to what you understand as a wish. Yet you are still unprepared to hear the reason from me, both because your amnesia has not yet lifted and because the very knowledge you seek would probably render you unfit to accomplish the task ahead of you should you receive it too soon."*

He stood and took two steps forward so that his face and mine were directly in front of each other. He seemed to be exactly my height.

"By the way," he said. *"Aubert was not a man of strong vision—a pious and good man, yes, but not a man of vision. He had some difficulty grasping the concept of Mont Saint-Michel, confusing it somehow with the Tower of Babel and the reaching of humankind too far into the sky. After explaining to him twice that I was but the messenger sent to deliver the good news of God's glorification on the island and his own pending immortality in the annals of humankind, I took the step of placing my finger on his head so that he might see for himself the vision of this most beautiful site as it appears today. It left a small red mark, not a hole. You see how men exaggerate?"*

I couldn't help but smile at this small revelation. And then he placed his finger on my own forehead.

"The images will flicker and then settle into a single scene," he said. *"You will be looking at a probable future, the one that we believe you will choose, but it is certainly not foreordained. If you are not prepared, or if you choose otherwise, then this will not occur."*

Images flashed through my mind, pictures of fire and smoke and a great shaking of the earth and twisting objects falling from the sky, and then I saw the gleaming white temple and the multitudes spread out before and around it, and I stood in front of them and spoke to them all the words of this Life. The scene faded slowly from my mind, and once again I looked directly into Michael's face, but this time with more understanding.

"May peace be with you, my friend," he said. *"Close your eyes now and open them only slowly when you can."*

The flash of light that erupted the moment I closed my eyes was startling. I placed my hands over my eyelids and only slowly moved them away after about a minute. Even then, I could not yet open my eyes. Finally, after several more minutes had passed, I carefully squinted and looked up. Saint Michael the Archangel towered above me in full white and gleaming armor. I could not look directly at his sword, which gleamed with the very light of divinity. I realized once more that I had absolutely no idea of the power of Michael, let alone of the One who had sent him. My pathetic brain could not begin to grasp the enormity of my situation. I could only hope that my soul was better prepared.

The next instant, Michael was gone, and Henry and I were in a cold, dank, musty and unimpressive stone hovel. The moonlight flowing through the small windows set high on the walls barely relieved the darkness inside. Only the sound of water lapping at the rocks below reminded me that there was a world outside, a world that apparently needed my help. I sat down next to Henry and placed his head on my lap as I waited for the dawn. I remember smiling. I had recognized the temple.

CHAPTER VII

THE TEMPLE

*H*enry moaned and regained consciousness as the first rays of the sun passed through one of the windows.

"Where am I?" he mumbled, quite reasonably.

"You are in Saint Aubert's Chapel, Henry," I said gently. "We made it, thanks to you, and I was able to fulfill my promise to Saint Michael the Archangel to address him at night in this chapel on October 16, the original founding date of the chapel on top of the mount. I apologize to you, Henry, for my confusion and for the distress that I have caused you."

He rubbed the knot on his forehead, still groggy and uncertain. "I remember slipping. Did I hit my head?" he asked.

"Yes, but we were able to stumble in together. The door was unlocked, and we entered. The chapel has sheltered us throughout the night. Come now, let me get you back to the abbey and your friends. I will advise the Cardinal of your incredible service in the face of my own recklessness."

"And ... and how did you hurt your own forehead?" he asked foggily.

"What do you mean?"

"The mark, the red circle on your forehead," he said.

I was about to say that I was unaware of any red circle, when I remembered Michael's words about Saint Aubert.

"Oh ... oh *that*," I stammered, trying to find a reasonable—and truthful—explanation. "That is a reminder not to follow the shadows but to trust my vision even in the darkest night."

"Oh," he said in turn, not quite understanding but willing in his condition to accept any explanation that sounded as if it might make sense.

We walked together slowly through empty streets back up to the Abbey, where I left Henry with friends who were not altogether pleased with my explanations or my dangerous insistence the night before on braving the elements to reach Saint Aubert's Chapel. Their attitude softened considerably when I told them that I would advise the Cardinal of their extraordinary assistance in helping me fulfill my vow to Saint Michael the Archangel. Then I trudged one more time back to my hotel and stared in the mirror in my room with wonder at the red circle practically glowing in the middle of my forehead. I left for Paris the next day and my return flight to Indianapolis.

So then. We are drawing ever closer to the conclusion of the narrative and a return to the present time as you know it. Have you been able to draw any conclusions of your own thus far? Have you been able to separate delusion from reality, or is it perhaps a fact that all reality is delusionary, that the only reality that we can ever know because of the amnesia is the *Maya* of the eastern religions? Moreover, don't you believe at times that each of us must live in a separate reality based upon the acuity of our senses, the level of our intelligence, our own individual body chemistries, our native languages, and the countries and communities in which we live, not to mention the differing joys and terrors of our childhoods, and that it is actually the height of arrogance for anyone to subscribe to the notion of a single reality and a single normalcy, and that indeed the entire edifice of psychiatry is built upon the shifting sands of competing theories about the nature of the conscious and subconscious minds, not to mention the counter-intuitive revelations of quantum mechanics, which you know suggest that all reality is actually subjective and that each of us creates a new reality with every passing second and every fleeting thought? Don't these things trouble you as you lie awake at night contemplating your own fallibility and the intellectual and moral clay feet of Freud and the other idols that you have chosen to worship in your rejection of the existence of the soul and the Creator of us all? Actually, I know they do. I have entered your mind on several occasions. I have seen the fear of death and the ultimate terror of absolute extinction that lurk in the shadows there, shadows that you cannot dispel with your focus on work and awkward attempts at play. If this is your reality, it is certainly not mine. I do not share in your delusions.

By the way, my real name is not Jake Daniels, of course. I'm sure that you have recognized that by now. Much of what I have written here can be checked for its accuracy, but most of the names are inventions. I do not want this to be too easy for you. I want you to follow the trail, as I have followed the trail. I want you to show the same determination to find me as I showed in finding Ariel. Oh, if you visit the locations, pore through newspaper archives, interview enough people, you will probably be able to piece it together. At some point, though, your quest will become spiritual. Every quest at its root is spiritual. Then I will be content.

Yes, I wrestled with the angels, as did Jacob, and I also have experienced holy dreams. Yes, I encountered Michael, as did Daniel, and I have determined to walk in the way of God, as did he. And yes, I affirm the reality of angels and of the One who sends His messages through them. But no, my name is not Jake Daniels, although it suits the purpose of the narrative.

The name is actually not important at this point. What is important is that I returned to Indiana and checked all of the arrangements for Allison. I flew back to Los Angeles and reported the events that I have described to you to the Bishop and Father Mark—and requested that the French Cardinal be advised of my enormous satisfaction with the support provided by the monks and nuns at the abbey. I also made a donation to the Benedictines in the name of those who served at the abbey. Then I rejoined Earl Dawkins in Tennessee and attached myself to him as a kind of preaching apprentice.

Don't be surprised by that. The Holy Spirit was always truly with him, and the same guardian angel watched over both of us. It was then that I began to call myself Jake Daniels. I believed that I could be located by the most powerful demons but that human followers had no such psychic abilities. The change in name would at least slow them down and perhaps protect my parents and others from them. I did not fear the remnants of the blood cults myself, but neither did I want them to interfere with the final phase of my preparations, as I had seen myself in Michael's vision addressing thousands of people before the temple of revelation, and I believed that I would have no second chance to deliver the message that had been so thoroughly etched into my mind: Love, Mercy, Compassion. With these three attributes alone, any human could depart from the path of destruction without forfeiting his free will. I needed to improve my public speaking skills dramatically—or so I thought at the time.

Unfortunately, the demons were never far from my thoughts. I reasoned—and this was confirmed by Raphael in a "dream" during that period—that the power of human thought that had given birth to the monsters could then be turned against us, as they had direct contact with our minds and enhanced psychic ability inherent in the impassioned and emotionally charged thoughts of men. The "screen" that Ahriman had used to show me the views of the world was only a lifting of the veil into his own mind. He had tried to penetrate mine, but it had already been sealed against him by the angels. Michael had apparently used Ahriman's psychic power against him by shifting his powerful intention to kill me into a vision of me embracing him.

Michael had told me very directly that I should "perfect" the already enhanced abilities that had been given to me, and I had taken this injunction very seriously indeed with the memory of Ahriman in mind. I focused the projection of love from my heart and the positive force of my intentions upon the formation of my thoughts every day for six months. At the end of that period, I was able to enter the minds of others with ease, move objects without touching them physically, and formulate reasonably accurate visions of the future myself. In other words, the powers of telepathy, psychokinesis, and precognition that had been reported by humans sporadically for thousands of years were real and available to all of us but only rarely controlled or understood. Within six more months, these had become as natural to me as any of my other senses or movements. If I told my finger to move, it moved; if I told the chair six feet away from me to move, it also moved. My ability to heal others had also increased exponentially.

At the same time, I worked very hard to harness those abilities. I did not wish to slam anyone else up against a wall accidentally or spontaneously force someone to grab his heart and stumble backwards out of an excess of affection or good feeling. I also limited my peering into the minds of others unless I could accomplish some undeniable good with it. None of this was as easy as it may sound, but I slowly managed not only to strengthen such abilities but also to control them reasonably well.

There were exceptions.

Earl and I had agreed to preach at a country revival meeting in a huge white tent in the middle of a forest clearing outside of a town in central Tennessee. Earl had long since acquired a widespread reputation along the preaching circuit as an unusually powerful and persuasive man of God who could lift any audience onto its feet as he testified to the love of Jesus. I had gradually improved my own preaching ability to the point that the name of Jake Daniels had also become known in the region, not least among the AA groups that I also addressed, as Jake was becoming viewed as a powerful antidote to Jack. Much of this was due to the love that I could by then modulate and send out to groups at the required levels, as well as my ability to "see" many of the problems that had driven people to drink in the first place. Of course, the healings among both the church groups and those struggling against alcohol did not hurt our reputations.

Earl had been healing people unconsciously for years—"Hey, and he'll cure yur lumbago for yuh, too, if only yuh ask." After we joined forces, though, his conscious ability to heal had improved rapidly. Healings were becoming commonplace at our appearances. The word spread.

People filled the chairs from front to back with others standing at the entrance. It was hot inside, and women were fanning themselves. Small children scampered up the side and center aisles and in the space in front of the stage. Earl was still better known than I on the circuit, and rightly too, so it was my responsibility to warm up the crowd and put them in the mood to receive the Spirit and move forward for the healings afterward. This particular crowd needed no warming up—and neither did I. The combination of the heat inside the tent, the genuine religious fervor of the participants, and my own driving need to perfect my skills as a speaker created a critical mass of radiant energy that could do no other than explode at some point.

"Are you ready to feel the love?" I asked the crowd.

"Yes, we are!" and "Praise God!" and "Give us the Word!" rang out around me. And then I made my first mistake.

I had intended to send a low-level burst of love for God and all of humankind into the entire audience in order to increase their receptivity to the words that would follow. Somehow, though, my own excitement and the unusually high emotions of the revival participants sent the energy off the scale. Everyone in the first several rows sat up straight and rolled their eyes, several clutching their hearts with pained yet beatific expressions. Those farther back also sat up straight, as if a strong wind had blown everyone backward in their seats, and those standing seemed yanked erect. Not a single sound could be heard in the tent for several seconds. Then the outpouring began, first as a low trickle of sighs and moaning and then as a torrent of words and cries as the dam of inhibition broke right down the middle, and the people embraced their neighbors and praised the Lord and asked forgiveness of their sins, and many dropped to their knees in prayer and others began to speak in tongues. And then I made my second mistake.

I had been concentrating for months on duplicating the compelling power of Ariel's voice. Yes, the other angels also spoke in commanding and powerful tones, and I had no doubt that they could easily duplicate the *compulsory* effect that Ariel had demonstrated in her brief conversation on the emergency line, but they had chosen not to do so with me. In any case, Ariel had been my model, and I had been working to match the sharp but somewhat sonorous sounds of *utterance* that could snap any audience to attention and keep it there. With the tent in serious uproar and the situation threatening to deteriorate into complete and perhaps dangerous chaos, I decided that there could be no better time to harvest the fruits of my labor—or at least to determine if there were any. I spoke into the microphone.

"The Lord commands you first to love him with all your heart and then your neighbor as yourself. Come to the Lord!"

Except for those in wheelchairs, every man, woman, and child in the tent stood, held the hands of those closest to them and slowly started moving forward, knocking over folding chairs everywhere as they came. My thoughts were racing.

"May the lame and the halt come first," I said.

The mass movement forward stopped, except for many of those in the front rows, including those in the wheelchairs, who continued to move forward. Two men simply rose out of the wheelchairs and slowly walked toward the stage. One elderly woman carrying crutches in both hands reached the stage first and looked up at me.

"Can the Lord heal me?" she asked. "I cannot walk."

"God bless you, Sister," I said in my normal voice, still holding the microphone. "You have walked to the stage carrying your crutches. Look at what you hold in your hands."

She looked from one crutch to the other and then raised them both above her head and shouted from somewhere deep inside her: "I CAN WALK!"

The two men who had risen from their wheelchairs both shouted at nearly the same moment: "I CAN TOO! PRAISE THE LORD!"

More shouts filled the tent and tears were flowing and a great rustling sound began to rise around us, as I could see the enormous desire to move forward pushing against the command to wait and the toppled chairs everywhere.

"Fold the chairs and move them carefully to the sides, and be careful of the children," I said even more forcefully, and within minutes it was done. I then directed that they move forward and that a line of chairs be set up behind them for any of the ill or elderly who might wish to use them.

"God bless you all," I said. *"Now sit so that everyone can see. Make room for your neighbor, and don't worry about your clothes. God looks at the inner cleanliness, not the outside."*

And then I made my third and final mistake that day.

Everyone sat down on the ground peacefully in a huge semicircle around the stage and looked up at me and Earl. Several of the elderly sat in the chairs behind them but far fewer than I expected. I gazed out at a sea of wet eyes and tear-stained cheeks, mixed with awe-filled expressions and the bursting excitement of those who had already been healed.

I noticed a boy in the back with a crutch, a latecomer, perhaps ten or eleven years old, who was limping forward from the entrance. Now you have to understand that I was far from immune to the emotion that pulsated inside that tent. I may have sent waves of love into the crowd and used the power of *utterance*, but those abilities stemmed from the angels and the Holy Spirit in the first place, and it was surely the Holy Spirit that was effecting the healings, not me, and I was just as swept up in the emotion and the power of the Spirit as everyone else. A small voice inside kept warning me to "tone it down" and moderate the power. Of course, that small voice might as well have been talking to Niagara Falls, since I did not yet know how to control the power completely, and I was near the point of not caring, as long as people were being healed and drawing closer to God. The boy limped forward slowly and painfully.

My intention was certainly good enough, as was my *intention*, obviously too good, as I had only wanted to lift some of the weight from his leg and ease his progress forward.

"Join us up front, little brother," I said to the boy into the microphone. "There is always room for one more in the House of the Lord." The crowd turned their heads to look at the boy, and I projected a pulse of love toward him from the area around my heart.

He lifted off the ground immediately and then began to fly in my direction about ten feet above the ground, picking up speed as he approached me. I was almost as stunned as everyone else— except Earl, or the transfigured Earl at that point. I felt the jolt from behind me at the same instant that the boy stopped in midair about two feet in front of me amid a giant collective intake of breath from everyone else in the tent. I stretched out my arms, and he dropped into them softly, wide-eyed and amazed, but safe and sound, gloriously sound. I set him down on the wooden floor of the stage and told him to walk down the steps on the side and sit in front. He was halfway to the steps in the perfect silence that permeated the tent before he turned and started to ask for his crutch. Then he looked down at his feet and then at me and came running back to give me a hug around the waist.

Once more the crowd erupted into an emotional frenzy fueled by the height of religious fervor and the actual proof of God's power in signs and wonders never before witnessed by any of them or even imagined possible in the degraded contemporary world.

Cries of "Hallelujah!" and "Hosanna!" and "Praise God!" filled the tent and the clearing beyond the tent and rang out into the countryside surrounding the clearing. Many in the crowd were praying fervently with eyes closed and weeping. Some had collapsed and were twitching uncontrollably. Others were hugging and crying and apologizing and asking loudly for forgiveness.

This was intensely and intimately real. Do not dare to look down upon it and consider it as anything other than the expression of genuine love for God and neighbor and heartfelt remorse for stumbling along the way of life that it was. My own need to practice control of the psychic gifts dissolved completely in the emotions and ecstasy of the people writhing and suffering and rejoicing before me.

The noise was deafening, but I easily heard Earl's voice behind me. "Go unto them," he said. "Touch as many as wish to be touched. Give of yourself and give up yourself."

I turned to look at him and felt the same shock that Father Mark must have felt when he first saw the aura around me. Earl was glowing, and I fully recognized for the first time, I think, that Earl was indeed a blessed vessel for the Holy Spirit, which descended upon him and performed its works through him. It was not Earl who had stopped the boy in midair before seriously injuring both of us or worse, but rather the work of divinity that somehow watched over and protected both Earl and me.

I handed the microphone to him and descended from the stage to walk among the people, touching their outstretched hands and kneeling with them to accept the blessings of the Holy Spirit. Then the voice that arose from Earl spread its amplified message throughout the tent and beyond: "And Jesus saw the crowds and he went up above them and opened his mouth and taught them, saying:

'Blessed are the poor in spirit, for theirs is the kingdom of heaven.

'Blessed are those who mourn, for they shall be comforted.

'Blessed are the meek, for they shall inherit the earth.

'Blessed are those who hunger and thirst for righteousness, for they shall be satisfied.

'Blessed are the merciful, for they shall obtain mercy.

'Blessed are the pure in heart, for they shall see God.

'Blessed are the peacemakers, for they shall be called sons of God.

'Blessed are those who are persecuted for righteousness' sake, for theirs is the kingdom of heaven.

'Blessed are you when men revile you and persecute you and utter all kinds of evil against you falsely on my account. Rejoice and be glad, for your reward is great in heaven, for so men persecuted the prophets who were before you ….'"

Earl's voice—and yet not Earl's—conveyed the entire Sermon on the Mount with a power and precision that utterly humbled me and reduced my attempt to imitate the compelling power of the angels' *utterance* to the kind of trick that it was—at least coming from me, a man, a mere human, I thought.

The voice that entered my head was crystalline sharp and pure: *"There is nothing mere about being a human."* I looked up at Earl standing on the stage and detected the slightest hint of a smile as he gazed at me and continued to repeat the words of Jesus without notes or mistake of any kind.

So then, it keeps getting worse from your point of view, doesn't it? Now I lay claim to supernatural powers and direct communication with the Holy Spirit. The problem is that you have not thought through your assumptions. Or perhaps you are afraid to think through your assumptions, because, if you do, the world that you know will dissolve before your eyes.

If you profess any religion at all, then you are going to find instances of flying or levitation as part of your holy text and fundament of your faith, whether we cite the flight to heaven of Muhammad on horseback, or the experiences of Ezekiel, or Jesus walking on water, or a series of Catholic saints who floated in midair, not to mention the various ascensions, including Elijah and the fiery chariot, or countless other examples. And there are the endless prophetic dreams and direct conversations with God.

Of course, if you consider yourself a hard-headed scientist with no time for such nonsense, then you not only separate yourself from the overwhelming majority of your fellow humans, but you also lock yourself into a materialistic dead end that is crumbling all around you under the odd but undeniable weight of quantum mechanics. Oh, and there are all those troublesome and irritating results flowing steadily out of the Rhine Institute and other scientific labs studying the paranormal with renewed scientific seriousness and all of the other pesky "unexplained" data that just keep piling up around your ivory tower. Showers of rocks falling from the sky? Haven't we been through all that centuries ago when scientists *knew* that rocks could not fall from the sky—until something more was learned about meteorites?

Look, I now know how much of this is going to turn out. The very existence of this text has helped point the way, and I have been able to see the broad outlines of the future. Certainly you and I will find ourselves in vastly different circumstances. I wish you well.

In the meantime, just know this, whether you believe it or not, that the Holy Spirit is active and among us as promised, and that Jesus said that these abilities would be found in those who believe: "*. . . they will cast out demons; they will speak in new tongues; they will pick up serpents; and if they drink any deadly thing, it will not hurt them; they will lay their hands on the sick, and they will recover.*"

If you are a believer but not a Christian, then your religion will profess something similar, with or without the serpents and the poisons. There is no God but God.

I truly believed that I had made three serious mistakes at the tent revival, yet the results—lasting and spectacular—said otherwise. Was my very "training" designed to help others, regardless of the final goal? That particular revival sparked a renewal of belief in the region that is alive to this day and growing. Those who were there can testify to it, and many others will know of it. Those who were healed will only smile at your disbelief and still prepare a home-cooked meal for you before you set out on the road again.

The figurative road beckoned me as well eventually, as I felt the approach of the cataclysm for which I had been prepared, as well as a peculiar but driving need to acquire forested property near the West Coast. When the time arrives for you to believe all that I have written, that bit of information will not be enough for you to find me. I said "near" the West Coast, remember. That includes a lot of states and a lot of territory, even before you try to decipher my real name.

Anyway, each of the angels in turn spoke of such property in my dreams, and the visions of it came to me almost nightly. I was puzzled, but I had long since learned to trust both the angels and the dreams, which were almost certainly sent by the angels in the first place. I embraced Earl Dawkins as the brother that he had become and flew to California to begin my search for the rugged land that matched what I was seeing in my dreams. That also provided me with a final opportunity to brief the Bishop, Father Martin, and Father Mark in Los Angeles before the defining event that lay before me.

* * *

The by-then familiar surroundings of the Bishop's office felt comforting to me, as did the presence of the Bishop himself and Father Mark, who had already advised me that Teresa had been invited to the Vatican for further examination and a personal meeting with the Pope. There were only three of us at the table. Father Martin's chair was unexpectedly empty.

"Has he returned to Rome with Teresa, then?" I inquired of the Bishop.

"No," he responded hesitantly and in an uncharacteristically subdued manner. "He, uh ... is being treated at the hospital now for injuries he sustained three days ago."

"I'm deeply sorry," I said in all sincerity. "What happened actually?"

"There was an exorcism, a particularly ... difficult ... one as it turned out." He looked down at his folded hands resting on top of the table.

"Forgive me, Your Excellency," I said after an uncomfortable pause in the conversation, "but you seem unusually reticent. Should I not be asking about Father Martin?"

"No, no, Mr. Daniels," he said with a low sigh. "You are gracious as always. It is just that his injuries were nearly fatal and you appear to be somehow involved with the event."

"What?"

"You see, I know you fairly well now, Mr. Daniels, and I know what your reaction is likely to be, and I am not at all certain that your response will be of any benefit whatsoever to Father Martin—or to you or to the boy."

"This is not the same boy who flew in an earlier exorcism, is it?" I asked.

"Why, yes, it is, in fact, the same boy. How could you know that?"

"Father Martin never mentioned a resolution to the case. And, in the meantime, I have encountered a flying boy myself, but one who flew on the wings of angels, Your Excellency. There is a pattern here that disturbs me, particularly if, as you suggest, my own name has been mentioned by the demon."

"The boy—the demon actually—roared out your name as he attacked Father Martin and nearly ripped out his throat with his teeth. Two other men could barely pull the boy off him in time, and they too suffered bite wounds. They were forced to tie his hands behind his back and lash his legs together. Father Martin's aorta was damaged but not severed. He lost a great deal of blood and flesh. The boy is now in a padded cell, Mr. Daniels. He cannot be controlled at home, and he is clearly a danger to both himself and others. His 'spells' had diminished so greatly until recently. Then the evil language began again, and he started to grow violent. His parents locked him in his room and called my office. Father Martin was here, and he ..."

The Bishop paused and stared at his hands again.

"Father Martin is a brave man and a devoted servant of God," I said. "I wish to visit him, Your Excellency, and then I wish to— no, I *must*—see the boy."

"Father Martin cannot speak, Mr. Daniels, and the boy is foul and putrid beyond comprehension. I do not believe that even you can help them."

"Then the time has come for new belief, Your Excellency—not in me, but in the power that acts through me and that gives all of us our very being. I have advanced, Your Excellency, not through any merit of my own, but entirely through the grace of God as conveyed through his angels and the Holy Spirit. You *know* that these powers exist and that their source is holy. You have devoted your life to them. It has been given to you and to me to witness them in action on the earth, not just to speak of them and to hope that they are real. We must use this knowledge and convey it and expand it and exult in it and trust in the grace of God beyond all else as we strive to love others as ourselves. We can do no other, you and I."

"And I," said Father Mark, who had been silent until that moment. "I fear no demon, Your Excellency. Christ cast them out and transferred that power to his disciples through the Holy Spirit, which is manifest in this man and which I feel growing in my own breast in his presence. He has said and I believe that all of us can reclaim the holy power inherent in us and lost in the long descent from Adam. Please grant his wishes, and allow me to accompany him, Your Excellency."

"So be it," he said after a short silence as he looked back and forth at each of us. "I will make the arrangements. May God bless you and keep you both."

"And you, Your Excellency," I added, "for I believe that you must also accompany us. Father Martin will not be able to bear witness to the Vatican, but you can do so even more powerfully in his stead. Are we not here together for a reason? Am I the only one who feels the bond among us?"

I boldly, perhaps too boldly, placed my right hand over his as it lay on the table. He seemed surprised but not displeased. Father Mark stretched from his spot across from me and placed his right hand over mine.

The Bishop closed his eyes, placed his left hand firmly on top of Father Mark's, and said, "Thy will be done."

Father Mark and I said in unison, "Thy Kingdom come."

* * *

The two appointments were scheduled quickly for the next day, Father Martin in the morning and the boy in the afternoon. Father Martin lay in his hospital bed in a private room, unconscious and breathing through a tube inserted below his neck. The doctor explained that he had suffered not only injury to the aorta but substantial trachea damage and shredding of his larynx. They also feared permanent brain damage due to the aortic injury. He was heavily sedated and being fed intravenously. Near miracles had been performed both in the ambulance and at the hospital in order to save him at all, but the prognosis remained poor.

We stood around his bed together like comrades in arms staring at a severely wounded comrade on a cot in a field hospital—and this time in the oldest conflict of them all. I asked the doctor if I could touch him, and, as he hesitated in formulating the best way to say no, I placed my right hand on his heart and my left on his forehead, closed my eyes, and sent a surge of love and healing energy into his body. He shook so violently that the tube popped from his neck, and then he stiffened.

"Get away from him!" the doctor shouted, rushing from the end of the bed to push me backward.

As I lifted my hands, Father Martin relaxed and opened his eyes. Rushing to reattach the tube, the doctor stopped in shock. Father Martin looked about the bed and then fastened his eyes on mine. He lifted his right hand slowly in my direction, and I took it firmly in mine.

"We are going to the boy," I said. "You did what you could, my friend. We will complete your work."

"He called your name," he whispered just loud enough for all of us to hear. "He said it's too late for you. Be careful."

"But … that's not possible," gasped the doctor. "He can't talk."

"He gives a pretty fair imitation of it, though," I replied. "Doctor, you and your colleagues have done a great job for a great man. But as a friend of mine once reminded me, 'There are more things in heaven and earth than are dreamt of in your philosophy.' This may be one of them. Please do not replace the tube; he clearly no longer needs it. But by all means do the tests to confirm what I say. And, thank you, Doctor, for saving the life of our friend."

We took turns shaking hands warmly with Father Martin and then with the doctor, who was in a daze. As we walked down the hallway together, we could hear him shouting, "Nurse!" His research plans were about to change.

The sense of elation that stayed with us through lunch and the drive to the sanitarium quickly dissipated as we passed the security checkpoint and through the perimeter walls of the facility. It was clearly no rest home but rather a hardened asylum for the criminally insane. The boy was only thirteen years old, but no juvenile center was equipped to deal with him. He possessed uncanny strength in his gangly frame, and he had torn open the throat of a priest with his bare teeth. Straight jackets would not stay tied to him, and he had the disturbing habit of throwing his feces at whoever entered his "room." He was, in fact, being held in a padded cell while the juvenile authorities tried to decide what to do with him. Sedative drugs and heavy doses of lithium were having no effect.

The gray-haired, aging director and two burly guards with an array of defensive equipment hooked to their belts walked with us to the end of an isolated hallway. "He has to be kept far away from other patients," the director explained. "They all grow worse if they are anywhere near him. I have never seen a case like this before, and frankly, we are all hoping that you will be able to advise us after you have seen him."

The Bishop and Father Mark both wore their Roman collars as usual. The Bishop had introduced me as an expert in "possession" cases, and he did most of the talking for us until we reached the door to the cell.

"The Bishop will not be entering the cell with us," I said. "We do not wish to expose him to the degradation that we understand lies inside."

"Oh, I think there must be some misunderstanding," the director replied. "We had never intended for any of you actually to enter the cell. We had hoped that observation would suffice."

"I must tell you, sir," I said, "that zoologists and veterinarians cannot treat the ills of dangerous beasts under their care without coming into contact with them. How much more important must it be then that we who are dealing with the pain and suffering of human beings be allowed to come into contact with them? We are professionals, and we know the dangers involved. If you wish for us to help *you*, let alone the boy, then we must be allowed inside."

"Please allow this," added the Bishop. "I trust these men implicitly."

After a quick exchange of views with the guards, the director nodded to us as one of them searched for the correct key on the ring attached to his belt. "The guards will lock the door behind you," he said, "and the Bishop can stand at the door slit, but, at the first sign of real trouble, the guards will enter and subdue the boy—harshly, if necessary. Do you understand this? The responsibility will lie heavily upon you if the boy is hurt, and I warn you now that any harm to the two of you must also lie at the doorstep of the church. As the guards are my witnesses, I advise you not to do this."

"We choose to enter at our own risk, sir. Thank you very sincerely for your concern."

"Then at least remove your clerical collar," he said to Father Mark. "He was apparently maddened by it in the case of the other priest and he ripped his throat in order to remove it."

"As God is my witness, sir," said Father Mark, "I thank you for your concern, but I choose to stand the test with God both at my back and my throat."

The director nodded to the guard, who inserted the key and slowly turned it in the lock after first sliding back the metal plate and peering through the exposed rectangular slit. "He's sitting on the floor in back," he said to us as the door swung open and we stepped across the threshold into the room. We heard the door lock behind us. My right foot ached horribly.

The smell of feces struck us sickeningly as we looked about the brightly lit room and saw the brown smears on the gray, padded walls. The boy sat naked against the far wall with his knees drawn up to his chest and his arms wrapped tightly around them. "There should be flies, you know," he said calmly in a voice that had not yet been lowered by puberty. Then, in a sudden and chilling transformation, the voice dropped two to three octaves as he grunted loudly, "I honor Azazel!"

The slight "tendril" of exploration that I felt in my head was nothing compared to the pressure that Ahriman/Satan had exerted. It is hard to explain, but I reversed it and sent it back to its origin along with a burst of love for the boy and all of God's creation. He screamed and unleashed a torrent of syllables that I knew belonged to a long-forgotten language once spoken by a best-forgotten people. Sensing renewed attack but feeling nothing, I turned my head immediately toward Father Mark. His eyes were closed, and his forehead dripped with sweat. I plunged into his mind, only to find a powerful block and another "tendril" writhing against it as it sought entrance into his thoughts and very being. I reversed that one also and propelled it back to its source with an even stronger sense of love for Father Mark and the extraordinary congregation of the Holy Angels Church.

Father Mark opened his eyes, and the demon roared in frustration through the mouth of the boy in guttural tones: "Der Knabe gehoert mir! Sheytan doendu! Du tabte! Her zaman kaybederin!"

Feelings of loss suddenly filled me, long-held feelings of regret and anguish, mixed with a sense of stumbling and falling away into the unknown. My thoughts flashed onto Earl and his terrifying fall from the cliff, and I remembered that the experience had led to renewal and ever greater power to help others, and I sent ever stronger waves of love toward the boy and the demon that plagued him.

"NO!' he shrieked in the boy's voice. "NO! It hurts! You *cannot* love those who hurt you! You *cannot*! You *cannot*!" And he launched himself toward me, pushing off with his feet against the wall behind him and sailing toward me in obscene imitation of the boy in Tennessee sweeping toward the Holy Spirit that would glorify and heal him. He bared his yellowing teeth in flight and reached toward me with his fingers twisting and his bloodshot eyes emanating the hatred of the demon.

When he was just over two feet away from me, I raised my right hand, and he stopped in midair, twisting and frothing, slashing at me with his hands and kicking his feet downward but not toward me, turning and gyrating like a cat preparing to fall on its feet after slipping from a ledge but never quite touching the ground, spitting and howling and finally hanging limply in front of me.

"Have you come to destroy me?" he asked weakly in the boy's voice.

"Be silent and come out of him," I said, repeating the words of Jesus from two thousand years in the past.

"Do not send me into the abyss," he begged.

"Come out now, or I will destroy you completely."

The boy's suspended body jerked, and a black form emerged from it and stood next to him. I lowered the boy to the floor and addressed the black, filmy mass—the very stuff of evil thoughts and dreams.

"It is not my intention to destroy, but rather to preserve human creation and help bring it back to the path of God."

At that instant, a horrible cackle arose from the boy at my feet, who leaped not at me but at Father Mark a few feet from my side. I had no time to react, but, again, the boy seemed to strike an invisible wall, as he stopped in front of Father Mark and twisted hideously as he reached desperately for the Roman collar only a few inches from his fingers. Father Mark stared impassively at the contorted figure in front of him. He was glowing brightly, and the power that flowed from him was infinite.

I held the first demon in my awareness and commanded of the second, still inside the boy, "What is your name?"

"Legion!" it replied in the savage, guttural tones that I had heard before. "We are Legion, and it is much too late to save the filth who gave us life. The Master has returned, and you, too, shall fall as before. This world is ours."

"Then why are you so helpless in the presence of the Holy Spirit?" I asked, knowing that Father Mark was indeed the receptacle for it. Nevertheless, his words evoked a strange sense of foreboding and regret within me.

"Why do you condemn us for filling the boy when this other energy fills the man?" the demon said with chilling contempt.

"Come out of him," I said simply.

A second black mass emerged on the other side of the boy, exuding not just evil but a hideous sense of utter despair and hatred of every living thing that did not share in it.

I turned to the first black shape and said, "Witness what happens to those of you who defile the Holy Spirit. Tell the others that the same fate awaits any that would enter the human temple again."

I held it fast in awareness and shifted my gaze to the second shape, which twisted in vain in order to escape or re-enter the body of the boy, who was sleeping in deep exhaustion at our feet. I concentrated on love for all living creatures and projected those feelings directly from my heart into the black mist. The edges of it began to glow and then peel inward like a newspaper cast into the fire. I then sensed and actually *saw* in some way a bolt of energy from Father Mark that exploded the demon instantaneously and left only tiny sparks that flickered for an instant and then disappeared.

I turned to the first shape and commanded, "Return to the abyss and tell what you have seen." It vanished.

The glow from Father Mark began to subside. "Are there others?" he asked.

"Not in the boy," I said. "I feel only peace in him now."

"The Spirit was so strong in me," he said quietly.

"I know. It has always been strong in you."

"Yet your presence seemed to magnify its presence in me. Are you truly only a man, Jake?"

"Oh, yes, Father, I am only a man, but I believe I now have the powers in the flesh that were intended for humans in the first place with the creation of Adam and that all of us can achieve them. The Holy Spirit is leading you in the same direction, my friend."

Both of us seemed to remember the Bishop at the same moment. We turned to see his eyes staring at us in shock and amazement. I walked over to the door and spoke to him softly through the viewing slit.

"Ask the guard to open the door, Your Excellency. The boy is safe now. We should speak with the director."

The guard opened the door cautiously, eyed the sleeping boy with apprehension as we left the cell, and then slammed the door shut again and locked it. Both guards had apparently been standing with their backs to the walls flanking the Bishop several feet away. Neither one seemed to have seen or heard much of anything.

The director was more than dubious when we told him that the boy was cured of his affliction and should be transferred at once to the infirmary.

"But how could you have achieved such a cure in only a few minutes? I have seen the strength and ferocity of him firsthand. I had never believed in demonic possession before, but this case had me seriously considering that possibility for the first time in my life. He came within a hair of killing your colleague, and he actually even frightened my guards. How can he now suddenly be cured?"

It was the Bishop who answered for us. "I cannot know what *you* would have seen, sir, as these two men were in the process of aiding the boy. My entire life has predisposed me to view the world in spiritual terms, and what *I* witnessed was a spiritual event that rid the boy of his affliction and served to illuminate the glory of God through the intercession of Our Lord and Savior Jesus Christ. You may choose to believe, if you wish, that he has suffered from a severe case of psychotic schizophrenia that reached a crisis point in the presence of such religious symbolism as the Roman collar worn by my fellow priests and the crucifix and holy water carried by Father Martin, and that Father Mark and our colleague Mr. Daniels used the same emphasis upon religion to reverse the process and anchor him again in our shared but so tenuous reality. The fact remains, however, that he has now been rid of the source of his affliction, and his vastly overtaxed body has been pumped full of medications that may well kill him if he is not given immediate medical attention in the infirmary. You approved our visit in the hope that we might be able to assist. This we have done, may God be praised, and now we advise you both professionally as spiritual and psychological counselors and personally on behalf of his parents to bring the boy into the infirmary. He is no longer a danger to anyone."

There was more conversation, but in the end, it was done. The boy lay unconscious for two days and remembered nothing about the last two weeks when he awoke. He was kept under observation for one month and released into the custody of his parents by the courts upon the recommendation of both the Bishop and a team of medical specialists, who could find nothing wrong with him, either physically or psychologically. Father Martin was released from the hospital without lasting injury three days after our visit. The Bishop and Father Mark met with the Cardinal, and all three flew together to Rome.

And I began my search for the promised land—that is, the forested, hilly and quite beautiful property that I continued to see clearly and sharply in my dreams. There is no need to go into great detail about it here. I followed my intuition, plain and simple. Intuition had become for me far more than vague feelings or "gut reaction." It was a new sense comprised of *intention*, awareness of "coincidence," acceptance of the essential unity of all things, and a loving trust in the grace of God. Intuition had become a powerful and reliable force in my life. Strengthened by the knowledge of my power over the demons, and by then in solid command of the other abilities that had been growing in me since I had first encountered the angels, I was filled with gratitude to God for my life and for all of the extraordinary attention that had been devoted to me. The more I expressed my gratitude and the more I aligned myself with whatever God's *intention* might be, the more powerful my powers of intuition became.

In short, I walked by the showcase window of a well-known travel agency across from my hotel in Los Angeles, saw a poster that reminded me greatly of the land in my dream, inquired about the location, rented a car and drove slowly in that direction over the next several days, stopping frequently at realty offices along the way to inquire about land prices and the availability of forest property. When I reached a small town that seemed oddly familiar to me, I stopped for lunch at a rustic restaurant and literally bumped into a man who turned out to be a real estate agent who had just acquired the listing rights to an isolated sixty-acre tract of land that sounded more than oddly familiar to me. I knew that it was the right spot long before we got out of his Grand Cherokee and walked around some of the property. He was asking for far more than I could afford at that point until he got a call on his cell phone from the owner, who advised him that he needed to sell quickly.

Too pat, don't you think? It worried me too for a while. I did not wish to be a puppet or to compromise the very free will and freedom of human creation that I felt I was meant to redeem from the disastrous uses that humankind had chosen for them. How would I or any of us deserve the unfathomable bows of the angels if we merely followed the script that was handed to us? True, the angels were no longer appearing to me in bodily form, and I sensed that it was important for me to accomplish my task without their direct intervention, as the whole point seemed to be for humankind to regenerate itself through its own intentions, thoughts, and ultimately actions. It was precisely that thought that triggered the understanding in me: I was not being led. I was in fact doing the leading, creating the circumstances and reacting to them, drawing upon deeper knowledge as the amnesia crumbled, and completing the arrangements that needed to be in place by the time the event occurred that could send humankind into a final bloody spiral that would hand the planet and the universe to the demons—and perhaps prove to God that the entire magnificent experiment could not work after all.

I returned to Indianapolis feeling deeply sobered by the responsibility that weighed heavily upon me. Yes, I truly and genuinely created my own life on earth, as do we all, through the intentions and thoughts that become action and form itself. I could not evade the responsibility for my own life, just as you cannot. I was the sum of every decision that I had ever made, both actively and passively, just as you are. And when all of those decisions by all of us are added together to form the global sum, then we are all responsible as well for the very direction of the planet and human life. Yet, in my case, I also had the opportunity and enhanced skills to be a catalyst for fundamental change that could cleanse the planet and point the way back to direct connection with God and the freedom to create in an atmosphere of love, mercy, and compassion.

I spent most of the day with Allison's beautiful form, receiving the reports of the physicians and caregivers and again reflecting on the enormous responsibilities that I had assumed. I was troubled, too, by the recurring sense of loss and regret that had been so recently triggered by the demon. And my right foot began to ache intensely.

The date was September 10, 2001.

* * *

The night was filled with dreams of the angels. They appeared both individually and collectively. The message was always the same: Remember! *"Remember Rumi!"* said Raphael. *"Remember Love, Mercy, and Compassion!"* said Gabriel. *"Remember that you have the abilities and intentions that you need!"* said Michael. *"Remember! Remember! Remember!"* they all said in unison.

And Ariel stood alone at last with her blonde hair blowing in the wind and her penetrating eyes boring into mine. *"Remember that I am always with you and always have been,"* she said, and vanished.

I awoke in my apartment feeling dazed and troubled. My foot ached. My mind whirled. The dreams were imprinted firmly in my consciousness, and the injunctions to remember and presumably *use* all that I had been taught could not have been clearer, yet there was something else stirring in my mind—the odd memories that did not seem to belong to me and yet were somehow also mine: I had a family. There was enormous love but also anguish, both our own and that of others. I had kept a record with messages for future generations and explained how they should be preserved, but I knew that much would be lost. Then there was the ineffable, glorious intensity mixed with fear and trembling, something that I could not describe or quite pinpoint.

I went into the bathroom, sat on the edge of the tub, and ran cold water onto my foot as I tried to probe the "memories" further and make sense of them. The injunction *Remember!* obviously carried two meanings, and both were resonating simultaneously in my racing mind.

I turned off the water and dried my foot and then hobbled into the living room to turn on the television and try to distract myself briefly so that my subconscious mind could work on the images that were bombarding my spinning brain.

I didn't understand at first. I suppose only a handful of people on the other side of the world did. Smoke was spilling from a gash in the side of one of the twin towers in New York City.

"BREAKING NEWS" was spelled out in large letters at the bottom of the screen, and the announcer was explaining that a private plane had apparently crashed into the building by accident. A strange and awful tragedy, I thought. Yet there was something else about the scene, something vaguely familiar and disturbing. And then out of nowhere the second plane crashed into the second tower in front of my eyes and those of the entire world. That cannot be an accident, I thought, not two separate planes striking the towers within minutes of each other. And then there was nothing else to be seen on the television networks apart from the tragedy as the entire nation focused on the burning buildings, and the reports began to flow in of the attack on the Pentagon and a fourth plane yet unaccounted for and finally the crash in Pennsylvania. And as I tried to absorb the events and the conflicting reports streaming into the news centers and to comprehend the possible motives of those who held human life so cheaply, I saw amid the fire and smoke the twisting objects falling from the sky that I now knew to be my fellow human beings, and I braced myself for the great shaking of the earth that I knew would follow, as the images on the screen matched the vision that Michael had granted me, and the towers crumbled and fell and the earth shook, and smoke and dust covered the scene of grotesque destruction, and all those who were still alive and running desperately to remain that way.

The name of Osama bin Laden was already being mentioned in connection with the airplane attacks even before the towers fell, as terrorist experts on screen were recalling the earlier attack on the World Trade Center in 1993, and I was again feeling the anger and disgust that had all but consumed me after the bombing attacks on our embassies in Kenya and Tanzania in 1998, before Azarias had swiftly arranged the trip to Konya and my absorption into the world of Rumi and brought me finally into the presence of God Himself.

"Remember Rumi!" Raphael had said. *"Remember Love, Mercy, and Compassion!"* Gabriel had said. And I did both in the days that followed, as the investigative reports pinpointing the attackers quickly flowed out to a grieving nation and Muslim crowds in the Middle East rejoiced over the slaughter of thousands of innocents in the name of God and praised the murderers themselves as holy "martyrs."

I remembered, and I fought the anger and disgust within myself, and I knew that I had to overcome them, for if I could not, I, with all of the divine intervention on my behalf aimed squarely at enabling me to overcome them, then who else could, and who else might conceivably convince others to do the same?

I focused on the lives that were lost and on those who had taken them, on the unspeakable perversion of Islam and the intentions of God, and I found abiding strength of purpose in probably the most loving, merciful, and compassionate words ever spoken on the earth: *"Father, forgive them; for they know not what they do."*

As I gradually overcame my personal anger and all too human thirst for punishment and revenge, a thirst that not only requires blood to satisfy it but also inevitably creates the same thirst in others in an endless cycle of bloodletting that has marked the history of humankind, I stumbled on the photograph that solidified my purpose and underscored my forgiveness of the 9/11 assassins. You must have seen it too, either in newspapers or the Internet—the exultant form of Satan clearly formed in the sky by the smoke rising from the burning towers. There was no mistaking him, and so the demons had not lied, and their master had indeed been regenerated by bloodthirsty men whose thoughts and intentions had become locked in death and destruction.

Then the reports of attacks on Muslims in the United States began to appear, and the threat to all of humankind and human creation finally became clear to me: The clash of civilizations could easily become reality, and the number of countries with

nuclear weapons had already increased dramatically and danger-
ously. If the clash grew and the very love of God could be perverted and twisted into motivation for blood and destruction by
the demons created by the perverted thoughts and intentions of
humankind itself, then Satan and his hosts would revel in the
ironies and rubble of an Earth made uninhabitable for human life
and the end of human creation in a universe that it had brought
into being. Thus would the experiment end and the intended gift
of free will become the noose with which humankind had hanged
itself.

And how was I, a single man, to prevent this?

The United States struck back in Afghanistan swiftly, destruc-
tively, and successfully. Osama bin Laden escaped—with help
beyond the comprehension of men, I am certain. The war on terror continued apace. The President had blundered and used the
word "crusade." Heavy pressure was placed on Iraq in order to
remove the threat of weapons of mass destruction, yet the very
focus on another Muslim country fueled the religious anger in the
region. The underlying clash of religion seethed.

I knew that I had to act, and I knew where I must act, but I did
not know when or exactly how—and I was on my own. There
were no more dreams and no more visitations. Human errors had
to be resolved by humans themselves, or the very thought of free
will would collapse upon itself and the reality would soon follow.

You think that you know the rest, of course. But you do not.
You do not even realize yet the absolutely pivotal role that you
have played in this drama.

You were not there, and the media were silenced, as you know.
For your sake, then, and for countless others, let me give you the
details as we rush together toward the conclusion of the narrative.

* * *

To say that I was on my own is not accurate. I was without direct divine help, but the circle of those who had touched the divine themselves was large and growing, and I had been the catalyst that had brought many of them together. I had connected individuals working in volunteer fields after their near-death experiences, and they were no longer afraid to discuss their experiences with others, who in turn had shared with still others. Information had been disseminated in the upper hierarchy of the Roman Catholic Church, and the thousands of Protestant worshippers and grateful reformed alcoholics that Earl and I had reached and Earl continued to reach were also spreading the word. There was a sleeping network in place, one that had been created almost accidentally as I had searched for the truth of my existence. Yet I could not yet awaken it and draw on it for support, with one exception—the chaplain's uniform.

I had not served in the military, and I knew almost nothing about military insignia or the correct way of wearing the uniform and the headgear. I needed help in acquiring the uniform and the knowledge, help that I received in a way that you can probably guess easily enough but I will not confirm.

Yes, I had a plan finally. I knew the temple and its location, and I had waited patiently for the sign that would tell me that my time had arrived. How else could my words have the widespread impact required for fundamental change in our ways of thinking except through dissemination in the mass media? And when would thousands of people be gathered together at the Jefferson Memorial in Washington, D.C., with the mass media present? The vision afforded to me by Michael could not have been clearer: *I stood at a lectern in a military uniform and addressed the thousands present and the millions watching the event on television at the Jefferson Memorial, the magnificent temple modeled on the Pantheon, housing the thoughts of a single man who seemed to have known two hundred years earlier about the struggle that we would face in changing our modes of thinking and freeing ourselves from the demons that encour-*

aged our lust for blood: "I have sworn upon the altar of God eternal hos-
tility against every form of tyranny over the mind of man. ... Almighty
God hath created the mind free..."

I had looked in vain everywhere for any notice of a large public event to be held at the Jefferson Memorial. In fact, large public
gatherings in Washington had been largely prohibited for months
after 9/11 out of concern for another attack. Most Americans had
not even known that the Vice President and representatives of the
key branches of government had formed a skeleton government
far from the city so that the country would not be leaderless if
Washington were decapitated in another attack.

Time passed with no sign of the gathering that I knew would
take place at the memorial—until the middle of June 2002. I had
not been idle all of that time—far from it. There was work to do
at the property, people to hire, and animals to acquire. Oh, yes, for
some reason there was to be an animal preserve, a place where
our homeless or mistreated cousins could find shelter and a new
chance at life. I couldn't have explained to you then why it had to
be. I only knew that it was necessary, and I felt enormous satisfaction as it began to take shape.

And then I saw it on an Internet news site in the middle of
June—a description of the events surrounding the upcoming special Fourth of July celebration in Washington. It was to be a day
of gratitude and renewal in the United States. The attack against
us had been avenged. Al-Qaida was on the run, and the Taliban
had been crushed and scattered. Pressure was mounting on Iraq
and other countries in the "axis of evil." A new world order might
yet be established by force of arms against every form of tyranny
over the mind of man, except for the fact that the world's religions were splitting ever farther apart and intolerance against
those of other faiths was rising. The photograph of Satan exulting
in the clouds burned in my mind.

And there it was in the news story—a televised concert by the
U.S. Marine Corps band and speeches in support of the troops to

be held at 2 p.m. at the Jefferson Memorial on July 4. The security for that event and all others that day was scheduled to be extreme.

I returned to Indianapolis and my apartment and began to write the speech, and I tore up one draft after another, day after day, growing desperate eventually at the prospect of saying anything to my fellow human beings that might possibly cause them to change their *intentions*, their very way of existing in a world ripping apart not from physical destruction but from spiritual ignorance and twisted thoughts giving birth to misshapen actions that created newly twisted thoughts in a demonic cycle of blood and agony.

And then I remembered that Moses also harbored severe doubts about his speaking ability, doubts worse than mine:

Then Moses answered, "But behold, they will not believe me or listen to my voice,

for they will say, 'The Lord did not appear to you.'" … But Moses said to the

Lord, "Oh, my Lord, I am not eloquent, either heretofore or since thou hast spoken

to thy servant; but I am slow of speech and of tongue." Then the Lord said to him,

"Who has made man's mouth? Who makes him dumb, or deaf, or seeing, or blind?

Is it not I, the Lord? Now therefore go, and I will be with your mouth and teach you what you shall speak."

In the end, it was Aaron who spoke for Moses, but the closest that I had to an Aaron was Earl, and I knew that our tasks were different, and that it was my responsibility and my honor and my burden to *"stand at the temple and speak to the people all the words of this Life"*—or I could choose not to do so. That was also still a possibility, and that would perhaps happen in an alternate universe in which a craven and corrupted Jake Daniels might value his own comfort and fear his own embarrassment so much that he would not fulfill the task that awaited him. If there was one thing I knew, however, it was that such a thing would not happen in my universe, and I prayed for the others that it would not happen in theirs.

I was certainly not Moses, neither in his greatness nor his fear of speaking, and I relied for strength on a text that was unavailable to him: "*When they deliver you up, do not be anxious how you are to speak or what you are to say; for what you are to say will be given to you in that hour; for it is not you who speak, but the Spirit of your Father speaking through you.*"

I set the computer and the paper aside and never touched them again, until now, of course, but that is not the same, is it?

So I trusted in the Holy Spirit to guide me and to provide the words at the crucial time, even though I could not speak to it or see it or even comprehend what it was, beyond the certainty that it was the energy of God Himself.

The day arrived, the day that you think you understand, and the reason that I have been writing this now for the last three days. You did not suppose that it could be so long, did you, or that I could do it so fast? You should now understand how that was possible, but I am certain that you do not yet accept it. No matter.

I had the well-fitting Army uniform with correct patches and insignia, including the small crosses and the colonel's wings, the hat, the tie, the belt, and the shoes, and I knew how to wear them and how to salute and how to carry myself. I did not yet know how I would reach the lectern or why I would be allowed to speak, but I had seen the vision, and I knew that both would occur.

I checked out of the same Marriott Hotel near Key Bridge where I had first stayed during my search for the Azeri in what seemed like another age altogether. My billfold with all of my identification and my return flight ticket were secured in a large sealed envelope that they had agreed to keep in their safe for me until my return upon payment of a one hundred dollar deposit. I had been tempted to walk once again, but the heat and humidity would have crumpled the uniform and perhaps dampened my spirit as well, and I wanted to look as cool, collected, and *authentic* as possible. The bell captain signaled for a cab for me.

The driver dropped me off at exactly 1:30 p.m.—or perhaps better, 1330 hours—at the small parking lot at the rear of the Memorial off of the 14th Street Bridge, and I walked around the building on a small sidewalk that opened on to the tidal basin and the beautiful marble steps that led up from it to the memorial. Several soldiers in uniform saluted me on the way, and I proudly returned the salute. At the end of the sidewalk, a young Marine saluted briskly and asked if I would like to have a program. I returned the salute and accepted the program.

"Semper Fi, Sir!" he said as he saluted again.

"All the way!" I responded as I saluted him in return. I then passed through a metal detector.

Hundreds of people were already sitting on the steps, and hundreds more were beginning to find their seats. Metal folding chairs for the band were located in a semicircle in the open area at the base of the steps, but the Marine musicians had not yet taken their positions. A low platform with colorful bunting around it and a lectern in the center had been placed to one side, and three rows of additional folding chairs had been set up at a ninety-degree angle to the band. Armed policemen and MPs were standing at strategic points all around the memorial.

I sat down near the bottom of the steps next to a group of animated young people, university students apparently, smiled at them warmly and exchanged pleasantries, and then examined the program. There would be a color guard and the playing of "The Star-Spangled Banner," an invocation by a real chaplain, a speech by a U.S. Congressman, a speech by the Deputy Commandant of the Marine Corps, followed by the concert itself, which would be broken by a brief intermission, and then the benediction at the end by the same chaplain. Nothing was scheduled to occur at the intermission.

Several minutes later, members of the band in their magnificent dress uniforms walked to their seats briskly in single file and stood at attention. When they were all in place, they were given the "at ease" command, and they sat down and began to adjust their instruments. People were still flowing into the area and looking for seats on the steps. Others simply chose to stand. There were easily fifteen hundred people already seated or still seeking out the best remaining vantage points. The dignitaries walked in together from a holding point on the side and took their seats.

A Marine captain in dress uniform stepped to the lectern and announced, "Ladies and gentlemen, please stand as the colors are presented, and remain standing until the completion of our national anthem." The three-man color guard walked across the open area in precision, stopped and turned in front of the platform and presented the colors. The captain nodded at the Marine conductor from the platform, and the orchestra began to play the anthem.

I saluted the flag and held the salute along with all of the real military personnel in the crowd. It was not a fake salute, even though I was certainly a fake officer and chaplain, and I knew that I was violating a series of statutes by pretending to be both. Nevertheless, I had no difficulty whatsoever in saluting the flag of the country of my birth, a flag that symbolized the struggle to establish and maintain a free society based on the ideals of the Declaration of Independence and the Constitution of the United States of America. Of course, we are still in the process of trying to match those ideals with reality, and we often fall woefully short of their fulfillment, and many of us do not even know what they are or even care. And many are just as ignorant of the religious foundation upon which the country was created and the near universal religious convictions of the founders, as well as their noble insistence that the state itself be prevented from dictating any particular form of religious observance or practice. Yes, how many Americans today could with a straight face and an honest heart declare that "with a firm reliance on the protection of Divine Providence, we mutually pledge to each other our lives, our fortunes and our sacred honor"? Yet the ideals themselves remain alive, however tarnished, the flag still flies over the land of the free and home of the brave, and the world is a better place for it.

Nor could I or would I ever denigrate the heroism and sacred honor of those who had risked and lost their lives to defend the ideals symbolized by that flag. **Yet, O Lord God Almighty, let us end both the necessity and the belief in the necessity for them to do so, I thought. Let us end the spilling of guts and the crushing of skulls and the rotting of limbs and the flowing of blood and the poisoning of minds and the torturing of our own souls. Let us end it now before the power to end it is taken from us by the demons, both real and imagined, that plague us in mind, body, and soul.**

Those thoughts filled my mind as I suddenly knew that the young Marine who had handed me the program was well along a chosen path that ended horribly in an unknown place called Fallujah, where he would lie propped up against the wall of a shattered house with both his legs blown off at the knees and blood flowing freely from the horrendous wounds and two skinny dogs waiting for their opportunity to feed about ten feet away from him, and he would die with "Semper Fi" on his lips and in his heart, and he would be a true hero in every sense, and what little was left of his body would be rotting in a grave before he had turned twenty-one.

Yes, I believed what Gabriel had told me, and I knew that such suffering and loss was in some way freely chosen by the boy as a way of dealing with other tragedies or providing spiritual growth in himself and others, but the way to obviate the need for blood and destruction in the future was to end it now, both in physical and spiritual terms.

My heart burned with a passion to lengthen the boy's life and give him other opportunities to improve his spiritual being without resorting to the violence that would almost surely claim his life and end his time on earth for further growth. More important, without fundamental change, there might soon be no opportunity for any soul to return to the earth because it would be made uninhabitable for human bodies. Only Satan and his hordes would dance in the poisonous dust of a nightmare world, and hell would truly exist after all.

The invocation was short, ecumenical, and effective. The speeches that followed were intensely patriotic and unashamedly militarist, teetering perilously on the edge of jingoism. The individual sentiments in praise of our troops and the advances made against those who had either planned or facilitated the attacks on 9/11 could hardly be challenged, but there was no mention of the civilian lives that had already been lost or those that would be in the fog of war, no mention of the families of the killers that we were hunting, no mention of the utter perversion of Islam by al-Qaida that made it appear to be a religion of death and destruction, no mention of the looming and actual clash of civilizations, no mention at all of the death and suffering that we were unleashing as the centerpiece of our strategy to prevent death and suffering in our own country.

The concert began, but it only served to heighten my emotions and underline my resolve to fulfill my task finally and address the crowd and the nation in a way that I hoped would plant the seeds of change in enough minds to start the transformation that was so essential for all of humankind. After a stirring rendition by the entire orchestra of the "Marines' Hymn" to great and deserved applause afterward and a fine interpretation of "When Johnny Comes Marching Home," a young and lovely African-American Marine sergeant stepped to the microphone to the right of the conductor and began to sing an a cappella version of the moving spiritual "Swing Low, Sweet Chariot," with the orchestra joining in on the chorus.

I was looking down at my feet when she began to sing the famous refrain, but my head jerked upward automatically as she sang the first stanza in a beautiful soprano voice:

> *I looked over Jordan, and what did I see?*
> *Coming for to carry me home,*
> *A band of angels coming after me,*
> *Coming for to carry me home.*

I needed no other sign, nor did I need to see them standing in front of me, for the band of angels had indeed come after me and had prepared me and led me to a shining and decisive moment in my own life and perhaps in all of human history. I had not accepted the chariot ride homeward after the truck crashed into my car in Indianapolis, and I would not accept it now or ever until my task was accomplished. Swing high, sweet chariot, I thought; I have too much more to do.

Two more selections were played, but I could not begin to concentrate on them, as the program in my hand listed "The Battle Hymn of the Republic" as the last piece to be performed before the intermission. The words and the music lifted me up again, as they had when I first visited the capital. I looked at the rostrum and the positions of the guards. I saw that the dignitaries were preparing for the intermission. The Marine captain stood next to the microphone. Television cameras and their operators were located at three different positions. I could easily move down three steps and then cross directly to the platform no more than thirty feet away. The orchestra was bringing the music home, and I mouthed the words of the last stanza as the crescendo peaked:

Glory, glory, hallelujah!
Glory, glory, hallelujah!
Glory, glory, hallelujah!
His truth is marching on.

The crowd stood and applauded wildly. The orchestra members stood and bowed and then filed off together to the left to nearly a minute of sustained applause. The captain spoke into the microphone: "Ladies and gentlemen, we will now have an intermission of twenty minutes." He turned and followed the dignitaries, who had already left their designated seats to return to the roped-off VIP area on the right for refreshments. As he moved, so did I. No one stopped me, and no one tried. Why would anyone question a high-ranking Army chaplain? I stepped onto the platform and turned the microphone back on.

"Ladies and gentlemen," I began, "may I have your attention please. I have been chosen to say a few words to you during the intermission." The television camera operators had already taken off their headsets, but I could see them quickly donning them again and speaking into their microphones. The light on the head-on camera blinked red.

"We are here today to honor our troops and to celebrate the independence of our great country." People were stretching and talking to their friends and family members. Small children were chasing each other in the open area. I scanned the crowd and looked to my left to see the captain drawing the program out of his pocket and looking from it to me and back again.

"It is appropriate that we gather here today at the memorial of one of our greatest Presidents and one of the indispensable founders of the United States of America." The captain beckoned to another officer and one of the MPs.

"Inscribed in the walls of the temple above us dedicated to his memory are the words that should guide us in this time of conflict and loss of human life." The crowd noise was still heavy, but more and more people were turning their heads in my direction.

"Among those words are these: 'Can the liberties of a nation be secure when we have removed a conviction that these liberties are the gift of God?'" Two policemen had also joined the captain and the small group around him. The captain pointed to the enlisted sound man in uniform working the sound board in the first row directly in front of me, and the MP jogged briskly toward him.

"The force of arms alone cannot secure lasting peace for anyone and certainly cannot change the convictions of those who hate us." As the sound man reached for the power switch, I reached out with my mind and froze the controls. Many more in the audience began to sit down again. The light burned red on the head-on camera.

"It is to God Whom we must turn in order to thank him for the gift of liberty in our own country and to ask him for His help in securing it in other countries." The MP tried to disconnect the sound cord from the equipment, but I had already locked it in place. The MP ran back to the captain, who nodded in my direction after a brief discussion, and the MP and the two policemen began to step in my direction. The sound man continued to turn his useless controls frantically. Other guards converged on the VIP area.

"And I invite you now to hear the word of God." Bright, blinding light flashed off the water of the tidal basin, and a great hush fell over the crowd at last. The security detail approaching me hesitated and looked around in all directions. A sharp wind blew across the water. One of the policemen placed his hand on the gun butt at his side. They started to move forward quickly—and I spoke with *utterance.*

> *Nothing is new under the sun. Jesus predicted that this day would come. He said this, my countrymen: "Indeed the hour is coming when whoever kills you will think he is offering service to God."*

The policemen stopped dead in their tracks, and every face in the crowd was turned my way. The children stopped playing and stared at me. Nobody within range of my voice over the loud-speakers was moving. I hoped that the same effect would be transmitted through television sets across the country.

Those who murdered three thousand people from more than forty countries on 9/11 gave their own lives freely in the process because they believed that they were offering service to God. God said, "Thou shalt not kill." Anyone who kills is therefore disobeying God and not offering service to Him. Yet that also includes us, my fellow countrymen. The way to stop the terrorists is to change their way of thinking, not to kill as they kill, and that can only be done if we change our way of thinking.

We have been told before what we must do, first by Moses, then by Jesus, then by Muhammad, and by countless other prophets and genuine men and women of God. The way to change is simple. We have already been told countless times. Do only this: "You shall love the Lord your God with all your heart, and with all your soul, and with all your mind. This is the great and first commandment. And a second is like it. "You shall love your neighbor as yourself." Can we not do that? Can we not accept that the terrorists, however misguided and perverted in their intentions, are also our neighbors? And can we not accept that we all pray to one and the same God? Can we not do these things?

If you are Christians, then you must do these things, for Jesus has said this to you clearly:

"But I say to you that hear, love your enemies, do good to those that hate you, bless those who curse you, pray for those who abuse you. To him who strikes you on the cheek, offer the other also ... Be merciful, even as your father is merciful. Judge not, and you will not be judged; condemn not, and you will not be condemned; forgive, and you will be forgiven ... For the measure you give will be the measure you get back."

If you are Muslims, then you **must** *follow the words of the Prophet, for he has said this to you clearly: "If you show mercy to those who are on earth, he who is in heaven will show mercy to you ... One who is not kind to others does not deserve Allah's kindness .... He is an unbeliever whose neighbors are not safe from his injurious conduct."*

If you are Jews, then you **must** *follow the words of the Lord and his prophets, for he has said this to you clearly: "Thou shalt not kill" and "Vengeance is mine." Do not forget Joseph, when his brothers feared his wrath and sent him this message after the death of their father, Jacob, "Forgive, I pray you, the transgression of your brothers and their sin, because they did evil to you." ... But Joseph said to them, "Fear not, for am I in the place of God? As for you, you meant evil against me; but God meant it for good, to bring it about that many should be kept alive, as they are today."*

If you are none of these, ladies and gentlemen, yet worship the one God in other ways and other forms, then your religion, too, will demand love, mercy, and compassion from you. If you do not believe in God at all, as wrong as you may be, then you still must practice love, mercy, and compassion in order to receive them yourself.

And now I say to all of you on the Fourth of July in the shadow of the author of our Declaration of Independence, "We hold these truths to be self-evident, that all men are created equal, that they are endowed by their creator with certain inalienable rights, that among these are life, liberty, and the pursuit of happiness." Are we now going to deprive our enemies of the inalienable right to life with which they have been endowed by their creator and ours?

Love our troops, and yet love our enemies too. Show mercy to our enemies, so that they might show mercy to our troops. Practice compassion for those who hate us, so that compassion might soften their hearts and change their thoughts about us. Love, mercy, compassion. Love, mercy, compassion. Feel them, ladies and gentlemen, in your own hearts and spread them in your own lives.

I sent out the strongest burst of love that I could manage from the pulsating area surrounding my heart directly at the television camera in front of me. My control was clearly not as good as I had thought, though, as the effect did not stop there, and everyone on the steps behind the camera leaned abruptly backward and those standing at the top staggered and clutched their hearts. It was like a directional resonating wave. I could almost see it spreading ripples in the air like heat waves on the hottest day.

It did not touch those to the side or behind me, however. With the cessation of *utterance* and what appeared at first to be deep distress in the audience, the policemen charged ahead at the platform. I switched off the microphone and turned to face them.

The captain was shouting, and I could see other soldiers and policemen also moving in my direction. It was all too fast for verbal thought, but the images in my mind seemed to be moving very slowly, as if I were pushing the forward button on a VCR intermittently and watching the stopped tape unfold one frame at a time. The three approaching policemen had all drawn their weapons. The people on the steps were stretched out and limp. The cameraman in front of me was sitting down on the hard marble and shaking his head dazedly. My eyes shifted, and I saw that members of the Marine Corps band, each of them also a rifleman, of course, were converging on me from the right. My eyes shifted back, and I saw a man rise to his feet on the steps to the left just as I was preparing to confront the three closing policemen and rip their guns away psychically before making my escape in an appropriate but totally inexplicable manner to all those who might witness it. The man shook his head firmly from side to side, and I could see that it was Azarias, the same Azarias who had once said to me, "You have a divine task to fulfill. It should not surprise you to know that I also have a divine task to fulfill—in fact, more than one. That is why I have been here in Washington, D.C., in the very heart of the New Roman Empire." Yes, Azarias— and Raphael, of course—continuing his work in New Rome as its legions were on the march, and I was obviously part of it. And the light and the wind—Gabriel and Ariel. They were all there except for Michael, and I halfway expected a naked man to rise from his seat on the steps at any moment. I smiled at Azarias, turned back to the charging policemen, and raised my hands.

* * *

Now you are finally up to date, and you probably know far more about the legal—and extra-legal—procedures that brought me here than I do. The arrest was not made with kid gloves. The name tag on my uniform said Daniels, and the MP was the one who first addressed me.

"What in the hell have you done, Colonel Daniels?"

"I'm not a colonel," I said, "nor am I in the Army. My name is Jake Daniels for now."

"Whoever you are, you're sick," he said, "and you make me sick." The two regular policemen finished frisking me, and the MP removed my hat and jacket. "Cuff him," he said. They led me away in the opposite direction from the VIP area with my hands cuffed behind my back, and a civilian policeman on each side of me holding one of my arms. The people on the steps were still dazed but mostly smiling, and many were hugging each other or holding hands. As soon as we reached a point at the side of the memorial out of view of the crowd and shielded by bushes from the parking lot, one of the policemen jerked my head up by the chin and said to the MP, "Be my guest." He was a big man, not as tall as I am, but burly. "Thank you," he said and unleashed a straight, hard punch to my stomach. I could have stopped him. I could have done a lot of things. Yet the image of Azarias shaking his head decisively from side to side stayed with me. I stiffened my stomach muscles, but the blow still knocked the breath out of me and jolted my torso forward. "You miserable bastard," he said. "Too cowardly to earn the right to wear the uniform." Then he left, and I was quickly thrown into the back of a police cruiser and read my rights so quickly that I could hardly follow the words.

I was booked and charged on so many counts that they must have had trouble finding space for them on the booking sheet— incitement to public disorder, impersonating an officer of the Armed Forces of the United States, disturbing the peace, suspicion of treason, suspicion of assault, etc. I had no identification on me, and all I would tell them was that my current name was Jake Daniels. To say that they were unhappy with me is a bit of an understatement, of course. There were more punches and more abuse. After a couple of hours, I was left alone in an interrogation room and to my surprise not taken to a cell. No one breathed a word about a phone call or a lawyer. Perhaps half an hour later, three clean-cut men in suits entered the room and sat at the table with me. They apologized for any discomfort that I might have experienced at the station but advised me that I was in serious trouble not only with the District police but also federal authorities. Things could be done to help me. Strings could be pulled. All charges might even be dropped, but they would need my full cooperation. Again, you probably know more about this than I do. There must be transcripts, for example.

Let me repeat the parts that you need for your evaluation.

"Who helped you with this, Mr. Daniels?" asked the man who was obviously in charge.

"Do you want the truth, or shall I tell you something that you are more likely to believe?" I asked in reply.

"The truth, by all means."

"I have been helped by four holy angels of God, all of whom have prepared me for this day, in which I hope that I have fulfilled the divine task appointed for me and for which I was brought back from the dead."

There are certain statements that bring any conversation to a halt. Mine was apparently one of them.

After a considerable amount of time spent on exchanging glances and trying to suppress smirks, the man continued. "Are you going to pretend to be insane, Mr. Daniels?"

"Not at all. I have absolutely no wish to be thought of as anything but entirely lucid and competent, Mr. ... ?"

"My name is not important, Mr. Daniels, but yours is, I'm afraid. We have not found any match yet from your fingerprints, nor have we found anyone with your name who fits your description in our databases, but we will identify you eventually. It would be far better for you to tell us who you are now and help us find your associates."

"If there is truly a need for you to find my associates, sir, then I am certain that they will find you first."

"Are you threatening me, Mr. Daniels?"

"I thought that I was blessing you, actually."

"Let's stop the silly games," he said, suddenly growing angry. "If you want us to help you, then you will have to help us as well. What kind of gas did you use, and how was it released?"

At that point, a number of things began to make sense. I was clearly being interviewed by the FBI or another federal organization even more secretive. The effect on the audience had been noticed immediately, of course, and people were seriously worried about it, particularly since the anthrax investigation had grown intense and security concerns in Washington were off the scale.

"A U.S. Congressman and his wife and the Deputy Commandant of the Marine Corps were in that audience, Mr. Daniels, although they don't seem to have been affected. We know that there was an explosion of some kind marked by a flash of light and a sudden burst of wind that blew the substance into the crowd. Many of those people are under medical care as we speak. They appear to be in delirium, and, if the attack was made with nerve gas, as we suspect, then you may actually face execution. Now, do you want to cooperate with us, or do you prefer to take the fall for everyone involved?"

"I would be happy to cooperate with you, but you are not going to believe my answers, and I choose not to lie to you. There is too much at stake here, far more than you can possibly imagine."

"So there is a conspiracy then? Tell the truth to us, Mr. Daniels, and I promise to do everything I can to ensure leniency for you."

"Ask your questions, and I will tell you the truth."

"What is truth then, Mr. Daniels? Who are you, and who are the others?"

"I am a faithful servant of God, or at least I am trying to be, and the others are holy angels, except for a few friends with unusually powerful psychic abilities. That is the truth."

He sighed and looked at his two colleagues. "We could let the police soften you up some more, Mr. Daniels, but I think that might be too easy on you, and I suspect that you wouldn't tell them anything anyway. Let me spell it out for you so there will be no misunderstanding. We are living under Code Orange in Washington, and normal procedures no longer apply in this atmosphere. You may wish to coddle our enemies, and you may even be one yourself, but we do not wish to coddle them or you. We wish to destroy them before they can pull off another 9/11 or kill anyone else on our soil. Under these circumstances, I have the authority to hold you indefinitely as a suspected terrorist agent complicit in a serious attack on some two thousand Americans at the Jefferson Memorial today. I can and will incarcerate you outside the normal justice system indefinitely—*indefinitely*, Mr. Daniels—until you decide to cooperate with federal authorities. Do you understand what I have said to you?"

"Yes, of course I do."

"Will you then cooperate with us?"

"I have been trying to."

"Why did you take the microphone today and address the crowd?"

"I was trying to fulfill a divine task in which I have been instructed to spread the gospel of Love, Mercy, and Compassion. Without these, and without a change in the way of thinking that produces the demons, the entire creative output of the human race will very likely be lost in the near future, and any concerns that you may have about the power of love that I projected into the crowd today will be as trivial as a gnat alighting on a speck of the radioactive dust that covers the earth."

"We will see you at another time in another place, Mr. Daniels or whoever you are. We will know more about you then, and you will have had an opportunity to understand just how stupid you are."

They left the room, and I sat there alone for another hour or so, after which I was handcuffed again and taken to St. Elizabeth's, where I have been for the last five days.

Now, if you wish, you can compare what I have written with the transcripts of any interviews made available to you, and you will find that my text and the transcripts are identical. To underline the point, and to sidestep the possibility that no transcripts have been made available to you, what follows is a word-for-word repetition of the conversation in our own first meeting. You can, of course, ignore it as did Father Sweeney and pretend that my ability to remember such things is simply a symptom of my obsession and proof of autistic disturbance.

You made me wait for a whole day in a locked isolation room, Dr. Tomas. Your orderlies appear to have been trained as professional wrestlers rather than psychiatric caregivers. In fact, I feel rather certain that they are not your regular orderlies, are they, Dr. Tomas? I am actually under the care of another organization altogether. Be that as it may, this is what you said to me in the interview room with the large mirrors and the orderlies standing just outside: "You are here, Mr. Daniels, so that I can determine whether you are mentally ill or faking that condition in order to avoid facing the consequences of your actions."

"What if I am neither mentally ill nor faking, Doctor? How can you be certain that there are only two possibilities before we even begin?"

You were not pleased with that answer. It was at that time that I first looked into your mind, as my response released a wealth of information into your consciousness. I learned to my dismay, for example, that there was no national or even local television broadcast, that the producers had dropped live coverage during the intermission in order to run commercials and present updates of news, weather, and sports. The tapes had been confiscated as material evidence against me. The story did not appear in the newspapers beyond a line or two mentioning that a mentally ill imposter had tried to speak before the crowd. There were no photographs. The entire story had been suppressed by federal authorities on grounds of both national security, if I were a terrorist, and refusal to provide publicity, if I were merely a misguided publicity seeker. No one had died or even suffered any harmful effects. In fact, everyone seated on the steps and standing above them had experienced persistent feelings of euphoria and love of mankind. Something had clearly happened at the site, but the authorities did not know what it might have been. They were extremely interested, however, in both the odd and deeply troubling sound of my voice and the explosion of light and its apparent impact on the crowd. They had no idea who I was.

"Perhaps you would like to tell me something more about the angels who have guided your actions," he said, looking down at an open file in front of him. "That would be a good place to begin the evaluation."

"You will not believe me, of course, certainly not yet," I said, "but I refuse at this point to evade your questions or tell you anything but the truth. I have been blessed to meet my guardian angel Ariel and to receive guidance and training from the archangels Raphael, Gabriel, and Michael. I have been given a divine task to disseminate a new gospel based on three simple words: Love, Mercy, and Compassion. Humankind stands at a crossroads that will either lead it back to God and alignment with His intentions or hasten the spiral into a nightmare world inhabited and controlled by demons. Does that give you something to work with?"

You continued to write for another minute or two, and then you adjusted your glasses and leaned back in your chair. "I am going to administer a series of tests, Mr. Daniels—with your approval, of course. I trust you are willing to take them voluntarily."

"Yes, of course," I said. I gleaned from your mind at that point that the tests were intended to gauge my reasoning faculties, overall intelligence, personality type, and basic contact with "reality." Specific questions related to my "delusions" of angels would be interspersed in a way throughout the battery of tests that would help determine whether I was faking, as no one can maintain a perfect pattern of coherent response to a long series of questions about a story that he is making up on the fly. But there was something else on your mind, something more important to you than the tests.

"There is one other thing, Mr. Daniels, something quite important for both of us actually. It can aid immensely in helping you if there are genuine matters of psychiatric concern, and it can help free you from this institution if it is clear that there are no such matters. I am authorized to tell you, in fact, that all charges against you will be dropped, since no one has apparently been permanently injured by your actions, *if* you choose to cooperate with the federal authorities and help them in their investigation. They are particularly interested in the unusual voice effects that you demonstrated, and they seek your help in locating those who helped you commandeer the sound system and release whatever substance was employed to impact the audience. Please keep that in mind as we continue over the next several days. My request to you is this: I wish for you to sit down after our session today and write out a description for me of everything that has occurred between you and the angels and why this contact has led you to the events at the Jefferson Memorial. Will you provide me with such a written narrative?"

The word that danced in your mind at that instant was "checkmate." You will remember that, surely, since it was only four days ago, and now you must ask yourself how I could know that. A lucky guess? Please, Doctor, calculate the odds. You knew, or thought you knew, that such a narrative would either demonstrate the strength of my delusions or provide you with the material from my own hand that would allow you to probe through my story in future sessions and prove that I was a fraud.

"Of course, Doctor—on one condition," I replied.

"And what is that?"

"I do not wish to do this in longhand. That will be too cumbersome for me, as well as messy as I make corrections. The angels deserve better than that. I ask that you provide me with a computer and printer. I pledge to you that I will print out the narrative for you when it is completed and not use the computer for any other purpose."

"You realize, of course, that such an arrangement would not provide you with Internet access or any outside contact through the machine?"

"Yes, I do, nor do I seek any. I only wish to honor your request properly and to satisfy myself as to the quality of the narrative."

"Let me consider your request," you said.

"Please do," I said. "Otherwise, I will not prepare the narrative."

"Shall we begin our tests, Mr. Daniels?" you asked.

"I believe we already have," I responded.

That evening, shortly after I had finished dinner in my cell ("room" is really too generous, wouldn't you agree?), one of the orderlies rolled the computer, screen, keyboard, and printer over to my table on a cart, and we set it up together. Actually, my request must have been considered a stroke of luck by your friends, since they could monitor whatever I wrote at will. "I will need a ream of paper," I said to the orderly, and he left the cell to fetch it with a smile.

I had asked for the computer as a way of asserting myself and not allowing you to dictate entirely the terms of my confinement. I also intended to alter the machine in ways that would help confirm the validity of my narrative. I do have to admit to you, though, that I went to bed deeply depressed that evening. The message had not been disseminated widely after all. How could two thousand people or likely far less change the mode of human thought or effect a shift back from the brink of mass destruction and despair toward eventual reunion with God? I doubted that the effect would even be lasting in those few who had experienced it. I am a man, not a being capable of changing people's souls by loving them. Had everything I experienced been for nothing? Did Allison lie in coma in the end for nothing? How could I have been expected in one brief speech to bring about a mass transformation of humankind powerful enough to bring the demons to extinction by cutting off the evil thoughts and intentions that created them? Why had I been abandoned and left to rot in a mental asylum? What was Raphael's purpose in preventing my escape? Should I not even now use the powers given to me to make my escape?

These and similar questions flooded my mind unmercifully. And then, finally, I slept.

Allison was the first to address me. "I will be with you soon, my love," she said, glowing with health and smiling in a way that broke my heart. "Write the narrative," she added. Raphael appeared and looked at me quizzically. *"Do you really not trust me after all we have been through?"* he asked. I tried to assure him that I was just puzzled and heartsick at my failure, not in any way upset with him. *"Write the narrative,"* he said. Gabriel arrived and asked, *"Are my words to you to be lost? Write the narrative."* Then Michael appeared, wearing an incongruous fig leaf and chuckling. *"I will be with you soon, old friend. Now write the narrative."* Ariel appeared, smiled warmly for the first time ever, and said, *"The Holy Spirit is with you. Think where you are tonight. Write the narrative."*

I awoke with a jolt, feeling oddly refreshed, although the barred and meshed window told me that it was still pitch dark outside. All right, where am I tonight? I asked myself. I am in a locked cell at St. Elizabeth's Hospital in Washington, D.C., a historic and honored institution that serves as a state psychiatric hospital with ties to the D.C. courts and the Department of Justice. (Thank you for the pamphlet, by the way.) Then I thought of Michael being with me soon and flashed on to his official title in the Roman Catholic Church—*Saint* Michael the Archangel. And that made me focus on *Saint* Elizabeth, for the first time. And who was Saint Elizabeth? I asked myself. Why the mother of Saint John the Baptist, a prophet crying in the wilderness. And is that what I am to become, a prophet? And is that who I am, John the Baptist returned? No, the memories did not fit anything that I knew of the Baptist. He had no family. There was no tropical setting. But a prophet who might leave Elizabeth and carry a message of renewal into the world? Something jelled. I sat down and began to write this chronicle: "Maybe I was not out of my body long enough …."

About a day and a half ago, I realized the real significance of the chronicle, and I could see its impact in the future. I am truly deeply indebted to you for this, Dr. Tomas, although I doubt that you had a great deal of choice in the matter, regardless of the potential impact on free will, as you were certainly intended to make the suggestion. Perhaps you could have avoided it, but the pattern of your decisions must have indicated a very high probability that you would ask me to write the narrative.

What is a prophet without a book? I now have a book, and it is also now clear to me that my divine task actually centers upon this book, which is intended to be a new gospel that relies upon the teachings of Jesus and many others and yet offers a new and very simple message that cannot be mistaken and should resonate in all serious religions: Love, Mercy, and Compassion. *The short speech at the Jefferson Memorial was only a means to bring me here and force me to write the book.* Do you understand yet what it means for all of us to erase the past and begin again?

I realize only now that I misunderstood everything from the very beginning. Ariel did not save me from the car accident—she caused it. She blinded the truck driver with her radiance and distracted me at the crucial moment when I might have reacted in time to avoid the crash. She did not mistakenly look into my eyes when I was in my astral body; angels do not make mistakes. She did so on purpose so that I might start the journey that has led to my transformation and my awakening. I had forgotten everything, you see, as had Allison. Now, finally, I can remember accepting with both infinite joy and trembling the invitation to atonement and the possible regeneration of humankind. I thought that the fundamental importance of the task would overcome the amnesia imposed on embodied life on the earth, but it did not. I now fully understand why Paul had to be forcibly awakened into his role as the Comforter. I also finally understand the angels' insistence upon separating appearance from reality and discovering the hidden depths and meanings in all things, including myself. I was no better at discovering Azarias's real identity than I was in remembering my own, and I now challenge you to look within this very text for meaning below the surface. You should not bother yourself with searching for the name given to me by my parents in this life. My real name is much simpler anyway, and both my past and future purpose much more important.

There are some other, more prosaic things that you need to know. First, the difficulties that the federal technicians have had in breaking into the computer have nothing to do with their lack of skill. I am sure, in fact, that they are highly trained and proficient in their fields. I have simply locked it in a way that cannot be resolved when I am out of the room. In addition, the keystroke monitor is not broken; I simply prevented it from working properly until the book was complete. Also, after I print out the completed work and leave it on the desk for you, I will delete the text from the computer. This will not be a standard deleting process, since there will be nothing remaining on the hard drive afterward.

Maybe this could seem unfair, since it may appear to impinge on your exercise of free will, but all the probabilities that I have seen note a future in which this book has been published widely and been accepted thoroughly as a holy text required for the regeneration of mankind, or humankind, as I prefer. With that in mind, you should elect to save your time and energy in trying to destroy it or even ignore its fundamental insights into the human condition. You can't succeed in suppressing it. At some point in our foreseeable future, a man named David will ask for this text and a copy of your report; do not worry yourself but simply provide him with those materials and wish both him and me the best. This aside is intended for you, my former keeper, and there is more here than meets the eye.

The wall is beginning to disappear, as promised.

Be that as it may, I am now at last approaching the end of this long narrative. Michael lolls comfortably on the bed in my cell, enjoying my full return to consciousness. He smiles. I can now smile, too, as the full import of the task ahead and the next steps stretch before me. I will retrieve my billfold and ticket long before you have a chance to read this. This will certainly not be the last or only disappointment for you, as I will reach Allison before you understand how you might find her. She has been cared for very nicely at a chapel under the name of Saint Michael through the efforts of many friends and specialists right in the center of Indianapolis. Trust me please as I advise you that it will do you no good to follow up on this information. Yes, the walls in my mind have also finally disappeared, and we can only thank You for your blessings, O God, and for the second chance that You have given to our own souls, both mind and Allison's, and for the urgent redemption of sin that we now have a chance to offer humankind.

As I prepare to leave, I realize I do unite past and present in my swelling heart and the future in my mind and soul. I also accept that had I known the full truth earlier, I could not have borne the guilt and the repeated responsibility. The history has survived, though now altered. Time, so much precious time, has passed, yet I know the part on our life spans is true, and Allison and I will atone and intend to use our new life on earth to fulfill God's original intention.

Shanti, reader.

LOVE, MERCY, COMPASSION

EPILOGUE

I first encountered the two of them at a secluded nude beach in California. I know that will sound a little odd and perhaps even prurient, but it was anything but that. There were ten or twelve other people there, and all of them obviously felt the same sense of utter majesty that I did as they walked down the wooden stairs and onto the sand in short robes, arranging their blanket and towels and removing their robes and sandals before they continued strolling hand in hand toward the ocean. It was not just the physical beauty. Yes, they might have stepped out of a Renaissance painting by Raphael or another great master, but it was more than that. The golden sunlight seemed to shimmer around them, almost as if they had visible auras surrounding them. The way they moved, their sheer *presence* was startling and humbling somehow. This is the way we should be, I thought. This is the way that it must have been intended all along. Who *are* these people?

They returned from the ocean some twenty minutes later, smiling and laughing and visibly happy in each other's company. They seemed to complement each other, not just extremely well but perfectly. Their wedding rings sparkled in the bright sunlight. Everyone was staring at them and talking among themselves quietly. I was the only unaccompanied person there. After about five minutes, I stood up and walked over toward them. He saw me approaching and smiled. "Sit down, David," he said, and patted an open space on the blanket.

"I only wanted to—" I started to say.

"I know," he interrupted gently, "and we thank you sincerely for the compliment. Please sit down."

When I did so, she reached out her hand and said, "Welcome, David. We have been expecting you. We just didn't know exactly when it would be."

Already in awe of them, I was taken aback even more by the fact that they seemed to know me somehow. They were much younger than I am, but they both projected a maturity and self-confidence far beyond their years.

"Have we ever met?" I asked. "I can't imagine that I would ever forget you."

"In a manner of speaking," he said, "but then all of us forget so much, believe me." Then he also shook my hand, and suddenly I felt completely comfortable with them.

"You are a fisherman, aren't you, not professional but a sportsman?"

"Yes," I said slowly, "but I—"

"I am going to ask you something special, something holy in fact, something said a long time ago by someone far greater than I. Think about it carefully, and then give me your answer. All right?"

I nodded my agreement.

"Do you wish to become a fisherman of men?"

I had recently retired from a satisfying career with the federal government, and I had come to California from Arizona in order to relax completely on the beaches and think about my future. My wife was visiting relatives in Norway. I was not particularly religious, beyond a lifelong but nondenominational belief in the existence of God and His infinite mercy. "What does that mean?" I asked nervously.

"It means in the long term," he replied, "that you will be instrumental in reversing the disastrous current course of the human race. In the short-term, it means that we would like for you to join us at a special animal preserve in about three days and see for yourself what we are doing."

"Do you trust us?" she asked.

"I have just met you, as far as I know," I answered slowly. "I mean I'm not in a position to trust you really or not trust you. The two of you make an incredible first impression and—"

She touched my forehead lightly, and suddenly I seemed to be standing in a rugged but beautiful forest area. I saw the two of them, clothed, each of them holding a young child, one about three and the other perhaps two. They were laughing at something that the older child had said, and he or she was laughing in response. Two unusual antelope bounded behind them, and they all turned their heads to look at them. The scene abruptly shifted to the inside of a medium-sized building. I could see the forest through the windows. There were some twelve people, including what appeared to be both Roman Catholic and Eastern Orthodox priests, a rabbi, and several Buddhist monks, seated in a circle with their heads bowed in prayer. There was a series of framed photographs arranged in a circle on the back wall, and just as I started to focus on the faces, I was once again seated on the blanket at the beach.

"What just happened?" I asked in a daze.

"You had a glimpse of our home, partly with my wife's help, but partly also because you are able to have that glimpse. Not everyone can, in the beginning. There is a task waiting for you, David, a very important one. If you wish to accept our invitation, then we will see you at this location in three days."

He handed me a business card from the pocket of his robe. It spelled out the name of the preserve on one side in large letters, as well as a town and state in smaller letters beneath it. The other side was blank.

"Is it well-marked?" I asked. "What road do I take out of town to reach it?"

"There are no signs," he said. "When you reach the town, fol-low your intuition, David. *Intend* to find us, and you will. I know it sounds strange to you now, but without the right *intention*, you will not find us, nor will anyone else. But consider this, my friend: Isn't it a bit out of the ordinary that we are meeting here together comfortably at a rather secluded beach without a stitch of cloth-ing, and my wife and I both know your name before you can tell us, and you have already experienced a remarkable vision, and we have offered you a job that entails—how did I put it now—'reversing the disastrous current course of the human race'? If you can accept all of that, then it should not be much of a leap for you to intend to find us and succeed in doing so. What do you say?"

"Well, I don't know why exactly," I said, "but I do trust you, both of you, and I cannot deny the reality of the 'vision' or what-ever it was. I will find you. I will certainly intend to anyway. Thank you, both of you."

We shook hands again, both of them offering dazzling smiles, and I returned to my own blanket still in an odd daze, gathered up my belongings, and made my way back to the parking lot and changing area.

That is how we met.

* * *

There is no need for me to go into much detail about myself or the drive to the town listed on the card, and it is certainly not for me to mention the name of the town or the state. It was interest-ing, although not really surprising, to find that no one at two dif-ferent gas stations had ever heard of the preserve, nor had the waitress at the small restaurant where I stopped for lunch. After paying the bill and returning to my car, I closed my eyes and focused my mind on the two of them and the vision of them standing in the forest with their children, followed by the ecumenical prayer meeting or whatever it had been. I started the car after a few minutes, drove out of town, and turned left on the first side road off the highway. I just kept driving for another thirty minutes or so, enjoying the sunny day and the scenery with my mind open and free of clutter, as the road climbed ahead smoothly. I passed a narrow dirt road on the right eventually, one not unlike several others that I had already passed, and something immediately snapped me into alertness. *That* was the road. I turned the car around, made the left turn, and drove along the hard-packed and rutted surface for some ten minutes, bouncing heavily at times, until I came to an old-fashioned wooden fence about five feet high stretched completely across the road. There was nothing at all old-fashioned, though, about the security cameras and other electronic equipment not quite concealed among the trees on the other side of the fence. I got out of the car to inspect the fence, which swung open just as I reached it. I got back into the car and drove ahead about a hundred feet through what had become a rather thick forest when the road made a sharp right turn and opened into a spacious gravel parking area, where two big vans sat empty. Beyond the parking area stood a *real* fence made of steel mesh about twelve feet high and then leaning inward at the top. It stretched into the forest on both sides as far as I could see. There was no barbed wire. As soon as I got out of the car, I could see a jeep of some kind approaching the gate from the other side. This time the gate did not open, however. The driver got out and unlocked a door set into the mesh at one side of the gate, walked through and closed it carefully behind him, and then approached me with a wide smile and his hand extended.

"Welcome, David," he said. "They're expecting you."

"Who are you then?" I asked, less than politely, I'm afraid.

"I used to be a truck driver," he said. "The Lord works in mysterious ways."

The road to the compound was paved and smooth. We passed animals on both sides of us of all kinds and sizes as we drove slowly ahead, including lions and cheetahs peacefully stretched out in an open area no more than an uncomfortable fifty feet from us. A little further down the road, a small flock of sheep was grazing peacefully in the same open area.

"That can't be!" I exclaimed to the driver in amazement.

"I didn't believe it either at first," he said, "but there are a *lot* of things that are hard to believe here at first, neighbor. Take a look at the palm trees on your left."

The driver dropped me off at a long, rather low-roofed building at a compound that appeared well on its way to becoming a village, with a series of cottages and other structures dotting the area. "Go on in," he said. "You're expected."

It was the same large, open room that I had seen in the vision. The circle, too, was the same, but the people were different, and they were all sitting on cushions on the floor. I half expected to see him sitting nude in their midst, but he was dressed casually in jeans and a plaid shirt. He waved me over into their midst, placed a cushion for me next to him, and introduced me by my full name, although I still had no idea at that time how he could know who I was. It gradually became clear to me, both from the official dress of some of them and the course of the conversation, that all of them were religious leaders.

Several spoke of the need for wider demonstrations of what they had witnessed themselves, but he argued persuasively against it, as doing so on a large scale, he said, would inevitably smack today of David Copperfield and/or computer manipulation. His quotation from Jesus sealed the argument: "Have you believed because you have seen me? Blessed are those who have not seen and yet believe."

It became clear as they spoke that a network of religious leaders and others had already been formed and had established regular lines of communication. Then the conversation switched to "the Book," about which I knew nothing at the time. They agreed that the time had arrived for the chronicle to be published and the gospel spread. He explained that he could write it again, yet he knew from experience that the dangers of distortion and misinterpretation were simply too great if two copies existed with slightly different wording. Oddly enough, he said, he had written it himself but had not had time to read it, and his ability to recapitulate it precisely had therefore been compromised. He had been required to fulfill his promise to "the Doctor," and a certain Michael had assured him that the Book would be safe in the hands of the doctor anyway until the time arrived to retrieve it.

The time was *now*, he said, both because of the world situation and because the promised courier had arrived. All eyes then turned to me. I looked back at everyone and smiled sheepishly. I had no idea what they were talking about.

He also smiled and said, "There is much that I need to discuss with David, but I wanted him to be here to meet you and see for himself."

Then she entered the room with the two children—both of them boys, as it turned out. The children toddled into the middle of the circle and sat down there happily, turning their heads and smiling at everyone. She took her place next to him, and I and others slid to the side to make room. After the children scooted over to sit in their parents' laps, the tableau was overwhelming. What I thought I had imagined on the beach was proven to be unquestioned reality indoors, as all of them visibly glowed, and a faint aura of golden light surrounded them as a group.

"The older boy has been advised?" asked one of the priests.

"Yes," he said. "Constantly."

She leaned over to him and said, "Where is your brother, loved one?"

The boy leaned over, placed his arm around his younger brother and kissed him on the cheek. The smaller boy then hugged his brother. All of the visitors clapped their hands in unison, and then all of them simultaneously lowered their heads in prayer. Tears streamed down cheeks. I was totally in the dark, but I also lowered my head and closed my eyes.

"Shalom," he said softly after a few minutes.

And everyone repeated in unison just as softly and just as reverently, "Shalom."

As the meeting ended, and the two of them hugged everyone leaving to prepare for the evening meal while the children played at their feet, I took the opportunity to examine the photographs in circular formation on the wall, each hanging by silken threads from golden pins. I was stunned.

All of them appeared to have been taken in the very room in which I was standing, but the subjects were extraordinary. Even those I could not identify except from the hints of their clothing were obviously as important to their followers as the ones I knew immediately. Pope Benedict XVI stood between the couple, holding their hands and bearing an expression of exquisite serenity on his face. Ecumenical Patriarch Bartholomew, the world's greatest champion of the environment, stood in the same position with a beatific smile on his white-bearded face. The Dalai Lama with his famous smile encompassing the whole of humanity stood between them in another. A turbaned Sikh with his dagger on his belt held his place proudly. A man whom I somehow *knew* was the Grand Rabbi of Jerusalem stood in another. Another bearded man in clothing I didn't recognize somehow *radiated* Grand Mufti of Mecca. A Native American in full headdress and regalia stood in yet another, as did a Hindu man with a painted circle on his forehead and his hands in front of him with palms together. There were three others, two women and a man, who were dressed in casual Western clothes and who were not at all familiar to me. As I shifted my gaze from one photograph to another, the circle of photographs slowly and noiselessly moved one position clockwise so that a different photograph rested at the top. Only then did I really notice the barely perceptible circular track on the wall that marked the existence of the wheel upon which the photographs were placed.

"It turns every fifteen minutes to remind all of us that we are children of the same God and equally but differently blessed," she said from behind me. "And the circle is growing, David. It will take time, but now we have time and purpose again. We also know the mistakes to avoid, but we are not immune from them even so. Michael has said that the very terms of our existence compel us to create and expand our boundaries constantly and that our challenge is to do so without blocking God's intentions with our own. You don't understand any of this yet, do you?"

"No," I said honestly. "I am fascinated by everything I see and hear in this place, and most of all by the two of you and your boys . . . but I don't understand what it all means."

She smiled warmly and said, "You will, and soon. You will not only understand, but you will also begin to *remember* under his influence. Come, now, it's time for dinner—vegetarian, by the way."

* * *

It is not my purpose to give you all the details of the compound. Perhaps you should know that the fence is real but that it does not keep the animals in or unwanted animals, people, or other entities out. Something else does that. The former carnivores in the preserve eat neither meat nor blood but remain strong and healthy on a different diet. Conditions have been altered in ways far beyond my understanding. "Most of what you see is here for symbolic purposes," he said. "Yet symbolism is important. I have learned that everything is a symbol for something else."

To be honest with you, I had great trouble accepting the full scope of what he told me at first, but the proof lay all around me, particularly in their *presence* and unfathomable abilities, and the new quality and content of my crystalline dreams only confirmed it.

My task, simple enough on the face of it, was to retrieve the book from Dr. Tomas, who would be waiting to give it to me at St. Elizabeth's Hospital in Washington, D.C., and then to arrange for it to be published. It would then take on a life of its own, preparing the way for a public emergence of the couple and a worldwide cessation of violence, coupled with a renewed and direct relationship with the Creator of us all. A videotape of the speech at the Jefferson Memorial was also retrievable, and it was known that the impact on the audience of the audio and the blast of love at the end were both somehow captured on the tape. It was the combination of the uncanny impact of the tape on the numerous federal agents who watched it and the still unexplained escape—and disappearance of the wall at St. Elizabeth's—that had led the FBI and others to maintain their surveillance of Dr. Tomas and continue their search for "Jake Daniels." Moreover, his photograph and fingerprints had somehow disappeared from all databases, leading authorities to believe that a conspiracy of unknown magnitude existed within the government itself.

Should I become a person of interest myself, my record as an Army officer and high-ranking government official with multiple security clearances would provide a measure of protection from undue harassment until the book was in the public's hands. Oddly enough, from my point of view, no one at the compound expected the authorities to believe anything in the book anyway. The fruitless search would continue for a long time to come. There were certainly other ways to proceed, he told me, but they all required mental or physical coercion of a type that he had long since forsworn. There would be no real or threatened violence of any kind on his side in the process of spreading the gospel of Love, Mercy, and Compassion, including any conceivable violation of free will.

When I arrived at St. Elizabeth's and introduced myself to Dr. Tomas on behalf of Jake Daniels, he welcomed me with a strong embrace and said that he had been waiting for my arrival for a long time. He led me to his office and locked the door behind us, putting his finger up to his lips as he turned back to me. He quickly wrote on a sheet of paper, "The office is bugged. Please confirm what you seek." I responded immediately with the following message: "The text and your report." He smiled broadly and gave me another hug.

Then, with difficulty, he pushed one corner of his massive desk to the side, lifted up the carpet where the desk had been standing, and revealed a narrow combination safe built into the floor. He turned the dials, opened the lid, and withdrew a large and bulky manila envelope. Then he reversed the process and signaled for my help to put the desk back in place.

He again wrote on the pad of paper. "Installed long ago to protect most sensitive reports. Envelope contains text, report, and short letter to 'Daniels.'"

I unbuttoned my shirt, slid the heavy envelope into it, redid the buttons, and zipped my leather jacket up partway. The envelope bulged out from my chest and stomach and formed a straight line up near my neck, as if I were wearing a bulletproof vest. I motioned for the pad of paper and wrote, "This will have to do. Better than walking out carrying a large envelope."

He lifted his right index finger and motioned with his left hand for me to stay where I was. The next thing I knew, I was holding a potted bonsai tree against my chest. "Bit odd maybe, but should work," he wrote.

We walked out of the front door of the facility together and along a sidewalk leading to the parking area. He leaned over close to my left ear. "Tell him this," he whispered. "Bless you, neighbor. Just 'Bless you, neighbor.' He will understand." I nodded, and we shook hands awkwardly, with me cradling the plant.

He did understand, although I did not, until he showed me later at the compound how to read the message in the text. I left him with the originals of all the documents and then set out to find a publisher. That is another story.

I talked to Dr. Tomas on one other occasion, calling him from a pay phone in another state about two months later. "I'm planning to describe how I received the text when it is published, unless you tell me not to," I said. "I'll understand either way, but your name and your role deserve to be known."

"It would be the highest honor of my life by far," he said. "The short-term hassle will mean nothing in comparison to infinity, isn't that true?"

"Yes," I said. "I thought you would agree. With your permission, I also want to include the report and your letter. He gives his permission on the report, of course."

"Then please publish them. And say, if you will, that all of us require forgiveness, and I hope that will include me."

"That has already been accomplished," I said. "Good luck, neighbor, and God bless you."

"And God bless you, neighbor. God bless us all."

APPENDIX A

Psychiatric Evaluation and Incident Report

DATE: July 12, 2002

SUBJECT: Interim Report: Mr. Jake Daniels (suspected
             alias)

FOR: The Director

FROM: Dr. T. Tomas

REFERENCE: A. Discussion in your office, July 10, 2002

             B. Classified Agreement with DOJ, dated July 5,
             2002

Mr. Jake Daniels was delivered to our care on July 4, 2002, under pending agreement cited in Ref. B above. I did not meet with him personally until the morning of July 6, in order to review thoroughly the circumstances of his arrest and the transcribed texts of his earlier interviews with the police and federal authorities, as well as to provide time for him to reflect on his situation and to establish the prescribed framework of authority standard in these cases. Working assumption: Acting out mental illness in order to protect accomplices and/or avoid criminal prosecution.

He presented in that first session as a highly alert, well-spoken, confident, and completely unintimidated subject. His confidence bordered on arrogance, and it was clear that he had thoroughly rehearsed his story about angels directing his actions. I saw no purpose in challenging him at that point, whether his story was either a well-rehearsed ploy or genuine symptom of delusion, particularly as he agreed to take the battery of tests voluntarily that would help us both with the diagnosis and the ongoing planning for either his unmasking or his treatment.

The results of all the tests were so striking and unexpected that I repeated them in different formats and versions the next day, only to garner the same results. Mr. Daniels has an IQ of 200+ (see attachments I-J). I had read of such scores, but I had never encountered them personally before. There were no indications of psychosis, personality disorder, bipolar tendencies, or delusional behavior in any of the tests themselves (see attachments D, E, F). The California Personality Inventory and the standard Meyers/Briggs Type Indicator (see attachments G-H), which I administered on three separate occasions in different versions, revealed an almost perfect balance of personality types, as if he carries within him the potential for all human behavior. That is an exaggeration, of course, but, in point of fact, on the basis of the test results and my conversations with him, I could only conclude that he was perhaps the most well-balanced individual whom I had ever met, with the one glaring exception of his insistence upon encounters with angels. That being the case, it was safe to assume that he had been consciously and deliberately inventing the stories about angels. His intelligence is so great, however, that I felt then and still do now that I would not be able to catch him in any departure from the tightly woven story that he was telling about guidance from angelic beings who had warned him that the world was on the verge of being controlled and destroyed by demons.

Nevertheless, I had asked him during the first interview (Attachment A) prior to the testing sessions to prepare a written narrative for me describing his encounters with the angels, so that

I might use it in subsequent sessions to probe his story and reveal discrepancies in it. He agreed, on the condition that he be allowed to type his narrative on a computer. I accepted that condition, and he could be seen typing furiously whenever he was in his room and late into the night for three consecutive days.

Our next two interviews (Attachments B, C) went much the same as the first with no change at all in his oral narrative or description of the events that threatened mankind. In brief, he explained that human beings share in the divine power to create and that this is accomplished through thought alone and the active *intention* for something to happen or appear. He further explained that human thought and intention had so diverged from God's own intention that our souls had fallen away from God and been captured in the heavy matter of the "earth plane," as he put it, and had actually deteriorated so greatly from their original condition that their "evil" thoughts and intentions were bringing demons into being who would further encourage evil thoughts and actions in a grand vicious cycle that was leading to the end of human habitation on the earth. The angels had selected him as the one person who might reverse this process and bring the various earth religions together in a great ecumenical movement that would set us all on the road to salvation. When questioned repeatedly as to why he would be divinely chosen for such a cosmic task, he would only reply reasonably that he also did not know the answer. He did refer, however, to the fact of reincarnation and memories that were rapidly returning to him that would soon break through the "amnesia" that had been placed upon him as a human soul on the earth.

All of this would point, of course, to extreme megalomania and perhaps dangerous psychosis if he were not faking his condition, as we had believed was the case from the beginning. Nevertheless, there are other odd factors that need to be weighed here. Daniels has demonstrated either elements of strong psychic ability or the tricks of a master magician. Federal authorities now believe that he somehow induced mass hysteria in the audience at the Jefferson Memorial in strong measure through a strange verbal mechanism that they are still studying on the videotapes. Moreover, I witnessed a pencil fly across the table directly into his hand during one of the testing sessions when the lead broke on the pencil that he had been using. He did not call attention to the "trick" and did not seem aware that I had even seen it. He genuinely seemed to have accomplished the feat absentmindedly with no other purpose in mind than to continue writing. He also frequently referred in our conversations to matters in my personal life that he had no way of knowing, short of telepathic ability or hypnosis beyond my understanding. I have marked those segments in red in the attached transcripts. In addition, he did something to the computer in his room that completely blocked the federal technicians when they tried to examine what he had been writing while he was meeting with me in the testing area. They never could determine how he had so thoroughly locked the machine, nor could they find any trace of the requested narrative in any of the folders in the computer or in the hard drive itself after his disappearance.

I refer to all of this in preparation for the following discussion of that disappearance.

On the morning of July 10, 2002, at approximately 5 a.m., the orderly on night watch duty covering Daniels' ground floor ward heard shouts among the patients. There were three other men in the ward, all of them multiple offenders with serious psychoses. All three were pounding on the doors and wondering why they were locked up. All three were declaiming some variant of having "seen the light" at last. The orderly saw that Daniels' door was unlocked and open. He felt a breeze blowing through the hallway and was stunned upon reaching the door to Daniels' room to find that both Daniels and the entire back wall of his room had simply disappeared. A quick inspection revealed no sign of an explosion or debris of any kind. He called me at home, and I rushed to the hospital to see for myself. There was no wall, and Daniels was gone. I called you, the police, and the watch officer at the FBI, in that order, and activated our own emergency procedures. The orderly seemed dazed throughout that period.

As you know, upon examination later in the morning, all three of the other patients exhibited lucidity and mental stability far beyond their earlier states. All three are now working with their lawyers to arrange new hearings, and they have all spoken with priests or ministers. They tell the same peculiar story: Light from the hallway shone through the windows in their doors, light so brilliant that they could not look at it directly and had to shield their eyes. In a few seconds, they began to remember their pasts with unusual clarity and felt intense remorse for their actions, particularly those in which others were harmed.

The federal forensics experts have not yet filed their reports, but I am hearing unofficially that the word most often uttered in the labs is "impossible." The surfaces that surround the rectangular hole where the wall used to be are smooth and unbroken to such an extreme degree that no known explosive, cutting instrument, or dissolving agent could have been employed, including an advanced laser. Moreover, there was absolutely no debris of any kind, either inside or outside of the room. The wall simply disappeared in some manner.

Examination of the computer and related equipment has revealed nothing wrong with them. They are now working perfectly.

One other strange item may deserve mention, although no one has yet established any connection between it and the disappearance of Daniels. About fifty feet directly in front of the hole in the wall, in the wide grassy area at that part of the grounds, the police found a charred area roughly in the shape of a circle about eight feet in diameter, in the middle of which lay some smoking, putrid matter that has not as yet been identified. That discovery renewed speculation about the use of a giant laser, but there are too many objections to that theory, both practical and scientific, for it to withstand serious scrutiny.

We are left then for the time being with a great many questions and very few answers, and we are unlikely to know much more until the forensics reports are made available to us. To add to the mystery, the police have asked us if we took photographs of Daniels, because they cannot locate his mug shots, and their videotapes of him under interrogation have been found to be defective. We also cannot find any clear video of him on our security cameras. There seems to be some type of interference that shields his face whenever he comes into view. I have been advised that his face is also obscured on the videotapes confiscated from the TV networks for the same reason. Moreover, the burst of light in Daniels' ward that the patients have mentioned apparently completely "fried" the circuitry of the camera covering that ward.

You have asked me to speculate or to offer a theory about Daniels and his disappearance if no firm information is available at this point. I do so now:

I would readily stake my reputation on the fact that Daniels is not insane. That leaves only two possibilities: (1) He faked his delusions about angels, and he is a master magician and hypnotist with highly advanced knowledge of electronics and other scientific fields perhaps only accessible to a super genius. (2) His story about angels is real.

My scientific training and skeptical bent of mind point me strongly toward the first possibility. However, my background as a lapsed Catholic and even Occam's Razor lead me to the second. Beyond all of the other marked peculiarities in this case lie four facts that cannot otherwise be explained, at least not yet: (1) the current lasting feelings of brotherly love in the affected audience members at the Jefferson Memorial, including the agents who have watched the videotape, apparently; (2) the failure of a series of cameras to record his image; (3) the spontaneous recovery of the three patients in Daniels' ward; and (4) the total dematerialization of the wall.

It is my judgment that "Daniels" will not be found. I believe that we do not know his real name. For the first time in my medical career, I am coming to believe that we are more likely to find our answers in the paranormal than in our current knowledge of science. Nevertheless, I will continue to gather all of the information as it becomes available, and I will file a more extensive report in the near future.

Attachments:

A. - Transcript of interview on July 6, 2002

B. - Transcript of interview on July 7, 2002

C. - Transcript of interview on July 9, 2002

D. - Minnesota Multiphase Personality Disorder Inventory

E. - Rorschach Test, Exner Scoring Method

F. - Peters Delusional Inventory test

G. - California Personality Inventory

H. - Myers/Briggs Type Indicator (3 sets)

I. - Stanford-Binet 5 IQ Test (2 sets)

J. - Weschler Adult Intelligence Scale

APPENDIX B

Letter from Dr. Tomas (original in handwriting)

March 20, 2003

Dear "Jake,"

One of the night staff called me at my home near the hospital. After overcoming my shock at the disappearance of the wall and your escape from St. Elizabeth's, I found your manuscript on the table next to the keyboard with my name written at the top of the first page. After calling the director and the authorities from my cell phone, I took the manuscript to my office and read the last part first in order to determine what was on your mind prior to the escape. As you intended, I was doubly shocked to find that you actually had the ability to read my mind. I know, for example, that I did not say "checkmate" out loud. Your re-creation of our first conversation and the material in the interview transcripts was also verbatim and without the slightest mistake, as I verified later in my office after meeting with the police. In any case, my "friends," as you termed them, arrived shortly thereafter and were much more interested at first in the baffling disappearance of the entire wall than they were in what you might have been writing on the computer.

They confiscated the entire computer set-up, in any case, including the printer, and brought their own forensics team to work alongside the police in and around your former room with the missing wall. They interviewed me only briefly in the beginning but asked that I remain in the hospital at their disposal for further discussion. The director also asked that I write my own report on the incident as more information became available, and I had every reason then to remain in my office, where I scanned through the rest of the manuscript and determined with considerable soul-searching that I was not going to deliver it into the hands of those who were undoubtedly going to use it to capture you. I also knew that neither I nor anyone else outside of intelligence circles would in all likelihood ever see the manuscript again. I made my decision based on the uncanny and still unexplained disappearance of the wall, the proof in the manuscript of your ability to read my mind, your scores on the tests that I administered, and my grudging but rapidly growing acceptance of your explanation for what had occurred at the Jefferson Memorial.

I also did some fast checking of some of the details in the manuscript and discovered that many of the sites that you described actually exist. No one in the Catholic hierarchy in the Los Angeles region would speak to me about you, however. They offered a variety of reasons for not confirming knowledge of you or any of the essential details, but they all boiled down to a refusal to violate the sanctity of clergy privilege. As a psychiatrist, I could hardly argue the point.

In the meantime, I encountered my own problems with our "friends," as they had been advised by the orderlies that you had been working nearly nonstop for three days on a manuscript that I had myself requested from you. I confirmed that fact and then felt neither particularly proud nor ashamed in telling them that I could not help them in locating it. If there had been a manuscript, then perhaps you took it with you, I suggested to them. That fact could surely be confirmed by checking the computer itself, including the hard drive if you had attempted to delete your work. If nothing were there, then your "work" must have been a sham.

They have never been quite convinced, though. Among other things, they still suspect that it was somehow an inside job, even though neither they nor their best scientists can determine what happened to the wall, since not even a speck of dust from it was found either inside or outside the room. The part that most astounds their scientists and correspondingly reassures me of the rightness of my decision is that the surfaces of the adjoining walls that remain are so astoundingly clean and smooth, even down to the atomic level, that it appears that the wall simply dematerialized. This is not a development that pleases them.

I admit to you that I had difficulty deciphering your message to me in the text at first, but, as with any puzzle, it became extraordinarily simple once I understood it. By the time I could read it, I was more than prepared for its message. Practically any-one who eventually reads the manuscript should be able to deter-mine the truth of it before you did yourself, as your special amne-sia would have provided you with an impenetrable barrier beyond that of your readers.

In any case, my friend, if I may now call you that, I will resign from St. Elizabeth's immediately after passing these materials to your David whenever he should arrive. My position here will be compromised, and happily so, since I compromised it more thor-oughly long ago by working too closely with authorities who were not really interested in the mental health of certain patients, whose confidentiality I sometimes breached, and inexcusably so. It should please you to know that a formal and honorable agree-ment between St. Elizabeth's and the Department of Justice is now being discussed. There are also plans for construction here that will remove the embarrassing evidence of your escape, among other things. Enough of the adjoining bricks and other materials will be removed in order for the research to continue.

Finally, I look forward with pride and high expectation to the wider publication of the manuscript. However, it is clear to me that you can be traced through the police department in Indianapolis, the articles about the fire and the attack on you and your wife in the *Indianapolis Star*, and a host of other leads provided in your chronicle. I assume that you will have arranged for these avenues of investigation to be closed off in ways that I can hardly imagine, or that you will welcome the attempt by those of goodwill who may truly need to find you. Or, as I most fervently hope and pray, perhaps there will be no need for you and she to remain concealed in any way after the emergence of the new gospel.

I write this letter to you now because the international situation proves to me that your ongoing work and your presence among us are absolutely crucial to the well-being of us all. I ask for your forgiveness and your blessing. A double "Shanti" to you, my friend and neighbor.

Sincerely and most respectfully,
Tomas

AFTERWORD

I refer you to the paragraph in the last full page of the central text, in which "Jake" addresses Dr. Tomas as "my former keeper" and challenges him to "decipher" its hidden meaning. I could not find the message myself in that paragraph and those that followed until the key was revealed to me. Dr. Tomas had similar problems in the beginning. It is not that difficult to decipher, but may the reader who has eyes to see actually see, and may that reader know that "Jake" has planted similar messages throughout the text in order to underline the existence of codes in other sacred texts and the importance of delving below the surface meanings of this world and discovering the reality that is so often hidden from us by our all too human perceptions and expectations. Connect the first letters in each of the lines. "Jake" himself has demonstrated the lasting importance of being first.

Printed in the U.S.A.

B0056